Critical Acclaim for

Song of the Silent Harp

BOOK ONE OF THE EMERALD BALLAD SERIES

This popular novel of the Famine period glows with love and faith amid the hardships, and even cruelty, of life under absentee landlords in 19th century Ireland.

The author has created a cast of complex characters in a panorama that stretches from County Mayo to Dublin, London, and eventually New York where the Kavanaghs are to work out their destiny.

All the color and imagery of a film enliven this story as it unfolds against a background of aborted revolution, disappointed love, the elemental struggle for life fulfillment in a harsh society.

Rarely has a novel captured so authentically the enduring faith of the Irish peasant that sustains Nora Kavanagh through the tribulation and struggle of that harrowing period.

This is a compelling and uplifting read that adds to an understanding of Ireland in the last century.

EOIN McKIERNAN,
FOUNDER, IRISH AMERICAN CULTURAL INSTITUTE

Heart *of the* Lonely Exile

THE EMERALD BALLAD

BJ HOFF

HARVEST HOUSE PUBLISHERS

EUGENE, OREGON

Cover photos © Thinkstockphotos; Shutterstock; Wikimedia

Cover by Koechel Peterson & Associates, Inc., Minneapolis, Minnesota

Published in association with the Books & Such Literary Agency, 52 Mission Circle, Suite 122, PMB 170, Santa Rosa, CA 95409-5370, www.booksandsuch.biz.

The village of Killala in County Mayo, Ireland, does exist. The suffering that took place there and throughout Ireland during the Great Hunger of the 1840s was all too real and has been documented in numerous journals. Nevertheless, it is depicted herein by fictional characters.

Previously published as *Heart of the Lonely Exile,* book two of An Emerald Ballad series, Bethany House Publishers.

HEART OF THE LONELY EXILE
Copyright © 1991 by BJ Hoff
Published 2010 by Harvest House Publishers
Eugene, Oregon 97402
www.harvesthousepublishers.com

ISBN 978-0-7369-2789-5

About BJ Hoff

BJ Hoff's bestselling historical novels continue to cross the boundaries of religion, language, and culture to capture a worldwide reading audience. In addition to The Emerald Ballad series, her books include such popular titles as *Song of Erin* and *American Anthem* and bestselling series such as The Riverhaven Years and The Mountain Song Legacy. Her stories, although set in the past, are always relevant to the present. Whether her characters move about in Ireland or America, in small country towns or metropolitan areas, reside in Amish settle-  ments or in coal company houses, she creates *communities* where people can form relationships, raise families, pursue their faith, and experience the mountains and valleys of life.

A direct descendant of Irish ancestors who came to this country before the Revolutionary War, BJ brings a decade of historical research and strong personal involvement to The Emerald Ballad series. Her understanding of the Irish people—their history, their struggles, their music, their indomitable spirit—lends to her writing all the passion and power of her own Irish heritage. BJ and her husband make their home in Ohio.

For a complete listing of BJ's books published by
Harvest House Publishers, turn to page 377.

Acknowledgments

My warmest thanks and appreciation to Harvest House Publishers for publishing this new edition of *Heart of the Lonely Exile,* the second book of The Emerald Ballad series, and for their ongoing support and encouragement of my work. Much gratitude is due the late Dr. Eoin McKiernan for the information and assistance he so kindly and patiently provided throughout the development of this series. Thanks also to the following: the late Thomas Gallagher of New York City; William Hughes of Baltimore, Maryland; Patrick Mead of Lake Orion, Michigan.

Contents

Part Three
SPRINGTIME ANTHEM • RAINBOW VISTAS

A Pronunciation Guide for Proper Names

Aidan . . . . Ā'den

Drogheda . . . . Draw'he guh

Eoin . . . . Owen
(older form of John)

Finola . . . . Fi nō'la
(from Fionnuala)

Killala . . . . Kil lä'lä

Seanchai . . . . Shan'a kee

Tierney . . . . Teer'ney

How shall we sing the Lord's song
in a strange land?

PSALM 137:4 (AMP)

Donal, Son of Eoin

And through the dread, dread night,
And long, that steeped our island then,
The lamps of hope and fires of faith
Were fed by these brave men.

SEUMAS MACMANUS (1869–1960)

Ballina (Western Ireland)
1705

Donal the Twin, son of Eoin Kavanagh, sneaked away from his nephew's cottage before dawn on Sunday morning.

He took nothing with him save the Kavanagh harp slung over his back and his few meager items of clothing, wrapped and knotted onto a stick like a peddler's pack. Around his neck he tied his shoes—thin as pages from an old book; he would save them for later, when the snow came.

Half-sliding, then stumbling the rest of the way down the scrubby incline, Donal waited a moment to catch his breath before getting to his feet. Turning, he rubbed his bruised ribs as he allowed himself one final look at the dark hillside hut that had sheltered him for weeks.

While it grieved him to leave without a final goodbye to Taber and Ellen, he knew it was best to go like this, unnoticed. Now his nephew and family could in all honesty plead ignorance when the British soldiers came.

Ah, but he would miss them—would miss the children's laughter at early light, their evening prayers at sunset. It had been a grand thing to be part of a family again, if only for a brief time.

Blinking against the sudden sting in his eyes, Donal drew in a ragged sigh, then turned his face toward the north. For months now, a number of families in and near Killala had been pleading with him to return and resume a hedge school for their children. Perhaps God was speaking through last evening's narrow escape to call him away from the comfort and safety of Taber's home.

Still, it was a hard thing, harder now than ever before, for Donal knew that, this time, he would not be going back. From now on he would live as a fugitive in the wilds of Mayo, without hearth or home.

There were still good people willing to shelter a renegade schoolmaster or priest, of course—the kindly Brownes and the Elliots, although Protestants, had hidden him more than once. But it went hard for those who dared to harbor an outlaw Catholic schoolmaster, and Donal could no longer live with the fact that he might subject others—especially his own nephew—to the risk.

There was winter on the wind in this hour before dawn. Donal butted his head against the cold, wrapping his cloak more tightly about his throat as he started north. Even in the darkness, it was evident that the countryside had taken on the bleak appearance of early November. Gnarled tree branches, stripped of their leaves, writhed upward, specters in the cloud-veiled light of the new moon. The red bog had gone dull and barren, and the low mountains of Mayo loomed, desolate and lonely and forbidding.

A pool of melancholy stirred somewhere deep inside Donal's spirit, and he shuddered beneath his cloak.

He approached the small whitewashed cottage of Bran O'Gara, his closest friend—in truth, his *only* friend. Suddenly he stopped, startled by the sight of Bran's thin, birdlike figure swooping out the door, lantern in hand. Protected from the elements by only a threadbare jacket, Bran flailed his arms as he came running to the road to meet Donal.

"Faith, Bran, what are you doing roaming about at this hour?"

"And what else would I be doing but watching for *you*, Donal Kavanagh? Didn't I suspect you'd be sneaking out of Taber's house before dawn, what with the trouble last night?"

In his right hand, Bran clutched a small poke, which he now thrust at Donal. "Mary fixed a bite to tide you over until you reach wherever it is you intend to go."

Grateful, Donal nevertheless felt shamed. His friend had so little, yet gave so generously. "That is kind of you, Bran, but not expected. These are hard times."

"Ach, 'tis only some biscuit and taties. Sure, and we can spare that much for you, Donal."

"I do thank you, then. You are a kind man."

Lifting the lantern, the thin-faced Bran squinted his eyes and peered at Donal. "What I am is a man who thinks it a crime to hunt down a schoolmaster as if he were a felon!" he burst out, shaking his head with indignation. "'Tis a terrible thing when men must risk their lives to teach the children!"

Donal nodded, meeting Bran's eyes in the light from the lantern. "Aye, it does seem a bitter thing when knowledge is outlawed in a land that holds learning so dear."

"'Tis not *knowledge* the British have outlawed!" Bran spat out. "'Tis being *Irish* they have made a crime!"

Again Donal nodded in sad agreement. "Aye, and that would seem to be the truth."

Putting a hand to his friend's sleeve, Donal attempted a smile. "My deep thanks to you, Bran. I will not forget your kindness. But I should go now."

In the wavering light of the lantern, Bran's face was lined with anger and despair. "Aye, it will be light soon. Go, then, Donal. And God speed you!"

Donal forced himself not to look back as he left his friend standing alone in the road. He would miss Bran, almost as much as he would miss his nephew, Taber, and his family. God be thanked for them all; they had risked much for his welfare.

But it was folly itself to dare the devil more than once, and so he had decided to leave before daybreak. Once the soldiers realized their prey was no longer about, they would certainly let up on their harassment of Taber and his family.

It chilled his blood to think how close he had come to being taken last night. It would have meant gaol—or worse—for his nephew. The soldiers had been almost halfway up the hill when little Mary had sounded the warning.

Donal had known for some time they were onto him. He'd barely escaped being caught just last week, when he and his band of raggedy scholars had sheltered themselves behind the hedges on the hill to study the Latin and the Greek. Though he got away clean that time, he knew he'd been spotted; sure, and his red hair was hard to miss.

The soldiers had shown up every day since, lurking at the foot of the hill to spy out the cottage, then finally trekking up to the front door last night.

Only his nephew's quick wits had given Donal the extra time he'd needed. With a quick word of explanation, Taber had flushed the children from the front door, sending them at a run into the yard, bawling and yelling like terrified calves as they went. Their mother immediately took off after them, flapping her skirt and shrieking at the top of her voice, as if to murder them both for whatever offense they supposedly had committed.

The distraction had been just enough to allow Donal to escape out the back of the cabin and make his way up to the glen. Thanks be to God, the soldiers had not brought the hounds along with them!

Upon returning to the cottage much later, he learned that the soldiers had been rough with the family, nearly provoking Taber to a foolish outburst. Donal knew then he had to go.

And so here he was on the road, as he had been many times before, and all for the crime of teaching Ireland's children.

He stubbed his bare toe on a stone and yelped, waiting for the pain to subside before going on. Limping down the deeply pitted road, Donal clenched his teeth from the pain in his toe and the cold ground stinging the bottoms of his feet.

"What kind of a land is it," he mused with a great sorrow, "when it is unlawful to teach a child—even one's own?"

For years now, all education had been forbidden to Catholics, including the right to employ a Catholic teacher or to educate one's children at home. Why, he could not even act as guardian to a child among his own relatives!

The list of Forbiddens was endless. Because he was a Catholic, he had no vote, could not bear arms, enter a profession, or hold public office. Nor could he buy land. Why, it was even illegal for him to attend Mass! And the priests—they were hunted down with bloodhounds, just like the schoolmasters! To compound the wrong, those Protestants—and there were many—who would protest the heinous laws by aiding a Catholic friend or neighbor soon found themselves in as much trouble as if they had committed the trespass themselves.

This was a time of terrible shame for Ireland, and that was the truth! Priests and schoolmasters had to be smuggled to the Continent if they were to receive an education of any sort. Some never returned—and yet a surprising number *did*. Like Donal, they made their way back to Ireland, hiding out like common criminals in the hills, meeting with their students or congregations among the rocks, while sentries took turns keeping watch for the soldiers. Some were slaughtered where they stood when the British came upon them without warning.

To avoid persecution—and to keep their lands—many of the Irish adopted the Protestant faith, even intermarrying with daughters of British landlords when possible. Such was the course Donal's twin brother had taken. Indeed, Fergus seemed to have turned his back not only on his faith but on his family as well. Twice he had tipped information to the soldiers about Donal's whereabouts, and once had even attempted to lead the troops to the hedge school. Only a warning from an alert scholar had saved Donal from capture.

For his betrayal, Fergus inherited their father's humble cottage and few belongings, despite the fact that Donal was the firstborn by minutes. The one thing left to Donal was the Kavanagh harp—and that was only because Fergus didn't want it.

Taber, Fergus's son, had grown to be a fine young man, embracing all the values his father had rejected. Over the years, the lad had come to be like a son to Donal, whose wife and infant son had died of typhus. Indeed, only because he loved Taber and his family so fiercely could he bring himself to leave them.

Ah, but one day…one day, they would be together again, if not on this side of heaven, then on the other. Then he would no longer be an exile in his own land, would no longer be forced to roam the hills alone. One day the exiles would come together at last: together with the Lord.

And so, in spite of the pain of leaving his loved ones, in spite of the prospect of loneliness and deprivation awaiting him, Donal was able to smile just a bit through his tears. Stopping, he tucked Bran's gift of food into his pack with the rest of his things, then retrieved the harp. Bracing the old instrument against his shoulder, he turned his face to the horizon.

Down the road toward Killala, in the cold hours of predawn, Donal

Kavanagh walked on toward his destiny. And as he went, he strummed the small minstrel's harp and sang the unchanging promises of his God:

"And the redeemed of the Lord shall return, and come with singing unto Zion, and everlasting joy shall be upon their heads.... They will know gladness and joy, and all sorrow will flee away...."

PART ONE

SUMMER BALLAD

New Horizons

Have mercy on us, O Lord, have mercy on us...
We have endured much ridicule from the proud,
much contempt from the arrogant.

PSALM 123:3-4

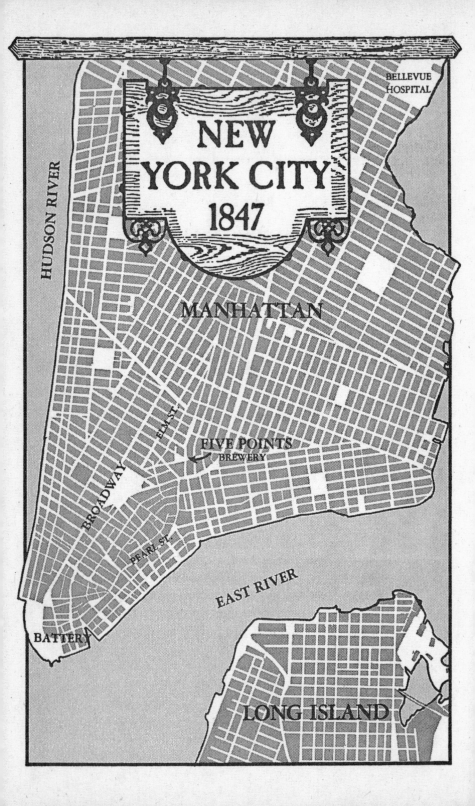

1

Friends Old and New

Youth must with time decay...
Beauty must fade away...
Castles are sacked in war...
Chieftains are scattered far...
Truth is a fixed star....

FROM "AILEEN AROON" GERALD GRIFFIN (1803–1840)

New York City
August 1847

It was a fine summer evening in the city, the kind of sweet, soft evening that made the young delight in their youth and the elderly content with their lot.

On this evening Daniel Kavanagh and Tierney Burke were indulging in one of their favorite pastimes—stuffing themselves with pastries from Krueger's bakery as they lounged against the glass front of the building. As usual, Tierney was buying. Daniel as yet had no job and no money. But Tierney, with a week's pay in his pocket from his job at the hotel and a month's wages due from his part-time job at Patrick Walsh's estate, declared he felt rotten with money and eager to enjoy it.

It had been a good day, Daniel decided as he polished off his last sugar *kucken*. His mother was visiting, as she did every other Saturday, delivered as always by one of the Farmington carriages. Every Saturday without fail, a carriage either brought her to the Burkes', or came to collect Daniel for a visit at the Farmington mansion uptown, where his mother worked.

In truth, Daniel thought he preferred the Saturdays he spent at the

Farmingtons', for then he could visit with his friend, Evan Whittaker, and the Fitzgerald children, as well as his mother. He enjoyed his temporary living arrangement with Uncle Mike and Tierney, but often he found himself missing the daily contact with his mother and the Fitzgeralds—especially Katie.

The thought of Katie brought a smile to his face and a sting of worry to his mind. Katie was both his friend and his sweetheart; they would marry when they were of age—that had been decided long ago.

So committed to their future plans was he that Daniel paid little heed to Tierney's relentless teasing about his "lassie." The fact was that Katie Fitzgerald had been his girl from the time they were wee wanes back in the village, and he did not mind who knew it. But Katie had ever been frail, and the famine and the long, horrific ship crossing had taken a fierce toll on her.

Daniel could not help but fret about her health. He would have thought the good, plentiful food and proper medical attention she was receiving at the Farmingtons' would be enough to have her feeling fit by now. Instead, she scarcely seemed improved at all.

Still, as his mother had reminded him just today, three months was not really so long a time—not with all the troubles Katie had been through. "You must be patient, Daniel John," she had cautioned him. "You must be patient and faithful with your prayers."

He was trying to be both, but it was hard, all the same, not to worry.

Shifting his weight from one foot to the other, Daniel turned his attention to Pearl Street. Although darkness was gathering, most of the neighborhood seemed to be in no hurry to return to their cramped living quarters. The sultry August atmosphere carried the sounds of children playing, mothers scolding, dogs barking, and men arguing. Most of the voices were thick with Irish brogue, although German and an occasional stream of Italian could also be heard.

Almost as thick as the cacophony of immigrant voices were the odors that mingled on the night air. The ever-present stench of piled-up garbage in the streets had grown worse with the recent warm temperatures; the fumes from sewage and animal droppings were more noxious than ever.

Still, there was no spoiling the pleasure of such a fine evening. Besides, Daniel was growing accustomed to the aroma of New York. Indeed, the smell rarely bothered him at all these days; it was negligible compared to the stench of Ireland's rotten potato fields and the countless dead bodies lying alongside the country's roads.

"So, then," Tierney said, downing a nut *kipfel* in one bite before wiping his mouth with the back of his hand, "will they tie the knot soon, do you think? Your mum and my da?"

It was a question Tierney seemed bent on asking at least once a week, a question that continued to make Daniel feel awkward—almost as if his mother were somehow under an obligation to marry Uncle Mike. More and more Tierney's prodding put Daniel on guard, made him feel the need to defend his mother—never mind that he secretly harbored the same question.

"I don't suppose it's for either of us to guess," he muttered in reply. "Sure, and Mother does care a great deal for Uncle Mike."

Tierney gave a curt, doubtful nod, turning the full intensity of his unnerving ice-blue stare on Daniel. "If that's so," he said, "then why is she still holding out?"

Daniel bristled. "It's not that she's *holding out*," he protested. "She just needs more time, don't you see? They haven't seen each other for more than seventeen years, after all! She can hardly be expected to jump into marriage right away!"

Tierney regarded him with a speculative look, then shrugged. "You're right, of course," he said cheerfully, shoving his hands into his pockets. As if no friction whatever had occurred between them, he tilted a quick grin at Daniel. "I expect I'm just impatient because I'm wanting to see them wed."

Not for the first time, Daniel found himself disarmed by his quicksilver friend. The older boy had a way of making abrasive, outrageous remarks, then quickly backing off, as if sensing he had caused Daniel discomfort.

Tierney had an incredible energy about him, a tension that sometimes made it seem that any instant he might leap from the ground and take off flying. He was impatient and blunt, decisive and headstrong. Yet he had an obvious streak of kindness, even gentleness, that could appear at the most unexpected moments.

Living with him was akin to keeping company with a hurricane. Wild and impetuous one moment, eager and conciliatory the next, he was entirely unpredictable—and a great deal more fun than any boy Daniel had ever known.

He liked Tierney immensely. In truth, he wished his mother *would* marry Uncle Mike so they could be a real family.

"If they *do* get married," Tierney was saying, watching Daniel with a teasing grin, "you and I will be brothers. How do you feel about that, Danny-boy?"

Daniel rolled his eyes, but couldn't stop a smile of pleasure. "Sure, and won't I be the lucky lad, then?"

Tierney wiggled his dark brows. "Sure, and won't you at that?" he shot back, perfectly mimicking Daniel's brogue.

꩜

Avoiding Michael's eyes, Nora stared at the flickering candle in the middle of the kitchen table.

The silence in the room, while not entirely strained, was awkward, to say the least. Nora had sensed Michael's impatience early in their visit. She thought she understood it; certainly, she could not fault the man for wanting more of a commitment than she'd been able to grant him thus far.

On the other hand, she didn't know how she could have handled things between them any differently. From the day of their reunion—Nora's first day in New York City—she had done her best to be entirely honest with Michael. She had told him then—and on other occasions since—that she cared for him deeply but could not marry him for a time, if ever.

In the weeks and months that followed her arrival in New York, Nora's life had changed radically. All that she had once held dear, everything familiar, had been mercilessly torn away from her. She had lost her home and her entire family except for Daniel John. Yet much had been given to her as well.

God had been good—and faithful. Daniel John had a home with Michael and Tierney, and she and the orphaned Fitzgerald children were safe and snug in the Farmington mansion with Lewis Farmington and his daughter, Sara—people who must be, Nora was certain, the kindest human beings God ever created.

Aye, she had fine lodgings—even a job—and she had friends, good friends: Michael, Evan Whittaker, Sara and Lewis Farmington, and Ginger, the Farmingtons' delightful housekeeper. There was more food on her plate than she could eat, and a fire to warm her bones for the coming winter. Had any other penniless widow-woman ever been so blessed?

Yet when it came to Michael, something deep within her warned her to wait, to go slowly. There were times when she wanted nothing more than to run to the shelter of the man's brawny arms and accept the security he seemed so set on offering—the security of a friendship that dated back to their childhood, the security of marriage and a home of her own. But in the next instant she would find herself drawing back, shying away from the idea of Michael as the solution to her problems.

She needed *time*, perhaps a great deal of time. Of that much, at least, she was certain. Time to heal, time to seek direction for her life. *God's* direction.

And time to forget Morgan Fitzgerald...

"The Farmingtons seem more than pleased with your work for them," Michael said, breaking the silence and jarring Nora back to her surroundings. "They cannot say enough good things about you."

Struggling to put aside her nagging melancholy, Nora smiled and made a weak dismissing motion with her hand. "Sure, they are only being kind," she said. "'Tis little enough they allow me to do. I suppose they still think me ill, but in truth I'm feeling much stronger."

"I can believe that," Michael said, studying her with open approval. "You're looking more fit each day. I think you might have even gained a bit at last."

Surprised, Nora glanced down at her figure. She *did* feel stronger physically, stronger than she had for months. "Indeed. Perhaps with all this fine American food, I'll grow as round as Pumpkin Emmie," she said, trying to ease the tension between them with reference to daft Emmie Fahey, one of the terrors of their youth.

"You've a ways to go, there," Michael said, meeting her smile. "But you *are* looking more yourself, lass, and that's the truth."

Unnerved by the way he was scrutinizing her, Nora glanced away. "Our sons are becoming good friends, it seems."

Michael, too, seemed relieved to move to safer ground. "Aye, they are," he answered eagerly. "And I couldn't be happier for it. Your Daniel is a fine boy—a good influence on that rascal of mine."

"Oh, Michael," Nora protested, "I think you're far too hard on Tierney! He doesn't seem nearly the rogue you paint him to be."

With a sigh, Michael rose from the table to put the kettle on for more tea. "I'm the first to admit Tierney's not a bad boy. Nevertheless, he can be a handful. And unpredictable—" He shook his head as he started for the stove. "Why, I don't know what to expect from the lad one minute to the next, and that's the truth."

"It's not an easy age for him, Michael. Don't you remember how it was, being more grown-up than child, yet not quite either?"

Nora could have answered her own question. Michael had never seemed anything *but* a man grown, had never appeared to know the meaning of childishness or uncertainty, at least not in the time she had known him.

Returning with the kettle, he offered Nora more tea. When she declined, he proceeded to pour himself a fresh cup. "What I remember most about being a boy," he said with just the ghost of a smile, "was trying to keep you and our lad, Morgan, out of the soup."

Nora glanced quickly away. "Aye, you were like a brother to the both of us," she said quietly.

"It wasn't a brother I wanted to be to *you*, Nora," he said pointedly, pausing with the kettle suspended above his cup. "That was your choice, not mine."

"Michael—"

He looked at her, setting the kettle down between them. "Is it still Morgan, then?" A muscle at the side of his mouth tightened. "Is *he* the reason you cannot bring yourself to marry me?"

"*No!* No, Michael, it is *not* Morgan! I've tried to explain all this before. I thought you understood..."

His gaze on her didn't waver. "Nora, I have tried. But I'm not blind, lass. I see the way things are."

Nora looked away, but she could still feel his eyes on her. "What do you mean?"

"I mean that Morgan Fitzgerald still occupies a large space in your heart—perhaps so great a space there will never be room for another."

"Michael—"

He waved away her protest, saying nothing. Instead, he went to stand at the window, his back to her. He stood there for a long time in silence. At last, he drew in a deep sigh and said quietly, "We'd be good together, I think. We could build a fine life, a good home—watch our boys grow to manhood." Stopping he turned to face her. "Perhaps we could even have more children..."

He let his words drift away, unfinished. As he stood there, his gaze fixed on her face, the frustration that had hardened his expression earlier faded, giving way to a rare tenderness. The grim lines about his mouth seemed to disappear, and his eyes took on a gentle smile.

"We go back a long way, you and I," he said softly. "And our boys—why, they're well on their way to being brothers already. Ah, it could work for us, Nora! You must see that." Shoving his hands down deep into his pockets, he stood watching her. "I know I cannot offer you much in the way of material things just yet, but we'd have enough, enough for us all. And things will improve, I can promise you that. I have prospects on the force—"

"Oh, Michael, you know none of that matters to me!"

With three broad strides he closed the distance between them. Bracing both hands palms down on the tabletop, he brought his face close to hers, his eyes burning. "What, then, Nora? What *does* matter? Tell me, lass, for I'll do whatever I can to make this work for us. I swear I will! Tell me what I can do to convince you to marry me."

Nora remembered he had asked her that same question once before, when he was still a young man preparing to go to America. He had done his best then, too, to convince her to be his wife.

That had been seventeen years ago. *Seventeen years, and her answer was still not what he wanted to hear.*

"Michael, you know you have ever been…special…to me."

He said nothing, simply went on searching her eyes, his large, blunt hands now clenched to fists atop the table.

"I *do* care for you…" She *did*. She was not immune to Michael's appeal, his almost arrogant handsomeness, the strength that seemed to pulse from him. But more than that, and far deeper, were the memories that bound them, the friendship that even today anchored their affection for each other. She could not bring herself to hurt him, but neither could she lie to him!

Suddenly, he stunned her by grasping both her hands in his and pulling her up from the chair to face him. Holding her hands firmly, he drew her to him. "And I care for you, Nora," he said, his voice gruff. With one hand he lifted her chin, forcing her to meet his relentless gaze. "I have always cared for you, lass, and that's the truth."

Trembling, Nora held her breath as he bent to press his lips to hers. Irrationally, she almost wished Michael's kiss would blind her with love for him, send stars shooting through her. Instead, she felt only the gentle warmth, the same sweet, sad affection she had felt for him all those years so long ago when he had kissed her goodbye, regret brimming in his eyes, before sailing for America.

He knew. He said nothing, but she felt his knowing as she stood there, miserable beneath those dark, searching eyes that seemed to probe her very soul. Gradually he freed her from his embrace, setting her gently away from him with a sad smile.

"You have been through a great sorrow," he said huskily. "And I am asking too much of you, too soon. I'm sorry, lass. Perhaps it's just that I'm anxious for you to realize that when you're ready, I will be here. I will wait."

"Oh, Michael, please—don't..."

He put a finger to her lips to silence her. "Enough sober talk for tonight. Why don't we have us a stroll? We'll go and find the lads and see what they're up to."

Relieved, Nora nodded, managing a smile. "Aye, I'd like that."

Michael smiled, too, watching her with infinite tenderness. Framing her face between his calloused hands, he brushed his lips over her forehead. "Remember that I am still your friend, Nora Ellen. No matter what happens—or does not happen—between us, I will always be your friend."

Nora could have wept for gratitude at his understanding, his gentleness. "Thank you, Michael," she whispered. "Thank you for being the man you are. And thank you," she added fervently, "for being my *friend.*"

2

Before the Night

It was a time when thoughts and violets bloomed—
When skies were bright, and air was bland and warm.
JAMES CLARENCE MANGAN (1803–1849)

Dusk was gathering, but the evening was still sweet-scented and warm.

Nora was keenly aware of the mixed glances that greeted her and Michael on their evening stroll. Most of the looks directed their way were friendly. A few women raked her with sharp, grudging stares, and one or two shifty-eyed men stepped smart in an obvious attempt to avoid Michael's eye. The rougher-looking youths steered well clear of him, too, while pretending to be not at all cowed by his close scrutiny. One young woman, whom Nora immediately pegged as fresh, gave Michael a bold, painted smile, causing him to scowl and turn red.

For the most part, however, they appeared to be a good-natured lot who openly approved of Officer Burke and his lady friend.

Michael seemed to know everyone they met and was diligent in inquiring after "the wife's health" or "the lad's whereabouts." They stopped now for a moment to chat with the peg-legged Cooley Breen, who presented them with a wide grin and a cup of hot chestnuts.

Suddenly, a little girl on the stoop of a nearby tenement screamed. Nora whirled around to see one of the countless pigs that freely roamed New York charging toward them. With an angry sound of disgust, Michael pivoted to shove Nora behind him. Crouching, he gave a terrible fierce roar at the pig, then lunged as if to attack it.

The porker stopped, sizing Michael up with a speculative glare. After a moment, as if uncertain whether the man meant business, the pig finally veered and lumbered across the street.

Seeing pigs running wild as hyenas on the streets of New York City had been one of Nora's biggest surprises when they first arrived. The pigs were not the only scavengers running free, of course. Huge rats scurried everywhere, and packs of wild dogs traveled from the mansions on Murray Hill to the slums of Five Points, feeding at will on the ever-present garbage that littered almost all the city streets. Occasionally a cow or a horse also sauntered onto an avenue, giving spectators a good laugh when the "coppers" gave chase.

Michael again took Nora's arm, and they continued on. As soon as they rounded the corner to Pearl Street, they spied Daniel John and Tierney in front of Krueger's bakery. Nora smiled at the sight of them, she and Michael slowing their stride as they approached.

Lounging against the storefront, the boys appeared to be deep in conversation. Tierney, obviously caught up in his own words, sliced the air with his hands for emphasis, while Daniel John stood smiling and nodding.

Watching them, Nora realized with surprise that the boys could easily pass for blood brothers. Although Tierney, the older of the two, was not quite so tall as Daniel John, it was obvious they would both be big men when fully grown. Each had blue eyes, Tierney's lighter and more intense, Daniel John's a deep blue and somewhat hooded. Tierney's thick hair was straight and dark, with the satin sheen of mahogany, while Daniel John's black curls were somewhat untamed but just as thick. Each boy had a long, narrow face, but where Daniel John's was hollow-cheeked and melancholy, Tierney's was impish and often flushed with indignation or anger.

"They are handsome lads, and there's no denying it," Nora said with soft pride.

They had stopped walking altogether now, and Michael smiled faintly, his gaze on his son and Daniel John. "Aye, they are that, and with faces as Irish as a map of Erin."

"We are blessed, Michael. God has been good in spite of all we have lost."

He looked down at her. "Do you mean that, Nora? With all you have suffered, it's no small thing that you can speak so."

For a moment the old, painful memories wrenched Nora's heart anew.

She shivered as once again she saw her husband's lifeless body carried across the threshold of the cottage; the angry, flushed skin and wild eyes of Tahg, her eldest son, caught up in the throes of fever; her black-haired Ellie, the poor, wee lass who died before ever she reached her seventh year.

Nora had to squeeze her eyes shut for a moment against the pain. "They are in God's arms," she murmured, more to herself than to Michael. "It helps me to remember that He holds them all to His heart."

Michael regarded her with a look of shared sadness, then resumed walking. When they reached the boys, Nora was immediately aware of Tierney's disconcerting appraisal, almost as if he were expecting some sort of announcement. Daniel John also greeted her and Michael with a questioning look. As soon as Nora met his gaze, he turned away, but not before she saw a glint of disappointment flicker in his eyes.

Obviously, the boys were hoping for a match. Perhaps it was irrational, but Nora suddenly felt a stab of guilt. Could it be that in her uncertainty she was failing her own son—and Michael's, too?

For a moment, she wondered if she shouldn't simply fling her pride and doubts to the wind and give in, give both boys what they seemed to want so badly. On the heels of that thought, however, came the familiar touch of restraint, the faint, inexplicable caution to wait.

Forcing a smile for the benefit of the boys, she said teasingly, "Is it sugar I see on your upper lip, Daniel John?"

The tension broken, he licked the sugar from his lip. "Tierney's treat," he said, grinning, elbowing the other boy as they moved in front of Nora and Michael.

Nora did not miss the fact that Tierney remained silent all the way back to the flat. Despite her attempt to ignore his rebuff, she felt his resentment like a blow.

The Farmington carriage was waiting as the four of them approached the flat. "Uriah's early today," Michael remarked, carefully guiding Nora around a circle of small boys playing marbles in the street. "I had hoped you could stay and visit a bit longer."

As soon as the elderly black driver saw them approach, he leaned from the carriage. His usually cheerful countenance was deeply lined; Nora knew at once something was wrong.

"Miss Nora, I'm to take you back right away!" he called out, his voice trembling with urgency. "It's little Miss Katie."

Nora put a hand to her throat. "Katie? What about Katie, Uriah? What's happened?"

"She took worse this afternoon. Could hardly get her breath, the poor child! She's awful sick, Miss Sara says. They've called for Dr. Grafton, but Miss Sara, she said you'd want to come soon as I can get you there."

Nora heard Daniel John's quick intake of breath. Meeting his stricken eyes, she tried to hide her own fear.

"I'm going with you," he said, already starting for the carriage.

Nora glanced at Michael, who nodded, saying, "Send word if you need me."

3

Valley of Shadows

They brought her to the city
And she faded slowly there.

RICHARD D'ALTON WILLIAMS (1822–1862)

Nora sat unmoving in the dim shadows outside Katie's room. Across from her, Daniel John braced on the edge of a chair that Sara Farmington had pulled into the hall from one of the bedrooms. His head was bent low, his hands clasped; Nora knew he was praying.

The doctor had been with Katie for more than an hour—a bad sign, Nora feared. What with the Fitzgeralds being of the Roman faith, a priest had also been sent for—surely an even more ominous indication that Katie's condition was grave indeed.

Shifting uneasily on her chair, Nora found her thoughts going to the night Katie had been born. The birthing had been a difficult one for Catherine, Katie's mother. Nora had stayed with her friend throughout the long hours, and when the two of them finally beheld the weensy red-haired infant, they had first laughed at her terrible frown, then cried with joy that she was healthy and whole.

Dear Lord, has it really been eleven years ago? She could remember Katie's pinched little face as if it were but yesterday. Poor wee thing, she had never been strong, not really. Like a wisp in the wind, she had failed to thrive throughout her childhood, drifting through the years in a quiet, unobtrusive way. When the Hunger came, she continued to fade, growing thinner and thinner until at last she was little more than a shadow of herself.

Even now, after all this time of basking in the protective care of the

Farmingtons, the lass continued to fail. Over the past few weeks, Katie's breathing seemed to have grown more labored than ever. She picked indifferently at her food, when she ate at all, and recently had taken to lying abed later and later in the mornings. Nothing the doctor did seemed to make any difference.

We are losing her. Sick at heart, Nora steeled herself to face the truth in order that she might be strong enough to help her son face it.

Poor Daniel John. What would he do without his Katie? The two of them had grown up nearly inseparable, each shadowing the other throughout their childhood. The affection between them had been a gentle, childish thing, but, given time, it might well have deepened into something more lasting. Now, as she sat watching her son, Nora knew with a dread certainty that there would be no more time for Daniel John and his Katie.

Merciful Lord, he has already lost so much...his father, his brother, his little sister, his home. How much more must he bear?

She looked up at the sound of voices to see Sara Farmington ascending the winding staircase. Just behind her came one of the largest men Nora had ever seen, nearly as big as Morgan Fitzgerald himself. Sara Farmington was a tall young woman, but this man towered over her. His well-tailored suit and immaculate linen marked him at once as a gentleman, in spite of the vast span of his shoulders and his heavy black beard. He had a full head of curly hair, black going to silver, but as he approached, Nora saw that he was younger than she might have thought at first glance.

She knew who he was right away: Pastor Jess Dalton. Sara Farmington often spoke with great enthusiasm about the famed abolitionist preacher. Mr. Dalton was to fill the pulpit recently vacated by the pastor of the Farmingtons' uptown church. In addition, arrangements had been made with the Ladies' Home Missionary Society for him to establish a mission in Five Points, the city's most scandalous slum district.

A former chaplain of the U.S. Military Academy at West Point, Pastor Dalton most recently had served the pulpit of a wealthy, influential congregation in Washington, D.C., where his abolitionist sympathies proved extremely unpopular. His arrival in New York City coincided with that of another controversial preacher, the minister of the newly established Plymouth Church in Brooklyn. Indeed, the new Brooklyn minister, Henry Ward Beecher, was a friend of Pastor Dalton, had traveled from his former pastorate in Indiana to perform the Daltons' wedding service at West Point. And now, by coincidence, they had both arrived in New York at the same time.

The preacher stopped to be introduced before going into the bedroom. Despite his size, Nora sensed him to be a man of great kindness. His voice was quiet and warm, his eyes soft with compassion as he bowed to Nora and solemnly shook Daniel John's hand.

"It's kind of him to come," Nora said as he closed the bedroom door behind him. "What with us being strangers, and Katie a Catholic."

"I don't believe things like that matter to Pastor Dalton," said Sara. "He seems the sort of man who cares about *everyone,* not merely those of his own congregation. Oh—and did I tell you, Nora, that his wife is also from Ireland? She's absolutely delightful—you'll love her! She appears to be a good deal younger than Mr. Dalton," Sara went on, "but they're obviously devoted to each other. You'll meet her soon, if you're serious about wanting to help out at the mission house."

"Aye, of course, I'm serious," Nora replied distractedly. "And Daniel John said he would help, too. Didn't you, son?"

She had to ask again before the boy answered. Dragging his gaze from his hands, he looked at her blankly for a moment, then nodded. Wincing at the bleakness in his eyes, Nora was glad when he agreed to accompany Sara to the kitchen, where the younger Fitzgerald children were awaiting word of their sister.

Pausing on the stairs, Sara turned back for a moment. "I sent Uriah to collect Father and Evan from the yards, Nora. I knew Evan would want to be here with you and the children."

Nora felt a grateful rush of relief. She and Evan Whittaker had formed a close friendship during the months since their arrival in New York, a friendship that had begun during their voyage across the Atlantic and continued to deepen as they settled into their new lives.

Employed as a personal secretary to Lewis Farmington, Evan roomed in the small cottage behind the Farmington mansion.

Most evenings he dined with Nora and the children, and they had taken to spending their Sunday afternoons together as well.

Nora realized her friendship with the slender, diffident Englishman might strike some as a bit peculiar. With his silver-blond hair and wire-rimmed spectacles, he appeared timid and unassuming, an impression emphasized by his frequent stutter. But Nora had come to know Evan's heart, had discovered behind the shyness and reserve a good, kind man with an unmistakable strength of character and a self-sacrificing spirit. Wasn't his empty left sleeve proof enough of his courage and selflessness? The man had risked his life—and lost his arm—in an effort to help a group of Irish strangers, herself included.

Time and close companionship had deepened Nora's admiration for her English friend to a genuine fondness. She thanked the Lord daily for Evan Whittaker. She was grateful, too, that Daniel John set such store by the man, for surely he would need the comfort of Evan's presence before this night was done.

In the bedroom across the hall, Dominic Carroll, the priest, completed the last rites, then motioned Jess Dalton to approach the bed.

The feverish face of the little girl appeared lost among the plump mounds of bedding all around her. Her hands, transparently thin, clutched the blanket; her small mouth was locked partly open in labored breathing. She was no longer conscious.

Jess Dalton had prayed at many bedsides; he was no stranger to the sickroom of the critically ill. He had witnessed much suffering, many deaths—but the sight of a dying child never failed to cause his spirit to moan in fresh anguish.

Nodding to the priest, whom he had met on numerous occasions before tonight, Jess looked over at the doctor, standing on the other side of the bed. His face gray with fatigue, the physician shook his head sadly. "She is almost gone, I'm afraid."

While the priest held the little girl's hand and prayed a final benediction, Jess Dalton sank to his knees beside the bed. Closing his eyes, he sought the Savior's mercy for Katie Fitzgerald, a little girl who had known more than her share of trials in her brief lifetime.

He knew the story of the Fitzgeralds, of course; Sara Farmington had spoken of the mother's death, the father's slaying before the ship ever sailed, and the incredible suffering the entire family had endured while still in Ireland. He knew about the famine that had claimed the child's health, the torturous voyage across the Atlantic that had sapped what little strength she had left.

"Oh, Lord, in Your mercy, make this crossing an easy one for Katie Fitzgerald. May your angels bear her up and bring her safely and speedily into Your presence...."

The pastor had scarcely begun to pray before the rattle of a sigh came from the little girl's throat, followed by a muffled sound of despair from the doctor. Clenching his big hands even tighter, he waited.

When he finally looked up, the doctor again shook his head, this time with sad finality. The priest continued to hold the child's hand. Jess Dalton's broad back slumped, and his eyes burned as he resumed his prayer.

"May this child, for so long ill and hungry, now delight in Your kingdom and feast at Your banquet table for all eternity. Jesus, gentle Shepherd of our souls, receive yet another small lamb into Your welcoming arms, and grant her peace, eternal peace, with You."

4

Hope of Heaven

Hope, like a gleaming taper's light,
Adorns and cheers our way;
And still, as darker grows the night,
Emits a brighter ray.

OLIVER GOLDSMITH (1728–1774)

Over the next two days, Daniel was aware only in the vaguest sense of the arrangements taking place for Katie's wake and funeral service.

He knew that both his mother and Sara Farmington, as well as Ginger, the housekeeper, had worked constantly to get things done—but he had only a faint idea of what sort of things they were doing.

Part of him—a part somehow detached from the cloak of grief that enfolded the rest of his being—took note of the fact that the room in which Katie had died was almost completely shrouded in white. A white satin cloth draped the small round table by the window, with a vase of white roses and fern its only adornment. White napkins discreetly covered the pictures and looking glass, and baskets of white flowers replaced the toiletries on the vanity.

On the bed itself, draped with white linen and silk ribbons, Katie lay, wearing a simple white dress, her reddish-blonde hair and golden red eyelashes the only color about her. Had it not been for the crucifix and sprig of holly placed upon her breast, she would have looked for all the world as if she were sleeping.

The Fitzgeralds and Kavanaghs being virtually unknown, and their status in the household being somewhat undefined, only close friends of the Farmingtons came to pay their respects. Occasionally Daniel heard subdued voices and quiet footsteps in the hallway as his mother and Sara Farmington greeted strangers who came and went, but for the most part the house was silent—the silence of death.

Miss Sara had arranged a very nice funeral service for Katie in the small chapel attached to the mansion, but now that the service was nearing its end, Daniel was anxious for it to be done with. The room was warm and decked with flowers. Their cloying scent made him almost ill.

He had eaten little and slept even less since Katie died, and that, combined with the closeness of the room, caused him to be weak and light-headed.

The priest had officiated at the service, but apparently Miss Sara had asked Pastor Dalton to be there as well. As the service came to an end, the big curly haired preacher stepped up to the front to offer a prayer and read from Scripture.

Daniel was remotely aware of soft weeping, coming mostly from his mother, beside him, and wee Tom, on his lap. Even the mute Johanna wept, her grief for her sister issuing forth in strangled-sounding sobs that made Daniel's own throat ache.

He did not cry, at least not aloud. As he drew Little Tom closer to him, his heart wept in silence, his spirit grieved, but he shed no tears for Katie. Even when Mr. Dalton prayed with deep feeling and eloquent words, Daniel could not cry.

It wasn't that he was deliberately trying *not* to cry. Indeed, he did not understand the dryness of his eyes. Was he so unfeeling, then, that he could not shed a tear or two for his own Katie, his best friend in the world since childhood? Guilt-stricken, he had attempted to force the tears any number of times since her death, but to no avail.

Had his heart grown hard from all its loss, battered to stone by wave after relentless wave of death? How could he *not* cry for Katie? Katie, with the green eyes that glittered like emeralds in the mist at the sight of a spring morning's rainbow. Katie, who had bandaged his thumb the time his whittling knife had slipped, then kissed it to make it heal properly. Katie, who had called him her hero-lad, ever trusting him to turn bad to good and clouds to sunlight. Katie, his own Katie, lying cold and stiff and life-less in the small white coffin.

He had failed her. In the end, he had been able to do nothing to help her, nothing at all. He had not even been with her when she drew her last breath. And now she was gone from him, gone forever, and he felt as if she had taken a part of himself with her. Something inside him had withered and turned brittle, crumbling to dust and destroying all his feelings, his hopes…and his tears.

Evan Whittaker took one look at Daniel's face as the funeral service neared its end and knew a mighty conflict was raging inside that young heart.

His own heart ached for the boy, and for Nora and the other two children. The loss and the grief represented in this room would not be quickly assuaged. They had endured too much—and lost too much—for life to be easy ever again.

Yet they survived. And while their survival alone attested to God's power and His mercy, He had accomplished much, much more for them all than mere survival. He had been gracious beyond anything they could have hoped for, providing them shelter and sustenance and the support of friends such as the Farmingtons, Michael Burke, Pastor Dalton. These friends were God's own messengers sent to ease their arrival in this new land.

Evan's gaze went to Nora, seated directly in front of him. Her diminutive form looked woeful and lost between her tall son Daniel on the one side and the brawny Michael Burke on the other. She wore a black crepe armband over the sleeve of a black dress—one of Sara Farmington's dresses. As Evan watched, she stroked the thin crepe over and over in a distracted, nervous gesture of despair. Sergeant Burke laid a protective hand on her arm, frowning down at her as if he feared she might faint at any moment.

Evan shared Burke's concern for Nora. Yet he had also come to realize that she was not the timid, helpless unfortunate he once thought her to be. More and more he saw her taking charge of her surroundings. Both Sara Farmington and Ginger, the housekeeper, frequently praised Nora's quiet efficiency as she kept things running smoothly and in good order about the house. The Farmingtons also claimed her to be an excellent helper in the mission work at the church.

Evan sensed a kind of drive in Nora these days, a resolve to be adequate for whatever task was at hand. No question about it, she was a far stronger and more confident woman than he would have believed her to be—and obviously growing stronger all the time.

Glancing at Michael Burke, he felt a moment's resentment that the broad-shouldered police sergeant seemed totally oblivious to Nora's new strength. Instead, he seemed intent on handling her as if she were some sort of delicate figurine, a china miniature that would shatter to pieces if he did not carry her around on a silk pillow.

For an instant Evan wondered nastily if the Irish policeman thought to convince Nora to marry him by convincing her of her *need* for him. Just as quickly, he pushed the thought away. He was being unfair. Burke was a good man—a sterling fellow, to be sure—and obviously he only meant to do right by Nora.

The man doted on her, that much was clear. As for Nora's attitude toward the sergeant, Evan found it somewhat puzzling. At one moment she would gaze at Burke with what appeared to be genuine affection; the next instant, she would seem almost evasive in his presence.

Suppressing a sigh, Evan dragged his eyes away from the back of Nora's bowed head. He simply must not think about her in such an...*intimate* way, must not speculate on her relationship with Michael Burke. He and Nora were friends, good friends, and he would not have that spoiled by a hopeless, foolish longing that she would surely find outrageous. If she were ever to suspect how deeply he cared for her, her trust would be rent, their friendship ruined forever.

Evan could not bring himself to even imagine such an existence. He had resigned himself long ago to a life without Nora's love. But he could not envision a life without her presence.

Katie was buried in a small Catholic graveyard. A soft summer rain began to fall as they came away from the graveside service. Nora counted it as welcome; a cloudless sky was not a good omen for a funeral.

Immediately she chastised herself for paying heed to superstition. She was a Christian, not a pagan, and shouldn't be mindful of the old tales.

But that was easier said than done, for wasn't she Irish? Michael claimed that the Irish, in any land, were never quite free of their ancient dark fears and echoes of doom. Glancing at him as he helped her into the Farmingtons' carriage, Nora thought somewhat testily that Michael was one Irishman who seemed resolved to rid himself of every trace of the ancient ways.

Her thoughts roamed without direction as the carriage bumped over the dirt road leading back to town. He had become quite the American, Michael had. It was this very thing that at times seemed to be the main source of contention between him and his son.

Odd, how Tierney, who had been born and raised in America, wanted nothing more than to live out his Irish heritage to the fullest, while Michael, an Irishman through and through, seemed indifferent toward his roots. Nora sometimes thought that if the two of them, father and son, could bend just a bit toward each other, their relationship would be greatly improved. But Michael was a stubborn man, and Tierney equally hardheaded. There was no telling if they would ever accept each other's differences.

"Nora? Are you all right, lass?" Seated close beside her in the carriage, Michael took her hand and looked at her with a grave expression.

She nodded. "I'm weary, is all. I expect we are all worn to a frazzle. I don't understand why Daniel John insisted on walking back from the graveyard, or why Evan thought he must accompany him. Sure, and they will both catch cold, especially Evan. He is not a bit strong yet."

"You fuss over that Britisher as if he were family," Michael muttered.

At Nora's sharp look he colored. "I'm sorry," he said grudgingly. "I know he's been the good friend to you, but you've enough to worry about without fretting over *him*."

"Aye, he *has* been a good friend to me, Michael—to us all," Nora answered, barely controlling her impatience. He did seem bent on resenting Evan Whittaker, and for the life of her, she could not understand why.

"Where would we all be now, I'd like to know," she said pointedly, "had that *Britisher* not risked his very life for us."

Michael remained silent, which only quickened Nora's exasperation. If he were so intent on being more American than Irish, he should *also* give over the old Irish hatred of all things English!

"Nora?"

She gave him a hard look.

"Perhaps you'd like me to stay with you this afternoon?"

Hesitating, Nora realized that what she wanted most was to be alone. "No, thank you, Michael," she said. "I have much to do. Things are in a shambles, with all the confusion of the past few days."

"They won't be expecting you to work about the house *today*," he persisted. "Sure, and you must realize by now that you're much more than just a servant to the Farmingtons. Sara counts you as a friend. She'll understand if you need some time."

Nora gave a quick nod. "Aye, Sara has been more than kind to me. As has her father. But I *need* to be busy, Michael, don't you see? It *helps* me. I cannot bring myself to sit and brood on Katie." She paused and looked away. "'Tis not that I don't mourn the lass, for, sure, I do," she went on to explain. "Katie was as dear to me as blood-kin. But now her suffering is done, and she's at home with our Lord."

Sadness gripped Nora, a sorrow multiplied by the memory of all the brutal deaths she'd seen in recent months. Life had to go on, certainly, but her life—and Daniel John's—would never be the same again. Katie, dear Katie, was dead and buried, and Nora was left with an empty numbness, a bone-deep weariness. Mourning would come later, perhaps—or perhaps not. She could not help but wonder if she had spent all her grief, burying the last of her feelings with those she had loved so dearly in life.

Michael had not seen it—the hollow-eyed Hunger, the fever, the despair, the hopelessness. Perhaps he would never understand. And she hadn't the energy to explain it all to him. Instead, she simply said, "The time for grieving is past, Michael. I need to get back to work."

Michael looked at her intently. "It's just that I want to help, Nora."

Immediately she regretted her sharpness with him. "Oh, I know you do, Michael!" she said quickly, squeezing his hand. "You're a grand friend, and what I'd ever do without you, I don't know!"

Inexplicably, his expression darkened, and he turned away, leaving Nora to wonder what she had said to put him off.

❧

Neither Evan nor Daniel spoke most of the way back to the Farmingtons'. As they walked along in silence, Evan savored the warm droplets of rain that had begun to fall, lifting his hand to touch the moisture on his face. The day had been sultry and oppressively close; even this brief respite was welcome.

Concerned for Daniel, who was obviously agonizing, Evan moved to break the silence between them. "D-Daniel—I know Katie was very... special to you. P-Perhaps it would help," he suggested cautiously, "if we t-talked about...what's happened?"

The boy merely shook his head, making no reply as they walked on.

Groping for just the right words, Evan stopped and put his hand to Daniel's arm. When the boy turned and faced him, the misery in his eyes tore at Evan's heart.

"D-Daniel," he ventured again, dropping his hand, "D-Daniel, there is something I would say to you."

The boy stood without moving, his pain-filled gaze polite but distant. At almost fourteen, he already topped Evan by two or three inches. Distressed by the depth of suffering that emanated from the youth, Evan hesitated, glancing around at their surroundings.

There was a quiet along this lonely road, so near and yet so removed from the noise of the city. With the rain gently stirring the trees and the sounds of New York subdued to a murmur, Evan felt a comforting kind of peace enfold both him and the boy.

"You have had m-much more than your share of sorrow, D-Daniel," he said at last. "And I wonder if, right at this moment, it doesn't seem as if there m-may never again be anything else in your life *but* sorrow."

Evan stopped, feeling a knot of despair clench at his own chest as he searched the boy's wounded eyes. Yet he felt the need to reach beyond Daniel's pain, his thin mask of composure. "I sense, too, son, that you are feeling somewhat...g-guilty...because there was n-nothing you could do to save your friend."

Daniel blinked and seemed to stiffen.

Sensing he had struck a chord at last, Evan went on. "Daniel, you've had a t-terrible loss, and you m-must grieve. It's all right to grieve, son," he said softly. "There is no shame in grief. But in the m-midst of your grief, you m-must also accept the fact that there was nothing you c-could have done for Katie. *Nothing*," Evan repeated.

An old, raw agony rose in the boy's eyes, and Evan winced at the pain staring out at him.

"She always counted on me," Daniel choked out. "She thought—she thought I could fix anything, make everything all right—"

Again Evan took the boy's arm. "Yes, I know. And with g-good reason, I'm sure. You were a wonderful friend to her, D-Daniel. Your m-mother has told me all about you and Katie."

The boy blinked, then turned his face away. "We would have married… someday," he said quietly. "We had already promised each other."

Evan released his grip on the boy's arm but continued to watch him, his mind reaching for wisdom, for some word that would help. He again felt the youth's pain, heard the ache in his voice.

"Daniel," he said hoarsely, "you are very young. Too young, perhaps, to h-hope for heaven—and yet I sense that is exactly what you m-must do."

"What do you mean?"

Touching him lightly on the shoulder, Evan managed a faint smile. "Heaven seems…so far away when you're young. Almost…a-a dream. But as young as you are, D-Daniel, you *must* hold the hope of heaven in your soul, to guard against d-despair and disillusionment."

Daniel's frown deepened. "I don't understand. I want to," he added, "but I don't."

Even glazed with sadness, the boy's eyes were true and noble. For an instant, Evan caught a glimpse of the godly man Daniel Kavanagh would grow to be, and he thought it would be a fine thing indeed to watch him age and mature.

"God has given you a-a pilgrim soul, D-Daniel," he said softly, momentarily tightening his grip on the boy's shoulder. "Today you feel yourself to be an exile, a stranger in this n-new land. Someday, p-perhaps, you will return to visit Ireland, and when you d-do, I fear you will be all the more aware of your state of exile. Even Ireland will n-no longer be home to you, n-not really."

God had given him the words he sought, and Evan went on with conviction. "Oh, Daniel, I p-pray that you—and I, as well—will grow to love this new land, this America! Yet I know in my heart that n-neither America nor your Ireland—nor m-my England—will ever really b-be home for us. We are p-pilgrims, you and I, Daniel. *All* of us are pilgrims, leaving our c-countries, crossing the ocean, journeying from one c-continent to another, as we m-make our way to our real home in heaven.

"Now, can you see m-more clearly how it is with Katie, son? She is at *home*—in her *real* home. Your Katie's exile is finally ended. She is at home with her Savior. No d-doubt she has already m-moved into her very own mansion—one of the mansions the Lord promised to prepare especially for her.

"And one d-day, Daniel, you—and I—we will go home, too. Although it m-may not seem so, at your age, son, the time passes far more quickly than we can imagine. This life—why, it's n-nothing but a fleeting whisper, compared to eternity. So hold your hope of heaven, son...and k-keep a pilgrim soul. Katie has gone home. But you and I—we, too, are on our way."

Silence hung between them for a moment. Then, with a tortured sob, Daniel took a step toward Evan. A tear spilled over from one eye, then another, until an entire trail of tears ran unheeded down the boy's cheeks.

With his one arm, Evan drew the boy against him, feeling the thin shoulders give a shudder, then begin to heave.

"That's it, son," he soothed, his own eyes burning with unshed tears as he held the boy close. "You go right ahead and c-cry. Weep for your Katie now, but only for a time. One d-day soon the two of you will laugh and rejoice again together."

No longer able to contain his own tears, Evan wept with Daniel Kavanagh for all that had been lost...and all that would be gained, in God's time.

5

A Plan and a Prayer

Fell are thy tall trees that erst branched so boldly,
Hushed thy sweet singers that once warbled free;
O the bleak fortune that now clasps thee coldly,
When, Isle of Ruin, shall it pass from thee?
JOHN SWANWICK DRENNAN (1809–1893)

Dublin
October

William Smith O'Brien's arrival at Nelson Hall was the one bright spot in an otherwise dismal month for Morgan Fitzgerald. He welcomed his old friend into his grandfather's spacious library with an enthusiasm he felt for few others.

As always, the handsome, elegantly attired O'Brien looked as if he might have stepped straight off the pages of Burke's *Landed Gentry*. In his mid-forties, the leader of the Young Ireland movement was still lithe and incredibly youthful in appearance.

Smith O'Brien was a Protestant landlord who had sat in Parliament for more than fifteen years, pleading Ireland's cause. Second son of the wealthy Sir Edward O'Brien, he claimed descent from the high kings— in particular, Brian Boru, supreme Monarch of Ireland in the early eleventh century. Educated in England at Harrow and Trinity, O'Brien was a gentleman, an aristocrat, and a patriot.

Although many of O'Brien's critics thought him cold and arrogant, Morgan Fitzgerald knew better. Oh, the man was somewhat vain, he supposed, and his mannerisms might be a bit stiff-necked at times. But to Morgan's way of thinking, these were minor flaws in a man so fiercely devoted to his family, his friends, and his country. While it could be argued that his personality inspired more respect than affection, his friendship for Morgan, from the beginning, had been warm, undemanding, and constant.

One thing could be said for the Young Ireland leader: he had the courage to stand for his convictions. Only last year, his refusal to serve on a committee to which he'd been appointed had earned him a month's imprisonment in a cellar beneath the clock tower of Westminster—and the dubious distinction of being the first MP to be imprisoned by the House of Commons in over two hundred years. The man's loyalty was beyond reproach; he was unswervingly committed to Ireland's good and the country's ultimate freedom from British rule.

"Fitzgerald, I must admit that until now I found it near impossible to imagine you in such opulent surroundings. Yet seeing you here, like this—" His gaze swept the room in appreciation. "I declare you almost look to the manor born."

Morgan curled his lip, waiting until Smith O'Brien sat down before lowering his own long frame into the chair across from him. "Hideous, isn't it?" he said, giving a disparaging lift of one hand. "This is the only room in the entire mausoleum that doesn't cause my nerves to rise up and scream in protest."

O'Brien smiled. "You're just missing the open road, you old tinker." He smoothed the front of his waistcoat, settling himself into the chair. "How's your grandfather, Morgan? I haven't seen him in weeks."

"He's off to London at present. Making what he refers to as his 'last visit.'"

O'Brien frowned. "Has he failed so much, then?"

"Aye, he grows dangerously frail these days," Morgan answered. In truth, he was greatly worried about his English grandfather—the old man had been looking pale and drawn and even slightly ill just before he left for London. "I did my best to dissuade him from leaving, but he insisted he had affairs that must be settled."

"If you don't mind my asking, how are the two of you getting on by now?"

Morgan waited until an elderly male servant had laid out tea and left the room before replying. "The old man is a tolerant sort," he said. "I'm sure I try his patience to the limit with my restlessness, but he continues to urge me to stay on. This is *his* idea, as you know," he added sourly, "not mine. Although I'll admit I've grown fond of him. In truth, I find myself missing him—a fact that would surprise him very much, I'm sure."

"Your staying here must mean a great deal to Sir Richard," O'Brien responded. Stirring his tea in thoughtful silence, he darted an uncertain glance at Morgan. "I was sorry to hear about your niece. That was a hard thing."

Morgan gave a short nod, swallowing against the knot that rose in his throat. He had received Daniel John's letter only a few weeks past, notifying him that Katie Frances had died in New York City. He had been partial to the wee, frail lass, and it still pained him to think of her gone.

"You've suffered great loss over the past months," O'Brien remarked, his expression solemn.

Morgan glanced away. "No more so than others in Ireland," he replied. "Less than many. It has been a year of terrible loss for the entire country."

Staring into the fire, O'Brien nodded. "And only God knows when it will end—or if it ever will."

For a long time they didn't speak, but simply sat drinking their tea and watching the flames leap and dance over the logs. Finally O'Brien broke the silence. "I trust your writing goes well," he said, watching Morgan refill their cups with fresh tea. "Your last piece for *The Nation* was excellent."

Morgan gave a short laugh and helped himself to a biscuit. "Mitchel hated it. I think he fears I've turned traitor with my recent insistence on caution."

O'Brien's patrician mouth turned down. "Mitchel is wasting himself with his obsessive attachment to Lalor and his erratic visions of sweeping England into the sea."

Morgan shrugged, swallowing the last bit of biscuit. "Mitchel's convinced the country must rise. Some are listening. He's greatly admired, you know. There's no denying his good intentions, that's certain. Mitchel is a patriot to the death."

"He's also wildly impractical," O'Brien pointed out, placing his cup carefully on the table. "He's become a fanatic, and the both of us know where that can lead."

Again there was silence. Morgan did not want to follow this path in the conversation. More and more lately he sensed the approach of yet another cataclysm for Ireland. His country was dying, his people starving to death by the thousands. Yet in the midst of the horror, certain voices demanded rebellion. *"The people must rise,"* they were saying. *"They must defy their English landlords and reclaim the land for Ireland."*

As Morgan saw it, the first job of the people was to *survive.* At this moment in Ireland's tragedy, the best they could hope for was life itself. Food was far more vital to a starving people than ideology, jobs and education more important than political rhetoric. Perhaps freedom from England's iron boot would come, one day. But for now it was little more than a wild-eyed patriot's dream.

He looked over at O'Brien. "You're still going to Belfast, I assume?" he asked bluntly, knowing the answer.

Smith O'Brien nodded, looking slightly uncomfortable. "And you?"

Morgan shrugged. "I told you I would go. I think it's a daft idea, but I will go."

O'Brien eyed him with dry amusement. "You really do detest Belfast, don't you?"

Morgan leaned back in his chair. "It is a terrible, grim city, you must admit."

"Morgan, I know you're only going to watch my back—"

"Now that's the truth."

O'Brien shot a quick glance at Morgan. "But I think these meetings are important to the movement, and in spite of your reservations, I believe you'll agree, once we're there. I *do* wish you'd plan to speak, along with the rest of us."

Nobody in Belfast has a mind to listen to a gentleman like O'Brien, Morgan thought testily. Much less would they heed a redheaded poet's plea for peace and reason. He already knew he would not open his mouth in Belfast, but it seemed important to O'Brien that he go, so he said only, "We will see once we're there."

As if he realized the subject was distasteful to Morgan, Smith O'Brien moved to break the tension. "Good enough." He smiled and shifted in his chair. "Tell me, have you given any thought to what you'll do once your grandfather is gone? Will you stay here, at Nelson Hall, do you think?"

Stirred from his disgruntled mood, Morgan looked at him. "Stay?" He shook his head. "No, I'll not stay. At least, not year-round. The place annoys me. I'd soon grow soft and lazy here. No," he said again, this time even more firmly, "this life is not for me. You know I must be on the road, at least a part of the time."

"But you *are* Sir Richard's heir," O'Brien pointed out. "He means for you to have his entire estate, isn't that so?"

"Aye, he does, and I already have plans for this place," Morgan said, locking his hands behind his head. "I haven't discussed my ideas with the old man yet, but I suppose in good conscience I should, and soon."

Smith O'Brien looked interested. "Ideas? What sort of ideas?"

"I'm thinking of turning the place into a school," Morgan replied, smiling. The simple act of voicing his plan made his blood run a little faster with excitement.

"A *school*!" O'Brien repeated, leaning forward. "Nelson Hall?"

"Aye," said Morgan, his smile widening as he savored the thought anew. "It's ideal for it, don't you see? All those moldy old rooms above, the rambling hallways, the excellent grounds—think of the scholars it would hold!"

"A classical academy, then—is that what you're planning?"

"In a way. I intend it to be an academy for all ages," Morgan explained, perching forward on his chair and gripping his knees. "Perhaps even for older lads who might not have been able to manage much education. I want to open doors to those who sincerely crave an education but haven't the means to get into one of the established academies. And there will be no restrictions based on religion," he added emphatically. "It will be a school where both Catholic and Protestant can come and learn together. And *live* together."

O'Brien stared at him. "What an *extraordinary* idea! But a quite wonderful one," he added quickly. "You'll serve as the master yourself, of course?"

Giving full vent to his enthusiasm, Morgan rose and went to stand with his back to the fire. "When I'm here. But I'm committed to the writing, you know—and to do it justice, I must have the freedom to travel, to keep in touch with the country. I hope to find one or two scholars to do the job when I'm away."

O'Brien laced his fingers together, nodding thoughtfully. "I think it's an absolutely splendid plan! You don't think Sir Richard will object, do you?"

"No, not at all," Morgan said with a faint smile. "As a matter of fact, I think he'll be every bit as enthusiastic about it as I am." His expression sobered for a moment. "I'm just a bit hesitant to bring it up, you see, since it would involve a mention of his passing."

"You could wait," O'Brien said. "After all, if you intend nothing until he's gone—"

Morgan shook his head. "I can't do that. I know he's made me his heir, but none of this is mine, don't you see? I feel a stranger to it all. No," he repeated, turning to face the fire, "I will tell him what I plan. It just seems a bit awkward, that's the thing."

For a moment he stood, relishing the heat from the flames. Too many winters spent on the road in years past had left him with a chronic ache that plagued his legs and his shoulders without mercy. He almost dreaded the thought of November coming on. An open fire in every room was a continual delight for him, one of the few features at Nelson Hall that gave him any real pleasure.

Turning to face Smith O'Brien, he said, "You will stay the night, I hope? I've been planning an evening of chess ever since I learned you were coming."

"Ah, yes, I'm looking forward to it!" Smith O'Brien got to his feet and joined Morgan in front of the fire. "Who knows when we'll next find time for a quiet evening such as this."

Morgan searched his old friend's features. "Aye, and that's the truth, William. From what I am hearing, things may not be quiet with you much longer."

O'Brien met his eyes, but said nothing. Morgan puzzled over the expression he encountered there, convinced it couldn't be fear he was seeing. In all the years they had been friends, he had never seen a glimmer of panic in Smith O'Brien's steady, piercing gaze. Yet tonight he could swear that an unfamiliar look akin to dread lurked behind that carefully controlled expression.

Smith O'Brien watched Fitzgerald's face. He was suddenly tempted to confide his dream. Just as quickly, he dismissed the idea. He and his old friend had been apart for months, had not enjoyed a leisurely, companionable time like this for what seemed an age. He would do nothing to mar the pleasure of the evening; only God knew when such a time would come again.

Besides, it was only a dream. He had never been given to foolish notions and flutters about such things, and he recoiled at the very idea that the big, granite-visaged Fitzgerald might think him womanish if he were to reveal his apprehension. No, he would keep his silence.

It was just that it always seemed so real—so dreadfully, chillingly real. And it came more and more often lately. It must have invaded his sleep a dozen times over the past few months.

First there would come the mist, dense and cold and dark. Then, as if rising up out of the ground itself, a ring of black-shawled women and youths would appear, their wraps draped over their heads as they bemoaned something in their midst, something just beyond the dreamer's range of vision. Their whispers would rise until they began to keen and shriek, as if teetering on the very edge of madness.

He would approach them. Slowly, ever so slowly, he would creep up to the outer fringe of their circle, unwilling to see what distressed them so, yet unable *not* to look. As he neared the ring of shadowed, faceless women, the woman nearest him would turn, step out, and face him.

Always, it was the same woman. Standing so close he could feel her breath on his face—a cold, vile breath, as if corrupted—she would freeze him in the path of her crazed eyes and begin to chant in a hoarse, thick whisper, "Have you heard about Fitzgerald? He is fallen…Fitzgerald is fallen…"

Almost immediately, the other black-garbed women would stop their moaning and turn to face O'Brien, staring at him with eyes filled with horror. One after another they would take up the chant, whispering, then wailing, splitting the night mist with a near-deafening madness, filling O'Brien's head with a dangerous pounding.

"Have you heard about Fitzgerald? He is fallen…Fitzgerald is fallen…."

With a shudder, O'Brien lurched toward the library table, his hand trembling as he attempted to refill his cup. He could feel Fitzgerald's eyes on his back. Swallowing hard, he hesitated until his composure returned enough that he could face his friend.

Killala

In his room, Joseph Mahon penned the last few words of the day's journal entry.

His hand was stiff, his knuckles gnarled from long years of enduring the cold, wet Atlantic winds. Like many of his fellow priests, he had kept a journal for years. Before the Hunger, he had been lax in keeping it up-to-date; now he attempted to make an entry every night.

He felt he had little time remaining to chronicle the events of the famine; he was besieged these days with a near disabling weakness. But as one of the few in the village who could read and write, he sensed a keen responsibility to record the horrors in his parish as long as he had the strength to hold a pen.

Earlier in the year he had exacted a promise by way of correspondence with Morgan Fitzgerald that the younger man would claim the journal once Joseph was gone, Morgan had agreed to see to it that Killala's tragedy, at least as Joseph had been able to record it, would be preserved. And Fitzgerald had promised to add his own recollections from his time spent in Mayo, as well.

The dread famine, with its accompanying plague of disease that had felled most of Ireland, had been particularly vicious in this remote western corner of the island. What had happened here must not be forgotten. Like numerous priests who sacrificed precious moments of sleep in order to detail the suffering of their parishes, Joseph Mahon would write the truth as he saw it—so long as his God gave him the strength to write at all.

> Today I performed last rites for three children. The Hagen lad died of consumption, but Mary Stevens and Liam Connors literally starved to death. By tomorrow the Connors' baby girl will also be dead.
>
> The village is at its lowest point in two years. There was no sign of blight this summer, but owing to the lack of seed potatoes, the acreage planted was miserably small—not nearly enough to help the poor people. Besides, they are far too weak and sick to harvest even the scantiest of crops. All relief works and soup kitchens are now shut down. There is no recourse left to the people except to starve.
>
> Yet, even now, Trevelyan—who has virtually dictated all relief measures—is insisting the crops are "wonderful" this year and, as always, maintains that the exports of corn and other grain should continue as usual. The rest of the corn, of course, is claimed by the landlords for their rent.
>
> With O'Connell dead, and Smith O'Brien only beginning to gain any authority with Young Ireland, there is no one to speak

for the people. Except, of course, for Morgan Fitzgerald. Unfortunately for the masses, his commonsense approach and appeal for caution is not what most of the so-called leaders wish to hear. They prefer Lalor, with his impossible doctrines, and Mitchel, with his visions of insurrection....

Joseph paused, the pen trembling as he was gripped by a terrible, sinful wave of hopelessness. His entire body shook as he penned his last words for the day:

May God have mercy on our souls, for we are trapped by an Evil too vile to imagine. Our entire country would seem to be host to an Enemy far more inhuman than the English, more savage than Bloody Cromwell. We are captives of an ageless Adversary.

God help us all, for hell has loosed its demons on all of Ireland.

6

The Church in Paradise Square

It is an easy thing to pray,
No want or sorrow knowing—
It is an easy thing to say,
"I praise God for bestowing."
But try to pray and try to love,
Pain wrung and soul' degraded—
The Lord God judges "crime" above,
But not as man has weighed it.

MARY KELLY (1825–1910)

These days, Sara Farmington spent two Sabbath evenings a month worshiping in a tent. No doubt it would astonish most members of her uptown congregation to learn that these informal church services in the Five Points slum ranked high among her favorite—and most meaningful—worship experiences.

Jess Dalton had wasted no time in taking the Word to the slums of New York City, targeting Five Points as his "Number One Mission." A large, sturdy tent had been hurriedly erected in the center of Paradise Square—the ludicrous name of the triangular space into which the five major streets of Five Points converged. In addition to Pastor Dalton, two Roman Catholic priests and a Baptist minister took turns offering outdoor services on Sunday evenings.

Already dubbed the "Big Tent" by local residents, it was only a temporary arrangement until an adequate, affordable building could be located. In the meantime, the crowds increased with each service.

This Sunday evening was no exception; the "Big Tent" was filled to overflowing. Because of the growing number of supplicants after services— underprivileged residents of the slum who stayed to beg for food or clothing or, in some cases, nothing more than some human warmth and kindness— Sara had fallen into the routine of accompanying the Daltons on their Sunday evenings. Most times Nora and Evan Whittaker came, too, but today Sara's father was treating them and the Fitzgerald children to a ferryboat ride and a tour of Staten Island.

This evening, as was always the case, not everyone in the service had come to worship. There were the usual number who wandered in and out of the tent merely to satisfy their curiosity or ease their boredom. Others arrived intoxicated. Whatever their circumstances or motivation, however, none would be turned away.

By now Sara knew what to expect. Should anyone prove disruptive, Pastor Dalton would simply halt his sermon and wait for a nearby policeman to remove the troublemaker from the tent. After the service, however, he would have a private conversation with the offending party. Although nobody seemed to know the gist of these discussions, it was observed that, more times than not, the mischief-maker would show up the following Sunday, seemingly penitent and respectful.

Jess Dalton was making a difference in Five Points. By touching a heart here, and another there, he was beginning to change lives for the better. Sara had never heard preaching quite like that of the big curly haired pastor with the compassionate eyes. The man seemed thoroughly comfortable with all kinds of people. Whether standing in the pulpit of his prosperous church on Fifth Avenue or in a tent surrounded by the destitute and downtrodden, he had a way of communicating the loving heart of God in a simple but compelling way. No "hellfire and brimstone" preacher, Pastor Dalton nevertheless managed to instruct and convict in a quiet, steady voice that never failed to convey the gentle warmth of Christ's forgiving love.

Sara could not imagine anyone coming away from his sermons unchanged. Certainly he had caused her to do some thinking about her own life.

This morning's sermon at the church on Fifth Avenue, for example, had stirred a discomfiting look at a flaw in her nature she would have preferred to ignore. Perhaps because it bordered on hypocrisy—a sin from which Sara would have believed herself exempt—she had, up until now, avoided confronting it.

It wasn't merely that she occasionally caught herself feeling smug, much like the sanctimonious Pharisee who considered himself better than other sinners. No, this was something more treacherous, more complicated than simple self-righteousness.

Listening to Pastor Dalton, Sara had been seized by an uncompromising conviction of her own sin. Shaken, she at first tried to retreat into denial. After hours of contemplative prayer, followed by an intense bout of soul-searching she had come to admit that her critical, judgmental attitude toward members of her own social circle—including members of her own congregation—was every bit as sinful as the attitudes she was forever condemning in *others*.

Sara knew that among her friends she was considered to be a "good Christian": fair-minded, generous-natured, and unswervingly dedicated to benevolence and good works. She had been raised in a household which upheld the principle that a "good Christian" was to give and to serve in proportion to the level of one's own prosperity. The more one prospered, the more one strived to mitigate the suffering of those less fortunate.

Her father, while unconventional to the point of raising eyebrows among the more tradition-bound of his class, was unflagging in his devotion to Christian service. Her lovely, genteel mother had died when Sara was only five, but Clarissa Farmington's kindness and generosity were legendary, not only among her household servants, but among tenement dwellers and Christian workers throughout the city.

Although Sara only vaguely remembered her mother's soft voice and sweet smile, she was ever mindful of her legacy. Inscribed upon Clarissa Farmington's gravestone and upon her daughter's heart were the words: *Many women have done excellently, but you surpass them all.*

Sara made every effort to follow in her mother's footsteps as she ministered in her own way to the lost and impoverished souls in the city's slum areas. Active in the Ladies' Home Missionary Society of her local congregation, she also spent hours every month as a volunteer for the Infants Hospital.

She had no reservations whatever about going among the most degraded poor wretches in the Five Points slum, knew no fear of the drunks who lined up in the alleys to beg in broad daylight. She was not repulsed by the poor hygiene or appalling physical handicaps she encountered in the tenements. To her, poverty, illness, and even degradation were not nearly so offensive as was the apathy and scorn she observed in many of her contemporaries.

Like her mother, she looked after their household help with diligence and real affection. Ginger, their West Indies housekeeper, received a handsome salary and more time off than any servant on Fifth Avenue. Like their other household servants, she was treated to generous gifts and favors throughout the year.

For years, Sara had lived what she thought to be a selfless, humanitarian existence. She would have no part in the discrimination and cruelty exhibited by many of her contemporaries toward the immigrants pouring into the city. Where others shrank from any form of involvement with these "undesirables," Sara opened her arms to embrace them. She truly did not understand society's aversion toward the impoverished and the oppressed, could not seem to help involving herself in the lives of others. It went against her very nature to turn her back on someone in need.

But Pastor Dalton's sermon that morning had jolted her to a shattering realization: *She was not what she thought herself to be, nor were her motives quite so pure as she was sure the Lord would like.*

The message had struck her with such force that she had written down the closing words:

"Charity is not merely an act of giving. It is an attitude. It does not demand or set conditions. It does not harbor expectations. True Christian charity is borne of a spirit large enough and great enough to look past the prejudices and weaknesses, the pettiness and the sin of the human heart and see the love of our Lord and Savior reaching out to all mankind, whatever their condition."

Now, as the pastor reached the closing of his evening message, Sara was once more jarred by the conviction that today the Lord had spoken to her in unmistakable terms, exposing an ugly sin in her life—a sin she had deliberately ignored for years. Jess Dalton's final words were for her:

"Christian charity is defined at the cross, the great equalizer of all time. When Christ looked down from the cross, He didn't see rich or poor, fools or saints, slaves or enslavers, bankers or beggars. He saw sinners—sinners in need of a Savior. He didn't qualify His love or His forgiveness—and we have no right to put conditions on ours, either. He loves that difficult neighbor you can't abide, that wretched opium eater, that pompous, hypocritical alderman with

the fat cigar—He loves them all—just as much as He loves you and me. And He calls us to love with the same unconditional love!"

The blood hammering wildly in her ears, Sara swallowed against the lump in her throat. How many times had she silently condemned a member of her own congregation for exhibiting what *she* interpreted as Pharisaism, prejudice, or indifference?

How many among the circle of her acquaintances and friends had she judged as heartless, denying them her respect, goodwill, and affection? Why, she had actually severed relationships—old family ties—because she deemed the other party to be selfish or without social conscience!

"He loves them just as they are, and we should thank Him with our every breath that He does! Where would any one of us be if our Lord could love only spotless, sin-free souls who lived up to His expectations?"

Her condemning spirit had secretly demanded that her friends and acquaintances live up to Sara Farmington's *expectations* before they could be counted worthy of her affection.

God forgive me, I've tried and judged others as if I somehow had the right to condemn their hearts. Yet, by withholding understanding and love from those I found lacking, I am as guilty as those I've condemned!

Sara sat in stunned silence, oblivious to the movement around her. The service was over, but still she sat, intent and isolated within the shell of her own contemplation. Suddenly she jumped and gasped when a broad shoulder squeezed in next to her.

Michael Burke smiled down at her with a quizzical expression. "Miss Farmington—I'm sorry, did I startle you?"

Sara blinked, taking a moment to recover. "Sergeant Burke—I—no! No, that's quite all right. I must have been…lost in the sermon."

"Aye, he gives a powerful message, doesn't he?" the sergeant replied. "Unfortunately, I had to miss most of this evening's—we had an entire gang of disruptives to handle before the service ever started. I'm just now getting back to the tent." Burke stood and extended an arm to her. "These Sunday evening congregations are growing fast," he observed, waiting for her to rise, then escorting her to the tent's exit. "We have to put on an extra man or two most every week."

"You said there was trouble earlier—what happened?"

His lip curled with distaste. "Just a gang of drunken Irishers in a mood to rile the crowd. A normal occurrence down here."

"But surely all the troublemakers aren't Irish?"

He looked at her, his eyes still hard. "As it happens, they usually are," he said bitterly. "Our lads and lassies from the Emerald Isle account for the largest population of the Tombs—the city jail. We haven't the cells to hold them all, and the problem is only growing worse."

His biting candor about his own people made Sara feel awkward and embarrassed for him. "Many of them are desperate, I'm sure—"

"Begging your pardon, Miss Farmington," he interrupted, "but I hear that excuse far too often. Oh, the Irish in the city are in dire straits, there's no denying it. But a vast number of them bring on their own grief—or at least add to it—simply because they can't keep their faces out of the bottle!"

Sara could almost feel the man's anger as the harsh words poured from him. "They drink because they can't find work," he went on. "They drink because they miss the 'ould country.' They drink because they believe themselves to be disadvantaged and persecuted. They drink for any number of reasons, but many, I'm afraid, drink just because they love to drink!"

His bitterness pierced Sara's heart. She sensed that Michael Burke's anger was motivated by shame and grief for his people. "It seems we're always harder on our own, Sergeant," she said softly. "I've had to deal with that particular…problem…myself recently."

His left eye narrowed slightly, a mannerism Sara had come to recognize as a sign of skepticism or puzzlement.

She managed a rueful smile. "It's the very thing I was chastising myself about only moments ago. I've always been too quick to criticize my peers, I'm afraid. I suppose we simply expect—or *demand*—more of those we consider 'our own kind.' And when they don't live up to our expectations, we tend to strike out at them. I'm only now beginning to realize that I have a great deal more forgiveness and understanding for total strangers than I do for the very ones I call my friends."

Searching her face, the sergeant lifted one dark brow. "You are a painfully honest young woman, Sara Farmington—*Miss* Farmington," he corrected quickly.

Inexplicably flustered, Sara glanced away. "*Sara* will do just fine, Sergeant," she assured him. "I believe we've known each other long enough by now to dispense with the formalities."

"That being the case," he countered with a grin, "you might want to know that my name is not *Sergeant,* after all. It's *Michael.*"

"Oh...yes. Yes, of course," Sara stammered, feeling ridiculously young and awkward under his amused scrutiny.

"Nora and the children—they're well?" he asked.

"Oh, yes, they're fine!" Sara said, relieved at the change of subject. "As a matter of fact, Father took them and Evan Whittaker on the ferry to Staten Island this afternoon. I'm sure the children will love it, but frankly I'm afraid Nora wasn't all that excited about being on the water again, so soon after their ocean voyage."

The sergeant made no reply for a moment. When he finally spoke, Sara wondered at the sharpness in his tone. "Whittaker went with them, you say?"

"Whittaker?" Sara stared at him blankly. "Oh—yes! Yes, Evan went along, too."

His dark brows dipped lower, his mouth again went hard. "They seem to have become great friends, Nora and Whittaker." Again, the unpleasant edge in his voice.

"Why...yes, I suppose they have."

"Not exactly a common thing between the Irish and the British. But, then, according to Nora, Whittaker is not your ordinary Englishman."

Good heavens, he sounded almost...*jealous!* Jealous of *Evan Whittaker*? For an instant, the idea caught Sara up short. *Could* Nora possibly be interested in the Englishman—romantically interested, that is? It was no secret around the Farmington mansion that Evan was sweet on *Nora*—Ginger clucked her tongue in sympathy for the "poor mon" at least once a day. But with the handsome, virile Michael Burke just waiting in the wings for her to accept his proposal, it had never occurred to any one of them that perhaps Nora's interest might lie elsewhere.

Sara felt a faint stirring of something akin to hope. Just as quickly, she shook it off. Of course Nora didn't care for Evan—*that* way!

And whether she did or not, Sara had no call to go getting wild ideas about Michael Burke! Even if by some remote possibility Nora *should* happen to be out of the picture, why would the police sergeant give an uptown spinster like herself a second glance? New York was filled with younger—and prettier—Irish girls.

The man was an Irish policeman, for goodness' sake! And she *was* Lewis Farmington's daughter, after all. Farmingtons didn't carry on over Irish policemen, even foolish, old-maid Farmingtons like herself!

"Miss Farmington? *Sara?*"

Sara blinked. Michael Burke was staring at her with a decidedly curious expression. "Yes—I'm sorry?"

"I asked how you came? Is Uriah waiting for you?"

"Oh, no—no, I came with the Daltons, actually."

"Well, then, would you like to walk a bit, until they're ready to leave?"

When Sara hesitated, he put in quickly, "Not in the Points. I was thinking we might start toward Broadway."

"I—well, I *should* stay and help…the pastor and Kerry may need an extra pair of hands." Now, why had she said that? She *wanted* to go, wanted to be with him.

He waited, smiling at her in the most disconcerting manner.

"Well, perhaps just a *short* walk," she said uncertainly, looking up to study the evening sky with feigned interest. "But I'll need to tell the Daltons."

He nodded, his smile widening.

Sara turned with a jerk and headed toward the Daltons, who were still surrounded by those few evening worshipers reluctant to leave. She was thoroughly disgusted with herself. What *was* there about Michael Burke that threw her into such a dither? He had the most unsettling way of making her feel like a silly, empty-headed schoolgirl!

Watching Sara Farmington and Michael Burke make their way out of Paradise Square, Jess Dalton attempted to carry on a disjointed conversation with his wife. There were frequent interruptions from the worshipers still filing past, but by now he and Kerry had grown skilled at communicating in fragments.

"What do you make of Sara and her policeman?" he asked in a low voice. Jess had seen the two together on other occasions, chatting after services usually, both looking somewhat stiff and uncomfortable in each other's company.

"What I think is that they're trying awfully hard to ignore their feelings for each other," Kerry replied, smiling cheerfully as she greeted the Widow Ransom.

Surprised, Jess continued to smile as he said goodnight to Willie

Toothman and his pretty wife, Sally, who was very much in the family way. "So you believe there *are* feelings there?"

"Faith, Jess, only a blind man could not see the sparks flying between those two!" Kerry paused to give poor Vida Ransom a hug. "And why are you looking so amused?" she said after the widow and her daughter went on by.

"I was considering the implications of a millionaire's daughter being paired with an Irish policeman," Jess murmured. Turning back to the worshipers, he gripped the dry, gnarled hand of Cletus Denvers, intoxicated as usual. Putting a hand to the man's shoulder, he said, "It's good to see you here, Cletus. You'll come back again next Sunday, I hope?"

Kerry looked up at him. "Sara's not all that clever at disguising her feelings, is she?"

Jess shook his head, both in answer to her question and as a greeting to a young woman who refused to meet his eye. Her face was garishly painted, her hair frizzed, but he had noticed her among the crowd on more than one occasion. "Good to have you. Please come again," he said warmly, shaking her hand. She hurried from the tent, still avoiding his gaze.

Kerry's eyes softened as she watched the woman scurry outside the tent. Keeping her voice low, she said, "Do you suppose the sergeant is aware of Sara's…interest?"

"Not likely," answered Jess with a tired sigh as his gaze took in several worshipers still milling about the tent. "I believe the sergeant is too busy dealing with his own feelings to notice Sara's."

"Oh, d'you think so, Jess?"

He didn't miss the hopeful note in her voice.

"I recognize the signs," he said, solemnly, "having been badly smitten myself a few years back."

Her sharp little chin snapped up. "You make it sound somewhat like hydrophobia."

He pretended to consider her retort. "It does carry some of the same symptoms, I suppose."

"And am I to assume from that remark, then, that you are no longer smitten, Mr. Dalton?"

He grinned at her. "Not at all, Mrs. Dalton. Just like hydrophobia, my condition has no known cure."

She attempted a severe frown, reminding him, "We were discussing Sergeant Burke and Sara Farmington."

"*You* were discussing Sergeant Burke and Sara Farmington. I was counting the shamrocks in your eyes."

"You are daft."

"And it's entirely your doing."

"We should be getting home," she said, ignoring the squeeze he gave her hand. "Where has our son taken himself off to, d'you suppose?"

"If he's true to form, we'll find him at the chestnut stand on Mulberry by now."

"Jess," Kerry said thoughtfully, "that limp of Sara Farmington's—do you know how she came by it?"

Jess nodded. "Her father told me. She was born with one hip out of alignment. The doctors could do nothing to correct the problem."

"Another condition with no known cure?"

"Apparently," he responded. "But I must say, the condition doesn't seem to slow Miss Farmington down very much."

"I've noticed," Kerry mused. "And it certainly doesn't seem to affect Michael Burke in the least, either."

Dalton looked down at his wife with an affectionate grin and raised one eyebrow.

"Jess, I'm wondering—" She stopped, but he heard the slight rolling brogue in her voice that invariably meant she was plotting something.

He cocked his head and waited, intrigued by a stray copper curl that had escaped the confines of her bonnet.

"D'you truly think Sergeant Burke might be interested in Sara?" Without waiting for his reply, she hurried on. "I have an idea—why don't we invite the two of them to go home with us for dessert? There's at least half of Molly's chocolate cake left over—plenty for all of us. Sara will be riding back with us anyway, and you know how I do enjoy her company... and you admire Sergeant Burke, you've said so yourself...it would be an opportunity to spend some time with the two of them, as well as giving *them* an opportunity to be together..."

When she finally stopped, Jess said only, "Mightn't that be awkward?"

Kerry's mouth drew to an impatient pout, which he never failed to find delightful. "Why would it be awkward?"

"Well..."

"Because *he's* an Irish policeman and *she's* Sara Farmington?" she challenged shrewdly.

"Certainly not!" He frowned at her. "But according to Sara, the sergeant is almost betrothed to Nora Kavanagh."

"*Almost* is a long way from the real thing," she huffed. "Especially in this case. It seems to me that Nora Kavanagh is more interested in spending time with Evan Whittaker than Sergeant Burke."

He stared at her. "It seems that way to you, does it?"

"It does. And that poor Englishman looks at her as if the sun daily rises in her eyes."

Jess sighed. Hadn't he learned long ago there was no arguing with the Irish? "Your intentions are the best, love, but I honestly think we might be well-advised to wait. Just for a while."

Knitting her brows together prettily, Kerry considered his words. "Oh, pshaw! But—perhaps you're right. Sara does seem determined that Nora and the sergeant will wed."

He nodded. "Sara's a determined young woman."

"But no match for the Irish, should Sergeant Burke have a mind to court her."

"Which you believe he does."

"Well…I'm not saying *he's* aware of it just yet. But, yes, yes, I believe he does."

Laughing, Jess took her arm and started out of the tent. "You are incorrigible, Mrs. Dalton."

"Just you wait and see, Jess," she countered smugly. "I have one of my feelings about Sara and the sergeant."

Having learned that Kerry's "feelings" were not to be taken lightly, Jess wisely remained silent.

7

Confrontation

Like a tide our work should rise,
Each later wave the best;
Today is a king in disguise,
Today is the special test.

JOHN BOYLE O'REILLY (1844–1890)

On Saturday night, Daniel and Tierney had their first real argument. Their natures being as different as they were, it was only natural they would have a falling out every now and then. They had fussed more than once since becoming roommates. But tonight was the first time Daniel had seen Tierney truly riled with him.

He had occasionally glimpsed the blistering, white-hot anger that seemed to lurk deep inside Tierney. It would spark and blaze without warning, never failing to catch Daniel off-guard when it did. Even so, this was the first time he had encountered it on such an intensely personal level.

Had the hour not been late, forcing them to keep their voices low, what began as an argument could have easily turned into an ugly row. And all of it over a part-time job.

It had been a nice enough evening to begin with. At Tierney's urging, Uncle Mike had taken the both of them to a meeting sponsored by some of the city's journalists—a meeting to raise funds for Ireland. There had been a great display of patriotism in the hall, both Irish and American, and Daniel had felt pleased and proud of his connection to both countries.

Later, lying in bed, Tierney on his sagging mattress and Daniel on the makeshift cot Uncle Mike had moved in for him, they rehashed their week.

Only when Tierney raised the subject of Daniel's taking an after-school job at the hotel did the argument catch fire.

Tierney seemed to find it unthinkable that Daniel would not sign on at the hotel in a shake. "Are you daft? What do you mean, you don't think you *want* the job?"

At Daniel's whispered caution, he lowered his voice. But his tone lost none of its harshness as he went on. "I've been pestering Walsh for weeks to find you something better than sweeping up. And now that he's about to make a place for you in the lobby, you don't *want* it?"

Hurt and somewhat surprised by Tierney's sudden flare of anger, Daniel hurried to explain. "It's just that I talked with Dr. Grafton last week, don't you see, and he admitted he needs some help in his office. He's willing to take me on at once."

The room was dark, but the rude exclamation from Tierney's bed told Daniel his friend was plenty sore, all right. "Doing what? Emptying people's slops?"

Why was it so important to Tierney *where* he worked? Raising himself up on one elbow, Daniel tried to explain. "What the doctor has in mind is that I'd be keeping the office tidy—looking after supplies and the examining room—that sort of thing." The same flush of excitement he had felt when the physician agreed to try such an arrangement now washed over him again. "He said he might even take me with him on calls from time to time. I wouldn't be allowed to do much, of course, but it would be grand experience for me."

Tierney let out a muffled sound of disgust. "And what will the doctor be paying you for this fine position?"

Daniel felt more than a little foolish when he realized he hadn't actually discussed salary with the doctor. "We—we haven't exactly settled on that just yet. But I'm sure it will be more than fair. Dr. Grafton seems a fine man, Tierney, and a truly excellent physician. He was grand with Katie."

"Not grand enough to save her life."

Daniel's jaw clenched with resentment. "It was too late for Katie," he muttered hoarsely. "She had been ill for years. What more could any doctor have done? I still say I can learn a great deal from him."

Tierney's bed creaked as he jolted upright. In the dark, Daniel could not see his friend's face, but he had no trouble imagining the other boy's dark scowl. "Patrick Walsh gives his people more than a generous wage!

You can't tell me that old sawbones will even come close to paying you what you'd make at the hotel!"

Daniel's hurt turned to anger. "Don't call him that!" Pushing himself up, he swung his feet over the side of the bed. "As for the money, that's not the most important thing for me. 'Tis the experience I'm after. That, and a job that—counts for something."

A long silence hung between them. Stung by Tierney's sullen refusal to even try to understand, Daniel groped for patience. "Tierney, you know it's all I've ever thought to do," he said, keeping his voice low. "I've wanted to be a doctor my whole life long."

Tierney's reply was a sharp grunt of disgust.

Dragging in a deep breath, Daniel went on. "I thought you understood. I'd rather make less money and have the experience. For later."

For a time, Tierney made no reply. When he finally answered, Daniel heard the exasperation in his voice. "Aye, for later. But this is for *now*." He paused. "Walsh would be offering you a rare chance," he went on, his tone less harsh now. "You've seen how it is for us in New York: the decent jobs are for everyone else but the Irish!"

Daniel could not argue the fact. In the newspaper ads, on the signs posted in windows, the hostile warning blazed: *NO IRISH NEED APPLY.*

It was almost a foregone conclusion that the Irish immigrant would find a closed door on any job worthy of mention. When one of the more fortunate ones managed to find a place with decent wages, he grabbed at it, knowing the opportunity might never come twice.

Still, Daniel felt the position with Dr. Grafton *was* a good job for him—an ideal job, considering his plans for the future.

"You're going to need money for your schooling, I should think." Tierney's tone was still grudging, but no longer angry. "You could tuck a lot more away working for Patrick Walsh than with any old doctor."

Daniel wanted his friend's understanding, but he wanted an end to the bad feelings between them even more. "I imagine that's true," he admitted. "What I'll do is, before I decide either way, I'll talk to Dr. Grafton and find out about the wages. I won't work for nothing, that's certain."

Tierney muttered, "I should hope not," then rolled onto his back. "I'm only trying to help you, you know."

"I *do* know!" Daniel quickly assured him. "And I'm grateful, truly I am.

But the thing is, just as you want to do what matters to *you,* I need to do what matters to *me.* You understand that, sure?"

"I understand that what matters to me is money," Tierney shot back. "And you're going to need your share of it, too, Danny-boy. At least until you're a stoved-up old sawbones getting rich off all the society stiffs."

Daniel shook his head at the other boy's foolishness, smiling a little. "That's how it will be, do you think?"

"No doubt about it! You'll have an exciting life, boyo—taking warts off the thumbs of bankers and bleeding the blue blood of foolish old maids like Sara Farmington."

Daniel stiffened. "Sara Farmington isn't an old maid—and she's not a bit foolish, either!"

Tierney made an ugly retort that bordered on profanity. His crudeness both angered and wounded Daniel. Sometimes it seemed that Tierney held nothing sacred—nothing, that is, except for Ireland.

"The Farmingtons have been great friends to us," said Daniel, his voice tight with resentment.

"The Farmingtons feel *sorry* for you," Tierney snapped. "You're nothing to them at all but another cause, can't you see that? A 'good work'— that's what you are."

Daniel swallowed. "That's not so. Miss Sara and my mother have become true friends."

"Grow up, Danny-boy! People like the Farmingtons don't make friends with Irish immigrants! Miss Sara and all her bustling about in the slums— the old man and his charity—that's their way of salving their consciences. That's all you are as well, and you'd be wise to face it!"

Daniel sensed he should be angry at Tierney's charges. Yet hadn't he questioned the Farmingtons' motives himself, and more than once? Hadn't a nagging whisper of doubt crept into his thoughts about their benefactors, causing him to wonder if the Kavanaghs and the Fitzgeralds might not represent still another "project" to Miss Sara and her father?

"You've seen for yourself how kind Miss Sara is," he challenged Tierney, trying to ignore his own faltering conviction. "And not just to Mother, at that. What about her concern for Johanna? Engaging a tutor for her, making the rounds of the doctors, with her—how can you even think she's not sincere?"

"And who wouldn't be good to Johanna?" Tierney shot back. "Still, it's all part of their do-gooder notions, I'm telling you. You just don't want to see it, is all."

Tierney's flinty irreverence never extended to Johanna Fitzgerald, Daniel noticed. Whether it was her inability to hear or speak, or just her shy, genuine sweetness, Johanna invariably evoked a softening, even a gentleness in Tierney that seemed at odds with his usual cynicism.

When Tierney spoke again, the last remaining trace of anger was gone from his voice. "There's a girl at school—she died just last week of the same thing that made Johanna as she is. The scarlet fever. She wasn't but thirteen."

After a solemn moment between them, Tierney did one of his quicksilver changes in mood. "Ah, well, when the illustrious Dr. Kavanagh here hangs out his shingle, we'll have an end to that sort of thing, don't you know? No doubt, he'll have a cure for everything from bunions to baldness."

Relieved to hear the teasing note return to the other's voice, Daniel hesitated only a moment before picking up his pillow and tossing it at Tierney's head. Immediately Tierney flung his own in return, and soon the feathers were flying.

A gruff warning from Uncle Mike in the next room put an end to their fun, but not before the pillow fight accomplished what Daniel had hoped for: the return of Tierney's raucous good humor.

Later, while Tierney slept, Daniel lay awake in the darkness of the room. In the street below a dog barked, then another, followed by a loud clang of rubbish containers and a drunken shout. After a moment there was the sound of laughter and shuffling feet.

Tired of tossing, and uncomfortably warm in the closeness of the room, Daniel finally gave up on sleep. Quietly, he got out of bed and tiptoed across the floor. Glancing back once at Tierney's sleeping form, he then crept out the window onto the narrow strip of roofing Uncle Mike jokingly referred to as "the balcony."

The balcony at night was one of Daniel's favorite places. Up here, behind the low railing that rimmed the roof, he could get away from the worst of the street smells and the people. On an especially quiet night, he could almost pretend he was back in Killala, sitting on the hillside, looking down on the village of his birth.

Still troubled, he plopped down, leaning against the wall and hugging his knees. He hated the fact that he and Tierney had argued. Despite the differences in their temperament, they had become best friends, and every dispute they had was like a thorn piercing his heart.

It was true they had little in common. While Daniel was content to sit quietly and strum the harp, Tierney would rather let off steam in bare-knuckle boxing. Daniel took to public school like a starving man at a banquet; Tierney detested it, doing only what he must to get by and keep Uncle Mike at bay. Indeed, it seemed his only interest in school was having fun with the other lads that followed him about, dogging his steps, imitating his every move.

Tierney was a natural-born leader, and that was the truth. For himself, Daniel much preferred the companionship of one or two close friends. He liked people well enough, but craved quiet times more. Tierney, on the other hand, seemed to thrive on being the center of attention.

Small wonder, Daniel thought with a faint smile. When Tierney spoke, others listened. He had only to make the smallest suggestion, and it seemed the other boys could not carry out the idea fast enough. And when he showed his temper or displeasure, the others wasted no time at all in working themselves back into his good graces.

Aye, we are different, all right, Daniel thought, resting his head against the wall. Tierney was a doer; Daniel himself was a dreamer. In truth, he had a softness in his nature that at times embarrassed him. It took little enough to bring tears to his eyes or a lump to his throat. Tierney, though, was entirely unpredictable. Moody, even sullen, one moment, he could turn the rogue in the blink of an eye. There was a darkness to the older boy's nature that Daniel found almost frightening. At times he glimpsed a hardness in his friend's soul, a ruthlessness he thought might quickly turn mean if provoked.

Uncle Mike saw it, too, he was sure. No doubt that's what accounted for his attempts to keep such a tight rein on Tierney.

Yet, Daniel wasn't so sure but what Uncle Mike's unyielding discipline didn't make Tierney more rebellious than ever. The two of them were forever at a standoff.

Most often, Uncle Mike was a kindhearted, good-natured man. But when it came to his son, he could be awfully hard and unyielding. Daniel thought his mistake might be in trying to force Tierney into his own way of doing things, instead of being a bit more tolerant of their differences—which were considerable.

At times, he felt almost sorry for Uncle Mike. He was baffled by Tierney more often than not, and his confusion seemed to show itself in anger. But Daniel had seen the hurt in the man's eyes after a row with his son, and it grieved him.

He also knew that to broach the subject would only bring Tierney's wrath down on his head. So he kept his silence, aching for Uncle Mike, but understanding Tierney's frustration as well.

Giving a long sigh, he stretched, then got to his knees. For a moment, he watched a rib-thin spotted pup foraging among the garbage piled along the edge of the street. Then he turned and eased himself back through the window.

8

A Self-made Man

He with body waged a fight,
But body won; it walks upright.
Then he struggled with the heart;
Innocence and peace depart.
Then he struggled with the mind;
His proud heart he left behind.
Now his wars on God begin;
At stroke of midnight God shall win.

W. B. YEATS (1865–1939)

Patrick Walsh leaned back in his chair, contentedly watching the smoke from his pipe spiral toward the library ceiling. In truth he preferred a cigar to the pipe, but every red-faced Irish politician he knew smoked a cigar, and so as a matter of principle he did *not*.

Walsh had made a career of escaping his undistinguished beginnings in Ireland. Without really denying his heritage, he retained the best parts of it, at the same time disavowing even the most trivial commonplace traits most often associated with the Irish.

His father, the owner of a failed pub, had died while still a young man, leaving his wife with three little girls and an only son. Out of sheer desperation, Patrick's mother had taken them all off to Cork, where she earned a meager living as a seamstress and laundress. There was never money for anything more than mere survival; luxuries such as education, nice clothing, or holidays were nonexistent.

Even as a child, Patrick had possessed an acute loathing for their poverty and the ugliness associated with it. Being poor meant being wretched—dirty, ragged, and hungry. In the city, it also meant being despised.

When he was fifteen, with no more than a fleeting thought for his weary mother and young sisters, Patrick stole the passage money for America. On the day he sailed, he said a final goodbye to Ireland. He had no intention whatsoever of returning.

He entered Boston harbor with nothing but high hopes and grand expectations. It took only a week to confront the sobering reality that for the first time in his life, he would be forced to work if he were to eat.

He lasted only a few months on the Boston docks, loading cargo. He begrudged every moment he spent there, viewing the punishment of hitherto unused muscles as a kind of injustice wreaked upon him because he was poor and without connections. His resolve to escape the trap of poverty grew in proportion to his increasing aversion to hard work.

Patrick's education had been sparse and sporadic. With the help of one of his mother's clients, he had managed a few terms, but his formal schooling had taught him only the basics. His mind was quick and agile, however, and he learned much about politics, business, and society, relying on secondhand books and discarded newspapers. Although he hadn't a notion as to how he would one day attain financial success, he never doubted for a moment that he would.

Less than a year after arriving in the States, Patrick made his way to New York City. He already knew from his extensive reading that New York was no better than Boston when it came to prejudice and contempt for the Irish. Still, he felt that in New York he would find his luck, and he was impatient to make that discovery.

Patrick believed in luck, believed it was reserved for those with the wits to seize it when it beckoned. Already convinced that he was destined for good fortune, he deliberately ignored New York's docks and headed uptown.

By now he owned a decent pair of trousers and a clean shirt.

He had grown tall, maturing to good looks. When he presented himself to the desk clerk at the Braun Hotel, he made a neat, even pleasing appearance. The ferret-faced clerk informed him, however, that there were no openings. None at all.

Of course, even if there *had* been an opening, the clerk added with a spiteful curl of his lip, the hotel was not in the business of hiring the Irish. Nor, he added, were any of the other "decent" businesses in the city.

Patrick's first real stroke of luck occurred right there, in the hotel lobby, that Monday afternoon in early autumn. As it happened, John Braun, the hotel's middle-aged German owner, was there, nosing about the premises to see what sort of excesses he might discover on the part of his staff. Watching the German, Patrick sensed he was somebody of means. It took only a few minutes of keeping his ears open to discover Braun's identity.

At that point, Patrick slipped into one of his flash-fire changes that would stand him in good stead for years to come. The green Irish youth was transformed to an experienced, sharp-witted young man with the gift of the blarney and a ruthless penchant for seizing the advantage.

Near a small group of businessmen across the lobby, two aging bellmen were struggling with a hefty pyramid of luggage. Not wasting a moment, Patrick sprinted across the lobby to hoist a bulging valise under each arm. "I'll get the heavy ones, gents," he said cheerfully, shooting the elderly porters an engaging smile as he started off toward the stairs. Nodding their approval, the businessmen followed.

In a short time, he returned to the lobby and boldly presented himself to John Braun. "Your desk clerk said you do not hire the Irish, sir, which is a mistake, as you can see. I'll work for less than any of your more experienced men, and you'll get twice the work for your money. Perhaps there's lighter work about the establishment that the elderly gents could manage."

Taken with Patrick's audacity, Braun stood staring at him for only a moment before breaking into a horsey laugh and hiring him on the spot. It bothered Patrick not in the least that his boldness eventually cost the two old bellmen their jobs.

From that day on, he made it a point to ingratiate himself not only with John Braun, but with the desk clerk and even the kitchen help. In no time at all he was being described as "quick," "industrious," and "a good enough sort for an Irisher" by the entire staff.

With the patrons of the hotel, however, Patrick made his best mark. They took to his charm like fleas to a dog, easily impressed by this fine-looking, well-mannered youth who had an answer for every question, a solution for every problem. It was not long before Patrick Walsh was considered indispensable.

His charming usefulness did not escape the notice of John Braun. Within months Patrick was promoted to the desk, then to assistant manager. By the age of eighteen he could do no wrong in the eyes of his German employer, who had no son on whom to lavish his paternal instincts.

Braun did, however, have a daughter. Alice Braun was twenty-three, short and squat like her mother. She was a good, dutiful daughter who seemed to accept her plainness and lack of appeal by devoting herself to her parents, her church, and her two cats.

When Braun invited Patrick home for dinner one night, the crafty young Irishman immediately saw how things were. Alice was the only daughter. Her parents both adored her. And, most importantly, she wasn't likely to find an acceptable suitor on her own.

By playing to Braun's personal liking for him and plying his considerable charm with Mrs. Braun, Patrick managed to turn his first dinner invitation into a weekly custom. During these occasions he was propriety itself, staring at Alice only a bit too intently, allowing his hand to linger on hers only an instant longer than might have been necessary.

Mostly, he concentrated on Alice's mother, sensing her to be the real force in the family. Within a short time, he had ingratiated himself with the formidable Ula Braun until she fairly simpered every time he stepped over the threshold.

Poor Alice still seemed incapable of anything more flirtatious than to peep at Patrick over the dumplings, her round cheeks flushed and damp. After a few weeks, Patrick took things a step further, requesting a private audience with John Braun.

During this meeting, he candidly admitted his affection for Miss Alice. Yes, he acknowledged, there were a few years between them—but Miss Alice seemed so young, so sheltered, that in truth he felt years *older* than she, rather than younger. Besides, it was a fact that the hardships he had endured in Ireland had matured him quickly. Oh, of *course,* he realized that Miss Alice was leagues above him in every way—he had not found so fine and pure a woman in all of Ireland, after all. But could he possibly dare to hope that the family would consider him an acceptable suitor?

At first, Braun was stunned, then overwhelmed to the point of tears. He assured his young employee that social station had never been of major concern to *him*, although of course it had to be considered in relation to Alice, since she deserved only the best. Still, he thought himself a good judge of character, and as far as he could tell, Patrick's was exemplary. There was no substitute for sobriety, integrity, and hard work, now was there?

There *was* one matter which *did* concern him, however, that being Patrick's Roman faith. His church was his own business, of course, and Braun had never been much bothered by the Catholics. Still, with Alice being a devout Lutheran, it was a subject of some concern to her mother and father.

Sober-faced, Patrick expressed his understanding and stated that he quite understood such parental concern. He would, he offered, give the matter serious consideration.

In the meantime, could he call?

He found it incredibly easy to woo Alice. She was already wild about him, he knew; the only thing left was to break her out of her shell and convince her that *he* was wild about her as well.

They went for long walks, during which he coaxed her to talk about herself, sensing that nobody aside from her parents had ever shown her the slightest interest until now. He made it a habit to compliment her, paying her the kind of attention that would have turned the head of even a more worldly, confident young woman.

The first time he kissed her hand, the poor thing almost fainted. The first time he kissed her lips, he thought she would weep.

They were married six months later. Having given serious consideration to his Roman faith and deciding it could present a hindrance in attaining his goals, Patrick cheerfully rejected it and became a Lutheran.

John Braun presented the newlyweds with a home on Staten Island and a fine new carriage. In addition, he handed over to Patrick full ownership of the hotel where he had first employed him.

In Alice, Patrick gained a slavishly devoted wife who asked no more from her existence than to make him happy. To be fair, she *did* make him happy. Patrick liked his comforts, and Alice saw to it that he lacked for none. Their home was tasteful and bright, peaceful and snug. His children were well-behaved, albeit rather dull, and Alice did her best to keep her weight from getting out of control. She was affectionate, supportive, and fiercely protective of her husband and family.

In return, Patrick played the fond, if somewhat distracted, husband. Although he might lose patience with her from time to time and grow snappish, he always stopped short of hurting her. He found himself unwilling to deliberately wound the spirit behind those adoring round eyes.

His affection for Alice was quite genuine—the kind of emotion a man might hold for his favorite house dog. Although he found his wife rather pathetic, he had an undeniable soft spot for her. But if the truth be known, his deepest motivation for marital harmony was the maintaining of his own comfort. He avoided situations that would cause Alice pain more out of the desire to keep his well-ordered life intact than out of any consideration for her feelings.

Thus he kept his infidelities few and discreet, usually indulging in an occasional assignation when out of the city on business. He was wise enough to know the adoring Alice was no fool. More to the point, he knew John Braun would never forgive a man who humiliated his daughter. Patrick was therefore exceedingly careful to ensure that Alice never had reason to doubt his affection.

It bothered him not in the least that his feelings for his wife ran scarcely deeper than those he might have lavished on a pet. The truth was that Patrick was not capable of caring deeply for another human being, could not really attach himself to anyone or anything for more than a token relationship.

He was utterly self-centered and totally without conscience. His ambition, his desires, and his comfort mattered far more to him than did his wife and children. Alice had been a means to an end, and he was not without gratitude. But he could not help it if, most of the time, he simply tolerated her.

As for their children, Isabel, the oldest at twelve, was a ringer for her mother. Plain and plump, as heavy in mind as in body, she was not the little girl Patrick might have chosen. Even less to his liking was the eight-year-old Henry, whom Patrick thought to be incredibly fussy for a small boy. Patrick more often than not avoided both his children, for they bored him.

Somehow, he could not envision either of the two inheriting the varied Walsh enterprises, which were by now considerable. In addition to the hotel where he had gotten his start, Patrick now owned another pretentious uptown establishment, plus half a dozen moderately priced boardinghouses in lower Manhattan. Using his managers as a front, he also held the deed on three grog shops and a number of dockside taverns.

His most extensive holdings, however, were in the Five Points slum. The tenements were a veritable gold mine for landlords like him, far more profitable than respectable property. As many as five families could be crowded into one room. Whereas well-to-do tenants could demand repairs, the poor were afraid to demand anything of the landlords. If the beggars got behind in their rent, they were evicted at once and immediately replaced.

Run-down taverns abounded in the miserable slum, and Patrick owned more than his share of them. But all of his holdings in the area were deeded and leased in names other than his own; not a hint of scandal or illegal activity could be allowed to smear his reputation or endanger his family.

In the past year he had discovered a new, highly lucrative enterprise. Using a middleman in England or in Ireland, he would purchase, under the name of a broker who did not exist, the entire list of steerage passengers for several of the immigrant ships coming over. When they arrived, two or three runners hired especially for the purpose quickly herded the bewildered immigrants off the ship, whisking them away to various tenements along the docks or in Five Points—all of which were owned by Patrick.

Once they arrived, the unsuspecting immigrants forfeited all their worldly goods—to be held as "security" until they found work—as well as their remaining funds, which went to pay the exorbitant rent for their lodgings. The entire venture was almost entirely free from the risk of exposure. Neither the middleman who arranged the purchase nor the runners had any idea of Patrick's identity.

Patrick could number on one hand the men who knew the truth about a single one of his vast business activities. To these few he paid a ridiculously extravagant salary in order to guarantee their silence.

To those who thought they knew him best, Patrick Walsh was a paragon of virtue, a family man, and a shrewd but honest, highly successful businessman. To the members of his church, he was known as a good-natured, generous Irishman who had made something of himself—a man who cared for the poor and the widow. To his in-laws, he was a prince. To his wife, he was a king. To his children, he was a sometimes stern but always cheerful papa who seldom expected more from them than that they do well in their studies and not annoy him.

In his own eyes, Patrick Walsh was a success, a self-made man whose luck had held and whose prospects looked brighter with every sunrise. It bothered him not in the least that a great deal of his wealth came at the expense of the downtrodden poor from his own homeland.

Hadn't Christ himself said they would always have the poor among them? To Patrick's way of thinking, he was actually doing the poor wretches a service, providing them affordable lodging as well as drink in which to drown their troubles.

After all, somebody was always quick to turn a profit from the ignorant Irish. It might just as well be him.

9

Unnatural Enemies

We dreamt of a freedom akin to the wind's
For the skill of our hands, and the strength of our minds;
But we wake to a chain that confounds and controls,
With its amulet circle, our limbs and our souls—
To the cold chain of poverty—binding us all
In the fathomless depth of our national fall.

JOHN DE JEAN FRAZER (1809–1852)

Michael Burke and Denny Price stood in the middle of Anthony Street attempting to aid a cart driver, whose wagon full of manure had overturned.

The owner of the wagon, an aging Irishman Michael knew only as Pete, was one of the many small contractors in the city who made his living doing what nobody but the Irish were willing to do—clearing New York's streets of the waste of thousands of horses.

The city's manure problem had surpassed the garbage dilemma. By now, there were enough stables in New York to house at least fifty or sixty thousand horses, horses that furnished the power for all the city's public and private transportation: they hauled garbage, pulled carriages and omnibuses, towed milk wagons and fire wagons—they even hauled incoming railroad cars into the city.

The resulting tons of waste presented New York with what almost seemed an insurmountable task of disposal. Although the worst problem existed between the Battery and Canal Street, few districts were exempt. It had fallen mostly to the Irish, desperate for employment of any sort, to load the waste from the stables into containers and haul it away by cart to the manure scows docked at either side of the city.

Overturned carts were a common occurrence. With the wagons precariously unbalanced by overloaded barrels and boxes, it took only a deep rut or a sudden turn to tip the wagon onto its side.

When this happened, it was the driver's responsibility to clean up the spilled load and get on his way as quickly as possible. That was easier said than done, however, for with the other wagons and carriages flying by, it was all the poor cartman could do to get his wagon back on its wheels and manage even a cursory cleanup.

If a policeman happened to be nearby, it was expected that he would help, the assumption being that a copper was long past having his sensibilities offended—besides, weren't the lot of them Irish, in fact? But even a policeman would shun the odious job if at all possible.

Michael Burke was no exception. Whenever he happened upon one of the overturned carts, he would actually moan aloud and do his best to think up a means of escape. Denny Price carried on even worse, spitting out his disgust in a terrible harangue before grudgingly conceding to help.

Presently, Michael and Price were both out of sorts. The aging driver's clumsy attempts to clean up his stinking spill had only created more of a mess. Grumbling, the policemen now put their own broad shoulders to the wagon, forcing it back onto its wheels.

Bracing himself to face the rest of the job, Price stood for a moment, scratching his chin. "You shovel it in, and I'll hoist the barrels," he suggested, looking at an undetermined point past Michael's head.

"We'll *both* shovel it in, and we'll *both* hoist the barrels!" Michael countered, grabbing a shovel from the wagon bed and thrusting it at Price.

"What about your back, then?"

"What *about* my back?" Michael stopped to look at him.

"Why, wasn't it yourself just complaining last week about your back?" With a frown of concern that appeared almost genuine, Price leaned on the shovel and looked at Michael. "The day we moved the captain's household for him."

"Aye, but that was last week, wasn't it now?" Michael grated, taking up the other shovel. "Let's just get on with it, why don't we? The sooner it's done, the sooner—"

At that instant a shout and the slap of running feet made them both whirl around to look.

Squire Teffon, a tavern keeper from Five Points, came barreling toward them as fast as his short little legs would carry him. *"Police! Police! There's a riot in Paradise Square!"*

It took Michael and Price only an instant to react. Exchanging a relieved look and a guilty grin across the overturned barrel between them, the two policemen dropped their shovels and took off at a run, leaving the hapless Pete shouting curses in their wake.

As soon as they reached the open square in Five Points, they spied a band of angry, shouting men. Clubs were already waving and threats flying as Michael and Price muscled their way through a gathering crowd of observers, then charged into the midst of the melee.

For an instant it occurred to Michael that shoveling manure might have been the better choice—certainly the safer.

With amazement he saw the big curly headed preacher, Jess Dalton, right in the thick of the fracas. Michael thought the preacher must be either a fool or a very brave man indeed, for he stood like a wall in front of four young black boys who were obviously frightened out of their wits.

Even unarmed, the preacher posed a formidable barrier. With his suit coat hanging open and his dark mane of hair blowing wildly in the raw November wind, Dalton stood with both burly arms outflung in front of the frightened boys as if to shield them. He looked for all the world like an Old Testament prophet protecting the people of the Lord from an attacking pagan army.

Michael had grown to like and respect this big rock of a man, and the scene he now encountered was somehow no surprise. There was a steadiness, a quiet strength about the preacher that hinted of a backbone of iron behind the smooth, rich voice and the cheerful demeanor. No namby-pamby Bible toter was this man, Michael sensed. It was already being said around Five Points that the preacher was no fool, that he was every bit as smart as he was big, and just as tough, too—no small accolade among the residents of the notorious slum.

The look Dalton now turned on Michael and Price held a glint of relief, but he made no move to relinquish his protection of the frightened boys. It was only Dalton and the terrified youths against at least a dozen Irish laborers, but Michael somehow thought the preacher's presence might serve to even the odds.

Behind the menacing Irishmen, the crowd of onlookers was drawing closer. A quick glance told Michael this bunch would do more than cheer if violence broke out. Their eyes blazed with excitement and blood-lust, and some glared at him and Price with undisguised hatred.

"I don't like this a bit," muttered Price. "The two of us won't be stopping this bunch of ruffians."

"Perhaps our guns will," Michael said, doing his best to ignore the fear churning in his stomach. "I'm going to the preacher. You stay here—and keep your gun at the ready."

Roughly, he parted two scowling toughs, who spat on the ground as he slammed by them into the center of the square.

"What's happening here, Pastor? What's this about?" With his gun trained on the circle of angry men, Michael kept his voice low.

"It seems there's a strike at the pipe factory, and these boys were hired in place of the regular workers." Dalton's voice was hoarse. "They accused them of having guns, but they don't. They're little more than children."

Strikebreakers. Michael sized up the situation at once. The boys were young, but not too young to trigger a bloody brawl, especially if the Irish strikers believed they were armed. Fights between the Irish and the blacks were all too common. Nothing set off a confrontation any faster than a black man taking a job an Irisher considered rightfully his.

Keeping his gun leveled on the mob, Michael eyed the cowering youths. "*Do* you have weapons—any of you? The truth, now!"

All four boys shook their heads vigorously.

One of the strikers—a big, hulking man with hostile eyes—now stepped forward. Michael immediately swung his gun toward the man. "Stop there! Stand where you are."

"What's this, then?" sneered the brute. "You're as Irish as the lot of us. Sure, and you'd not fight for the likes of *them?*" He jerked his head toward the black boys.

"I've no mind to fight for the likes of *anybody!*" Michael snapped. "And I'd hate to use this," he said, raising the gun a fraction, "to avoid such a fight. So why don't you and your boyos get away before I change my mind?"

For an instant his eyes went to Price, who was still standing just outside the band of men, his own gun at the ready.

"Those black monkeys are stealing work from your own people, man!" roared the big Irishman. "Would you have us starving here in America as we did in Ireland?"

The man's red eyes and slightly slurred speech told Michael the attacker had had a drop too much, which meant he was even more of a threat than he might have been otherwise.

"We'll settle no labor disputes in the streets! Now, get away, or the lot of you will spend the night in the Tombs." Michael's voice was quiet, but his pulse was pounding in his ears. True, he and Price had the guns, but still there was no telling what they might try if their tempers were fired by the drink.

"You'll have to arrest us all then, copper!" shouted a new voice, a harsher one.

A small, pinched-faced man with black hair and black eyes stepped up beside the bigger tough. "Is that what you'd be thinking of doing— *Officer*?"

The challenging sneer of the little man's face made Michael's blood boil. "Why, I figure that's your choice," he replied, voicing a note of calm he didn't feel. "Though it does seem a terrible waste of time."

"If you value your thick neck, you'll back off—*copper*," growled the small dark-haired man. "Captain Rynders will take care of us, well enough."

"*Rynders!*" Michael's face tightened. "I should have known you were a part of his riffraff."

The muttering of the crowd swelled to an angry buzz. Michael would have given a month's pay just then for the sight of a Black Maria filled with policemen.

The man's narrow, pinched face contorted with anger. At the same time the big striker beside him took another step forward.

Michael's jaws locked, and his hand tightened on the gun. "Stay back— both of you!"

Unexpectedly, a shout went up from the onlookers as two or three of the other strikers moved in. Instinctively, Michael took a step backward, then stopped. If he let them intimidate him, he was done for. They'd take the black boys and likely him and Price as well.

"*I said stay back!*" he roared, sweeping the front line of them with his gun.

Suddenly, Michael spied a small newsboy at the edge of the strikers.

Billy Hogan—a good, spunky little lad. Just last month Michael had rescued him from an assault by a bunch of gang members intent on emptying the boy's pockets and taking over his corner.

The lad now locked gazes with Michael, who nodded slightly toward Mulberry Street. The boy understood. Edging backward a step at a time, he quickly slipped out of the mob and took off at a great run.

Michael prayed the lad would bring help and bring it soon!

Out of the corner of his eye, he saw the preacher shift his weight. Instinctively, he stiffened. His instincts told him this was no ordinary street row. These men wanted blood. Even a man of the cloth was at risk among thugs like these.

"You men," Dalton said suddenly, stretching up on the balls of his feet to the full extent of his considerable height, "drop those clubs before someone gets hurt! These boys have done nothing wrong! They want to work, that's all. There's no sin in that!"

At once, a shout went up from one of the men brandishing a club. "They want *our* work!"

The crowd roared encouragement, screaming, "Get rid of the blacks! Teach them a lesson!"

The preacher looked at Michael. Michael looked at Price.

Suddenly, the big laborer and his smaller companion leaped forward, clubs raised to strike. Aiming his gun in the air, Michael fired. It stopped them for only an instant. The heavy-shouldered Irishman now lunged toward the preacher, while the smaller one came at Michael. Michael had time to fire the gun only once more before he was hit by the dark-haired striker.

A roar exploded from the mob as Michael was knocked to the ground. Dust filled his eyes and burned his nostrils. His gun went flying.

With a half moan, Michael kicked upward, plowing both feet into the striker's stomach with as much strength as he could muster. The man cried out, then sprawled backward.

The crowd went wild, like beasts on a rampage. Still on the ground, Michael saw the preacher swat the hulking Irisher away as if he were only an annoying bee.

His eyes stinging, Michael clambered to his feet, looking wildly over the ground for his gun.

Denny Price came charging into the center of the fray, firing his gun into the air. "I'll not aim high again, boyos!" he yelled, taking a defiant stance close to Michael. "'Tis your heads next time, you spawn of the devil!"

The crowd roared even louder. Spectators milling about behind the strikers shouted out encouragement, some cheering the policemen and the preacher, others egging on the strikers to attack.

Suddenly a gun exploded. Michael whirled. The dark-haired striker was holding *his* gun, aimed right at his head!

The striker's mouth twisted in an ugly smile. "Either your partner gets rid of his gun, copper, or I get rid of *you*."

Beside him, Price muttered under his breath. "Sure, and we're in the soup this time." Then he turned his gun on the striker. "Take it *from* me, rat-face!"

Suddenly, one of the black boys behind the preacher broke and started to run in the opposite direction, as if to escape.

Dalton shouted and whipped around, trying to stop the boy, but he was too late. The dark-haired striker with Michael's gun fired at the boy, hitting him high in the middle of his back.

With a sickening thud and a terrible scream, the boy hit the ground. The preacher ran and fell to his knees beside him.

Now the mob went berserk with blood-lust, cheering and roaring like savages.

Without warning, Michael saw Price move to charge the dark-haired striker with the gun. The hoodlum fired when he saw the policeman coming, but Price dropped low, his gun steady. One well-placed bullet in the striker's gun arm took him down, sending the pistol skating over the ground.

Michael lurched forward to retrieve his gun. At the same time, the big red-faced Irisher who had started it all hurled himself at the preacher, who was still on his knees beside the injured black boy.

Dalton whipped around just in time, rolling sideways to escape the striker's charge, then lunging to his feet. With formidable strength, the preacher flung the big Irishman into the crowd.

Stunned, the striker crumbled, landing in a dazed heap amidst his cronies.

When another angry striker lunged out of the crowd toward the preacher, Dalton easily shoved him aside. The striker lost his balance and went sprawling onto the ground.

His gun now in hand, Michael whipped around and fired into the air. Price, too, got off a warning shot, but the crowd had turned savage. The two policemen were no match for their rage.

Suddenly a shout went up from Mulberry Street. Some in the crowd turned to see where it came from. Another angry cry sounded, and two more policemen, both carrying nightsticks and guns, shoved their way through to the center of the square.

The taller of the two fired his gun in the air as he came. His partner, a burly bald man, roared like an injured bear, *"Move back—move back right now, or you'll be shot where you stand! Spread out and disband immediately!"*

The din gradually ebbed and died away. There was some grumbling, a few angry protests, but little by little the crowd began to back off. At last they broke apart and dispersed, muttering and casting resentful looks back over their shoulders as they went.

The other two policemen helped to herd them out of the area while Michael and Price went to Dalton. The preacher was again on his knees beside the fallen black boy, the rest of the youths huddled close by.

"Is he dead?"

Dalton shook his head, raising his face to look at Michael. "No, but he's bad. We need to get help for him right away."

"Doc Hilman's probably in," offered Price. "He's just a few doors up, on Mulberry."

"Go for him, why don't you," said Michael.

Cradling the unconscious boy's head in his lap, the preacher's eyes never left the youth's face. "You'd best tell the doctor to hurry," he said quietly.

10

The Cry of the Victim

The pharisee's cant goes up for peace,
But the cries of his victims never cease.
JOHN BOYLE O'REILLY (1844–1890)

Michael and Jess Dalton stood in the dingy hallway that served as a waiting room while Dr. Hilman worked on the injured black boy. Two chairs on the wall across from them were occupied by an elderly man and his frail, crippled wife.

Outside, the last of the late afternoon sunlight was ebbing, the shadows growing long and deep. The waiting room had taken on the damp chill of evening.

"Who is this *Captain Rynders*?" the preacher asked. "I keep hearing his name mentioned around Five Points."

"Isaiah Rynders," Michael said, scowling. "He's a gang boss. A gambler and a knife-fighter, too. He owns a number of dives in Paradise Square." He paused, looking at the preacher. "He's also a Tammany politician."

"Dangerous?"

"Mean as a snake—and more deadly," Michael replied without hesitating.

They remained silent for a time. "The boy will need hospital care," Dalton finally said, his voice low.

Michael looked at him wearily. "He's a penniless Negro, Pastor. It's not likely he'll get hospital attention."

"He's only a child!" Dalton protested. "They certainly wouldn't turn him away—"

"Of course they'll turn him away! The Negroes have no rights in New York—things are as bad for them as the Irish, if not worse."

Leaning against a decaying wall, the preacher hugged his big arms to himself and studied Michael for a moment. "If that's so, Sergeant, what accounts for the enmity between the two?"

Michael frowned. He would not have thought Dalton naive, but perhaps he was.

"Oh, I'm aware of *how* things are," the preacher put in quickly. "Half of the brawls that go on down here seem to be between the Negroes and the Irish. But it's still difficult for me to understand *why*, especially knowing the history of both. Why do two persecuted peoples insist on persecuting each *other*?"

Michael considered the big preacher's words. It was a matter he himself had given much thought to, having been forced to put down countless battles between the two factions over the years.

"I understand what you're saying, Pastor—it would make more sense that our troubles bring us together, not divide us."

Dalton nodded.

Michael drew a deep sigh. "Aye, so one would think. Yet any policeman in the city will tell you that persecution only breeds more persecution, just as crime seems to breed still more crime."

The pastor studied him, saying nothing.

"I imagine part of the problem, at least for the Irish," Michael went on, "is that the blacks compete with us for the jobs we're so desperate for—and for the same *kinds* of jobs, at that. There's little available to the Irish in the way of work except for the lowest, meanest jobs in the city: laborers, manure-cart drivers, housemaids, washerwomen. And it's the same for the Negro, don't you see? Both groups vie for the same jobs, but the Negro will work for even less than will the Irish. And they'll do anything at all—anything—to earn their bit of pay!"

"Breaking strikes, for example."

Michael nodded. "And worse."

The preacher raked a hand down his beard and looked toward the doorway. "I suppose it's difficult *not* to resent a man who seems to be taking food out of your family's mouths."

"Exactly," Michael agreed. "Oh, that's not the only reason the two are always at odds, of course. I sometimes think we Irish are our own worst enemies."

Dalton turned back, frowning. "How so?"

"Well, Pastor, we're a clannish bunch, it seems to me. Perhaps all the years England has kept our faces in the dirt accounts for some of what we are." Michael shrugged and smiled grimly. "There was no improving our lot, don't you see? We were denied all the things we might have used to better ourselves: education, political involvement, job opportunities—why, we were even forced to suppress our language, and the Catholics their religion! I expect all that time of being treated like mindless savages has bred a kind of natural distrust in many of us, made us suspicious and even resentful of those outside our own circle."

The preacher gave a slow nod. "Caused you to turn inward, you mean. Center on yourselves."

"Aye, I should think so. Ourselves and our country—Ireland. Perhaps that accounts in part for our fierce patriotism, our secret societies, and the like. That being the case, we turn on anyone else who might seem to pose a threat."

"The persecuted become the persecutors."

"Aye, exactly. I'm not saying it's right, mind, but merely trying to explain things as I see them."

The pained, sorrowful expression on Dalton's face piqued Michael's curiosity. The man truly seemed to *care* about people—about the Irish, the blacks, the people who couldn't defend themselves. And Michael couldn't help but wonder where Dalton's interest came from.

He already knew a bit about the pastor's father, of course. A lawyer and a labor reformer, Andrew Dalton had also been known throughout the East as a scrapper—a crusader for the rights of the working man. Apparently, championing the underprivileged was a tradition in the preacher's family.

Of course, with his wife being an immigrant herself, that might account for Dalton's concern. Yet there was the matter of his name. "Begging your pardon, Pastor," Michael said, "but I can't help wondering: With the feeling you seem to have for the Irish—and with your name being *Dalton*—is it possible you have some family roots in the old country yourself?"

Dalton smiled. "More than possible. My grandfather came from Ireland. He was a printer," he went on to explain. "He got himself into trouble with the English authorities, printing 'inflammatory materials'. His intention was to go back to Ireland once his offenses were forgotten, but he met my grandmother here and stayed." He paused, then added, "And there's my wife, of course. She immigrated only a few years ago. So you can see I have strong ties to Ireland and its people."

The big pastor lifted his regretful eyes to Michael. "What will it take to change things, Sergeant? What can the *church* do to make a difference for the Irish—or the Negro? It does seem that the solution ought to begin with God's church, but I confess I sometimes wonder where to start."

Michael met his look. "I would ask you this, Pastor: Where *is* the Lord's church? Where was it—other than a brave few, of course—when the Irish were dropping by the thousands along the road, dying of starvation and the fever?"

Tasting his own anger, Michael knew he should stop. This was a man of God he was addressing, after all. A man of the *church*. But the spurs of resentment and disillusionment in his soul drove him on. "Where is the church when the black slave is torn away from his wife and his babies and put in chains or when he's beaten to a bloody pulp for accidentally looking into a white man's face?"

The preacher's eyes were pools of sadness. He did not speak, but merely shook his great head.

Michael's voice grew hoarse from the acrid sting of bitterness. "You ask me what the church can *do*, Pastor. Well, I ask you: What has it *done*? Where has it been? Where, exactly, is it now? Right now?"

Dalton delayed his reply, looking off into the distance for a moment. Turning back to Michael, he finally said, "That's a fair question, Sergeant. With no easy answer. One thing I'm certain of: It's not the celebrated saints who always achieve the greatest things for the Lord. The greatest orators, the fieriest preachers, the most eloquent writers—they do a fine work, and we need them, every one. But it seems to me that the Lord often uses the smallest soldiers to gain the greatest ground—one victory at a time."

The pastor's good-natured face creased with a smile, but his eyes burned with the zealous faith of the patriarchs. "The reality of the Lord's church has little to do with great cathedrals and congregational meetings. I suspect its presence in the world is less dependent on hymn singing and sermons than on compassion and love.

"I'll tell you where God's church is, Sergeant: It's with the aging Quaker widow ladling soup to an endless line of starving Irish peasants."

As the pastor spoke, Michael watched him carefully. Sensing the man's passion, his fervor, he felt a faint stirring in his own spirit. The intensity of the preacher's words drew Michael into the very center of the flame that burned within Jess Dalton's spirit.

This was a man on fire…on fire for God.

Michael's interest quickened, and the preacher nodded, still smiling. "Yes. And it's with the emaciated, ailing priest who has given his own meals in order to feed the starving children in his parish. It's inside the prison walls with the repentant felon who spends the remainder of his life telling his cell mates about the changing love of Christ. It's with the circuit-rider evangelist in his worn-out clothes on his run-down horse, who gives up hours, and even days, teaching Negro slaves to read and write. It's with fine young women like Sara Farmington who are willing to leave the luxury of a Fifth Avenue mansion to nurture dirty, lonely children in a rat-infested tenement."

The preacher put a hand to Michael's shoulder—a big, calloused, ever-so-gentle hand. "And it's with the honest, noble-hearted policeman like yourself, Michael Burke," he said softly, "who puts his life on the line every day to make the city a safer place for decent people."

He paused, gazing intently at Michael for a moment before going on. "Don't you see, Sergeant, the church is where it's *always* been. In the humble, servant hearts of all those who are willing to be the helping hands of the Savior. *That's* where the church is."

Michael swallowed against the lump in his throat, his eyes locking with the kind, knowing gaze of the preacher. The unspoken understanding between them brought an unexpected thrill of joy to his soul.

Aye, he thought with dawning conviction, *indeed, that is where the church is. And it is also with this soft-spoken, heavy-shouldered preacher who is willing to risk his life defending four frightened Negro boys in the middle of New York's greatest shame.*

11

The Music of the Heart

The happiest heart that ever beat
Was in some quiet breast
That found the common daylight sweet
And left to heaven the rest.
JOHN VANCE CHENEY (1848–1922)

Early Monday morning, Evan Whittaker stood at the large, wide window of Lewis Farmington's office in Brooklyn, looking out over the East River to the tip of Manhattan.

As always, he had shared his employer's carriage, then the ferryboat, to the shipyards. Parting company when they arrived, Evan came inside to his office, leaving Mr. Farmington to walk about the yards, browsing and inspecting, just as he did every morning.

This was Evan's favorite time of day. There was still more than an hour before the actual workday would begin, but already the river teemed with a great forest of ships, their tall masts swaying, as white sails and the flags of many nations waved in the cold November wind. All up and down the shore, clippers and schooners, ferryboats and sloops moved in pursuit of the day's business.

Like the morning itself, fresh and poised on the threshold of a new beginning, the busy traffic on the river seemed to point to the city's exciting promise.

"This is the day which You have made.... Oh, Lord, I rejoice...I am glad in it...."

Evan voiced his praise aloud as a song, immediately putting his fingers

to his lips in surprise. How long had it been since he'd broken out in singing, simply because his spirit could not contain his joy?

He loved to sing—partly for the sheer joy of the music itself, and
partly for the pleasure that came when he could express himself without
the stumbling block of a stutter. In music, his words flowed without hesitation, unhindered by the stops and starts that marred his speech.

His strong tenor voice was, in fact, the one gift of which he might
have been slightly vain, had it not been for the lack of opportunity to use
it. Other than joining in the Sunday worship hymns, his times for vocal-
izing were few.

Nora had caught him at his solitary singing once this past summer, in the
gardens behind the mansion on Fifth Avenue. It had been one of those perfectly lovely August days when everything in sight, from the serene clouds
above to the tiny violets blooming alongside the garden lane, looked to be
painted in place by the brush strokes of the Master. Touched by the beauty of
his surroundings and moved by gratitude for the return of his health, Evan
had begun to sing a simple, poignant hymn from his childhood.

At that moment, Nora had unexpectedly appeared, causing him to
freeze with embarrassment. Quickly, with the kindness so much a part of
her nature, she had put him at ease, commenting almost shyly that it was
"grand to hear the song of his heart."

To his surprise, she went on to ask if he'd like to learn an old Irish tune
that was one of *her* favorites from childhood. She spent the next half hour
teaching him a lovely little children's song—*I Wish I Had the Shepherd's
Lamb*—coaching him first in English, then in her mysterious Gaelic language.

Now as he awaited the arrival of his employer, Evan caught himself
smiling again at the memory. It had been a special time—a gift, really—
to hear Nora sing the happy little tune in her soft, almost childish tones,
and laugh at his feeble attempts to learn the Gaelic. The myriad colors of
the flowers, the sweet-scented warmth of the afternoon, had seemed to
make the garden a magic place that, for the moment, belonged only to
the two of them.

"P-Perhaps I should take up your Gaelic in earnest," Evan had said,
laughing at himself. "It would certainly hide my pesky old stutter."

Nora's expression had immediately sobered. "Does it bother you so
much, then? I didn't know."

"Well, I d-don't suppose I'll ever be fond of it," Evan returned with a deprecating shrug, "b-but I've learned to live with it well enough."

"It's odd, you know," she replied after a moment, "but I seldom even notice it. I doubt that I ever would if you didn't poke fun at yourself so."

Oh, she was wonderful! She was simply...splendid! She would never know the moments of pure, crystal joy she brought him with her acceptance, her patience, and her small words of praise and affirmation. It wouldn't *do* for her to know, of course, for she might be offended if she ever became aware of the depth of his feelings.

"Well, you certainly seem a happy man this morning, Evan! You look as contented as a cat in the sunshine."

The booming voice of Lewis Farmington jarred Evan from his reverie, and he turned, embarrassed at being caught daydreaming like a schoolboy.

The lithe, dapper Farmington strode briskly into the office. "I expected you'd be waiting for me. We might just as well get started, I suppose. I should be making some notes on those drawings Cannon dropped off last week."

"I'll have to go and get them," Evan offered. "They're still in Mr. Donaldson's office, I believe."

"In a moment." Mr. Farmington dropped down into the huge leather chair behind his desk. "Wonderful view, isn't it? I never tire of it. Makes a man feel as if he's a part of something important, somehow."

Evan came to stand at the front of the desk. "Why, yes," he said, relieved that the older man thought his euphoria was due to the view. "It d-does at that."

"I have something for you." Lewis Farmington's sun-bronzed face creased to a broad, good-natured smile. "If you're interested, that is. Do you happen to like the opera, Evan?"

"The opera? Why, y-yes, very much," Evan answered, watching as Mr. Farmington opened his desk drawer and removed an envelope.

"Good, good! I have tickets for the opening at the new Astor Place Opera House next week." Farmington fumbled through the contents of the envelope. "Let's see, now—ah, yes, *Ernani,* that's what they're doing. Some young Italian composer—"

"V-Verdi," Evan offered. "Giuseppe Verdi."

"Yes, well...I like to listen to the music, but I don't know much about the composers. Will it be any good, do you think?"

"A-As a matter of fact, I attended the opening p-production in London t-two years ago," Evan said. "It was excellent."

"Oh, you've seen it before? Well, was it good enough that you'd care to see it again?"

"Again? Oh—yes, yes, of c-course, I would."

"Fine. Here are tickets for you and Nora."

Evan stood staring at the two tickets in his employer's outstretched hand. "For N-Nora? And me?"

Lewis Farmington glanced up. "Why, yes, even if Nora's not an opera fan, I'm sure she'd enjoy seeing the new theater. It's supposed to be quite something, you know."

Evan stared at him. "I—I doubt that N-Nora even knows what opera *is*."

Farmington seemed to consider that for a moment, then nodded. "Yes, I expect that's so. It should be quite an experience for her, wouldn't you say?" As if the matter were entirely settled, he went on. "I'll escort Sara, and you can escort Nora. The ladies couldn't go without us, of course—no ladies are admitted without escorts. Oh—and another thing, Evan, we mustn't forget—admittance will be restricted to those wearing kid gloves."

Evan blinked. "Are you...s-serious, Mr. Farmington?"

His employer chuckled, leaning back in the chair. "Isn't that a hoot? They're already calling it the 'Kid-Glove Opera House' around town. The whole idea sounds like something Astor himself thought up, if you ask me. He's a caution, the old scoundrel."

New as he was to the city, Evan had already heard a great deal about the eccentric John Jacob Astor—the "landlord of New York." Astor, a German immigrant, had started out in New York City as a baker's helper, later moving on to work for a Quaker fur merchant, flogging moths from the pelts in storage. He was now reputed to be the richest man in America.

"You *know* M-Mr. Astor, sir?" Evan asked, impressed.

Farmington's expression sobered. "Yes, I know Astor, poor soul."

Evan frowned. *Poor soul? The man who owned Manhattan?*

Farmington smiled a little, as if he had read Evan's thoughts. "He *is* a poor soul, believe it or not. Oh, he's a rich man, all right! He's accumulated enormous wealth, as you know. Made most of it in the fur trade. And real estate, of course. The man raked in a fortune during the Panic. Bought up mortgages from those who couldn't make their payments, then foreclosed."

He frowned. "There's always a great deal of money to be made at the expense of others, isn't there, Evan? And goodness knows, Astor has made more than his share." Shaking his head, he went on. "He's in his eighties now, and still hoarding every dollar as if it were his first. I fear he doesn't enjoy his money very much these days. He's weak as an infant. In fact, when I last saw him, he was drooling like a pup and could scarcely speak. Has to be watched every minute."

What a difference, Evan thought, *in the ways men handle their money.* Some, like Lewis Farmington, made their money work *for* them. Others, and it sounded as if Astor might be one of them, simply worked for the money, became obsessed with it—frequently *possessed* by it.

In the short time he had worked for the man, Evan had already observed that Lewis Farmington was, if not actually indifferent to his wealth, certainly unimpressed by it. At times Farmington almost seemed to view his fortune as a challenge. He apparently enjoyed using his money to make a difference: in the city, in his church, and in the lives of those less fortunate.

"Well, now, about the opera—" Farmington's voice jarred Evan out of his thoughts.

"Oh, yes—well, I w-wonder…"

"You needn't worry about the kid gloves, Evan. Sara, I'm sure, will be more than happy to lend Nora a pair, and you're certainly welcome to borrow a pair of mine."

Evan's pale face flushed, and he glanced down briefly at his empty sleeve. Farmington's eyes followed the glance, as if suddenly he realized his mistake.

"I'm sorry, my boy," he said gruffly. "I didn't mean to—"

"That's quite all r-right, Mr. F-Farmington," Evan stammered.

"I'm an old fool," Farmington blustered. He fixed an intent gaze on Evan's face, and his tone softened. "You know I'd never deliberately—"

"I know, Mr. Farmington," Evan said. "I've h-had quite a t-time getting used to the idea m-myself. P-Perhaps I could w-wear one glove and c-carry the other…" He paused, and a twinkle filled his eye. "Mr. Astor's people might not let m-me in unless I had both."

"Then you accept my offer?" Farmington beamed, obviously relieved that Evan hadn't taken offense at his blunder.

"Well…well, thank y-you very much, Mr. Farmington." Evan faltered.

"It's just that...I can't help but wonder if it wouldn't be b-best to offer the extra ticket to—to Sergeant Burke."

Evan drew in a deep breath, swallowing down his disappointment. It had been a difficult suggestion to make, but it seemed only right, in view of the way things were with Nora and the policeman.

For a moment Lewis Farmington said nothing. His dark eyes probed, making Evan uncomfortable.

"Evan—" He stopped, cleared his throat, then began again. "Evan— I'm going to say something to you, and if I'm altogether out of line, you just tell me so, and I'll mind my own business."

Astonished, Evan hastened to protest. Farmington, however, waved him off with a quick movement of his hand. Leaning forward in his chair, he folded his hands on the desktop and said firmly, "Sit down, son."

With a jerk, Evan lowered himself to the chair. He felt a sudden stab of apprehension, wondering if he had somehow failed in his work.

He found that difficult to believe. As recently as two days ago, he had overheard Mr. Farmington praising him to Silas Donaldson, the ship-yard's assistant manager.

"Evan, I'm a good deal older than you," said Mr. Farmington, "and I'd like to think that, after all these months of working together, I have your trust."

Taken aback at his employer's blunt announcement, Evan stared at him in confusion. "Why...why, of course, you d-do, Mr. Farmington!"

"Good." Mr. Farmington linked and unlinked his fingers several times. "Then I wish you'd confide in me—man-to-man."

Evan stared at him blankly. "C-Confide in you, sir?"

"Yes. About Nora. You're sweet on her, aren't you?"

Looking up from his hands, Farmington met Evan's horrified stare straight on.

"I—I don't—"

"Well—*aren't* you?"

Evan tried to swallow, failed, bit his lip instead. "I...ah...I am very *fond* of N-Nora, of course. We went through a h-harrowing ordeal together... and we've become awfully g-good friends over the past few m-months. At least, I like to *think* our friendship is special, but—"

"Good heavens, man—there's nothing wrong with being smitten over a fine young woman like Nora Kavanagh! What I'm wondering is why, if you're taken with her, you don't *do* something about it?"

Stunned, Evan could do nothing but sit and gape at his employer. Had he made such an obvious spectacle of himself that even Lewis Farmington had seen his feelings for Nora?

"Well?" His employer looked at him with an openly quizzical expression.

Feeling more foolish by the moment, Evan groped for a reply. "I…I'm n-not sure I understand, sir."

Farmington's dark brows shot up. "Why, what is there to understand, son? Why don't you *court* the woman?"

His pulse thundering in his ears, Evan moistened his lips and managed only, "*C-Court* her? *Nora?*"

"Yes, yes, court her!" Farmington said, nodding impatiently. "Haven't you ever courted a woman, Evan?"

Evan's mortified silence was his only reply.

His employer searched his face. "Good heavens," he said slowly, "you haven't, have you?" Leaning back still more, he crossed his arms over his chest as he studied Evan. "Well, perhaps it's high time you did. Court a woman, that is."

Miserable, Evan turned away, toward the window, where only moments before the view had held such promise. "I…I c-couldn't do that, sir."

Farmington's response came after a long moment. "Because of your arm, I suppose?"

Turning, Evan met the older man's gaze. "Yes," he choked out, feeling as if he were about to strangle. "B-Because of my arm." He paused, pulling in a ragged breath before he could go on. "And also b-because of M-Michael Burke. Even if—if I were…whole…I c-could never have the conceit to think N-Nora would prefer me to—to him. They were childhood friends, they're both Irish—and Sergeant B-Burke is…well, he's an impressive k-kind of man. B-Besides," he hastened to add, "there's the fact that they're…practically b-betrothed, after all."

Evan did not—would not—mention the other reason that Nora might be hesitant to accept Michael Burke's proposal.

Mr. Farmington did not know about the bond that had apparently existed between Nora and Morgan Fitzgerald, the Irish patriot-poet who had helped to save them all from utter destruction. But Evan secretly wondered if Fitzgerald wasn't the reason Nora had not yet agreed to marry Michael Burke.

Lewis Farmington regarded him with a measuring look. "I know it's been assumed Nora and the sergeant would marry," he said. "But I see no evidence of any real affection between the two. And I'm not at all convinced there ever will be."

Surprised, Evan asked, "B-But why? I happen to know Sergeant Burke stands r-ready to m-marry Nora—all she has to d-do is say the word."

Farmington nodded agreement. "But she *hasn't* said the word, has she?" He continued to scrutinize Evan with an unreadable expression. "I don't pretend to be an expert in these matters, but it seems to me that if Nora had the kind of feelings for the sergeant that lead to marriage, she'd have acted on them by now. At least, she'd be a bit more enthusiastic about spending *time* with the man. No," he said, getting to his feet, "I may be middle-aged and absentminded, but my instincts are still sound enough. And my instincts tell me that Nora is not in love with the sergeant."

He raised a finger as if to emphasize his point. "Therefore," he said with a meaningful look, "you have just as good a chance as the next fellow. And one thing more: My observation is that Nora is not the sort of woman to mind a missing limb. Surely you know that much about her by now, son?"

Evan wasn't sure which unsettled him more, his employer's awareness of his true feelings for Nora or the man's kind gaze and his use of the word *son*. "Mr. Farmington, I d-don't know quite what to say," he began. "I feel—"

"Oh, pshaw! You feel embarrassed that I've noticed you're sweet on Nora. Why, that's nothing to be embarrassed about!" Again he wagged a finger at Evan. "The only thing you should be concerned about is the fact you aren't taking steps to win her! Let me tell you, if I were a few years younger, I'd give it a go myself. She's a delightful woman!"

"Why, y-yes, she is...b-but..."

"Tell me something, Evan—how, exactly, do you see yourself?"

Puzzled, Evan frowned. "Sir?"

"How do you *see* yourself?" Farmington repeated. "As a *man* who has only one arm? Or as *only* a one-armed man? It will make all the difference, you know. Let me tell you what I think, Evan: I think *Nora* sees you as a *man,* and that the fact you're without an arm is only incidental to her. I believe Nora is already very fond of you, and you'd do well to press your advantage while you still have it!" He paused, smiling brightly. "That's what I think! If you want the woman, Evan—then *court her*!"

Evan stared at him, dumbfounded.

"Say, do you want these tickets or not?" Mr. Farmington asked, again extending his hand.

As if in a dream, Evan accepted the two tickets, then stood staring down at them.

Farmington beamed. "Good for you! Now, then, if you'll just fetch me those drawings from Donaldson, we'll get to work."

Evan finally managed to swallow, though his mouth still felt like cotton batting and his heart was hammering like thunder.

Lewis Farmington's dark brows quirked impishly. "By the way, if you decide to explore the subject further—the subject of *courting*, that is—I'd be happy to give you the benefit of my experience. My courting of Sara's mother was quite successful, as you may have gathered."

Dazed as he was from the entire conversation, Evan could not suppress a smile. "Th-Thank y-you, sir. Perhaps I'll…just take you up on that."

After his assistant left the office, Lewis Farmington continued to stare after him.

Leaning back in his chair, he stroked his chin and reflected on Evan Whittaker. Solid gold, that one. Even minus an arm, and despite that plaguing stutter, the slender, fair-haired Englishman was unmistakably a man of honor and real strength of character.

Too bad Evan didn't see the attraction he obviously held for Nora Kavanagh. Now, *he* had seen the magic between the two more than once, had just as quickly seen that each was unaware of the other's feelings.

One thing he was convinced of: If Nora held an affection of any kind for Sergeant Burke, it was of the sort that good friendships are made of—not marriages. With Evan, on the other hand, she lighted up like a shooting star. Why, her entire countenance changed when the man walked into a room! Those large sad eyes of hers would suddenly go all soft with a smile, and she'd actually turn pink if he drew near her.

But Evan was just too unassuming, entirely too self-effacing to notice. *Even if he should become aware of Nora's interest,* Lewis Farmington wondered, *will he have the cheek to respond?*

And what was his *own* interest in things between the two? He was fond of them both, of course. He'd like nothing better than to see them together—if the Lord willed it so.

Still, he wasn't certain his motives were entirely unselfish. There was Sara to consider. His daughter had more than a passing fondness for Michael Burke; he had seen it months ago. The girl could deny it all she would—and deny it she did, every time he attempted to broach the subject. But he knew his daughter, and he knew beyond all doubt that she was enamored with that Irish policeman. Moreover, he wasn't at all convinced the sergeant wasn't somewhat taken with *Sara,* in spite of his professed commitment to Nora Kavanagh.

Going to the window, he stood staring out at the ships in the harbor—many of them built by Farmington Shipyards. Lewis wasn't certain he liked the idea of his only daughter being sweet on an Irish policeman, although Burke did seem a good man. Certainly, he was handsome enough to turn a girl's head. More importantly, however, he sensed an unshakable integrity about the policeman. Burke seemed clever, too—clever and ambitious. With the right contacts and a measure of opportunity, even an Irish policeman could advance himself.

Farmington sighed. Irish was Irish—no two ways about it—and a large part of the city despised them. For Sara to involve herself with an Irish policeman would mean immediate and total rejection by her contemporaries.

A scandal, that's what it would be. Lewis Farmington frowned at the thought. Then his features smoothed, and he relaxed. After still another moment, he smiled.

Sara was not a girl to back down in the face of scandal. As long as she believed herself to be in the right, she would not budge.

He turned and went back to his desk, perching on the edge of it instead of taking the chair. He had to laugh at his own foolishness. Here he was, wasting valuable time speculating about other people's romances, when he had a mountain of work waiting for his attention.

What he ought to do, he supposed, was to put some energy behind his *own* personal life. From time to time he had thought about remarrying, but courting was such a bothersome business. Once had been enough. His marriage to Clarissa had been a good one. Sometimes he missed her desperately.

But to go about wooing a woman again?

He grimaced. No, indeed. It was one thing to scheme about Evan's love life—and even his daughter's—but he would be content with that. For all the encouragement he'd been so quick to lavish on Evan, he personally found the idea of courting a woman entirely too much trouble.

No, he would stick to his ships. At this stage in his life, he liked things to be predictable. And romancing a woman, he thought dryly, was *anything* but predictable.

12

Arthur

The children with whom I have played,
The men and women with whom I have eaten,
Have had masters over them,
They have been under the lash of masters....
Their shame is my shame, and I have reddened for it,
Reddened for that they have gone in want,
While others have been full.

PADRAIC PEARSE (1879–1916)

Arthur Jackson woke up trapped in a dream.

He knew he was awake because the pain racking his body was too excruciating to be anything but real. Yet the room in which he found himself was like no room he had ever seen.

It was big, with a high cream-colored ceiling. Almost one entire side of the room was glass—tall windows framed by ivory, drawn-back drapes. Obviously, the room belonged to somebody rich. Yet somehow the room seemed *friendly*. The wallpaper was all soft-colored roses. A big padded rocking chair sat by the window, as if inviting somebody to come rock in it. A fire burned low in the fireplace, and there were lots of books, some lying open around the room.

The bed in which Arthur lay was immense, with four high posts and a plump, lavender-scented comforter. It was the kind of bed he might have imagined for a king. *For sure,* he thought, *not many black boys had ever woke up in such a bed!*

His eyes didn't want to stay open and kept fluttering shut when he tried to focus them. When he was finally able to fix his gaze in one direction, it came to rest on a thin-faced, redheaded boy sitting close to the bed.

Arthur blinked. The boy was just a kid, probably no more than nine or ten. But his big green eyes held a sober expression that made Arthur wonder if he might not be older than he looked.

Arthur wanted to sit up for a better look at the room, but as bad as it hurt to take a deep breath, he thought he would surely pass out if he moved.

The boy stood, but kept his distance. "I'll get my mother," he said. His words sounded peculiar, but he talked so quietlike that Arthur couldn't tell what was different about him. "She said I should come for her the very minute you woke up. Don't be trying to move, though—you're bandaged all the way around. I expect it hurts." He caught a breath, still peering closely at Arthur. "Just...just you be lying real still until I can get my mother."

"Who you?" Arthur was surprised at the sound of his own voice. He sounded weak and raspy, like his daddy sounded after working all day in the hot fields.

The boy had started for the door but stopped, turning around at Arthur's question. "I'm Casey. Casey-Fitz, my family calls me. Casey-Fitz Dalton." Again he moved to go, but hesitated. "What's *your* name?"

"Arthur. Arthur Jackson." An unexpected pain seized his back, then shot upward into his chest. Arthur gritted his teeth.

The redheaded boy frowned. "You shouldn't be talking if it hurts. The doctor said you might be having a terrible fierce pain for several days. He sent some medicine for Mother to give you when you need it."

At that, the boy lifted his hand, as if to caution Arthur. "Just...wait right here, now. I'd best be getting my mother. She'll be cross if she finds out I didn't come right away."

Before Arthur could ask him anything else, the boy dashed out of the bedroom, slamming the door behind him.

Arthur pondered his situation with growing uneasiness. He had heard something in the boy's voice he didn't like. A certain way he worked his tongue, a kind of sing-songy sound.

Irish. The boy was *Irish!* Irish, like the strikers in Five Points.

The memories churned up in him, spilling over and flailing out at him with dizzying force. *The strikers yelling. Then the riot. Clubs and guns. The big curly headed preacher-man who had tried to help. The policemen who came running. And then a gunshot.*

The pain was no memory. It was still inside him—maybe not as hot and as shattering as when it had first roared through him in the street, but still bad enough that he couldn't draw an easy breath.

The man who had shot him had been Irish. The Irish seemed to hate all black people.

The Irish said the black boys were taking jobs from decent *white folks*. Especially *Irish* white folks.

Arthur didn't know about that. He hadn't thought to take anybody's job, not on purpose. He was just trying to make enough money to keep from starving to death.

When the laborers at the pipe factory struck for better wages, there was no lack of black boys like himself eager to take advantage of the situation. All he wanted was a job—*any* job. Some of the older Negroes had warned the younger boys to stay clear of the picket line. But most of the Irishmen walking the line had appeared so drunk that Arthur thought he could just skedaddle right through their midst without being stopped.

He'd done just that for three days, but then he'd got caught, along with three other boys. The strikers had been mean drunk and after blood. Even the coppers had their hands full trying to beat them back.

He knew he had been shot; he remembered waking up, just once, and only for a minute or two. A gray-haired man who said he was a doctor was bending over him.

But how had he ended up here, in a fancy bedroom he'd never seen before, being stared at by a boy who surely looked and sounded like an Irisher?

Again, he made an attempt to move, to push himself up. This time the pain made him cry aloud. He squeezed his eyes shut, feeling sick to his stomach.

The door opened. Arthur looked up to see the redheaded boy come walking quietly into the room. With him was a woman who Arthur reckoned to be the boy's mother, though she didn't hardly look old enough to be *anyone's* mother.

She had red hair, too, darker than her son's. She was just a little woman, not a whole lot bigger than the boy, but dressed nice—like a lady.

Seeing her frown, Arthur swallowed. His heart skipped and raced as he wondered what to expect.

But when the woman reached the bed, she smiled at him. "Hello, Arthur. Casey-Fitz told me your name. How are you feeling? It's good seeing you awake at last."

Arthur drew as deep a breath as he could manage, relieved that the woman didn't seem about to throw him out of bed. Still, he couldn't find his voice to answer her.

Her smile faded, and the frown returned. "If you're in pain, Arthur, I have some medicine I can give you."

Arthur *was* hurting, but at the moment he was a lot more interested in finding out where he was and who these people were—and what he was doing here. "It's not too bad, ma'am," he said, watching her closely.

Standing beside the woman, the Irish boy stared at Arthur. He, too, was frowning. "This is my mother," he said. "Mrs. Dalton. She's been taking care of you—with Molly's help, of course."

Arthur looked from the boy to his mother.

"Molly is our housekeeper," she said. "And a grand nurse as well. I'm not very good at taking care of sick people, I'm afraid, but Molly is the best. And she says you're doing just fine, Arthur, so you're not to worry at all."

"Where—" Arthur wet his lips. "Could ya tell me where—"

Mrs. Dalton looked at him, then put a hand to her mouth. "My goodness! Of course, you want to know where you are! I should have thought of that first thing! Well, now, would you be remembering Mr. Dalton, Arthur? The preacher who helped get you to the doctor after…" She paused. "After the shooting?"

Arthur nodded at the thought of the big black-suited preacher-man who had used his own body like a human shield in the thick of the riot.

"This is his house. I'm his wife, and Casey-Fitz here is his son. Jess—Mr. Dalton—made arrangements for you to stay with us until you recover."

Arthur's eyes widened. "Stay *here*?"

The woman smiled. She regarded him almost as if she sensed his suspicion. "That's right," she said quietly. "Don't you remember telling the doctor you had no place to go, Arthur?"

Arthur shook his head. "Don't remember nothin'."

The woman's cheerful expression sobered. "No, I expect you don't recall very much at all about what happened to you. Well, that's perfectly all right, Arthur. You're quite safe here with us, and more than welcome to stay as long as necessary."

Arthur stared at her. Every reply he could think of stuck in his throat. His gaze went to the boy, who was watching him with undisguised curiosity.

Was this really happening? Arthur couldn't remember anybody in his entire life speaking as kindly to him as this woman had. 'Course, he didn't remember his mama—she'd been dead too many years. But he was sure if she had ever talked to him so sweetly his brain would have somehow stored it up for keeps. Daddy—well, Daddy had always treated him fair, but he was a gruff man, all the same.

But this woman, this *Mrs. Dalton*—she made him feel as if she actually *cared* about him. As if he were worth something.

He blinked, realizing she was talking to him. "We mustn't be tiring you any more," she said. "Molly will want to fix you some warm broth, now that you're awake. I'll just go down and let her know." She started to turn, then hesitated. "You rest, Arthur. I'll send Mr. Dalton in the moment he gets home. He'll be wanting to say hello, I'm sure."

The boy hesitated after his mother left the room, although she called him to follow.

"She meant what she said, you know," he told Arthur. "You can stay as long as you like. Da's forever bringing home company to stay the night or even a few days. They like having people in, you see." He paused, cocking his head a bit. "So do I. It'll be swell, having another boy around for a change."

Arthur reached up slowly and ran his hand through his hair. He blinked in surprise. It felt clean and cotton-smooth. How long had it been since his hair had been clean? He'd had no way to wash it since leaving the river.

Who had done such a thing for him?

He stared at the redheaded boy. Casey Dalton was obviously hoping for more conversation.

"How—how old you be?" Arthur asked, clearing his throat.

"Nine. Almost ten," the Dalton boy added quickly. "You're older."

Arthur nodded. "Near 'bout thirteen."

Casey Dalton considered Arthur for another moment. "Everybody is always saying I seem older. Maybe we could be friends."

Arthur stared at him, not trying to hide his skepticism. "I'm a Negro."

The younger boy met his eyes with a steady look. "I'm Irish."

Arthur glanced away, fixing his attention on a framed picture of a green-covered hillside on the opposite wall. "I don't reckon I mind that you're Irish," he said, slowly turning back to the younger boy.

"Well, then…I don't expect I mind that you're a Negro," answered Casey Dalton.

Still, Arthur hesitated. "What about your folks?"

The Irish boy considered the question. "That's their bed you're sleeping in."

Arthur's eyes bugged and his mouth went slack.

"Mother told my da you ought to have the best mattress. The one in the best guest room sags a bit, and we haven't put a bed in the other spare room just yet."

He paused. "Mother almost always has her way."

Later that night, when everybody else in the house was asleep, Jess and Kerry Dalton lay talking in what the family referred to as the "best guest bedroom."

"Now that we know the boy is going to be all right," Jess said dryly, "do you suppose we could move him in here and reclaim our bed? This mattress was not made to hold a man of my size."

Resting her head on her husband's big, sturdy shoulder, Kerry smiled contentedly. She was about to drift off to sleep. "Soon," she murmured. Yawning, she added, "He's still in too much pain to be moving about."

"Many more nights on this mattress and *I'll* be the one who's in too much pain to move about."

Kerry laughed softly in the darkness and buried her face against his neck. Then, abruptly, she pushed herself up on one arm to look at him. "I almost *forgot*! Tell me about your talk with Arthur! What did you find out about the boy?"

Flinging one forearm up over his head, Jess groaned. "Oh no! Not now!"

"Yes, now! I want to know everything!"

He laughed at her. Plumping two pillows against the head of the bed, he propped himself up, then pulled her back into his arms. "Stay close, and I'll tell you."

"Everything," she reminded him, settling back into the warmth of his embrace.

"There's not that much to tell, actually." He kept his voice low as he talked. "The boy's a runaway, just as we figured. But a runaway with his father's blessing."

"What do you mean?"

As Jess explained, he stroked her hair with gentle fingers. "He said his daddy and an uncle made a few dollars for themselves by hiring on at a nearby plantation for night work. About two months ago they gave Arthur the money and told him to make his way north. He didn't want to leave— he was afraid to come alone. But his father is lame, and the uncle wouldn't leave. Anyway," he went on, "he had quite a time of it, getting here."

"A bad time, d'you mean, Jess? What happened?" Kerry shifted in his arms so that she could look at him. His bearded face was haloed in the faint wash of moonlight filtering through the drapes, and she smiled a little as she looked at him.

"Well, he almost got caught first thing, before he ever got out of Mississippi. A neighbor's overseer spotted him and set the dogs on him. He spent one entire night bobbing in and out of logs in a mill pond to keep from being caught." Tracing the line of her cheek, then her chin with one finger, he went on. "He said he came close to getting shot more than once before he reached Ohio. Some people in Cincinnati gave him food and helped him across the river."

"To think of going through such a thing alone—and he's so young! Why, he's only a child, Jess!"

"Black children grow up fast in the South, Kerry." Jess's voice was grim as he tightened his embrace. "They don't really have a choice."

Kerry understood the truth in his words. She had read a number of Jess's own writings, as well as the works of others, about the plight of black slaves in the South. The horror-filled stories, especially of the women and children, broke her heart every time she thought of them.

"What about his mother?" she asked quietly. "He had to leave his mother, too?"

"She's dead. The boy doesn't remember her at all."

"No wonder the poor child seems so lost and alone! And to be injured and laid up as well."

Jess's voice in the darkness was strained and quiet. "One thing he said to me, I can't forget."

"What, Jess?"

"When I was explaining to him that he could stay here for as long as he needed to, he asked me right out why we were doing all this for him. I told him we tried to do the things we thought Jesus would do."

He stopped, saying nothing for a moment.

"And?" Kerry prompted. "What did he say to that?"

"He asked me," Jess said, drawing a long breath, "if I really believed Jesus would do such things for a *black boy*."

Kerry swallowed against the knot in her throat, then lay thinking in silence for a long time. When she spoke again, it was a near-whisper. "You know, I can remember, back in Ireland, thinking nobody had ever suffered as much as the Irish. But I know better now. Sometimes it did seem that we were slaves of the English, but in truth we were only slaves of their political system. But the black folk—why, they're bought and sold as if they were no more than *animals*!"

"It won't always be that way, love," Jess said quietly, his voice growing thick with sleep. "The day will come when they will break their chains. God never intended any man to live enslaved."

"And men like you will help them break those chains," Kerry whispered, mostly to herself. "Then frightened young boys like Arthur Jackson won't have to run away any longer to find their freedom."

His breathing had grown even and shallow. He was asleep. Kerry kissed his cheek ever so gently, then nestled more snugly into the safe, warm haven of his arms.

In the quiet peace of the bedroom, she breathed her last prayer of the day for this big, godly man who, when she was still little more than a child herself, had taken her in, given her a home, and made her his legal ward.

Eventually, thanks be to God, he had also made her his wife.

13

Secret Sighs

Love tender, true I gave to you,
And secret sighs....

FROM WALSH'S *IRISH POPULAR SONGS* (1847)

It took Evan three days to muster the nerve to speak with Nora about the opera—three days of talking himself into the idea, then out of it; three days of convincing himself she would enjoy the evening, then agonizing with himself that she would rather stay home alone than spend it with *him.*

One evening, before going to his cottage, he stopped in the library on the first floor. He was leaving the room when Nora appeared in the doorway. "Evan? You're home early today. There's nothing wrong?"

Evan shook his head. "Mr. Farmington had a b-board meeting in Manhattan and insisted on d-dropping me off early b-before he went. I was just p-putting some designs on his d-desk that he wants to review later this evening."

He smiled at her. No doubt she was wholly unaware of how lovely she looked. She was wearing his favorite dress, a soft blue wool that deepened the gray of her eyes to dark smoke and heightened the faint blush of her fair skin. It pleased him to see how healthy she looked! Despite her slenderness and the air of fragility that seemed to continually hover about her, she appeared entirely recovered from the worst ravages of the famine.

Evan knew he should take this opportunity to ask Nora about the opera. He was keenly aware of the tickets in his suit pocket; he had carried them next to his heart since Monday. Yet he couldn't quite bring himself to approach the subject. In an effort to ignore the tickets, he groped for a less threatening topic of conversation. "The house s-seems awfully quiet. Where is everyone?"

"Sara went off to the church building to help set up a mission display for the weekend. And Ginger is in the kitchen, helping Cook."

Evan chuckled. "You mean *annoying* Cook, d-don't you?" The friction between Mrs. Buckley, the Farmingtons' cook, and Ginger, their West Indies housekeeper, was an acknowledged fact throughout the household. Theirs was an ongoing but harmless sort of rivalry; Evan suspected it had more to do with the stark contrasts in their natures than any real antagonism between the two. The mild-mannered, self-assured Ginger had a way of ignoring whatever she chose, while the hot-tempered Mrs. Buckley liked a good argument every chance she could find.

She already had it in for *him,* Evan knew. He had been relegated to her bad graces the moment his British accent first landed upon her ears. Evan believed the Irish cook's attitude reflected the enduring Anglo-Irish enmity rather than any personal hostility. In fact, he had come to find Cook's rancor a somewhat amusing challenge, and enjoyed baiting her by employing the most excessive of British mannerisms in her presence.

He suddenly realized that Nora was regarding him with a quizzical stare. "Are you quite well, Evan?"

Distracted, Evan traced his mustache with one finger. "Well? Oh—yes. Yes, of c-course."

Should he ask her now? Was this the right time? Was there a right time? Should he ask her at all?

"Nora—"

Nora tilted her head, waiting, still peering at him with worried eyes.

"I…I was won-wondering—" Evan stopped, shrinking inwardly at the sound of his inane stammering.

"What is it, then, Evan? You *aren't* well, after all, are you now?" Nora insisted, her frown deepening as she leaned closer.

Her closeness only flustered him all the more.

"Oh, I'm f-fine—r-really!" he assured her. "It's just that…I've b-been wanting to ask you…something…" As usual, when he was under pressure, the dreaded stutter exploded full-blown. "The th-thing…is, M-Mr. Farmington was k-kind enough to offer t-tickets to the op-opera, and I…I won-wondered if p-p-p-perhaps…you would allow m-me to…escort you."

There! It was done, and as he'd feared, she was staring at him with a look of dismay. More than likely, she was stunned by his presumption and struggling for a tactful way to refuse.

"Opera tickets? What sort of tickets would that be, Evan?"

"What sort—oh…well, the opera is *Ernani*. It's to b-be the opening p-production for the n-new Astor P-Place Opera House. In two weeks."

"I see. And these are Mr. Farmington's tickets, you say?"

Evan nodded, not trusting his voice.

After a moment of hesitation, Nora turned her face away. "I—I don't believe I know what an *opera* is, Evan, that's the thing."

Evan instinctively put his hand to her shoulder, appalled that he might have embarrassed her. "Why, an opera is—is n-nothing but a musical stage p-play, Nora. I think you'd enjoy it, I really do."

Nora turned back to him. "A play, is it? A *musical* play?"

Evan nodded, reluctantly dropping his hand away from her shoulder. "That's right. The story is often a somewhat w-weak little plot about d-doomed lovers with actors and actresses who sing a great deal, but the m-music is usually quite b-beautiful."

"Well…I do like music," Nora said uncertainly, reaching a hand to tuck a loose strand of hair back in place.

Evan's gaze followed the movement of her hand, intrigued by its smallness. "Mr. F-Farmington even offered the k-kid gloves required for admittance," he said, smiling.

Nora's eyes widened, and Evan chuckled, explaining about the outlandish admission requirement.

A doubtful expression crossed her features, and he quickly reassured her. "It's just p-pretentiousness on the part of the management. You mustn't m-mind that sort of foolishness, Nora."

"But I'd have no dress fine enough, I'm sure, if it's as grand an occasion as all that."

"N-No matter *what* you wear, you'll b-be the loveliest woman there, I can promise you that!" Mortified by his unexpected outburst, Evan immediately turned away.

After an awkward moment of silence, during which he braced himself for Nora's refusal, he felt a light touch on his arm. "Thank you, Evan," Nora said with quiet dignity. "It's kind of you to be asking me, and I—I would be more than happy to go to the opera with you."

At his quick intake of breath, she hurried to add, "If Sara will help me manage a suitable gown, that is."

Overcome, Evan fought to contain his monumental relief and delight. "Oh—I'm *sure* she will, Nora! M-Miss Sara obviously enjoys making other people happy—especially you! Indeed, I wonder if she ever thinks of herself at all."

"Aye, and isn't that the truth," Nora said, smiling. "But Evan," she said, suddenly serious as she dropped her voice to a conspiratorial undertone, "about the kid gloves: does it strike you now and then that rich people have no end of cracked notions about the most unimportant things?"

As always, her ingenuousness delighted him. "Why, y-yes," Evan agreed soberly, "it has occurred to me from t-time to time."

In another impulsive gesture that was quite unlike him, he suddenly gave in to the desire to take Nora's hand. When she made no pull to move away, but rather stood smiling shyly at him, Evan felt as if the dawn of a high summer morning had risen in his heart. Just for a moment, he almost felt a whole man once again—indeed, he somehow felt *more* a whole man than he ever had in the past, even in the time before he had lost his arm.

It was as if Nora somehow…completed him, filled the empty spaces in his heart and made him whole. She could not replace his missing arm, of course, could not change the fact that he was maimed. But what she *did* do, without her ever realizing it, was to *add* something to him—something new and wonderfully fulfilling.

It was a gift only Nora could give.

In her room later that night, after most of the household had retired, Nora sat in the small rocking chair by the fire, thinking.

Inside, the house was quiet, but outside, the cold November wind whipped a fury about the mansion, whistling through the wrought-iron fence that surrounded the grounds, rattling a loose pane of glass somewhere in back.

The moan of the wind made Nora think of their final winter in Ireland—the relentless storms off the Atlantic; the cold, damp cottage; the lack of food. Shivering at the memory, she glanced about her cozy little bedroom, snug and warm with its honey-colored furniture and creamy silk walls, the soft rose carpet and the black marble fireplace where a fire always burned.

She was struck anew with amazement at all that had happened to them in a matter of months. Even now, it took her breath to consider the things the Lord had done for them.

From the moment of their rescue from the coffin ship by the kind-hearted Farmington family, her life had seemed more dream than reality. Not only had Lewis Farmington and his daughter, Sara, given her a position in service and the shelter of their luxurious home, but hadn't they offered their friendship as well?

This in itself never ceased to overwhelm Nora, that these two people, who socialized with the cream of New York, would deign to befriend a group of raggedy Irish immigrants!

And just see what they had done for the Fitzgerald children! Why, they pampered wee Tom like the pet of the family, and Sara had even hired a private tutor for the deaf Johanna.

And Evan—they had taken him to their hearts as well, seeing to it he received the very finest in medical attention, then giving him employment as Mr. Farmington's own personal assistant at the shipyards.

She smiled at the thought of Evan. Indeed, lately it seemed she could scarcely think of him *without* a smile. Nora wondered if the man had even a thought of how much she cherished his friendship, how greatly she treasured his kindness to her and the children.

Her smile softened as she recalled Evan's stumbling attempt to invite her to the opera. Here she was, an uneducated Irish woman who did not even know what an opera *was*, and he treated her as if she were royalty, as if her presence was a gift he could never deserve. Dear man! Dear, dear Evan, who offered her so much without ever being aware of it.

Guiltily, she realized that she thought of *Evan* more often these days than she did Michael. But wasn't it only natural, with both of them living in such close quarters and being employed by the same family? And they *were* friends, after all, good friends.

You're supposed to be friends with Michael, too…more than friends, if truth were told….

Nora rose from the rocking chair with a jerk, uncomfortable with the direction her thoughts were taking. Sure, and no decent woman—especially a widow-woman with a son almost grown—should be entertaining thoughts of more than one man; yet of late it seemed that hers insisted on roaming among *three*.

Evan had come to mean more to her than she would have ever believed possible. Michael, of course, continued to offer *his* friendship—and his name, should she agree to marry him.

And, always, like an undercurrent beneath a deceptively calm lake, ran the memory of Morgan Fitzgerald—a memory that, to Nora's great surprise, seemed to be ebbing and drifting further away with time.

He had not hanged after all, thanks be to God. Indeed, he was out of gaol and had astounded them by discovering an English grandfather with whom he was living in Dublin—a grandfather who had immediately set about making Morgan his sole heir!

She was relieved that Morgan was safe, thankful that his neck had been spared—but in some inexplicable fashion, the very fact that he was now out of harm's way had served to push him to the back of her memories. Perhaps because she no longer spent so much effort fearing for his life, so much energy in prayer that God would spare him—perhaps that was why she had finally been released from her obsession for the man.

When the letter had come telling them of his pardon, her first foolish thought had been that now…perhaps now, he would come to her. Just as quickly, she had dismissed the wild notion. Nothing had changed with Morgan, except that he was in a better position than ever to spend his life and his passion for Ireland. He had made his choice long ago, had wed an island rather than a woman, and there would be no separating them—now, or in the future. Morgan belonged to Ireland. He always had. He always would.

She would never forget him. He was a part of her life that, even though it no longer existed, could not easily be put away and forgotten. He had been her first love—a wondrous, great, and fiercely painful love—and she did not think she would ever think of Ireland without a thought of Morgan as well. But that's all he would ever be for her—a memory.

With thoughts of Morgan came the image of Michael as well. They were much alike, those two—the friends of her youth. Morgan, ever the wild poet, had swept her heart away with his passion and power. Michael, the rock-steady support, had always waited on the sidelines for her to turn to him. She loved them both, and always would. But now, in the present, Michael was here, still waiting, wanting to protect her, to shelter her.

Sure, and it was a fierce temptation for Nora to say yes to Michael's offer of marriage. Michael wanted it; Tierney wanted it; even Daniel John wanted it. The security Michael held out to her was a powerful attraction; he would take care of her and Daniel John.

But something in Nora rose to the surface in the face of the mighty temptation to be *cared for*—a memory of a prayer she had prayed near the end of those long, terrible days on the *Green Flag*. She had asked God to give her the strength to depend upon Him alone, to make her equal to the challenges that lay before her.

And hadn't He answered that prayer, after all? Hadn't He opened the door to a new life, a life determined by His direction? Aye, God had given her a chance to prove herself, to trust in Him to care for her. And now, in Michael's insistent proposal, she found herself drawn backward to the old way of life she had known in Ireland. And she knew she could not go back. She could never again be Nora, the girl; God had grown her into Nora, the woman.

Suddenly Nora understood her vague reluctance to accept Michael's offer of marriage. It seemed so *logical* to marry him; yet somehow it didn't seem *right*. If she married Michael, she would become, once more, the dependent, protected woman, overwhelmed and swallowed up in his strength. And she knew, instinctively, that she had passed beyond that portal when she stepped onto the *Green Flag* to come to America.

Michael loved her, in his own way—of that Nora was certain. But she needed more than love and protection. She needed...*respect*, the kind of respect she found in her friendship with Evan Whittaker. He knew her not as the girl she had been, but as the woman she was. And he accepted her—cared about her—for herself. He treated her not as a child to be coddled, but as an equal, an adult, a woman to be honored.

It was hard, ever so hard, to let go of the past! And yet she must. Even if she had to live her life alone, she must look only to today, and to the future. God had opened the door. For the sake of her son...and for the sake of her own life...she must be done, finally done, with yesterday.

❧

Later that night, Sara Farmington found her father dozing at his library desk over a stack of ship designs. As quietly as possible, she edged his teacup a few inches away from his hand so he wouldn't knock it over when he awakened.

She should have remembered that the slightest noise would rouse him—he was a man who thrived on little sleep and came instantly awake at the least movement.

As he did now. With a muffled grunt, his head came up and his eyes snapped open.

"Don't go taking my tea, daughter! I was just resting my eyes for a moment." He gave a huge stretch, yawned, and, watching her over the rim of the cup, took a deep sip of tea that was, Sara was certain, quite cold.

He refused her offer to make fresh tea, motioning instead that she should sit down across from him. "Now tell me what you've been up to this evening, why don't you? You disappeared right after dinner, and I haven't seen you since."

Taking the chair on the other side of the desk, Sara eyed her father with amusement. "Actually, I've been conferring with Nora about a proper gown for the opera," she replied dryly.

His dark eyes fairly snapped. "Hah! So he asked her, did he?"

"Oh, yes. He asked her—if we're talking about Evan. I suspected it was entirely your doing; it seems I was right."

Her father shrugged, lifted both heavy brows, and shot her an ingenuous look. "I had extra tickets. I thought the two of them might enjoy seeing the new opera house."

"I'm sure they will." Sara folded her hands in her lap.

"Well, neither of them ever does anything but *work*," her father argued, waving a hand with a defensive air. "Work and church—that's their life! I believe they need to have some fun, don't you?"

Sara arched an eyebrow, but said nothing.

Her father stared at her for a moment, then grinned. "Surely you've seen that the man is enchanted with her."

Drawing in a deep breath, Sara nodded reluctantly. "So it appears."

"Well, you needn't sound so put out. I think they'd be splendid together."

"Father…" Sara paused uncertainly. "What about Michael Burke?"

"What about him?" her father shot back, his forehead creasing in an obstinate frown.

"He's expecting Nora to marry *him*."

"Oh, pshaw!" Lewis Farmington reared back in his chair, his chin thrust forward in a terrible scowl. "I'm getting more than a little sick and tired of hearing how Nora and Sergeant Burke are going to be married—*one day*! If Nora wanted the man, she'd have done something about it by now! And if he was as serious about her as he fancies himself to be, he'd have carried her off long ago! Let Evan have a try, I say."

"For goodness' sake, Father, you make it sound as if this were a *foot-race*!"

He smiled slyly. "A fair enough comparison. Two suitors vying for a lovely woman's hand—yes, I think that sums it up rather nicely."

Exasperated with him, Sara got up from the chair. "You're dreadful! You must be one of the busiest men in New York, and here you are playing matchmaker."

"I should think you'd encourage the idea of a courtship between Evan and Nora."

Uncomfortable under his close scrutiny, Sara glanced away. "Why would you think that?"

She could feel his eyes locked upon her, even though she refused to look at him.

"Well…they're obviously drawn to each other. You seem to care about both of them. And—"

When he stopped, Sara held her breath, waiting for what she was sure would come.

"It would settle this thing between Nora and Sergeant Burke. I thought that might be to your liking."

Sara turned to face him, doing her best to manage a noncommittal expression. She found his dark eyes gentle, but appraising.

He knew.

Sara almost moaned aloud. "Father—"

"It's all right, my dear. You needn't defend yourself to me, nor should you feel the slightest need to deny or admit anything. I'm not at all sure how I feel about your…attraction to the sergeant, because to tell you the truth, his so-called attachment to Nora has made it unnecessary for me to examine my feelings up until now. However, if Nora is even half as taken with Evan as he obviously is with her, the time may soon be coming when both you and I will have to make an honest evaluation of our feelings about Michael Burke."

Sara stared at him in dismay. She moistened her lips and found them bitter and dry. She attempted to smile. "Father, you're really making entirely too much—"

The tenderness in his eyes gave way to an expression of fatherly concern. "Sara, let's just—wait and see, shall we? I think that's the thing to do. For now."

He could read her too easily. He always could. She could not—would not—lie to him.

"Yes, Father," Sara said quietly. "We'll do just that. We'll—wait and see."

14

Lament for the Land

Day after day, mile after mile,
I roamed a land that knew no smile.
AUBREY DE VERE (1814–1902)

Killala (Western Ireland)

Joseph Mahon sat hunched over his journal, his head nodding, his burning eyes drifting in and out of focus.

Lately, his right eye had taken to twitching and drooping, making it next to impossible to write legibly in the dim candlelight. Fatigue, more than likely. He had never known this kind of exhaustion. There was no part of his body free from the ache of weariness. Even his teeth, the few he had left, pained him from daylight to dark.

At the height of last winter's misery, he had managed three or four hours of fitful sleep most nights, enough to keep from keeling over through the day. But for weeks now, rest had been sporadic. Few nights passed without his being awakened by a desperate parishioner who came begging food or last rites for a family member. Joseph could no longer remember when he had last slept more than an hour or two at a time.

The days were frantic and turbulent, crammed with endless work and packed with heartache. Like most of the other priests in the county, Joseph somehow made the time to write numerous letters to the relief officials. In addition, he attended every meeting he could, relentlessly plaguing every last mother's son of them, trying to eke out some sparse sustenance for his people.

His efforts in this regard were the least of his tasks, of course. Above all else came the ceaseless duties of comforting the suffering and ministering to the dying, all the while trying in vain to find some slight vestige of hope—in lieu of food—for the starving.

Of late, Joseph, like many among the clergy, had also taken to nursing those who were ill. A number of physicians in the area had themselves succumbed, victims of either the Hunger or its shadowing fevers. Disease and death wildly outdistanced the supply of both doctors and clergy. Physicians, priests, and Protestant ministers were dying in ever-increasing numbers.

In truth there were days when Joseph found himself almost longing for death, his deteriorating flesh crying out for rest, blessed rest. But then he would remember his people and their dependence on him, and with an exhausted sigh he would once more pray for the strength to go on.

Now his head nodded, and he jerked awake. Steadying his pen, he waited for the trembling of his hand to cease. He had become obsessed with keeping the journal, with the need to record what he could of the horrific conditions in his parish—conditions which were, he knew, representative of most parishes throughout County Mayo and much of the rest of Ireland.

What was happening to the people must be remembered. The survivors…the world…must somehow, someday, be required to take notice of Ireland's suffering.

Propping his elbow on the table, he braced his head with a fist and renewed his writing:

> Now that winter is upon us again, it is to be expected that things will be even more dreadful than before. No longer does a day pass in Killala without death, and throughout our poor Mayo the suffering defies all imagining.
>
> This evening on my way to investigate a rumor about the Hegartys, I passed through scenes one could not envision except in their worst nightmares. The streets now swarm with gaunt wanderers, roaming aimlessly to and fro like lost souls cast into the void. Homeless and hopeless, they are near naked—starving, some raving with madness, they will upon occasion mob one who appears in better circumstances than they.
>
> The children and the aged are the worst. They break the heart with their pitiful swollen bellies and their bewildered, pleading

eyes. Oh, God, they are enough to crush the strongest of spirits, the stoutest of hearts!

But I digress from my accounting of the Hegartys. Their mean abode is off to itself a ways and appeared deserted when I reached it. Silence reigned; at first I thought the entire family had left to go on the road, but when I entered I found the ghastly reason for the quiet.

Poor Nessan and Mary were both dead, propped together in the corner on a mound of filthy straw! The babe was dead as well, in Mary's arms. The other three children—more specters than living beings—were huddled beneath a piece of soiled horsecloth. Only one, wee Kathleen, found the strength to whimper when she saw me.

I went at once to fetch Dr. Browne, and, the Lord bless that good man, he helped me to bury Nessan and Mary and the babe before taking the sick children to his own house!

The kind doctor is a shadow of himself, and I fear he will not be long after helping those he treats with such charity. God help us, we are all dying, some more slowly and painfully than others…but we are all of us dying. The land itself is dying, and that is the truth.

Joseph stopped, laying his pen down long enough to remove his spectacles and rub his burning eyes. He shook his head in an attempt to stay awake, but he was almost numb with fatigue.

A hood of darkness slipped down over his head, masking his vision. He bent over the table and put his head down upon his folded arms. He would rest his eyes, then, for a moment.

Only for a moment…

In his Spartan, drafty bedroom at Nelson Hall, Morgan Fitzgerald was packing for a trip he did not want to make.

He regretted now that he'd agreed to accompany Smith O'Brien to the Belfast meetings. That in itself would not be such a bad thing, although he found the northern city bleak and depressing. It was more the fact that Meagher, McGee, and Mitchel were also going. All three were avowed militants, bent on stirring the people to a rising—and all three thought Morgan had gone soft.

He crossed to the bureau and rifled through the clean linen stacked in the middle drawer, checking to see what he might have forgotten. Returning to the open valise on the bed, he stood staring down at it, his mood growing more and more dour.

In truth, the only reason he had agreed to the trip at all was his concern for Smith O'Brien. The man had made himself some real enemies over the past months, as had most members of the Young Ireland movement, either wittingly or unwittingly.

Oddly enough, it was not the Orangemen—the northern Protestants—who worried Morgan most. He suspected O'Brien's *real* foes were a number of troublemakers bent on destroying the entire Young Ireland organization, along with its leader.

They had been at their mischief here in Dublin for some time now, as well as in Limerick and Tipperary. More than one Young Irelander had been attacked on his way home from a night meeting last summer, including Mitchel and Meagher.

These days the Young Irelanders were accused of an entire assortment of sins and seditions, from O'Connell's death last May to a wave of atheism, racism, and political unrest. Smith O'Brien, in particular, had come under heavy criticism, both for his support of "secret societies" and for "hobnobbing with the gentry" at the expense of his commitment to the common folk.

A Protestant, O'Brien had joined both the Catholic Association and the Repeal movement. At first he had worked well with Daniel O'Connell, the most popular hero in Ireland, both of them endeavoring toward the same ends: relief for the famine victims and repeal of the union between Ireland and England.

When the time came, however, that O'Connell insisted all members of the Repeal organization disavow physical force or armed rebellion, a number of dissidents refused. With such men at the front as Thomas Davis, a young Protestant barrister and poet from Cork, Charles Gavan Duffy, and John Blake Dillon, the Young Ireland movement was born.

Through its journal, *The Nation*, the movement began to attract some of the finest minds in Ireland, both Protestant and Catholic, and the aristocratic Smith O'Brien gradually became one of the most prominent figures. With the acquisition of John Mitchel and John Martin, however, an increasingly militant tone began to issue from *The Nation*. More vigorous language in favor of rebellion arose; stirrings and murmurings for a rising of the people grew louder.

After the death of Daniel O'Connell, his son's weak and ineffective leadership all but destroyed the Repeal movement. With this weakening of "Old Ireland"—O'Connell's followers—the radical, militant John Mitchel began to speak out with even more force. Smith O'Brien continued to insist he would have no part in a rising, but Morgan sensed that in spite of his protests, O'Brien was being caught up in the wake of rebellion.

And where do I stand in all this? Morgan asked himself, restacking the contents of the valise to make room for his pen and papers. After years of indulging in violence and renegade activities, he had been spared from the gallows by an English grandfather whose existence had been unknown to him until a few months ago.

Right on the heels of this unexpected pardon came a renewal of his faith, a spiritual reawakening Morgan would have thought impossible for an outlaw such as he. Turning back to his Savior, he found he had not been forsaken as he had once thought. Like the Prodigal Son, he had thrown himself, sins and all, at the feet of a forgiving Father, to find himself healed and accepted.

He desired to do nothing that would grieve the Lord who had so graciously restored him. Although he was still a Young Irelander, still committed—at least in principle—to the movement, he had begun to feel more and more uncomfortable with the militant turn of *The Nation* and its supporters.

His own belief that the dire straits of Ireland's starving people spelled certain failure for any attempted rebellion led him to disavow the fiery prose and militant verse of *The Nation's* leading writers. His refusal to use his pen in support of violence had made him many enemies within the Confederacy. Ironic, this, considering the enemies he'd already made *outside* the movement during his more rebellious, dissident days.

He knew himself to be caught in the middle: Unable to endorse the heedless militancy of Mitchel and his followers, he found it equally impossible to accept British rule in his own land. Ireland belonged to the Irish, not the Queen, and he was committed to doing all within his power, and within the confines of his conscience, to see the country free of England's boot.

So he continued to publish in *The Nation*, trying not to mind that his present works were received with little interest and even a degree of contempt. No longer was he revered as the *Red Wolf of Mayo*, the rebel-patriot who had inspired fear in the landlords and devotion among the peasantry. No longer did his Young Ireland contemporaries turn to him for counsel; most disdained even his company.

He was the grandson of an Englishman, a patriot whose voice could no longer be heard above the whispered rumors and insinuations about his loyalty; a poet whose words no longer stirred the hearts of fellow Irishmen, except to anger—anger that he would dare to call for common sense and brotherhood in a land of warriors and displaced chieftains.

Indeed, some Young Ireland members had gone so far as to label him a traitor to the movement, inferring that his inheritance from his grandfather had turned his Irish blood to English ice. The contempt of former comrades grieved Morgan more than he would have them know. Only O'Brien and two or three others within the movement continued to show him the same degree of loyalty and friendship as in the past.

O'Brien, especially, had remained unswervingly firm in his support. Morgan genuinely liked the aristocratic Young Ireland leader. He valued his friendship and trusted his integrity. Therefore, although he questioned his own judgment, he was prepared to see this trip to Belfast through to completion.

An unexpected knock at the bedroom door made Morgan straighten and turn. Surprised to hear his grandfather's voice, he crossed the room to let him in.

As soon as the old man entered, Morgan saw that he was having one of his frequent attacks of the rheumatism. It was all he could do to manage the few steps to the chair beside the bed.

It was a rare occurrence when Richard Nelson invaded the privacy of his grandson's rooms, and so his visit caused Morgan to wonder what he was about.

The old man's eyes went to the folded clothing on the bed. "So…" He paused on the word. "You are still going."

Morgan nodded, returning to the bed to sort the remaining few articles of clothing. "Aye, I am," he replied, avoiding the old man's searching eyes.

His grandfather said nothing for a moment, but simply sighed and continued to watch Morgan.

"I'll be away only a few days," Morgan said in an attempt to make conversation. "When I return, we'll start in on the library again." Some weeks earlier, at the old man's request, he had begun the monumental task of cataloging his grandfather's vast, magnificent library.

"It's not the library I'm concerned about, as I'm sure you know," said Richard Nelson, his pale hazel eyes regarding Morgan with a worried expression. After a slight delay, he went on. "Belfast is not friendly to the Young Ireland movement these days, I'm told."

Morgan continued his packing. "Nor is Dublin, for that matter."

"That's quite true, but at least in Dublin you have friends among your enemies."

Morgan said nothing.

For a few moments the old man was silent. At last he said, "I had hoped you might separate from these... Young Ireland people altogether. You've already distanced yourself from some of their politics."

Morgan straightened and turned to face the old man, who was now leaning forward, his thin hands clinging tightly to the chair arms. "You told me you respect much of what Smith O'Brien is attempting to do within the movement. And I happen to know that you like and admire him as a person. He is the reason I'm going to Belfast."

Richard Nelson drew his mouth into a disapproving line. "You are going as his bodyguard."

Surprised at the old man's perception, Morgan attempted a dry laugh. "I would hope you'll not say such a thing to Smith O'Brien. He has enough worries without being told he needs someone to guard his back."

"The young fool needs more than protection these days!" His grandfather's hands were white-knuckled on the arms of the chair. "He needs to choose his place and stick to it. O'Brien is trying to be all things to all people, and if he isn't careful he's going to spread himself so thin he'll accomplish nothing."

Morgan made no reply, but in truth he feared that the old man might be right. In a deliberate move to change the subject, he sat down on the edge of the bed, saying, "You haven't told me the news from your talk with Clarendon."

The fourth Earl of Clarendon, an old friend of Richard Nelson's, had reluctantly accepted the Lord-Lieutenancy of Ireland this past summer. His grandfather made no secret of the fact, however, that he held no real faith in his friend's ability to help the country.

"There is no good news, that much is certain," Richard Nelson replied sourly. "Had it not been for the panic in the money market, things might have improved by now. There was a sizable sum earmarked for Ireland last summer, you know. But our esteemed Chancellor of the Exchequer now claims that England is dangerously short of money, thanks to the panic, and there will be no funds forthcoming for Ireland's relief."

Morgan uttered a sound of disgust. "There is *never* enough money for Ireland, so it would seem. It would have made no difference, had there *been* no financial panic. Wood and Trevelyan would have simply found another excuse—anything to avoid saving the Irish."

His grandfather nodded. "Clarendon is in a state about things. He admits to the Irish people's despair, feels England has pushed them too far. With such widespread hatred and desperation, he thinks a rising is a real possibility. He says there's been an alarming number of landlord assassinations everywhere, even some mutilations."

Morgan grimaced but said nothing. He didn't condone the acts, but he understood all too well the desperation behind them.

"Clarendon is convinced the murders are part of a planned rebellion," his grandfather went on. "He says the idea is to frighten the landlords enough that they'll simply give up on the land and leave, allowing the tenants to win by default. He's beside himself with worry. He even went so far as to request an Act of 'Extraordinary Powers' to impose fines and prohibit the holding of arms."

Morgan looked up.

Nodding, his grandfather explained. "Oh, his request was turned down, of course. The Prime Minister isn't about to give the Lord-Lieutenant of Ireland excessive authority. Clarendon, by the way, is threatening to resign."

Morgan pushed both long arms straight out, bracing his hands on his knees. "Clarendon's fears about a planned rebellion are without foundation, in any event. The people are in no condition to manage their own survival, much less a national rising."

His grandfather regarded him with a measuring look. "Clarendon believes the plans are being made by Young Ireland, not the people."

Morgan shook his head, then got to his feet. "O'Brien has retreated from all talk of a rising."

"But Mitchel and the others have not," the old man pointed out sharply. "And it would seem that many are listening to them."

Morgan gave a noncommittal shrug.

"There are even more who listen to *you*, Morgan. And your voice is sorely needed in Ireland. Don't...endanger yourself."

Morgan gave a wry smile. "I fear words on education and peacemaking are not the popular thing these days. The Irish have ever had a fierce love for rebel verse and inflammatory essays. And," he said ruefully, "I must admit to having written my share of both."

"The times are different now," the old man insisted. "The need today is for caution and reason."

Morgan looked at him, still smiling. "Ah, but the sons of Eire have never been fond of either, now have they, Grandfather?"

15

Binding Wounds and Broken Hearts

The dwellings of the virtuous poor,
The homes of poverty,
Are sacred in the sight of God,
Though humble they may be.

ELIZABETH WILLOUGHBY VARIAN ("FINOLA") 1830–1903

New York City

Daniel had been working for Dr. Grafton for over a month, but Monday marked his first time to accompany the physician to Five Points.

With the help of Pastor Jess Dalton, a weekly clinic had been established in the notorious slum. His congregation had reluctantly agreed to rent two rooms above Duke Neeson's pub until such a time as an entire building could be located for the use of the mission.

It had taken the pastor's intervention to convince the mission committee, but they finally agreed that using rooms over a pub for medical treatment of the poor was a viable alternative to having no facilities at all. From now on, Dr. Grafton would take turns with other volunteer physicians, treating walk-in patients and, as time allowed, making calls on some patients known to be bedfast or simply too ill to visit the clinic.

Arriving immediately after school, Daniel soon realized that the mission clinic would undoubtedly be his most hectic—and most distressing—experience as the doctor's helper. Both Uncle Mike and Tierney had warned him about Five Points, of course, and Pastor Dalton also had tried to tell him what to expect. But all their combined descriptions and warnings fell far short of the gruesome reality of the vicious slum.

Not since leaving the devastation of his homeland had Daniel been forced to confront such abject suffering, such unmitigated despair. Those who came to the mission clinic were not only ill and destitute; most were illiterate and wretchedly dirty. All seemed sad beyond imagining.

In a grim way, Daniel's former experience with the suffering and misery in his home village now worked to his advantage. Because of the horrors he had endured in Ireland—and on the coffin ship that had brought them to America—he could confront the agony of Five Points without revulsion.

In addition, Dr. Grafton's skill and willingness to teach made the clinic experience far more positive than it might have been otherwise. In his entire life, Daniel had known only two physicians: Dr. Browne in the village, a good man but sorely limited by a lack of proper equipment and medicines; and Dr. Leary, the surgeon aboard the *Green Flag*, a sad, drunken individual who had committed suicide at the end of the voyage. Limited as his experience had been, Daniel knew that Dr. Grafton was a fine physician—skilled, conscientious, and caring. It thrilled him to watch the doctor work, knowing he was learning in the process.

Today he seemed destined to learn more than his mind could take in all at once. In the two hours since he had arrived, the doctor had treated three boils, a baby with a scalded hand, an old man with a broken wrist, a young boy with a gunshot wound, and two cases of scarlet fever.

And the patients were still lined up in the hallway, waiting. In the midst of applying a poultice to a young mother's ulcerated arm, Dr. Grafton fretted aloud about the impossibility of the situation. "Why, we could bring them in for another two days straight and still not attend to everybody out there! And there are calls yet to make with Pastor Dalton."

Daniel nodded, feeling no less overwhelmed by the enormity of their task. He had seen for himself the milling lines of the ill and pain-wracked in the hallway and wondered how on earth so many had managed to pack themselves into the small, gloomy space.

Just then, Pastor Dalton stepped into the room and came to stand close by. "You didn't come down here alone, did you, son?" he asked, giving Daniel's shoulder a quick squeeze.

"No, sir, Uncle Mike wouldn't let me. He and Officer Price gave me a ride in the Black Maria."

The pastor nodded. "Good, good. It's no place to venture alone—I don't allow my son to come by himself either." Turning back to Dr. Grafton, the pastor said, "I can accompany you on calls whenever you're ready, Nicholas. It's getting late."

The doctor looked up with a frown of frustration. "I can't leave now! You saw that crowd in the hallway."

The pastor nodded. "But you can't possibly treat them all in one afternoon."

Dr. Grafton removed his spectacles for a moment to rub the bridge of his nose. "We've simply got to have more help, Pastor," he said wearily, replacing his eyeglasses. "The situation down here is a nightmare. A few hours a week doesn't even begin to make a difference!"

As he spoke, he carefully lowered the sleeve of his patient, then helped the pale young woman to her feet. "Now don't forget, Peggy, you must change these applications twice a day." His voice was firm but kind. "I'm sending plenty of lint pieces along with you; just apply the bread-and-milk poultice as I showed you, and then cover it with lint. Be sure to keep it clean—that's important."

The young mother stared at him incredulously. "Sure, and we've no bread or milk for the babies, Doctor, much less for a sore arm!"

Dr. Grafton stared back at her, an angry flush rising to spread across his noble features. "Yes. Yes, of course, I should have realized. Well, then," he muttered, fumbling inside his medical case, "take this." At her blank look, he stopped to explain. "It's a mild solution of nitric acid, to soak the lint pieces in. What you do is to soak each piece in a small amount of the solution and then apply them to the sore. And I want to see you here again next week."

"I have no money, that's the thing," the woman said softly, looking down at the floor.

"You're not to concern yourself with that. Just you be here next week so I can see how you're doing." When she didn't answer, he pressed his face closer to hers, searching her eyes. "Peggy?"

The young woman nodded. Before hurrying out the door, she darted a quick, grateful smile over her shoulder.

A collective wail went up in the hallway when Pastor Dalton informed the waiting patients they could not be seen until next week. Many grumbled angrily, while others only sighed, as if being put off was nothing new to them. Within a few moments they began to disperse.

As soon as the hallway was cleared, Daniel left the mission room with the doctor and Pastor Dalton, heading for the dismal streets of Five Points.

"Is your Uncle Mike still nearby?" the pastor asked Daniel once they were outside.

"Oh no, sir, he had special duty at the Astor Place Opera House tonight. For the opening, you see."

"Ah, yes," the pastor said, nodding. "Tonight is to be quite a lavish evening for New York society."

Daniel was uncomfortably reminded that the night was not only special for the society folk. His mother would be there, too, thanks to Mr. Farmington. In addition to supplying tickets for her and Evan Whittaker, he had even provided a carriage for them to ride in!

Daniel had concealed his uneasy surprise, had even managed to pretend a pleasure he did not feel when his mother first told him about the opera. His unsettled feelings had nothing to do with Evan Whittaker. Daniel was more than fond of Evan—indeed, he counted him a close, true friend. Nevertheless, his reaction to his mother's excited announcement had been fraught with conflicting feelings.

On the one hand, he was glad for her, pleased that she would have such a rare opportunity. On the other hand, however, he was seized with an odd sort of apprehension that she would be spending the evening with a man other than Uncle Mike. She was already spoken for, after all.

Spoken for, but not promised...

Why should that fact distress him so? He was getting as bad as Tierney, fretting over the relationship between his mother and Uncle Mike. And wasn't he the one *defending* her more often than not those times when Tierney happened to make an impatient remark about her keeping his da "at arms' length"?

Tierney. Wouldn't he be fit to be tied if he learned about this business of the opera? And there was an uncomfortably good chance that he *would*, what with Uncle Mike assigned to duty at the Opera House. If he should see Mother and Evan, then there was no hope of keeping it from Tierney.

As they trudged down one of the filthy, dark alleys off Paradise Square, Daniel told himself he was being foolish. Even if Uncle Mike *didn't* happen upon them tonight, his mother was too excited not to mention her experience. Perhaps she already had.

Stumbling over a loose stone in the street, Daniel twisted his ankle, but went on before the pastor or Dr. Grafton noticed. He winced, not from the pain in his ankle, but from the thought of how angry Tierney would be if he learned about the opera.

Tierney was determined that his da and Daniel's mother would wed. Why, he had virtually planned it all out in his mind before they ever stepped foot on American soil!

That was his way: Once he got an idea in his head, he would not stop until he saw it through to completion. If it occurred to him that events might not work out as he planned, he merely brushed the thought aside and tried a bit harder.

Stubbornness, Daniel thought with a grim twist of his mouth, *is one of the few things Tierney has in common with his da.*

It was nearing dusk by the time they reached their first house call, a rickety tenement on Cross Street. In front of the dilapidated building stood a number of young toughs with mean eyes and cruel mouths. When they made no move to let the doctor and his company pass by, Pastor Dalton simply parted them with a firm hand and a challenging smile.

Upstairs, on the second floor, the pastor led them down a dim hallway reeking with noxious odors. He stopped at a dark, scabbed door hanging by a single hinge. "The little girl I want you to see is five years old," the pastor told them, his voice low. "She's been extremely ill for weeks. Her name is Ellie—"

Daniel scarcely heard the rest of the pastor's explanation, his mind locking on the name. *Ellie* had been his little sister's name. Poor wee Ellie, dead of the Hunger and its accompanying fever when she was scarcely six years old.

Guiltily, he realized it had been some time since he'd thought of her. The memory of Ellie and his older brother, Tahg, who had died just before they sailed from Ireland, seemed to grow dimmer and dimmer with every month that passed. He wondered if it was terribly wrong that he no longer thought of them each day.

"She and one brother live with their father," Pastor Dalton was saying, his big arms folded across his chest. "The mother is dead, as are both grandparents. The father was a hod carrier, but lost his arm to blood poisoning.

Now about all he can do is visit the markets and carry baskets for buyers. He's a sober man, has signed the pledge—but he's a bitter, defeated man as well. Before her illness, little Ellie would beg for food. All they have now is what the boy earns cleaning streets. I thought if you could help the little girl, it might serve to help the entire family."

Inside, they were met by a small, bony man with a missing arm. Although obviously solemn and guarded, he appeared clean and respectable. He welcomed them with little show of enthusiasm, but his son, who looked to be about ten, seemed pleased and relieved that the doctor had come.

There was only one room, no bigger than the bedroom Daniel and Tierney shared. It held a dented cylinder stove, its pipe passing through a broken window. On one side of the stove was a small basket containing shavings instead of wood. There was some sort of food in a pan on top of the stove, but it smelled foul rather than nourishing.

In a dark corner to the right of the stove, a small girl lay on top of a heap of tattered rags. She did not move, did not even turn her face to take note of their entrance. But when Pastor Dalton dropped down beside her and murmured a greeting, her head lolled weakly in his direction, and she managed a faint smile.

"I've brought Dr. Grafton, Ellie," said the pastor, putting a gentle hand to the little girl's frail shoulder. "He knows you've been very ill and wants to help."

Still the child said nothing, and Daniel found himself comparing this wan, passive little girl with *his* Ellie, who at the end had shown much the same lifelessness.

The child made her first sound when Dr. Grafton knelt and began an examination of her throat. At her whimper of pain, he stopped immediately, studying her with a thoughtful expression.

Curious, Daniel moved in a bit closer. He caught the faint sour smell emanating from her, saw that her skin was damp with a light coating of perspiration, although the room was cold enough to chill him through his jacket. Her flushed cheeks and glazed eyes marked a high temperature; he wondered if she might not be in the beginning stages of scarlet fever, a disease that lately they had been seeing much of in Dr. Grafton's private practice.

The doctor drew aside the thin, tattered blanket, revealing severe swelling and redness around the child's wrists and elbows; even her ankles appeared inordinately large compared to her small, thin frame. With great gentleness, Dr. Grafton took her wrist, timing her pulse.

"How long has she been like this?" he asked, looking up at the father, who had come to stand near the little girl's feet.

"This poorly, d'you mean?" He frowned with a considering expression. "Two weeks, mebbe. Before that she was some fevered. Awful sore, too. She's been taking on worse for several days now. Won't even let me touch her but what she cries."

Turning back to Ellie, the doctor continued to study her. "You feel sore all over, child? Is that it?"

She nodded weakly. "It hurts."

"Hurts more when you try to move, does it?"

Again she nodded.

Dr. Grafton scrutinized her for another moment, then got to his feet. "Acute rheumatism," he said flatly. "One of the worst cases I've seen for a spell."

The father cleared his throat. "Is it something mortal, then, doctor?"

The doctor looked at him. "Mortal? Oh—no, no, it needn't be! But it *is* serious. Has the child been exposed for any length of time to the elements?"

The man merely looked at him blankly.

"Has she been out in the cold and rain for a long period of time? Perhaps when she wasn't feeling well to begin with?"

The man's eyes took on a glint of understanding. "Why...she was," he said, nodding. "On the ship that brought us over, we laid in water as cold as ice most of the way. For weeks, don't you see? We liked to froze to death, and that's the truth. Ellie, she seemed to take it hardest. She's never been strong, Ellie hasn't."

Daniel saw the doctor's face tighten, his mouth thin to a hard line, as if the father's reply was no surprise.

"Well, we must get to work on her right away," the physician said briskly. "And you'll have to help, so pay close attention."

Over the next few minutes, Dr. Grafton showed the father and son how to apply a mixture of wintergreen oil and laudanum to strips of cotton batting, then wrap them around the little girl's swollen joints.

"And you're to give her this every two hours until her temperature drops and she begins to feel better," the doctor said, handing the father a small bottle of salicylic acid.

While Dr. Grafton advised the father and his son, Pastor Dalton knelt beside the little girl's pallet. In a soft, infinitely caring voice that almost seemed a contradiction to the colossal size of the man, the pastor encouraged the child, then prayed for her. Daniel believed he had never heard such power as that which fired the big preacher's quiet, yet bold, words spoken on behalf of wee Ellie Higgins. Sure, and the Lord must listen closely to such a man as this!

Outside the building, Daniel asked, "Will she get better, Doctor, do you think?"

The physician regarded him with a troubled look. "We will hope so, but she is in the throes of a critical attack, son. This kind of rheumatism often shifts about in the body, and, depending on where it settles, it can do irretrievable damage. It does not help that the child was obviously frail before she took ill."

Before leaving Five Points, they called on three other patients: an elderly woman who had broken her hip from a fall down an entire flight of rickety stairs; a newsboy, beaten nearly senseless by his drunken father and given refuge by a black couple in the same tenement; and a young wife, little more than a child herself, near death with childbed fever.

With each patient, Daniel was struck anew by Dr. Grafton's seemingly endless store of patience and genuine kindness. Not only did he treat each affliction with consummate skill, but he treated the person with respect and consideration.

Someday, Daniel vowed to himself, *he* would be a doctor like Nicholas Grafton: a doctor capable of seeing, not only the needs of the body, but the needs of the heart as well. A doctor who saw a *person*, not merely a patient.

16

A Night at the Opera

A pity beyond all telling
Is hid in the heart of love.

W. B. YEATS (1865–1939)

Nora appraised her reflection in the mirror with a critical eye. She supposed she should feel grand—even elegant—after all the fuss and bother Sara Farmington had gone to getting her ready for this night.

What she felt, in fact, was more than a little silly.

She had been corseted, laced, and stuffed, like a bird ready for the roasting. And her nerves! Never had she been in such a state, she was sure of it. Perhaps a sensible dress would have made a difference. The frivolous gown that had been altered just for her was at least in part responsible for her discomfort; inside it, she felt clumsy and woefully conspicuous.

And those foolish little silk boots! Walking to the top of the stairs, Nora leaned forward just far enough to eye her white, silk-covered toes. Such vanity! If all this... *frippery* hadn't been Sara Farmington's idea, Nora would have deemed the entire display utterly sinful! But she had enough faith in Sara to trust her judgment about such things. Despite the obvious extravagance and unnecessary fuss, she could only assume she was still on the safe side of sin's gate.

Nora let her eyes sweep down the carpeted stairway to the foyer below. There, looking shy and magnificent in evening dress and white satin waistcoat, stood Evan, gazing down at his shiny shoes. His left sleeve hung empty against his side, and with his right hand he toyed nervously with his mustache.

At last he looked up and saw her. A light filled his eyes, a glow unlike any Nora had ever seen. Sure, he must think her a foolish, foolish woman, dressing up like a lady of society!

But Evan didn't seem to think any such thing. He extended his hand to her as she came down the stairs, saying, "Why, N-Nora, you look absolutely b-b-beautiful!"

Nora felt her cheeks redden under his wondering gaze.

"Are you r-ready to go?"

"Aye," she said. The room had suddenly gone warm, but Evan didn't seem to notice. He took her wrap from her and, with an awkward movement, attempted to place it around her shoulders.

At that moment Lewis Farmington burst into the foyer from his study. "Evan, my boy!" he began, then stopped and eyed Nora with a long, approving look. "Why, Evan, I do believe you will be escorting the most beautiful woman at the opera tonight."

Evan nodded and managed a "Y-Y-Yes, sir," while Nora's face flushed an even brighter red.

"Didn't want you to forget these, son," Farmington said. Slapping a pair of kid gloves into Evan's hand, he spun on his heel and disappeared into his study. "You go on ahead," he called back over his shoulder. "Sara and I will be along shortly."

Evan looked first at the gloves, then at Nora, then back at the gloves again. Bewildered, he quickly stuffed both gloves into his right-hand coat pocket.

Nora looked up into his face, her soft eyes forcing him to meet her gaze. Slowly, and without a word, she reached into his pocket and retrieved the gloves. After a quick glance, she tucked the left glove gently back into his pocket.

"Give me your hand," she said simply.

"Nora, I—I—"

"Give me your hand, Evan," she repeated. Dropping his eyes, he held out his hand, mutely, submissively, like a little boy.

With infinite tenderness, Nora shook open the glove and fitted it over Evan's extended hand. His whole arm trembled as one by one she smoothed the supple leather over his fingers. He could feel her touch beneath the leather, and when she turned his palm upward and bent her head to button the tiny pearl clasp at the wrist, he closed his eyes, afraid to breathe.

She was so close, so close. Dared he think that this small gesture of compassion, this moment of tenderness, signified more than just the kindly act of a generous woman? Could she hear his heart pounding, feel his pulse throbbing at the wrist under her delicate fingers?

At last Nora looked up, but she did not let go of his hand. Their eyes locked, and for a brief moment Evan thought he saw something—*something*—behind her expression.

"Evan—" she began.

"Yes? Y-Yes, Nora?"

"I—I want you…to know…"

Evan's heart raced. "Y-Yes?"

Nora dropped her eyes and drew her wrap around her. "I just want to thank you…for escorting me tonight. Sure, and I don't doubt it will be a fine, fine evening."

The spell was broken. Evan let out a deep sigh and smiled at her. "Sure, and it will be, lass," he answered.

Nora laughed lightly at his attempt to mimic the Irish brogue. He extended his arm, and together they walked out into the chill evening, where Mr. Farmington's carriage awaited them.

They were seated in the—the *balcony*, it was called. In truth, they were suspended in midair! The very thought of it—a floor in the air with red velvet sofas and armchairs!

Nora dared not lean too far forward. High places had always made her head spin. And yet she suspected that her light-headedness might be caused by more than the altitude.

Her plush chair was sandwiched between Evan on the one side and Sara Farmington on the other. She could feel Evan's nearness, even though their elbows were not touching. She studiously avoided looking at him, tried to put the thought of him out of her mind.

Looking up, she studied the opulent painting of three rather dandi-fied-looking men gazing down upon the stage. "Would you be knowing who those men on the ceiling are, Evan?" she asked, her gaze still fastened on the lavish ceiling.

Evan glanced from her up to the ceiling. "Why, yes, that's M-Mozart, of course. And Rossini, and…B-Bellini, I think. Yes, B-Bellini."

Nora nodded as if those names indeed meant something to her. After a moment, she could not stop herself from asking, "And who, exactly, would they be, Evan?"

He smiled at her. "They're c-composers, actually. Quite b-brilliant composers, all three of them."

One of the things that endeared Evan to Nora was the way he never made her feel ignorant. Not a bit. He treated her every question with serious consideration.

Nora knew that Evan was quite the well-educated man; to him, many of her questions might seem backward, even ludicrous. Yet never did he display the slightest hint of condescension toward her.

In that respect, he was like the Farmingtons. Although wealthy and privileged, neither Lewis Farmington nor Sara ever made Nora feel less than a person of value. They were kind at all times. They were thoughtful and caring, and not in the least patronizing toward Nora or anyone else who worked for them.

But Evan alone truly made her feel—*worthy*. Worthy and even a bit… special. Evan understood her, and that was the truth. She could not explain how he had come by such sensitivity, but he invariably knew what would strike enthusiasm in her, and just as surely seemed to understand what would anger her or cause her pain.

Stealing a covert look at his profile, Nora could not restrain a small smile. Sure, and God had blessed her with much more than a good friend in Evan Whittaker; indeed, He had brought a kindred spirit into her life.

❧

Obviously, she had no idea how very lovely she was. Out of the corner of his eye, Evan stole yet another glance at Nora, seated beside him. Her lips were turned up in just a hint of a smile, and he wondered what her thoughts were at this very moment.

The first act of the opera was nearly over, but the stage had held but a small portion of his attention. It was impossible for him to concentrate fully with Nora so wonderfully near.

The theater was warm, with every seat filled, and the faint scent of lilac at his shoulder was almost dizzying. The scent was, he was certain, Sara Farmington's doing; he doubted the idea of perfume would ever occur to Nora, whose very simplicity was one of the things he loved most about her.

He was nearly overcome with her nearness. Lewis Farmington had been right; she was quite the loveliest woman in the theater. Sara Farmington had seen to it that Nora lacked not one small detail in her appearance. Dressed in a gown of deep rose satin with a delicate lace flounce, she was exquisite. From the sprigs of flowers in her hair to the tips of those smart little silk boots that seemed to fascinate her so, she was nothing less than enchanting.

Her dark gray eyes, always enormous, tonight appeared even larger. Her wonder seemed to increase with the evening. Everything was new to Nora, of course—new and fascinating.

The theater itself *was* quite an achievement, Evan had to admit, with its one magnificent chandelier, the mosaic ceiling, the tiers and amphitheater all furnished with crimson velvet sofas and armchairs.

He found it somewhat lavish for his taste, but, then, Americans did seem to like things done up in excess. As for the performance itself, Teresa Truffi, the soprano portraying the sad Elvira, while no means a great singer, nevertheless had a certain quality in her voice that moved the audience nearly to tears a number of times, himself included. The tenor singing the outlaw Ernani's part, however, was mediocre at best.

None of this would matter to Nora, of course. She was wholly enthralled—and somewhat overwhelmed, Evan sensed—by the theater, the opera, indeed the evening itself.

Her profile was near rigid, as if frozen with awe at the action on stage. A wave of tenderness mingled with longing swept over Evan. It was all he could do not to touch her, but at the back of his mind was the ever-present caution that, no matter how much Nora might seem to cherish their friendship, that did not mean she would encourage anything more—no matter what he had felt earlier in the evening.

Unexpectedly, the words of Lewis Farmington came echoing through his thoughts:....*I believe Nora is already very fond of you.... If you want the woman, Evan, then court her!*

Evan blinked, hesitating only another instant before taking Nora's hand in his own. Incredibly, she glanced down at their clasped hands, then turned and smiled warmly into his eyes.

At that moment, the song in Evan's heart soared, rising far above the singers' voices to drown out the music of the orchestra.

Doesn't Evan look nice tonight?

Surprised, Nora realized she had never thought much one way or the other about Evan's appearance; certainly, she had never thought of him as—as *attractive*.

She was accustomed to seeing him in a business suit, used to his impeccable grooming. Why, Evan would never think of being caught outside his rooms, she was certain, without his hair neatly combed and his spectacles polished. Tonight, though, there seemed to be something different about him. Something almost...charming.

It was his smile, Nora suddenly realized. The man had such a warmth to him. She blinked at the thought, then restrained a smile of her own. Who would have imagined she would ever see warmth in an *Englishman's* smile?

But this was no ordinary Englishman. This was Evan. Evan, who had risked his own life to save her and her family, who, even when wracked with pain and fever aboard ship, had offered his protection to her for as long as she might need it. Evan, who had lost his arm as a result of his efforts in their behalf. Evan, with the kind heart and good soul. Evan, her very dear friend.

Impulsively, she squeezed his hand, and the warmth in his eyes enfolded her heart.

After the final curtain had fallen, the audience stood applauding, then chatting with one another. Nora was still shaken by the tragic, sorrowful finale. That poor girl—Elvira—losing her one true love, left with nothing except the prospect of a dutiful marriage to an aged nobleman she could never love.

Still unnerved by the powerful drama, she said nothing as they followed the Farmingtons out of the theater.

"You're awfully quiet, N-Nora," Evan said, studying her with concern.

Even with her arm anchored firmly inside his, Nora felt unsteady on her feet. "It was so sad," she said without preamble. "I didn't know music could be so sad and yet so grand all at the same time."

The crowd in front of them slowed as they began to empty from the theater, and Nora clung a bit more tightly to Evan's arm.

"I'm afraid m-most operas are sad," he said, smiling. "A few have happy endings, but not m-many. But d-did you *enjoy* it?"

"Oh my, of course, I did!" she assured him. "It was grand! And I do thank you for helping me with the story. Where did you ever learn to speak *Italian*, Evan?"

He laughed. "I d-don't really *speak* Italian. Just a few words, that's all— enough to help m-me understand what's happening on the stage."

Just outside the theater, the throng of people had come to a complete stop, unable to move because of the press of so many bodies spilling out onto the street at once. Nora turned to look at Evan while they waited. "You're an awfully smart man, Evan. You seem to know something about everything!"

A light flush rose to his cheeks. "But n-not very much about *anything*," he protested.

"Why, that's not a bit true!" Nora gave him a stern frown, then smiled. "You're the cleverest man I know," she insisted, studying his open, good face. "And quite the nicest."

His eyes went over her features with such a tenderness that Nora felt as if he had touched her. They stood that way for another moment, looking at each other with questions in their eyes as a strange, undefinable awareness hung between them.

Suddenly, from just outside the crowd, a gruff voice called her name. Nora whirled around, startled.

"Nora?" Michael's face was hard, his eyes glinting with incredulity as he parted the crowd to reach her. "What are *you* doing here?"

He stood as still as a stone in front of her, his jaw tight, his eyes flashing.

Irrationally, it struck Nora that he was far bigger and broader than she had once thought. For a moment she could see nothing but the front of his dark wool coat and the copper star pinned there.

Before she could attempt a reply, Michael glanced from her to Evan, then the Farmingtons. To Sara and her father, he offered a short but polite greeting; to Evan, he managed only a curt nod with a grudging "Whittaker."

Bewildered by the surge of guilt that came crashing over her without warning, Nora found herself unwilling to meet Michael's dark eyes. Instead, she fixed her eyes on the copper badge.

"I scarcely knew you in your finery." His words grated with unmistakable sarcasm.

Slowly, Nora dragged her eyes away from the badge, forcing herself to meet his gaze. Expecting to find his eyes as cold as his voice, she caught her breath in surprise at his stricken expression. Without really understanding why, she suddenly felt foolish and bitterly deceitful.

17

Unexpected Interlude

Last night we saw the stars arise,
But clouds soon dimmed the ether blue;
And when we sought each other's eyes
Tears dimmed them too!

GEORGE DARLEY (1795–1846)

Stunned and confused, Michael fought to keep his hurt from showing. Yet, he knew Nora had seen, could tell by the way she quickly glanced away from him.

She looked so…different. *Elegant*, that was the only word for her. She always looked sweet and fine, in her everyday gingham dresses and sensible hairdo. But this, now—this was something else, something that seemed too grand for Nora, too extravagant.

Standing there in her finery, with flowers in her hair, she looked uncommonly lovely and delicate. Her cheeks were flushed—with embarrassment, he sensed. He made no move to relieve the awkwardness between them, but simply continued to rake her face with a demanding stare.

Finally, he realized he was being rude and dragged his gaze away from her, only to find Lewis Farmington regarding him with a curious, measuring expression. But it was Sara who finally threatened to shake his composure. She stood, straight-backed and dignified as always, her level, knowing gaze brimming with something akin to pity.

Michael wanted to run. She had seen his hurt, then, as had Nora. He felt the fool for the first time in a long time, at least where a woman was concerned.

He groped for words, desperately wishing he had not even approached the foursome. "Well, now, Nora," he choked out inanely, "aren't you looking grand tonight? I did not know that you fancied the opera."

Her huge gray eyes held an appeal to which he could not, would not respond. He followed the movement of her hand as she dropped it quickly away from Whittaker's arm and touched a sprig of flowers in her hair. "I— Mr. Farmington and Sara invited…us…" Her voice faded, and she made no attempt to go on.

Lewis Farmington cleared his throat and said something vacuous about the large crowd. "Is this a special duty for you, Sergeant Burke?"

Michael directed his reply to Nora, continuing to appraise the uncertainty in her eyes. "I'm an assistant captain now, sir. And, yes, this is…special duty."

"Oh, *Michael*!" Nora cried, reaching out to him, then drawing her hand back when he simply stared down at it. "Your promotion came through at last. I'm—I'm so very happy for you," she said lamely.

Her pleasure appeared to be genuine, but Michael found no satisfaction in it. He was too taken aback by seeing her like this, dressed up like the grand lady, parading about with the Farmingtons—and on the arm of that…Englishman.

He had seen the way the two of them looked at each other. But, wait, now—*what*, exactly, had he seen? Nora could not possibly be…*interested*… in a man like Whittaker.

Could she?

Unable to stand and look the fool any longer—and unwilling to allow Sara Farmington any further glimpse of his pain—Michael lifted his chin and took a step backward. Somehow, he managed a lame smile.

"Well, I must be seeing to my men…make sure there are no problems," he said tightly.

Locking gazes with Nora one more time, he made a determined effort to conceal his conflicting feelings. "A pleasant evening to you all," he said with difficulty. Then, giving a short, stiff nod, he whipped around and walked away.

A knot of dismay rose to her throat as Nora watched Michael traipse off into the crowd. Seeing the slump of his broad shoulders, remembering the one fleeting glimpse of raw hurt she had seen in his eyes, she knew with a sick sense of guilt that she had wronged him, wounded him.

She could have dealt with his anger. But it was the terrible fierce look of betrayal in his eyes that she now found impossible to bear.

The pain she had seen before he concealed it had surprised her. Obviously, it was not seeing her here—but seeing her here with *Evan*—that had done the damage.

But why? He couldn't be jealous of Evan, after all! That would be too foolish entirely!

Suddenly, she knew it was *not* foolish. Michael *had* been jealous of Evan. No doubt he had seen them come out of the theater together, had seen her on Evan's arm, seen the two of them talking together, laughing together.

She felt a knife stab her own heart now at the memory of the pain she had encountered in Michael's eyes. She should have *told* him, told him long before now about tonight.

And why, exactly, *hadn't* she? It wasn't as if there had been no opportunity. She had seen him two or three times, at least, since Evan first told her about the tickets. She could easily have talked to him, explained about tonight.

Why hadn't she, then?

"Nora?"

At Evan's soft reminder, Nora blinked. Aware that both he and Sara Farmington were regarding her with uncertain expressions, she forced a smile.

For a moment she was unable to look directly at either one of them. Glancing instead at Mr. Farmington, she encountered a look of understanding, a gentle smile of reassurance.

"It's late," he said with his usual straightforward brusqueness. "I'll have our carriages brought around."

༚

Why hadn't she *told* him?

Michael agonized over the question all the way home. Rejecting a ride in the Black Maria, he walked, hunkered down against the cold sting of the night wind on his face.

In an attempt to throw off his anger and humiliation, he first tried to convince himself he was making too much of the entire affair. After all, it went without saying that the Farmingtons had arranged the whole evening. Certainly, neither Whittaker nor Nora could so much as afford the tickets, much less the required finery.

No doubt, Lewis Farmington had taken it upon himself to do a kindness for two people who worked for him. More than likely, that's all it was. *Then why hadn't she told him?*

Try as he would, he couldn't banish the question. If, as he would like to believe, the entire affair meant nothing at all to Nora, why hadn't she at least mentioned it before tonight?

The knowledge that Sara Farmington had been witness to his humiliation somehow grieved him almost as much as Nora's deceit.

Michael heard the whisper of pride rise to the surface of his emotions, and he could not deny it was one reason for his hurt. Seeing the two of them decked out in their finery, mingling with New York society, had made him face the painful reality of who he was.

An Irish policeman. Suddenly, his promotion to assistant captain meant nothing—nothing at all. The truth was that, no matter how hard he worked or how high he rose in the ranks, no matter how much he might better his lot in life—he was an immigrant—an *Irish* immigrant with little to offer a woman like Nora.

What *could* he offer her that would even begin to compare with what she already had? A three-room flat in a low-rent district. A policeman's pay that might support a family but would never do more than provide the bare necessities. And himself—a rough-edged copper with a mediocre education, whose manners at their best were blunt and crude.

Michael shook his head, muttering to himself as he strode along in the cold night. When Nora had come to America, he had believed—truly believed—that he could make a life for the two of them. With Morgan left behind in Ireland, he had hoped that her love for the man would diminish, that finally, after all these years, she would see her need for *him*. Besides, hadn't he promised Morgan to take care of her?

Yet, here she was now, on the arm of Evan Whittaker. Michael could deal with her love for Morgan. It was an old affection for a man much like himself—a man of strength and purpose. Evan Whittaker was—well, what kind of man *was* Evan Whittaker, after all? Intelligent, more than likely. Well-educated, even cultured. A different kind of man than himself, sure.

Did that matter to Nora? Was that what she wanted, then?

His wounded pride mingled with bitterness, and he almost choked on the lump of misery in his throat.

How it stung, to acknowledge his foolishness—and him a man grown! Why, he had thought to offer Nora so much—when in truth even if he offered her everything he had, it would be as nothing when compared to what was already hers!

Hours later, lying sleepless on her bed, Nora still could not shake the image of Michael's stricken, angry face.

There was no way she could have anticipated his reacting as he had. He had thrown her off-balance entirely with his unexpected harshness, his cold disdain, making her feel as though she had—betrayed him.

Could it be that Michael cared for her more deeply than she believed? Over the past few weeks, she had found herself questioning his feelings for *her* almost as often as she puzzled over her feelings for *him*. That Michael cared for her, she did not doubt. But what continued to puzzle her was the *depth* of his caring.

Some vague, nagging intuition caused her to question whether Michael's feelings for her were of the sort a man should have for the woman he marries. Nora could not shake the conviction that his affection was based more on memory, the old fondness of their youthful friendship—even on a sense of duty—than on any real depth of love.

No matter what Michael said, no matter how often he caught her eye when they were together or how tenderly he might happen to touch her hand, there were times when Nora almost felt that he had convinced himself he loved her, wanted to marry her, because he was lonely—or even because their *sons* desired the union!

Instinctively, she knew that if she were to confront him with her suspicions, he would deny them. It was almost as if once he had determined to marry her, he *would* marry her, no matter the reservations of his heart.

She should have told him before—long before—of her hesitation, of the nameless resistance in her heart to the idea of marrying him. She had only just recently identified it herself, and she doubted that he would understand. Michael still saw her as the young girl of his boyhood—how could he possibly understand the woman she had come to be?

Still, in her desire not to hurt him, she had hurt him even more.

Impatient with her sleeplessness, she flipped off the bedcovers and swung her feet to the floor. Grabbing her dressing gown, she shrugged into it and went to look out the window.

For a long time she stood, staring mindlessly into the stand of pines at the back of the grounds. With a sigh, she touched the cold windowpane, drawing a mindless design in the frosty vapor.

It was one thing to analyze Michael's feelings for *her*, but would she ever understand hers for *him*? She cared for him deeply—but did she care *enough*? The affection she felt for Michael was not the kind of love that would make her a good wife to him, the kind of wife he deserved.

Michael was a good man. Nora knew without even thinking that he would be a good husband—a *wonderful* husband.

He deserved a good wife, a wife who would love him with all her heart, who would be a comfort to him and an asset to him.

A wife with a true passion for him. The kind of emotional *and* physical passion Nora did not feel. She loved him as a *brother*, treasured him as a friend. But she had no true passion for him—no burning desire in her heart to share his life, no desire in her flesh to share his bed.

She felt her skin heat. Perhaps she shouldn't even be thinking in such a way. Perhaps a lack of physical desire should have no bearing whatsoever on her decision.

But without that desire, wouldn't she be cheating him? It would be an unforgivable deceit to wed him and deprive him of shared desire. If she married him, it would be a choice made out of need and weakness, rather than out of strength and love.

Yet, such a marriage *could* work, could it not? There was a great deal to be said, after all, for having friendship at the very foundation of a marriage. Indeed, wasn't friendship the very thing that sometimes led to a deeper caring, a special love?

Nora suddenly wished she could talk with Evan. He might not have answers for her questions, but at least he would listen. He would care and understand and try to help.

At the thought of Evan, she smiled. Somehow the thought of Evan *always* made her smile. His gentleness, his concerned, caring manner made her feel cherished, valued. She remembered the warmth of his closeness as she had stood, her arm linked in his, outside the theater. Her mind

flashed an image of the look in his eyes as she was putting on his glove—
a look of...what?

Of love?

Nora laughed aloud at the absurdity of the idea. Impossible—a cultured English gentleman and a country Irish widow-woman. Sure, and that was as likely a match as an immigrant Irish policeman with a society lady like Sara Farmington.

With another restless sigh, Nora pressed her cheek against the cold glass of the window. The night's excitement and turmoil had left its mark. She knew she would not sleep for hours. Her body was rigid with nerves, her mind filled with questions.

Questions without answers.

She stood looking out for another moment. Suddenly a movement caught her eye—there! Across the lawn near the trees, a solitary figure walked, one hand clutching the front of his coat, the other sleeve, empty, moving with the wind.

Evan!

A thought struck Nora like a physical blow. Her heart pounded wildly, and her pulse quickened. Could the man, also sleepless, be walking abroad on this bitter cold night—thinking of her? She watched as he paused, looking upward at her window, staring **hard**. At last he turned and walked back toward his cottage, just as Nora reached out to him, leaving her fingerprints on the frosty windowpane.

18

Fitzgerald Is Fallen

O, inspired giantl shall we e'er behold,
In our own time,
One fit to speak your spirit on the wold,
Or seize your rhyme?
THOMAS D'ARCY MCGEE (1825–1868)

Belfast

The Belfast Music Hall was grim, as always: a mean place, smoke-filled and noisy, the atmosphere hostile. Twice in the past hour the police had intervened to keep order, but their efforts had, for the most part, proven futile.

To Morgan's frustration, the crowd had scarcely heard O'Brien's speech at all. The man's patrician demeanor, his evident nobility, worked against him in a rough place such as this.

McGee and Mitchel had hardly fared better, what with the rattles and catcalls and out-and-out threats. Only Meagher, with his strong sense of stage presence as an orator, had been able to triumph over the opposition and heckling, making himself at least heard, if not entirely welcomed with enthusiasm.

The hall was filled with Old Irelanders, shrieking, whistling, stamping, and swearing in the barbaric accents of Ulster. Of all Ireland, Morgan favored the North least, mostly because of its grimness and hovering phantom of intolerance. He would be vastly relieved when all this was over and they could leave for home. As much as he wanted away from Belfast, even more did he want shut of all this talk of revolution.

While Smith O'Brien was still holding back from any planned peasant rising, Mitchel's speech had left little doubt as to *his* intentions. The man had a vision of the tenants rising as one, bursting their bonds, raising the green flag, and finally sweeping the British into the sea.

That was no vision, Morgan reminded himself. It was delusion. Amid them all, O'Brien was the only voice for sanity. And yet the voice was growing dimmer, Morgan feared. Smith O'Brien was tilting more and more toward Mitchel, toward armed rebellion.

When the pathetic attempts at speech making were done, someone raised Morgan's name, and soon a weak chant from the back of the room began to swell. Vexed, Morgan shook his head firmly. O'Brien tried to persuade him to speak, and Morgan snapped at him, more harshly than was usually his manner. "This mob is in no mood to hear a voice for reason, only the rattle of drums and the sound of muskets! What I mean to do is get us away, before things turn even nastier!"

Even as Morgan spoke he began to press O'Brien and the others from the hall. He had been witness to riots before, and he did not doubt but what they were only moments away from one.

Glaring back in the direction of the group chanting his name, he lifted a hand in protest, then continued to urge the other Young Irelanders through the crowd. Only O'Brien went with him; Mitchel and the others insisted on staying behind to debate with a group of mill workers.

They found the street outside almost as loud and raucous as the hall. Swarms of hard-looking men stood huddled in front of the dismal buildings, gathered around fires rising out of barrels, as they warmed their hands and grumbled, condemning both Ireland and the Queen in the same breath.

Tough-looking youths seemed to be everywhere, both lads and lassies, ragged and dirty and miserably thin. Most were running wild in the street. Others were begging money or food from the passers-by. Morgan thought again, as he had before, that Belfast's children were born old and desperate and hard.

In front of one building milled a group of women. Wives of those inside, more than likely, fearful for their husbands, more anxious still for the wages they knew would be spent on the drink once things got rowdy.

"Not exactly a resounding triumph, eh, Fitzgerald?" said O'Brien with a sardonic smile.

"Had you really thought it would be anything other than a failure?" Morgan bit out. At the moment, he was altogether irritated with O'Brien, Belfast, and politics.

Smith O'Brien shrugged lamely and put a hand to Morgan's shoulder. "I'm sorry, old friend. I should never have asked you to come. It wasn't worth any of our efforts, that's certain. The fault is mine, but I'm nevertheless grateful for your loyalty."

"'Tis done, and that's what matters," Morgan said, relenting somewhat. "The thing to do now is to leave this abominable place. I tell you, no other place in the world sets my teeth on edge as much as mean old Belfast."

"Yes," O'Brien agreed with a sigh, "it's not one of my favorite cities, I admit. Still, if we could have made any progress at all, it would have seemed worth—"

O'Brien stopped, both he and Morgan whirling around when someone behind them shouted a warning.

From out of nowhere, or so it seemed, came a squad of burly, mean-faced men charging toward them. Dressed in the rough clothing of laborers, they were waving bludgeons and roaring curses as they came.

Keeping his voice low, Morgan grabbed O'Brien by the arm. *"Run, William! Now!"*

For an instant, Smith O'Brien seemed transfixed, frozen. Not waiting, Morgan began to drag him into the street, hoping they could lose themselves in the crowd before their attackers could reach them.

But they were too late. The mob was upon them, fists flying, clubs coming down hard.

"Get away!" Morgan shouted at O'Brien. "Go for help!"

He could not hear his own voice for the cries around them. Their attackers were roaring, spitting out curses and threats, while all around them the swelling cries of the spectators in the street drowned out Morgan's and O'Brien's pleas for help.

Morgan snapped his big body back and forth like a whip, holding one assailant after another off O'Brien, who had all he could do to stand.

Around them the street had exploded into a full-blown riot, men fighting, women shrieking, children screaming. Morgan's blood raged with a blazing anger, yet his spirit was seized with a terrible coldness at the palpable presence of evil hemming them in. The swell of madness closing in on them seemed borne of demons rather than men.

His breath came hard and ragged. Pain sent flames of light streaking before his eyes, yet he dug his feet into the street and went on fighting. He caught a fleeting sense of savage faces, dark with hate and intent on blood.

He felt the metallic taste of his own blood as it tracked his cheeks to his mouth, heard the fabric of his shirt give and tear. His legs were lead, his chest caught in a vise of pain. He felt himself weakening, and he fought to stand. He was trapped, walled in, about to die.

Suddenly, the darkness shattered, rent to pieces by a thunderous explosion. A fire broke out in Morgan's spine, hurling his feet out from under him. A hot blaze of pain went roaring up the length of his body, and he toppled, hitting the cobbles with a terrible crash and a fierce, terrified scream.

"*God deliver me!*"

A final groan of protest ripped from his throat. Then the clamor of the night faded to silence.

By the time the other three Young Irelanders reached them, the police had managed to break up the mob of attackers, arresting all who did not escape.

Smith O'Brien was mostly scratched and battered, but not badly hurt.

Morgan Fitzgerald lay motionless. His face was bludgeoned and bleeding, his right eye cut from brow to cheekbone. He lay in a pool of his own blood. To those gathered near, the life seemed to be pouring out of his big body from the gunshot wound at the small of his back.

He was alive, but barely.

Annie Delaney had seen it all, from the ruckus inside the Music Hall to the attack on the two men—and then the shooting.

Her wee size had enabled her to sneak into the hall earlier without being seen. She had high hopes of engaging the sympathies of some of the better class of lads inside—of which there had proven to be few.

On a good night she would have been able to beg enough to see her through a week or more. This had not been a good night. She'd been leaving the hall almost empty-handed when the chant for *Morgan Fitzgerald* began, stopping her in her tracks.

Oh, she knew who the Fitzgerald was, Annie did! The other street sweepers might scoff all they liked when she claimed to be able to read, but she *could* read, and that was the truth! She might be but a lassie, and she might be on her own keeping—but she was not ignorant. Not Annie Delaney.

Before her real da had passed on and left her mum to take up with old Frank Tully, he had taught her to read some, enough to make out the news and the articles in *The Nation* he left lying about.

Of course, once Da was gone the lessons were finished, but Annie had not left off the reading. Even when she ran off, leaving her mum to old Tully, she took her clippings from *TheNation* with her.

Annie would not have left her mum except for Tully. The ape could not keep his filthy hands off her, and Mum wouldn't listen when Annie tried to tell her what her new husband was really up to.

Until the last bad incident with the dirty-minded sot, Annie had been able to fend him off by a swift kick where it hurt most or by simply darting past him and running off. He was clumsy and slow, and no match for her once she took off.

But one evening when her mum was working late at the linen mill, Tully climbed the ladder to where Annie slept. She was lying on her cot, reading. Worse luck for her, Tully wasn't so drunk this time that he hadn't the wits to block the doorway with his bulk. Her attempt to squeeze past him failed.

Annie screamed and fought like a wild thing, clawing at his eyes, kicking and biting. In the end she managed to escape before he could work his unspeakable acts on her—but not before his hands had turned savage. He went after her like a lunatic, pounding on her and tearing at her clothing, all the while shouting such depraved filth that Annie thought she would feel dirty and spoiled forever.

Finally, she managed to land a fierce blow against his throat, winding him enough that she got away and bolted down the ladder. By then he had pummeled her so hard with his fists that she carried the bruises and the soreness for weeks.

She knew she would carry the disgusting memories much longer.

She had run straight to the mill to wait for her mum's shift to end. But when Annie told her what Tully had done—even though she could see for herself how he'd beat on her—Mum had stopped just short of blaming Annie for the entire episode.

"Well, you're growing up is all," she muttered nervously, looking everywhere else but at Annie. "And Tully is no different from any other man when he's been at the bottle. It makes a man weak in the flesh. You'll just have to stay out of his way, you will! I can't say a word to him, or he'll be after beating up on the both of us."

Annie realized then that her mum was terribly afraid of Tully and would go on ignoring his wickedness—no matter what it might mean for her daughter.

Annie left the flat that night and never went back. She tied her few pieces of clothing on a stick, and went on the streets, carrying all her treasures in a small poke. Her da's books were her treasures—them and the verses of one Morgan Fitzgerald.

Da had fancied this poet more than any other writer, had even taught Annie some of her lessons from Fitzgerald's writings. Little by little she had come to know his verses by heart, and she could recite whole chunks of his essays. Da always said there was no denying the fact that Morgan Fitzgerald had a great, noble heart—and a voice for Ireland—if only Ireland would listen!

So tonight, when a small group at the back of the Music Hall had begun to call for Morgan Fitzgerald to speak, Annie had taken notice. And sure, hadn't she identified him easily enough? There was no mistaking him, his being the giant he was!

There he stood, scarcely any distance at all from her, trying to make his way out of the hall with one of the Young Irelanders who had spoken earlier—the dandified-looking fellow who talked like a Britisher, the one called *Smith O'Brien*.

Annie had caught the startled look on the big Fitzgerald's face when he heard his name, saw him shake his great head with its copper mane once or twice, then lift a hand in protest to those who were calling him. On his way out of the hall, he passed by her so close that she could have reached out and touched him, had she dared.

My, and wasn't he huge and fierce-looking at that moment, with that thick, bronze beard and those green eyes flashing fire? As resplendent as one of the old High Kings, and that was the truth!

But just see what he'd come to, lying in the street in a sticky pool of blood because of those apes with their fake Irish brogues! Why, they were no more Irish than the Queen herself, and that was the truth!

Annie knew who they were well enough—old pig-faced Johnnie Dorton and his cronies. A bunch of toughs from the mills who went around beating up Irishers for money. They'd done in two Catholic lads from West Belfast last month. While the motives back of their nasty business were always a mystery, it was no secret at all that most of their wages came from the soldiers.

And now just see what they'd done! With all the excitement and clamor in the street, nobody—including his political cronies—seemed to be paying any attention to the fallen Fitzgerald.

Furious, Annie pried her small frame in between two of the women at the front of the crowd circling Fitzgerald, then bolted toward him.

The three Young Irelanders were down on their knees trying to bring him to, while the mob in the street kept pressing closer and closer to the place where Fitzgerald lay.

Squeezing in among them, Annie dropped to her knees and listened to his chest. He was still breathing! The breath was coming in great, ragged gasps—but he was *alive*!

On her knees in the street, enraged with the mob milling about and doing nothing, she raised a grimy fist to the air and screamed: *"Don't ye know who this is, ye great fools? This is Morgan Fitzgerald himself, the nation's poet! Won't somebody be goin' for the doctor? Or will ye just go on flappin' your gums and lettin' the man die here, like a dog in the street?"*

One of the women in the crowd jumped, then took off running. Annie pressed closer to the slain Fitzgerald.

"Don't ye go dyin', Fitzgerald!" she demanded, her voice hoarse and desperate. "D'ye hear me, now? Wherever ye be, ye must not be dyin'!"

❧

William Smith O'Brien knelt on the cobbled street beside the great form of the unconscious Morgan Fitzgerald.

With only half a mind he took note of the small, sooty-faced youth with the straggling black hair and the tattered clothing. He paid little heed to the cries of the child, aware only in the vaguest sense of the other Young Irelanders hovering over Fitzgerald.

Beyond grief, O'Brien knew only guilt: guilt that he had bidden Fitzgerald accompany him to Belfast, guilt that his friend had taken a shot almost certainly meant for *him*.

He would have wept had his soul not been seized with a terrible, paralyzing chill.

It was the dream...

Horribly, eerily fulfilled, the spectral-like dream of the weeping women, with their dread announcement about Morgan Fitzgerald, now came gruesomely to life in front of his eyes.

"He is fallen...Fitzgerald is fallen."

PART TWO

WINTER LAMENT

Gathering Shadows

So I say, "My splendor is gone and all that I had hoped from the Lord."
I remember my affliction and my wandering, the bitterness and the
gall. I well remember them, and my soul is downcast within me.

LAMENTATIONS 3:18-20

19

A Pocketful of Money

Happier days may yet await us,
Scenes more pleasant glad the eye,
But even these shall not elate us
While o'er Ireland's fate we sigh.

FROM *LAYS FOR PATRIOTS,*
PUB. BY SAMUEL B. OLDHAM, DUBLIN (1848)

New York City
December

Sitting in his study late Saturday morning, Patrick Walsh turned to look out the window. The Burke boy was shoveling the snow that had fallen overnight, clearing the walk on this side of the house. With the ease of a much larger man, the youth scooped, lifted, then tossed the snow to the side, his movements smooth, almost rhythmic.

Walsh took one last sip of coffee, draining the cup. With a faint smile, he continued to watch Tierney Burke.

Tall and lean as a whip, the boy fairly hummed with good health and restless energy. He was a bright rascal, too. In some ways, he reminded Patrick of himself when he was younger. Clever and sharp as they came, as agile in wit as on foot—with an ambition designed more for excitement and adventure than for steady, hard work.

Tierney Burke already displayed the telltale signs of a certain ruthlessness that Patrick admired—the kind of relentless determination it took for an Irishman to succeed in America. His character was not without its weaknesses, of course—the most potentially damaging being the boy's near-irrational zeal for Ireland and all things Irish.

Walsh had despised it all his life, this misguided passion of the Irish patriots. He thought of it as the national madness, a madness that turned humdrum lives into romantic adventures, meaningless jobs into holy callings. It was the very spark that fueled their endless secret societies wherein plowboys became heroes—*martyred* heroes, more often than not.

The madness had crossed the Atlantic with thousands of immigrants, riding the waves to America only to run rampant among the tenements and push its way into Tammany Hall. Never quite able to escape the lure of mythical Old Ireland and its warriors, hotheaded youths bent on dying for Eire continued to espouse the *Cause*. Even the few who managed to succeed in the States regularly sent enormous chunks of their money back to Ireland—a foolish, sentimental gesture, as far as Patrick Walsh was concerned.

He had sensed, almost from the beginning, that Tierney Burke bore all the markings of one of those wild-eyed rebel zealots in the making. Yet the boy would bear watching, for with the right sort of guidance he might in time turn out to be useful in a number of ways. It was even possible that the young scamp's raging Irish fever could be turned to benefit.

Not for the first time, Patrick found a delicious irony in the fact that an Irish policeman's son had become, albeit unknowingly, a part of the Walsh "business enterprises." He had never met the boy's father, but the bullish Mike Burke had himself quite a reputation among the pub owners and gamblers of Five Points, that of a hardheaded, uncompromising copper who wouldn't bend. Honest cops held him in high regard, while those on the take thought him a fool.

In other words, he couldn't be bought.

Walsh picked up a long, narrow envelope containing a generous Christmas bonus for Tierney Burke. His smile turned faintly contemptuous as he thought of the boy's straitlaced father. It might shake a bit of the starch out of Officer Burke if his son were to end up on the wrong side of the law.

As things stood now, the boy had no knowledge of certain transactions being passed across the desk in the hotel lobby. His part was entirely innocent: He accepted envelopes and mailbags, routed them to the proper boxes, and made an occasional delivery for Hubert Rossiter or Charlie Egan.

Rossiter, the bookkeeper for numerous Walsh businesses, served as a middleman between Patrick and the brokers who sold steerage lists from the immigrant ships. Charlie Egan, a food inspector who had been on the

Walsh payroll for nearly four years, acted as manager for the Irish runners, who herded the immigrants off the ships, then delivered them to selected tenement houses in Five Points. Houses owned, as it happened, by Patrick Walsh.

The hotel, middle-class and respectable, proved an ideal place for Rossiter and Egan to funnel the steerage lists back and forth from the brokers. In addition, the safe in the hotel office served as a temporary "bank" for the operation's continuous flow of cash.

In one of Patrick Walsh's most lucrative ventures, thousands of dollars passed over the hotel desk every month, under the unsuspecting eyes of Tierney Burke. Walsh was beginning to wonder if it might not prove interesting to test the boy, find out exactly what he was made of and if he were worth grooming for bigger things.

Patrick considered the envelope in his hand. After a moment, he looked up, then tapped on the window and motioned the boy inside.

In the bright winter sunlight flooding his employer's study, Tierney Burke stood, cap in hand, waiting.

Walsh was taking his time coming to the point. Seated behind a gleaming, massive desk, he appeared relaxed and confident, as always. As he studied Tierney, his long, narrow fingers danced idly on an envelope in front of him.

"I've already told you I'm pleased with your work," he said matter-of-factly. "Both at the hotel, and here, at the house."

Unsure as to what was expected of him, Tierney merely inclined his head, saying, "Thank you, sir."

"Your father must be very proud of you," Walsh went on. He flashed a tight, fleeting smile that was gone before it ever reached his eyes. "We Irish set great store by good sons."

His remark caught Tierney by surprise. Walsh seldom referred to his own Irish roots. Indeed, the one thing that made the man suspect in Tierney's eyes was his blatant disavowal of his Irishness. Still uncertain how he should respond, he gave another small nod and a guarded smile.

"I believe in rewarding an employee for work well done," Walsh said, handing the envelope to Tierney. "You can think of this as a bonus—a

Christmas gift. This time of year, a young fellow like yourself can use a bit of extra cash, I should think."

Surprised, Tierney stared at the envelope for only an instant before accepting it. "Thank you, sir! That's very generous of you, I'm sure."

Walsh waved away his thanks. "You've earned it." With the impassive, measuring gaze that Tierney had by now grown used to, his employer continued his scrutiny.

Walsh's eyes were a pale, peculiar shade of hazel that in the natural light of day looked almost opaque. He had the long upper lip of the Irish, but otherwise his features bore no hint of his Celtic origins. His nose was straight and narrow, his mouth thin and somewhat cynical—giving him the impression of a continual sneer.

The light in the room faded to a less startling brightness as clouds moved across the winter sun. Shadows played over Walsh's face, changing his features to a cold, unpleasant mask. Tierney felt a momentary chill at the transformation. Walsh was a cold, hard man, he had no doubt. He had seen through his employer's agreeable, good-natured facade early in their relationship. The man was a fraud. Yet he did not actually dislike Patrick Walsh. While he might be a disappointment as a person, as an employer he could be tolerant and even generous.

Sensing that Walsh had more on his mind than presenting him with a Christmas bonus, Tierney planted his legs a bit more firmly, waiting.

"What are you planning to do with your life, boy?" Walsh asked unexpectedly. "You're reaching the age to make some plans, I should think. How old are you now—sixteen? Seventeen?"

"Fifteen, sir."

Walsh's eyebrows lifted. "I'd have taken you to be older. Well, then, perhaps you're too young to have ambitions after all."

"No, sir." Tierney dropped the envelope into his pocket and linked both hands behind his back. "I have plans."

"Career plans?"

"Eventually. First off, I intend to go to Ireland. When I can raise the money."

Walsh sat forward, his fingertips touching to form an arch on the desk in front of him as he regarded Tierney with a thin-lipped smile. "To live? Or just to search out your roots?"

"Both, sir."

Walsh shifted his gaze to his fingers. "I assume you've a reason. Most folks are bent on *leaving* Ireland these days, not going for a stay."

"Aye, and things will not improve as long as that's the case." Tierney's eyes flashed.

Walsh lifted his face, and Tierney caught a glimpse of amusement. Angered, the boy looked away.

"Don't be too quick to condemn all Irishmen for leaving, Tierney. There's more than one way to help the country, you know."

Tierney looked back to his employer. Walsh was smiling, but it was not the disdainful smile of a moment before.

"Leaving Ireland doesn't always mean abandoning her entirely," Walsh said. He spoke slowly, as if measuring his words with care. "Some of us choose to make a difference from over here. We can make a great deal more money in America than we ever could in Ireland. That being the case, there's nothing to say we can't use a bit of that money to help the country. Some of us, like your father and I, chose a different way. That doesn't necessarily make it the *wrong* way."

Tierney attempted to hide his impatience. "My father is a policeman, sir. There's little left over to send to Ireland, if we're to live. Da is one Irishman who won't be getting rich in America."

Walsh lifted one brow, still smiling. "But some of us will," he said quietly.

Tierney looked at him.

"I'm keeping you from your work," Walsh said briskly, pushing himself back from the desk and getting to his feet. "Perhaps after the holidays we can talk more about your plans. I can't help but admire your ambition, and if you're really set on getting to Ireland, you're going to need some money. Who knows, we may come up with a job with more—responsibility—for you in a few weeks. Something that will pay better than clerking at the hotel."

Walsh walked around the desk and started toward the door, making it clear that his young employee was dismissed.

On the way out, he threw an arm around Tierney's shoulders. "Now, I want you to treat that father of yours to a nice gift for Christmas. He may not make a lot of money as a policeman, but it's not because he doesn't deserve more! I, for one, have the greatest admiration for our police force."

For the first time since going to work for Patrick Walsh, Tierney squirmed beneath the man's touch.

Going back around the house, Tierney hoisted the shovel and resumed clearing the walk. He was keenly aware of the envelope in his pocket and chafed to know the amount within. But Walsh might be watching, and he was unwilling for the man to see his eagerness. The envelope would keep.

This was the first time Walsh had behaved in such an odd fashion, asking Tierney personal questions and speaking openly of his own Irishness—even hinting that he believed in helping the old country with gifts of American-made money!

What, then, accounted for his own feelings of suspicion and annoyance? Why had he been so put off, even uncomfortable, with the man's questions?

Partially, Tierney supposed, it was because he did not trust Walsh's sincerity. His instincts told him that Patrick Walsh was interested in little other than himself and in making more money. Nor did he swallow that ridiculous tale about helping Ireland. Walsh was too eager to forget where he came from—and to have everyone else forget it, as well. That kind of Irishman didn't send money back.

But what bothered him most, Tierney realized, was the fact that the man had obviously been patronizing him. From the moment the conversation had shifted to Tierney's interest in Ireland, there had been a glint of contempt, a hint of mockery in Walsh's manner that even now set Tierney's teeth on edge.

Uneasily, he realized that his employer's actions had caused a seed of distrust to take root, a seed planted earlier by his father. Da continued to insist that Patrick Walsh's reputation was not what it might be, that a number of his "business interests" were suspect. He made no secret of the fact that he questioned the man's phenomenal rise to success, what with Walsh being an Irishman in a city where the Irish seldom rose above the police force or the fire department.

It was a rare thing, indeed, for Tierney to concede the possibility that his father might be right. They seemed to disagree on everything lately, from what to have for breakfast all the way to politics and religion.

But he resented Walsh's probing and his condescending manner. The look in his employer's eye when he referred to Da and the police force had been patent contempt.

Tightening his jaw, Tierney flung another scoop of snow into the yard, stepping up his pace to get the job done. He and Da might have their differences—and in truth, they seemed to have a growing number of them—but it was another thing entirely to think that an orange-blooded Irisher like Patrick Walsh might dare to mock them.

Tierney thought again of the envelope in his pocket and its enticing contents. Walsh had said to get his da a Christmas gift, and so he would. What with the sum he already had stashed in the sock under his pillow, this unexpected bonus should give him enough to buy gifts all round.

He already had a fine knife picked out for Da. And he'd get Daniel a gift, too.

The thought of Daniel made Tierney wince, remembering the terrible row they'd had the night Da had run into Nora and the Englishman at the Opera House.

It wasn't Daniel's fault, of course, but Tierney was still steamed with Nora. He'd lost his temper and said some pretty rough things to Daniel about his mother. But what Daniel didn't seem to realize, or refused to admit, was the hurt Nora had brought upon Da.

He wished now he hadn't blown up as he had, and he was eager to set things right between himself and Daniel before Christmas. Perhaps the right Christmas gift would help break the ice.

He'd get a present for a few others as well, like wee Tom Fitzgerald, the poor, long-faced little tyke. He was soft toward both those Fitzgerald kids, and that was the truth.

Especially Johanna—Johanna with the sad eyes and silent voice. Tierney could make her smile well enough, could sometimes evoke a strange, voiceless laugh from her. He liked that. Somehow, it made him feel a man.

Aye, for Johanna he would buy a silk scarf. Something bright that would make her sad eyes smile.

"Hello, Tierney."

Tierney tightened his jaw and went on shoveling, digging at the walk a little more vigorously. He did not look up, but he was irritably aware of Isabel Walsh standing nearby, watching him.

He knew only too well that his employer's twelve-year-old daughter had a fierce crush on him. To date, Tierney had not worked a Saturday but what the lumpy Isabel, who seemed to have inherited all her mother's worst features, did not make a nuisance of herself at least once.

It was all Tierney could do not to be insulting. Something about the girl set his teeth to grinding. Indeed, all Isabel had to do was say his name, and he wanted to spit. He tried his best to avoid her whenever possible.

But here she was, decked out in one of those abominable fur-trimmed coats that made her look for all the world like a stuffed beaver. Balanced precariously on top of her fat sausage curls was one of those silly little plumed hats that reminded Tierney of a dead goose.

The girl was usually overdressed in heavy, ornate finery like some sort of European princess. Yet, like Mrs. Walsh, poor Isabel only managed to look squat and dull and frumpy in whatever she wore.

Tierney tried to be civil to both Walsh youngsters. Obviously, they were the darlings of their mother's heart, although he had observed Mr. Walsh's impatience with his children, especially with the fussy eight-year-old Henry.

He gave Isabel a cursory glance, pretending great interest in his work. Out of the corner of his eye he saw that she was holding a package, wrapped in shiny paper with bright ribbons tied around it. With dismay, Tierney knew at once it was for him.

"This is for you, Tierney," said Isabel, thrusting the package at him. "It's a Christmas present." She had a reedy, staccato way of speaking that always made her sound out of breath, as if she'd just run up an entire flight of stairs.

Reluctantly, Tierney straightened. Leaning on his shovel, he fixed his gaze on the mangy brown plumes adorning Isabel's hat.

"You oughtn't to be giving me a Christmas present," he said uncharitably. "I didn't get you anything. Or Henry."

Isabel stepped closer, extending her short arms straight out with the gift in front of her. "That doesn't matter, Tierney. Henry and me—Henry and I—will get a lot of Christmas presents. You probably won't, Mama says."

"Indeed," Tierney answered, straight-faced.

"Mama helped me pick it out," Isabel droned on. "She knew I wanted to get you something special."

"That was kind of her," Tierney replied evenly, wondering what sort of contraption made those cigar-sized curls that stuck out all over her head. He reached for the gaily wrapped gift as if it were a toad. "Thank you and Merry Christmas to you," he mumbled, immediately setting the gift down on the walk and hoisting his shovel. "I'd best get back to work now."

Isabel stood staring at him a full five minutes more, indulging herself in a meaningless monologue as she watched him work. Tierney muttered in reply once or twice, paying no attention to her whatever. Finally, she went back inside.

Tierney drew a long sigh of relief. He could almost feel sorry for Patrick Walsh, although certainly his employer would not welcome his sympathy. Still, there was no getting around the fact that Walsh's family fell far short of the man himself. Mrs. Walsh did seem a very kind woman and entirely devoted to her husband and children, but she wasn't the least bit attractive. Walsh's son was prissy and dull at best. And his daughter—well, sure, and that one would try any man's good nature.

No wonder Walsh showed little enthusiasm for anything other than making money!

Well, and wasn't it a fine thing to have money in the pocket, after all? Tierney could certainly appreciate the feeling. And now he had hopes of a job making even more!

Hoisting another shovelful of snow, he began to whistle. Christmas was coming, he had money in his pocket, and school was dismissed for the holidays. Tierney felt so good he could even allow himself to speculate on the contents of Isabel Walsh's gift.

20

Tearing Down Walls

Have we not all one Father? Did not one God create us?

MALACHI 2:10

Arthur Jackson was beginning to wonder if there was anyone in New York City who wasn't Irish.

He was staying in an Irish family's home. Oh, the preacher said he was born in America, but he was mostly Irish, all the same. The strikers who had ganged up on him and the other black boys—they had been Irish, too, including the one who shot Arthur. Even the policemen who had jumped into the riot had been Irish.

Now here came a doctor named Grafton with a boy—his assistant, they said—named Daniel Kavanagh. The doctor talked normal enough, but his boy didn't sound as if he was long off the boat.

His time in New York had taught Arthur that he should steer clear of the Irish, that they were the enemies and competitors of the blacks. But except for the strikers who had jumped him, all these strange Irishers were being so nice to him! It was hard to take, and pretty confusing to a black boy from Mississippi.

Never in his life had Arthur been touched by a doctor—until he got shot. And this one was a rich man's doctor, you could tell. He wore a fine suit and had a watch fob hanging from his waistcoat. And he had an *assistant*—the Irish boy.

Arthur wondered briefly if these two would still be so decent to him once Mrs. Dalton and Casey-Fitz were out of the bedroom.

But the doctor's hands were gentle as he examined Arthur's wound, then pressed the tender places around his back and ribs. He smiled a lot as he worked over him, as if he knew Arthur was skittish and wanted to reassure him.

The Irish boy also grinned at him now and then. Arthur wondered how a Paddy, and such a young one, managed to land a job with a gentleman doctor. This Daniel Kavanagh might be a little older than Arthur, but not by much, he'd judge. Still, he seemed to know what he was doing. He had all the tools and stuff ready and waiting, almost before the doctor told him what he wanted.

He must be awful smart, but where did an Irish boy get all that learning?

"Deep breath, Arthur. Again. Does that hurt?"

It hurt plenty, but Arthur just shrugged. His daddy had taught him not to whine about pain.

They had him sitting up in bed, which made his sides and chest hurt even more. The doctor pressed on a tender spot, and in spite of himself, Arthur yelped.

"Mm-hm," was all the doctor said.

That must have meant something to the Kavanagh boy, too, because he frowned, just like the doctor. When he looked at Arthur again, though, he smiled.

Arthur let out a long breath of relief when the doctor finally helped him lie down.

"Your lung still has a ways to go before it's all healed," said the doctor. "I'm afraid you're going to have to stay in bed a while longer."

"How come if I was shot in the back I hurt so bad in my chest, too?"

Smiling, the doctor closed up his black case. "Because part of your rib punched a hole in your lung. You're very lucky that bullet didn't go on through your heart."

Arthur swallowed. He didn't want to think about that.

There was a long, awkward pause between Arthur and the Irish boy after the doctor went downstairs to talk with Mrs. Dalton.

Finally the Irish boy broke the silence. "Do you go to school?" he asked.

Arthur shook his head.

"So you work, then?" the boy asked, tidying the night table the doctor had used during the examination.

"When there's work to be had, I do," said Arthur. Deciding the other boy seemed friendly enough, he asked, "How'd you get a job like this, with a doctor? You go to school for it?"

Daniel Kavanagh shook his head and came over to the bed again. "No. I mean, I do go to school, but just regular school. I got the job because Dr. Grafton happened to be needing an assistant at the same time I was looking for work."

Arthur looked at him curiously. "Can't see wantin' to spend so much time around sick folks. You like it?"

"Aye, I do. I want to be a doctor, you see, so this is a fine job for me to have."

Arthur nodded as if he understood, but he still reckoned this Irish boy might be kinda peculiar. Spending all that time with a doctor and sick people—it must get awful discouraging.

"Where do you live?" asked Daniel Kavanagh, putting both hands in his pockets.

Arthur shrugged. "Got a room in Five Points with some other fellows I know."

The other boy's expression changed.

"It's not so bad," Arthur muttered resentfully. He didn't want no Paddy feeling sorry for *him.*

Daniel Kavanagh nodded agreeably. For a minute Arthur felt as if he were looking right *through* him. But at least he didn't say anything else about Five Points.

"Ain't lived there long," Arthur said, yawning. "I come from Mis'sippi."

Daniel Kavanagh nodded. "Mr. Dalton told us. He said you ran away. That must have taken a lot of courage."

Embarrassed, Arthur kicked at the blankets with his feet. "Naw, just took a lot of runnin', that's all."

Daniel smiled, and silence descended between them again. This time Arthur yielded. "I can play the harmonica," he offered. As soon as the words were out, he was sorry he'd said it. Some fellows thought it was sissy to play a musical instrument.

But Daniel Kavanagh's face lit up. "Truly? That's grand. I play the harp."

Now *that* was a sissy instrument, Arthur thought. But the boy didn't seem embarrassed. He sure wasn't like any of the Paddies Arthur had met in Five Points!

"Maybe I'll bring my harp over sometime after you're feeling stronger. We could play some songs together. If you'd like to, that is."

Arthur's eyes bugged. Wouldn't that be a sight, though? A colored boy playing music with a Paddy!

"I don't know anybody else who plays music," Daniel Kavanagh said quietly. "Except for Morgan Fitzgerald, that is, and he's in Ireland. He taught me the harp, you see, and we used to play songs together sometimes."

Arthur had never expected to *like* a Paddy. Yet, something in the Irish boy's eyes tugged at him, and he found himself responding to what seemed like an offer of friendship on Daniel Kavanagh's part.

"Guess that'd be okay," Arthur said. "But I dunno how long it'll be before I got enough wind to play. I'm awful short of breath yet."

"Oh, don't worry! With Dr. Grafton taking care of you, you'll be feeling as good as new in no time at all! And I'll pray for you!"

Arthur stared at him, stuck for a reply.

Then the door opened, and Mrs. Dalton and Casey-Fitz came in with the doctor. Everybody seemed to be talking at once, and the noise made Arthur's head spin.

These had to be the strangest folks he'd ever met. They treated one another like family, and they treated him almost as nice. Even if they were always talking about the *Lord* and *praying*, none of it seemed put-on.

Some of their talk and proper ways made him uncomfortable, but he knew they didn't do it on purpose. And not a one of them seemed to pay any attention that he was black.

These were strange folks, all right. And now he'd met a boy who played a harp, just like an angel!

Peculiar as they were, he guessed he liked them well enough. They seemed good people, especially Casey-Fitz and Daniel Kavanagh.

Even if they were Irish.

❧

That night, up to his elbows in dishwater, Daniel told Tierney about his talk with Arthur Jackson. "He's on his own keeping entirely. Just think of being on your own in Five Points!"

Tierney grunted, obviously unimpressed.

"He was hurt, but he's getting better, thanks to Dr. Grafton." Daniel frowned as he scrubbed a grease-caked frying pan. "He's the same boy Uncle Mike helped to save from the strikers, you know."

Tierney lifted an eyebrow. "The black kid that got shot? The one the Daltons took in?"

Daniel nodded. "Arthur Jackson is his name. He plays the harmonica."

Tierney's indifference turned to scorn. "They *all* play the harmonica."

Daniel shot a look at Tierney. "What do you mean?"

Tierney shrugged and went on swiping the dish towel over a plate. "Colored boys. They all seem to play some kind of music. Jungle drums, mostly." He grinned, but there was no humor in it, only contempt.

Daniel swallowed down his anger. "That's an ignorant thing to say, it seems to me."

Tierney looked at him, a threatening glint in his eyes. "You're saying I'm ignorant because I don't like Negroes?"

"No, I'm simply saying it *sounds* ignorant when you talk so. Especially when I don't think you even mean what you say."

Tierney's eyes narrowed, but Daniel pretended not to notice. Turning back to the sink, he attacked the frying pan with a vengeance. Tierney was forever making cutting remarks about the Negroes or the Germans or the Poles—about anybody who wasn't Irish. Yet Daniel did not believe Tierney was as prejudiced as he let on. He half-suspected Tierney said some of the things he did because he thought it was *expected* of him.

In New York City, the Irish hated the Negroes, and the Negroes hated the Irish. And Tierney would be the last to go against the mold. He fancied himself as the tough man, one who would brook no questioning of his being thoroughly, unmistakably *Irish*.

Daniel could not help wondering if Tierney might not be more intent on convincing *himself* than anyone else. This was only one of the traits in his friend that had begun to worry Daniel lately. He was changing, Tierney was, becoming harder, more impatient—sometimes even unkind. But Daniel had been unable to determine just how much of this hardness was authentic, and how much was sham—a mask Tierney had chosen to wear, for whatever his reasons.

Uneasily, he sensed a wall going up around his friend—a self-erected wall—that was slowly shutting out everyone around him, including

Daniel and Uncle Mike. Tierney was building a fortress around himself—whether for protection or isolation, Daniel could not say. He only knew that he was beginning to feel left out, separated from his friend. It made him feel unhappy and increasingly troubled.

21

A Christmas Like No Other

And never was piping so sad,
And never was piping so gay....
W. B. YEATS (1865–1939)

Christmas Day, for the most part, was a festive, glad occasion, an occasion that, at the Farmington mansion, began weeks—even months—before it arrived.

The house was elaborately decorated. Dried flowers and leaves, carefully preserved from the past autumn, had been added to the profusion of evergreens in each room. Even the last rosebuds of the fall had been saved by dipping their stems in melted paraffin and wrapping the blooms in tissue paper. Stored in cool dresser drawers, they were retrieved and recut, then placed in warm water to grace the immense dining room table for this one day.

Christmas dinner was like nothing Daniel had ever imagined. For the first time in his life, he grasped the full meaning of the word *feast*—roast turkey and stuffed ham, stewed oysters and candied sweet potatoes, fried celery, lemon pudding and cranberry pie. And that was in addition to a seemingly endless assortment of fruit and nuts, decorated cookies and candies!

The entire day was a wonder. From the ornate decorations that filled the spacious dining room to the magnificent table spread in full splendor before them, it was an astonishing occasion altogether.

Glancing up from his half-empty plate, Daniel studied the immense chandelier overhead with some concern as to how firmly anchored it might be. Festooned with lush evergreens, brightly colored leaves and berries, it hung like a great adorned tree suspended from the high ceiling.

Across the room, Daniel's own gift to the Farmingtons rested proudly against the far wall. At the inspiration of his mother, he had made a large Christmas harp, forming its frame from some lightweight wood strips and stringing it with thin wire. Decorated with colored leaves, Christmas greens and tinsel, it stood as tall as a man grown, drawing attention to itself from any point in the room.

Sara Farmington had declared the harp "quite the most wonderful Christmas gift" she had ever received. Daniel had been enormously gratified with her enthusiasm. Both Miss Sara and her father had seemed genuinely impressed that he would go to so much effort on their behalf. In truth, it had helped him to feel less an outsider.

When the Farmingtons first insisted that everybody—Daniel and his mother, Evan Whittaker, and the Fitzgerald children—share their Christmas at the mansion, Daniel had worried that he might feel out of place. Miss Sara was a grand lady, and Mr. Farmington a prince—but his son, Gordon—"Gordie," the family called him—and his wife took on insufferable airs.

As it happened, the Gordon Farmingtons spent Christmas with the wife's family, considerably easing Daniel's apprehension. Throughout the entire day, Miss Sara and her father spared no efforts in making their guests feel at home. Gifts were lavished on them all. Ice skates and books for Daniel. A silver-handled mirror and a soft wool shawl for his mother. A huge sack of marbles and a toy train for Little Tom. For Johanna, a doll and a miniature tea set. And for Evan Whittaker, a fine leather-bound journal and a framed sketch of a pastoral scene—an English countryside.

Toying with his food, Daniel was disappointed that in the face of such abundance he had so little appetite. The headache and raw throat that had been plaguing him overnight worsened as the day wore on. He simply could not bring himself to eat more than a few bites of the banquet.

His mother had noticed, of course, chiding him for not eating more. Daniel pushed his food around on his plate and made no mention of not feeling well. Fretting about him would only spoil the day for her, and he refused to allow anything to steal the Christmas light from her eyes.

He grew more uncomfortable by the moment, however. The dining room was warm and oppressively stuffy, and he longed for an appropriate moment to excuse himself.

Biding his time, he could not help but reflect on the drastic difference between this Christmas and last. Last year in Ireland, with Da recently dead, food and money had been so scarce as to be a continuing source of despair. Christmas Day had passed almost unheeded, except for a service at the meetinghouse and the few small playthings his grandfather had whittled for the children. Mother had been silent and grieving, while Tahg, Daniel's elder brother, and his wee sister, Ellie, had both been too ill to take notice of the day at all. It had been a terrible Christmas—the bleakest in his memory.

This Christmas Day, now—well, it was quite different. The only imperfection to mar its joy—aside from his feeling so poorly—was the fact that Tierney and Uncle Mike had chosen not to share the day with the rest of them.

Miss Sara had invited them, but Uncle Mike had quickly declined. Too quickly, Daniel realized. Obviously, he was still peeved with Mother. As was Tierney.

Tierney had told Daniel what had transpired at the Opera House that night in late November. His light blue eyes had been glazed with anger, his tone hard and cold, when he related how Uncle Mike had encountered Daniel's mother and "the Englishman," the both of them "decked out in their borrowed finery."

For days afterward, Tierney had remained withdrawn and aloof toward Daniel, almost as if to punish him. Uncle Mike, too, had seemed excessively quiet and distracted. It came as no surprise, therefore, when he refused the Farmingtons' invitation; nevertheless, it was a great disappointment. At least Tierney had recently attempted to patch things up, resuming his usual teasing remarks and pranks over the past two days. And hadn't he given him a fine pocket knife, almost exactly like the one he'd bought for Uncle Mike?

Glancing across the table, Daniel met Johanna's eyes. Her hand went to the bright emerald scarf at her throat—Tierney's gift. Daniel winked at her, and still touching the scarf, she returned his smile.

Forcing down one last bite of pie, Daniel winced at the swollen ache in his throat. He was feeling more than a little ill now. He dared not delay in getting some air, else he would disgrace himself by being ill in front of everyone.

"Excuse me, please," he muttered thickly, pushing himself away from the table. Half-rising from his chair, he quickly gripped its back when the room began to spin. He swayed, catching his breath and hoping nobody had noticed.

He should have known better.

"Daniel John?" His mother's voice was sharp, her tone questioning. She left her chair and hurried round to him.

"Mother...I feel—I might be a bit ill..." he managed to choke out. Then the entire sea of faces round the table began to spin crazily out of control.

What had begun as a shining gift of a day ended in a nightmare for Nora, with Daniel John almost fainting dead away at the dinner table. Breaking his fall, Nora saw at once that the boy was afire with fever. More frightening still, his skin was blotched with a fine, bright scarlet rash.

Mr. Farmington half-carried him to the chaise in the parlor, then immediately sent Uriah for Dr. Grafton. While they waited for the doctor, Sara herded wee Tom and Johanna from the room; Evan stayed to help Nora with Daniel John.

The lad was restless, thrashing about anxiously on the chaise as he groaned and muttered meaningless, disjointed words. He seemed too ill to manage more than a nod or a small shake of his head when they questioned him.

Nora was beside herself with fear. "He's not making any sense at all, Evan!"

"It's the fever," Evan said softly, his forehead lined with a worried frown.

Nora looked from him to her son. "He's delirious, do you mean? But how...he was perfectly fine until the dinner! I don't understand..." She let her words drift off, unfinished. Putting a hand to Daniel John's brow, she uttered a soft gasp of surprise from the heat she felt with her fingertips. "He's so hot! And the rash..." She hesitated, staring at her son with growing horror. "Lord have mercy, I have seen this rash before!"

Evan put his hand to her shoulder. "Nora, I'm sure the d-doctor will be here any m-moment—"

Nora continued to stare helplessly down at the boy. "It was in the village, years past," she choked out, her voice trembling. "I remember... because of Johanna."

"Nora, it m-may not be the same thing—"

"Scarlet fever." Nora stopped and tried to get a breath, but could not. "'Tis called the scarlet fever! Johanna had it—that's why she cannot hear or talk!"

Whipping around to Evan, her voice rose with her fear. "'Tis the same thing, Evan—the scarlet fever!"

Evan started to speak, then seemed to change his mind as he gripped her shoulder more tightly.

"Scarlet fever," Nicholas Grafton announced within moments of his arrival. Indeed, it had not even been necessary to examine his young assistant. He had seen enough scarlet fever during his years of practice in the city—especially of late—to recognize the disease at first glance.

Guilt tugged at him as he continued to examine young Daniel. He had almost certainly contracted the disease from other patients; they had been seeing an increasing number of cases over the past few weeks.

The boy was feverish, the rash widespread. Bad throat already—swollen, and just starting to ulcerate.

Dr. Grafton straightened, turning to the mother. "How long since the rash appeared?"

"How long?" The woman stared at him with frightened eyes, all the while wringing her hands until they were white-knuckled.

The one-armed English fellow at her side answered for her. "Little m-more than an hour ago. We were still at d-dinner. Daniel seemed faint, and when we helped him away from the table he could scarcely walk. He complained of being d-dizzy and sick to his stomach."

Grafton gave a short nod. "The rash is fairly widespread already—probably started on his chest and back earlier in the day." He looked at the boy's mother. "I feel bad about this, Mrs. Kavanagh. Undoubtedly, he picked it up on calls. Daniel's not one to keep his distance from the patients—he's a fine assistant, willing to do whatever needs doing."

Sighing heavily, the doctor closed his medical case. "He's going to need a great deal of care and close attention. Will he be staying here?" Grafton found his young assistant's living situation somewhat peculiar, although the boy seemed content enough living apart from his mother—with his "Uncle Mike," as he called him.

Lewis Farmington was standing directly behind the mother. "Why, of course he'll stay here! Nora will want to be with him. Just leave instructions as to the proper care, Nicholas. We'll see that he gets everything he needs." He paused. "In addition to Nora, he'll have Ginger and Sara to help. They're both very good with illness."

"Yes, well, that's fine, but the thing is—scarlet fever is highly contagious. You still have two other children in the house, isn't that so?"

Farmington nodded.

"Johanna—Johanna has already had the sickness," Nora Kavanagh offered. The woman appeared to be more in control now, though still frightened.

As well she might be, Grafton thought. Scarlet fever was a treacherous disease. In addition to making a body miserably ill, it often wreaked havoc on the vital organs, at times causing irreparable damage. Sometimes it even killed.

"It was the scarlet fever that left Johanna—as she is," added the mother.

She meant the girl's deafness, of course. At Lewis Farmington's request, Grafton had examined the children when they first arrived from Ireland, had attended the older sister who eventually died of heart failure. He still remembered the younger sister, the deaf girl with the frightened eyes.

Nora Kavanagh turned her stricken gaze on the doctor. "Johanna—she was never able to hear or speak after she had the disease."

Grafton bit his lip, then nodded reluctantly. "That happens." He paused. "But we won't let it happen to Daniel, Mrs. Kavanagh. We'll bring him through this just fine. I'll keep a close watch on him, you can be sure."

Her uncertain smile took obvious effort. It occurred to the doctor that Daniel's young mother was surprisingly lovely for one who had endured so much tragedy. Although her delicate features bore shadows of past grief, there was a quiet, serene beauty about the woman.

"Daniel should be isolated from the rest of the household," he said, turning to Lewis Farmington. "Except for those who know for certain they've already had the disease. Of course, anyone here today has been exposed, so it may not do a great deal of good."

Lewis Farmington frowned. "I wouldn't remember whether I've had it or not, but it doesn't matter—I never get ill. *Never,*" he added confidently. He looked at his daughter. "To the best of my knowledge, though, Sara has never had it."

"I never get ill either," Sara Farmington said with equal assurance. "I must take after you, Father."

Farmington peered at his daughter with narrowed eyes, but she merely smiled at him cheerfully.

"Little Tom—Johanna's brother—I'd remember if he had it," said Nora Kavanagh. "I'm sure he hasn't."

The doctor looked at her closely. "And you?"

"Myself? Oh…well, more than likely, I did," she answered vaguely. "As a child, you know."

Grafton knew, all right. There would be no keeping the woman away from her son. She would expose herself without a thought, as would most mothers.

When asked, the Englishman declared he had scarlet fever as a boy. "I st-still remember the sore throat." Then, turning to Lewis Farmington, he suggested, "Why d-don't we move Daniel to my rooms in the cottage? That will at least separate him from Little Tom—and from M-Miss Sara, as well."

Sara Farmington waved a dismissing hand. "I'm not at all concerned about myself. But that's a good idea, Evan, if you really don't mind. It's going to be awfully hard to keep Little Tom away from Daniel otherwise."

During the next few moments, Grafton helped to move the boy to the cottage behind the mansion, then wrote out detailed instructions for his care. Unfortunately, there was little in the way of medication that would help. A few drops of belladonna, night and morning. Spirits of nitre. Otherwise, cool drinks, bed rest, and warm baths.

"We'll need to watch for ear infections and dropsy. If he should start swelling up, send word to me at once." Handing the belladonna to Daniel's mother, the doctor looked at her sharply. "Don't wear yourself out now, Mrs. Kavanagh," he warned. "There are plenty of others here to help look after your son."

The Englishman moved just a step closer. "You c-can be sure we'll all help, D-Doctor."

Dr. Grafton saw the way the man looked at Daniel's mother, saw, too, the grateful gaze with which she answered.

So that's how it was, was it? Odd match—an Englishman and an Irish widow. Still, it was good she wasn't alone. She was in for a difficult time of it these next few days.

As was young Daniel, poor boy. Few things caused the body more distress than this ugly illness. And there was exasperatingly little they could do.

Watch him closely, and pray, that was about all. It had been Nicholas Grafton's experience that, with scarlet fever, prayer was just about the only thing that seemed to make any real difference.

22

Vigil Before the Dawn

Life and death are in thy hand, Lord, have mercy!
RICHARD D'ALTON WILLIAMS (1822–1862)

Daniel knew it was night and knew he was awfully cold, for he was shivering hard enough to make his teeth chatter.

He was in a strange room, on a strange bed. No...no, it was not strange, after all. He had been here before, in Evan Whittaker's rooms. The bed was high, with a wide, deep mattress. A fine bed. But the room seemed to be circling the bed—or was the bed revolving? He desperately wished it would stop, for the movement made his head ache even more.

The heat raging over his body was like a blistering wind, seizing him and trapping him inside. He had never been so agonizingly hot in his entire life. A terrible thirst plagued him, but he was sure he could not force even a small sip of water down his swollen throat. The very act of swallowing was a torment.

He was confused by the room, frightened of the heat. When he closed his eyes, he saw nothing but a fog. When he opened them, he saw his mother leaning over him, hovering, her cool hand soothing his forehead. Evan Whittaker was there, too, watching him. And sometimes Sara Farmington, not smiling as she usually did, but instead thin-lipped and shadowed in the dim light.

He wanted to sleep, to drift away from the relentless pounding in his head and the pain in his throat. He longed for the sweet oblivion sleep would bring, but it would not come. Every time he closed his eyes and began to drift off, he would jerk awake again, more miserable than before.

Why did Evan Whittaker frown so as he bent over him? And Mother—Mother's face was so white. Like a specter, she was!

Somehow, the sight of her made Daniel feel guilty. He was worrying her again, and hadn't she had more than enough trouble? She should not have to worry about him....

He closed his eyes against the pain knifing through his head and his throat.

What was wrong with him? Was it the fever?

Was he back in Killala, then? Or aboard the coffin ship, the *Green Flag*—dying, like all the others, of the Black Fever?

No. He wasn't in Ireland or on the ship. He was in America. Why, then, was he so ill? Had the fever followed them here, to New York City?

He could not think. The effort made the hammering in his head seem louder still. With a long moan, he turned his face to the wall and again sought the blessed nothingness of sleep.

Evan could feel Nora's fear; the entire room seemed to throb with it.

Sitting beside her, near the bed, he was aware that her whole body was trembling, as if she, too, were in the throes of a relentless fever.

He took her hand, found her skin hot and clammy. Her other hand was drawn into a tight fist, pressed against her mouth as if to choke back a cry of despair.

Evan's eyes went to the boy. Daniel had not stopped his restless tossing and moaning since they'd put him to bed. By now the rash had erupted full-blown. In the flickering candlelight of the deeply shadowed room, the boy's skin appeared raw and angry. At the moment, he seemed lost in a fog of delirium, his only sounds an occasional groan or a muffled sob of pain.

Giving Nora's hand a reassuring squeeze, Evan got up to check the fire. He was keeping it low, according to the doctor's instructions that the room should be fairly cool but not cold. He hunched forward, poking the logs just enough that they wouldn't smother the flames. Straightening, he stood with his back to the fire, looking first at Daniel, then at Nora.

She leaned forward on the chair, gripping one of her son's hands between both of hers. Her eyes were huge, her features set in a rigid mask of fear.

Apprehension swept over him as he remembered a similar scene, this one in the small, mean cottage back in Ireland. Nora, white-faced and despairing, seated beside the bed of her elder son, gripping his hand as if to hold him back from the death that finally claimed him.

Chilled, Evan tried to shake off the memory. He was suddenly seized with the need to flee the room, to escape the air of foreboding that seemed to shroud his quarters.

When Ginger slipped quietly into the room at that moment with a tray of tea, he went to Nora and touched her lightly on the shoulder. "I'll be b-back shortly," he whispered. "I need a bit of air—and you n-need your shawl. It's too cool for you without a wrap."

She looked up at him with anxious eyes but made no protest as he started for the door.

꒷꒷

Evan tugged at his coat impatiently, exasperated at how even the most simple, ordinary act turned clumsy and difficult for a man with one arm.

He was reluctant to examine his sudden urgency to escape the cottage. God forgive him, he feared it was more cowardice than anything else. The sight of Nora hovering near Daniel's bedside, agonizing over the possibility of losing yet another son, slashed at his heart like a scythe.

Opening the cottage door, he stepped outside into a world of soft, white beauty, clean and silent. Over an inch of snow had fallen during the past few hours. With a graceful, almost dreamlike motion, large cottony flakes drifted to the ground.

Evan glanced down at his polished black dress shoes, then decided to go on. The snow on the pathway wasn't all that deep.

Welcoming the cold, bracing air, he walked slowly toward the "big house"—Mrs. Buckley's term for the mansion. In the late hush of the winter's night, the pale limestone structure looked more like an old world chateau than a family home. Its lines were French, its overall appearance one of restrained elegance: sturdy, yet graceful. Evan suspected that the mansion reflected more of Miss Sara's personality than that of her father. Mr. Farmington's taste, he sensed, would run more to top-heavy brownstones with turrets and cornices and lots of ornate iron battlements.

He stopped for a moment in the middle of the walkway, staring into the dense stand of pines that bordered the west side and rear of the mansion. His heart aching, he recalled Nora's stricken face. Daniel was all that remained of her family, all she had left after the brutal ravages of the famine and her journey across the Atlantic.

Dear God, what if she were to lose him, too?

Evan shuddered. As he resumed walking, his thoughts turned to his own family, which consisted only of his father and his aunt Winifred.

Just last week a letter had come from Father, a letter that disturbed him more deeply each time he thought of it. Containing mostly minor bits of news about Portsmouth, the pages had nevertheless hinted of what was, for his father, an uncommon degree of sentimentality.

Evan's mother had died just after his twentieth birthday. Over the years, his clergyman father, always a bookish, somewhat remote man, had become more and more reticent. Charles Whittaker's affection for his only son had been, for the most part, understood—but unspoken and largely undemonstrated.

In his most recent letter, however, his father had actually admitted to missing Evan—and missing him rather badly. He had even gone so far as to indicate that both he and Evan's aunt Winifred—Father's younger sister—deeply bemoaned the fact that Evan dare not return to England. When Evan defied his employer, the notorious landlord Roger Gilpin, he had shut the door on his own homeland. Gilpin had a long and vicious memory; he would not forget Evan's betrayal, or his own lust for retribution.

Of Evan's actions he said merely, "One must act according to God's direction as one interprets it." But he did hope Evan had not been too hasty in lending his aid to the victimized Irish at the expense of his own well-being. Gilpin was a powerful man, and he had no doubt been thoroughly incensed by Evan's abdication of responsibility. A mere employee's defiance was doubtless an act for which Gilpin would demand unmitigated justice.

To Evan's great surprise, his father had enclosed a small amount of money, with the admonition that Evan must not, under any circumstances, attempt to recoup his own savings from the London bank where he had formerly deposited it. "Do not give that dreadful man even a hint of your whereabouts, my boy. Not a hint."

Evan was still somewhat puzzled by the money. His father knew he was employed, after all, and earning a generous wage as Lewis Farmington's assistant.

Evan sighed. He *was* his father's only son—his only child. And Father was getting along in years. When Evan was growing up his father had seemed an elderly man, though, of course, he hadn't actually been *old*. Only a bit older than most of the parents of Evan's contemporaries.

Now, with an entire ocean separating the two of them, Father had only his sister—Aunt Winifred. And they were as different as a canary and a barn owl! Widowed twice and still attractive enough to turn male heads whenever she entered a room, Aunt Winnie was as outgoing and ebullient as Father was self-contained and laconic. Twelve years younger, at times she seemed more Charles Whittaker's daughter than his sister. She claimed to find her brother "as dry as old ashes," while Father, for his part, viewed Aunt Winnie as "flighty and altogether frivolous."

Yet they adored each other. Evan smiled a little in memory, a smile that quickly fled as he realized how greatly he missed the two of them. Over the past few months he had become more and more aware that people—especially family—gave a person a sense of identity and place. Like young Daniel, he, too, was an only son. It was a sobering but somehow reassuring thought to know his undemonstrative, often remote, father missed him.

With the thought, he was again overwhelmed by the enormity of all Nora had lost—and all she stood to lose if something were to happen to her only surviving son.

And so right there, in the middle of the walkway, despite the snow wetting his hair and stinging his skin, he began to pray aloud for Nora and her son—her *only* son.

"Lord, it is f-for You, Creator of life, to preserve Your creation or reclaim it. D-Daniel is Your child. Yet he is N-Nora's child, too, and she does love the boy so. She has lost so m-much, Lord—her other children, her husband, her home—only r-recently have the wounds of her grief even begun to heal.

"Oh, Lord…You who were willing to g-give up Your only Son, please have mercy on this frightened m-mother…and in Your compassion, spare her only son. Please, Lord…please spare Daniel Kavanagh."

Evan opened his eyes, brushing away the tears that had spilled over as he prayed, mingling with the wetness of the snow tracking his cheeks. Then, drawing his coat more tightly about him, he again started up the pathway toward the mansion.

23

Between Destiny and Despair

The buoyant step and the cheerful air
Will be reckon'd amongst the things that were;
The joyous shout and the thrilling strain
Will only meet a response of pain....
Tho' the heart be heavy, and dim the eye,
On Him, on Him we still rely.

FROM *LAYS FOR PATRIOTS*,
PUB. BY SAMUEL B. OLDHAM, DUBLIN (1848)

Belfast, Ireland

Joseph Mahon the priest arrived at the hospital in Belfast two days after Christmas. There he found Morgan Fitzgerald bundled in a wheelchair by the room's only window. Vaguely, Joseph noted that the window looked out on a stone wall.

Morgan turned as Joseph entered the room. The change in the young giant struck Joseph like a blow. The wind-whipped bronze of the younger man's skin had paled. His strong features were gaunt, sunken. The unruly copper hair had grown longer and wilder, framing the pain-ravaged face in an angry blaze of fire.

But it was the winter in Morgan's stare that seized Joseph's breath and brought the sudden sting of tears to his eyes.

God have mercy, what would it take to warm such a desolate spirit?

The room was as grim as a gaol cell, and the weak afternoon light scarcely relieved its gloom. As Joseph drew closer, Morgan's eyes registered surprise for just an instant. He gave a brief parody of a smile that did nothing to relieve the bleakness of his gaze. "Ah, but you are too late, Joseph. I have decided to live, as you can see."

Joseph stopped directly in front of him. "And aren't we all glad for that?" was all the retort he could manage.

With effort, he concealed his dismay at Morgan's appearance. Gray of face and too lean by far, the lad had a plundered, defeated look on him that chilled Joseph's heart. Ever burdened with the Celtic curse of occasional melancholy, Morgan now looked more devastated than morose, more vanquished than disconsolate.

"Grandfather sent for you, I suppose." Morgan's voice was flat and lifeless.

"He did, thanks be to God. How else would I have heard about the fix you have gotten yourself into this time?"

"And have you come as priest or friend, then, Joseph?"

Ah, Lord, such pain...such bitterness! Where to start praying for the lad... how to speak?

"I would hope I could be both, lad, but it is your choice," Joseph replied gently.

Morgan lifted a hand in an idle motion. "Only a priest would come so far to see a fool."

Joseph was not deceived by the quiet voice, the slightly mocking smile. Morgan Fitzgerald was in pain—and not the worst of it physical. "He is no fool who risks his life to save another. I am told that Smith O'Brien is alive because of you."

Morgan turned his face toward the window. With his broad shoulders slumped against the back of the wheelchair, his long, once powerful legs hidden beneath the lap robe, he looked ten years and more past his age.

An aging Irish warlord. Joseph could have wept for the once mighty oak, now felled.

Yet he would not show pity. God forbid that a man such as Morgan Fitzgerald ever think himself to be pitied!

"So, then, where is your grandfather?" he asked casually. "And how is his health?"

"He went back to the inn earlier, to rest." Without turning, Morgan went on. "He's worn himself out entirely, sitting with me. Even now, he has it in his head that he dare not leave me for a moment."

"He was badly frightened, Morgan, and worried. He does dote on you, you know."

"Aye," Morgan said dully. "He does." He turned now to look at Joseph, a weary, not altogether focused stare. "He should not have sent for you, Joseph. You look exhausted entirely."

Joseph shrugged. "At my age, there are worse things than exhaustion."

"You are not old, Joseph." Morgan's words were perfunctory, flat. "But you must be tired. How did you get here?" he asked after a moment, leaning his head against the wall behind the wheelchair.

"Why, your grandfather sent a fine coach for me! I traveled in great style, don't you know?"

There was no answering smile to his attempted lightness, merely a small nod. The green eyes that once danced with roguish humor or the glint of intrigue were now dull; the wide mouth, always so quick with a smile or a good-humored taunt, had gone slack. Only a faint shadow of the rebel of Mayo hovered about the wasted man in the wheelchair.

"Tell me of the village," Morgan said woodenly.

Clearly, his thoughts were on anything else but Killala. Yet Joseph seized the slightest opportunity to draw him out of himself. "Why, nothing has changed, except to grow worse. With another winter upon us, there is great despair. We will be wiped out entirely if more help does not come, and come soon." He paused. "The generous gifts from you and your grandfather have saved more than one family, Morgan. We are grateful. You do receive my letters?"

Morgan nodded, then pressed the fingers of one hand against his forehead, as if to still a dull ache.

"Morgan?"

Dropping his hand away, back to his lap, Morgan looked at him.

"What are the doctors saying?"

"Sure, and you know what the doctors are saying, Joseph," Morgan replied, looking directly at him. "I don't believe for a moment Grandfather sent a coach for your journey without a letter of explanation. You have already been told I will not walk again."

Grieved, Joseph sank down heavily on the edge of the bed. "I thought perhaps there might be some new word by now," he murmured. "Some change…"

A ghost of a smile touched Morgan's lips, then faded. "Just like a priest.

Ever expecting the miracle. Ah, Joseph, don't we both know that old Belfast is not the city for miracles?"

Joseph leaned forward, keenly mindful of the shattered dreams behind that marble mask. "When will you be able to travel—to go home to Dublin?"

"Soon, I imagine. There's little else they can do for me here, except ply me with laudanum and their bad Ulster jests." In that moment he seemed to falter. He glanced down at the floor. "The problem isn't so much the journey to Dublin," he said tightly. "It's more a question of…how I will manage once I get there. I will need…care, you see."

Morgan lifted his eyes. The look of agonizing humiliation that had settled over that once proud and noble face went straight to Joseph's heart. He wanted to weep. "Why…why, your grandfather will arrange all that, lad. He will see to excellent care for you, of course."

Morgan looked away. "Still, I am a great ox. Too big and ungainly to be easily managed. It will no doubt take some doing to find somebody capable of…handling me."

Joseph thought he would choke on his suppressed pity! Wringing his hands until they ached, he groped for words. "Morgan? The pain—is the pain very bad?"

The mask seemed to slip even more. "I will tell you the truth, Joseph," Morgan bit out, his voice hoarse, "some days I think I will go *mad* with it."

The unexpected, blunt reply pierced Joseph's heart. "But the laudanum—doesn't it help at all, lad?"

Morgan met his eyes. "Aye, it helps." One long-fingered hand went to his head, then raked down the side of his bearded face. "I had some a short while ago. But I'm afraid to take more than a bit of the stuff, don't you see?" He stopped, again glanced toward the window. "I'm afraid I'll reach the point I cannot do without it."

Joseph looked at him. For one frozen instant, he saw what the other had doubtless allowed no one else to see—even his grandfather. He saw the raw, unrestrained fear of a man who had seldom in his life been without power, the power of robust good health and a strong, mighty body.

A remnant from one of Morgan's own poems suddenly slipped in among Joseph's sorrowing thoughts: *I have become a man whose soul, like Eire's, is ever trapped between destiny and despair….*

Joseph rose slowly, staggering for a moment with weakness. He grabbed the bed railing to steady himself, then moved to Morgan.

He could not think what to say to his stricken young friend, and so he did the only thing he knew to do. Wrapping both arms around Morgan's wide, sagging shoulders, he pressed the great head against his chest and held him there, next to his heart, while he prayed for him.

Outside in the hall, Annie Delaney listened to the exchange between the two men. Obviously, the frail-looking priest and Morgan Fitzgerald were old friends, for the Fitzgerald had referred to him as *Joseph*, rather than *Father*.

When a long silence fell between the two, Annie risked a peek inside the room. Creeping closer to the door that stood ajar, she inched her face around the opening, just enough to have a look.

A lump swelled in her throat. The priest was cradling that grand copper-crowned head against his own chest. And he was praying. Praying for Morgan Fitzgerald.

This was a strange thing entirely! Annie could not imagine, try as she would, the hawk-faced Father Daly showing such gentle affection to even a wee child of the parish—much less a man grown!

She found it sad and yet strangely comforting, seeing the great Fitzgerald finally surrender to his pain. Through the weeks of his confinement, Annie had shadowed the man, evading the nurses in the hallway, sneaking in and out of the small alcove near his room. Not once had she seen the Fitzgerald's weary composure slip, even a little. Yet now he clung to the aging priest like a frightened boy.

Shrinking back into her hidey-hole, Annie pressed her lips together, thinking. He was fretting about going home. Humiliated, no doubt, that he would be dependent on others for his care. Sure, and couldn't she understand that? What was worse than feeling trapped by your own helplessness? And wouldn't it be an even harder thing for a man like the Fitzgerald than it had been for her? He was a great, powerful man. Probably he had never depended on another soul for a thing before this trouble had come upon him.

And now, just see the fix he was in! Sure, and the old man—the grandfather—would be of no help. Why, 'twas all he could do to make his way down the hall without stumbling! He looked to be a very old man. And ailing as well. Still, he was obviously rich, and so could afford the best of care for his grandson.

His grandson. Who would have imagined such a thing? Morgan Fitzgerald himself, grandson to an Englishman! What would her da have thought of *that*?

Annie sat very still, gnawing on her knuckles. It sounded as if he would be leaving soon. Leaving the hospital and going back to Dublin with his grandfather.

She let out a long breath. There was no accounting for the way she had grown attached to the big fellow. Why, she had never laid eyes on the man until a few weeks ago! Yet ever since that awful night outside the Music Hall, when he had fallen to the street with a bullet in his back, Annie had sensed in some strange, unaccountable way that he was to be a part of her life—and she a part of his. An important part, at that.

Perhaps because it was by his poetry that she had learned to read, had grown from a child with his words engraved upon her heart.

Or perhaps, she thought with a faint smile, she might be a bit fey, just as her grandmother Aine had been. Some had said she was purely daft, but Annie had thought her a wonder. She still missed her sorely, even though the old dear had been dead going on four years.

Grandmother Aine had known things. When the *banshee* would wail. When the cow would go dry. When disaster was lurking but a breath away.

Whatever accounted for it, Annie *knew* Morgan Fitzgerald. More than *knew* him—she *needed* him. And he needed her, though of course he could not know that as yet.

She did not intend to let him simply walk out of her life and—Annie pressed her fingers to her mouth in dismay. Fitzgerald could not *walk* out of her life, any more than he could *walk* anywhere else! Morgan Fitzgerald would never walk again—hadn't she heard it for herself?

Still, he would be leaving for Dublin, and leaving without *her*, unless she could prevent it. She did have an idea—but would the old man hear her out? And even if he did, would he take her seriously?

The silver-haired priest came out of the room. Watching him for only a moment, Annie got to her feet.

Perhaps he was the very one to give her idea a boost.

24

An Encounter with Annie Delaney

Oh! who can tell what things she hears—
What secrets of the faery spheres,
That fill her eyes with silent tears!
Sweet wandering fancy-charmed child,
With cheek so pale, and eyes so wild.
Oh! what shall come of this lonely dreaming!
THOMAS CAULFIELD IRWIN (1823–1892)

Faith, child, would you be causing a priest to fall on his face, then?" Joseph Mahon threw out a hand to brace himself against the wall in the dim hallway. The raggedy little urchin had darted out in front of him from nowhere, blocking his path and causing him to stumble.

"Sure, and I'm sorry, Father!" the child said breathlessly. "But I would speak with you, if you please. It's that important."

Joseph stared down at the thin elfin face, speculating as to whether this creature was a girl-child or a lad.

"And who is it wanting to speak with me?"

"Annie Delaney, your reverence." The pointed chin lifted, as if the name itself were a matter of pride.

The face was perky, if not altogether clean, capped by a shaggy riot of black, straight hair that seemed to grow wild, entirely without direction. Two black-marble eyes peered out from behind the hair, studying Joseph with an unsettling, solemn gaze. The clothes were wretched: a boy's cap, an oversized coat that looked as if it might have belonged to a drunken sailor, and a long, tattered skirt above boys' shoes and woolen stockings.

A street urchin. One of the numerous Belfast orphans on her own keeping, no doubt, living off what she could beg or steal.

Now regretting his sharp tone, Joseph softened. "And what, exactly, would you be hoping to discuss with me, Annie Delaney?"

Those disconcerting dark eyes measured Joseph for another full moment. "I would speak to you about your friend, Father. Morgan Fitzgerald. I'm hoping you might put in a word for me with the grandfather."

Joseph frowned. "A word for you? I'm afraid I don't understand, lass."

The thin shoulders straightened. "I'm asking your help in convincing the old gentleman to take me along to Dublin City when they go." She paused, swatting an unruly shock of hair out of her eyes. "To help take care of his grandson, don't you see?"

Joseph's first instinct was to laugh, but he sensed it would be a grave error. The child was deadly serious. "Well, Annie Delaney, I'm afraid you're a bit young to be the nursemaid for such a man as Morgan Fitzgerald. And a bit small." Joseph paused, lifting his eyebrows in a stern look. "Besides, what would your family be thinking of such an outrageous idea?"

The black eyes locked with his. Joseph caught a fleeting glimpse of a terrible pain in that young soul. "Sure, and there's no family to be fretting about me, Father. As to me age and me size, more than likely I'm older—and stronger—than you think." The child paused. "I'm nearly eleven, after all."

Joseph studied the strange lass with growing curiosity. She *was* older than he would have thought—if she were telling the truth.

Again the sharp little chin thrust upward. "If you're thinking that's too young for such a position, then you should be knowing I've lived some longer than me years—I've been on me own keeping for quite a spell, don't you see? And I'm educated as well, Father—I can read and write and do sums. I'm not ignorant."

Of course, she would not be ignorant. What child on the bitter streets of Belfast would be ignorant? But how to convince this curious wee lass that her schemes were out of the question?

"Please, Father, if you'd just try to persuade the old gentleman to take me on, he wouldn't regret it, I promise you."

Joseph was entirely at a loss for words. He found himself drawn to the child, did not want to be harsh with her. She was digging with the wrong foot, but he sensed she would not listen to such an incidental thing as reason. A man, even a priest, would be hard-pressed to topple Annie Delaney's dreams, he was sure.

Scratching his head, he drew a long sigh. Annie Delaney's gaze never wavered as Joseph groped for an acceptable response to her outrageous proposal.

≫

When Joseph met with Richard Nelson later that evening in the hospital waiting room, he found it difficult to describe his remarkable meeting with Annie Delaney.

What surprised him was that Sir Richard already knew about the peculiar wee lassie.

The aging Englishman sat in the rickety chair with the dignity of a monarch. Yet Joseph did not miss the trembling of his hands on the head of his cane or the quaking of his voice when he spoke. "Oh, dear, yes. The poor child has been hovering about the hospital day and night." He shook his head. "The nurses wanted to order her out any number of times, but I told them to let her alone, just so long as she doesn't disturb Morgan. She thinks we haven't noticed her, of course."

As he went on, his voice faltered, then took on new strength. Obviously, it was difficult for him to even speak of the incident that had felled his grandson. "Smith O'Brien says the child ran out into the street when Morgan was...shot. Began screaming at the bystanders to get help. Apparently she stayed right there in the street with him until the ambulance arrived. And she's been at the hospital almost every day since, I believe."

Sir Richard shook his head sadly. "I can't imagine what her family must be thinking, allowing her such freedom about the city!"

"She has no family—or so she says," Joseph put in.

The old man lifted tired, sad eyes to look at Joseph. "I was afraid it might be something like that. You don't suppose she's a bit dull-witted, do you? Shadowing Morgan as she does? It's most peculiar."

Joseph almost cracked a smile at the thought of Annie Delaney being dull-witted. The lass might be as flighty as a tinker's child—and certainly her behavior was somewhat odd. But dull-witted? Indeed, no! Why, hadn't she

marched out an entire parade of arguments—all surprisingly well posed—
to support her plea that Joseph entreat Sir Richard in her behalf? And there
had been something behind those intense black eyes—some clear, bright
glint of watchfulness—that signaled the presence of a sharp, even superior
intelligence.

"Whatever her reasons, she has fastened a great deal of hope on Morgan," Joseph said with a sigh. Inexplicably, he was reluctant to take the
child lightly. The fierce intensity, the solemn earnestness, of her plea had
moved him more than he would have thought.

"The child has asked me to speak with you," he said to Richard Nelson,
"in the hopes you might be persuaded to take her to Dublin, once Morgan
has recovered enough to go home."

Sir Richard stared at him incredulously, then gave a short burst of
laughter. "Why, the poor child! Was she serious, do you think?"

Joseph nodded, still disturbed by the memory of Annie Delaney's
fierce insistence. "Oh, she was serious, all right. The lass seems to fancy
herself involved with Morgan's life somehow. She is determined to go to
Dublin, to help take care of him."

"Good heavens! As if we haven't enough to deal with…" Nelson's words
drifted off, and he looked away, almost as if he had forgotten Joseph's presence entirely.

Joseph noted again how much the elderly Englishman had failed since
their first meeting in Dublin. His hands trembled continually, and his
every movement appeared to require great effort. He seemed to have aged
years in only months.

What *was* to be done about Morgan? Obviously his grandfather would
be of no help at all in the more practical aspects of his care. Faith, it was more
likely that Richard Nelson would soon need someone to look after *him*.

Joseph rose, wincing at the stiffness in his own aging bones. Going to
the window, he stood looking out. Dusk was gathering, and the candle-lit
windows of Belfast's shops and houses softened the mean gloom of the city.
He felt his own spirit darken with the dreariness of his surroundings.

"The child learned to read on Morgan's writings in *The Nation*," he
told Sir Richard, attempting to shake off his heavyhearted mood. "That
is likely one reason she feels so attached to him. He has become a type of
folk hero to her. You'd think she knows him, and knows him well, to hear
her speak of him."

"How peculiar," Sir Richard replied vaguely. "But of course, what she asks is quite impossible. She's only a little girl. She'd be more trouble than help."

Joseph turned to look at him. "What *are* you going to do, Sir Richard? Morgan will need a great deal of care, at least for an extended time, it would seem."

The poor man seemed beside himself with worry. "I have people looking into it now. He's going to need someone quite strong, of course. And thoroughly reliable." Nelson's voice faltered. "Certainly, I'll do all I can. But I'm afraid that will be precious little. I'm anxious to see him well settled…as soon as possible. If you could help us to find someone, I'd be most grateful."

Their eyes met, and Joseph shuddered at what he saw there. He had looked into the eyes of approaching death too many times not to recognize it when it stared back at him.

At the same moment a thought struck him about a companion for Morgan. He said nothing to Richard Nelson, wanting time to consider the idea. But it occurred to Joseph that he just might be able to help Morgan's grandfather with his dilemma.

Morgan had deliberately foregone the laudanum with the intention of being alert enough to catch his devious wee phantom. And, sure enough, there she was! A glimpse of shaggy dark hair and odd clothes—and she whisked out of sight!

"*You! Come back here!*" he ordered, leaning forward in the wheelchair.

He waited. When the doorway remained empty, he called again, this time more loudly. "*I know you heard me! Stop your skulking about and come here at once!*"

After a moment a face came into view, then the body attached to it—a small body, small and pathetically thin.

She was a disreputable-looking little creature—dust smudges on her chin, a scrape over the bridge of her nose.

"In here!" Morgan ordered.

She made no move, but simply stood staring at him with those bottomless black eyes.

"You're the imp my grandfather told me about. The one who saw me shot."

At last there was a sign of life. A stiff little nod of the head, a quirk of the mouth.

"I haven't the strength to shout at you from across the room. Come closer," Morgan commanded.

There was a long hesitation. Finally, hugging her arms tightly across her chest, she entered. In the middle of the room, she stood staring at him.

"So, then. Are you going to tell me your name?"

For a moment she seemed to consider his question.

"Annie Delaney. Annie Delaney is me name, sir."

Twisting his mouth at the grating Ulster accent, Morgan appraised her. Not quite clean, but more raggedy than dirty. She reminded him a bit of a hungry kitten.

How old? Eight? Nine? Perhaps older. "Well, Annie Delaney, I'm Morgan Fitzgerald. Should I be pleased to meet you at last?"

A grin broke across her face then, revealing a noticeable gap between her two front teeth. "Aye, sir, I should hope so."

Brazen little thing. "So—I am told you've been haunting my room, Annie Delaney. Would you be wanting to explain why?"

"Why...just to make certain you're getting better, sir. Sure, and didn't everyone think you were going to die?" Her eyes widened. Clearly, she had not meant to be quite so blunt.

Bemused by the gamin face and the bold air of assurance about the waif, Morgan lifted a questioning eyebrow. "And now that you know I will live, Annie Delaney, why do you still plague the nurses with your presence?"

Again came the grin, wider this time. "Your grandfather told them to let me be. So long as I didn't bother you, that is. Besides," she added saucily, "they can't catch me at all, don't you know?"

More than her share of brass. Morgan almost smiled back at her. "No, I don't imagine they could."

After another long pause, the lass's expression sobered. "In truth, I've been waiting for a proper time to speak with your grandfather. But today I decided I would talk with your friend the priest instead."

With the battered boy's cap perched jauntily atop the tousled hair and her hands thrust into the pockets of that abominable coat, she looked for all the world like a *Punch* caricature of the vulgar Irish street-child. All she needed was a broom.

"And what kind of important business would you be needing to discuss with my friend the priest?"

She considered him for a moment. The thin shoulders stiffened slightly, and Morgan realized Annie Delaney was not quite so confident as she would have him believe.

But by the time she gave her reply, the impudent tilt of the head and the cheeky grin were back in place. "Why, to tell you the truth, sir, I was hoping he could convince your grandfather to take me along to Dublin City with you, once you're feeling up to going home."

Morgan stared at the scrawny lass with a mixture of disbelief and growing sympathy. Obviously, she was somewhat daft. Just as obvious was the fact that she was looking for a home. It made him sad to realize there was nothing he could do about either of Annie Delaney's predicaments.

25

Whisper of Hope, Sigh of Regret

Come! Come to us, Angels of Hope and of Healing,
With chaplet of snowdrop and plumes of the dove...
RICHARD D'ALTON WILLIAMS (1822–1862)

New York City

Toward evening on the third day after Christmas, Daniel's condition seemed to take a turn for the worse. Lewis Farmington sent word by Uriah to Dr. Grafton, while Evan stayed at Nora's side.

Throughout the day, the boy had refused all nourishment, except for an occasional sip of lime water. His entire body was raw with the scarlet rash, and his skin felt moist and sticky. Apparently, his swollen throat gave him the most distress; at times he seemed near tears with the pain. Yet the fever itself had abated somewhat.

Nora was frantic with worry and reeling from exhaustion. Each time she tried to stand, Evan hovered near in case she should swoon. She had had precious little sleep for three days, had eaten only a few bites of the meals Ginger insisted on bringing to the cottage. She looked ghastly, and Evan found himself praying as fervently for her as for Daniel.

He drew a long sigh of relief when Dr. Grafton finally arrived, stamping his feet and apologizing for not coming sooner.

The snow that had begun Christmas night had turned into a major storm, virtually paralyzing the city. "I did my best to get here yesterday," the doctor explained, "but it was hopeless. The streets were simply impassable. Not that they're much better today."

Evan stood at Nora's elbow throughout the examination, half-fearing what they might hear. But when Dr. Grafton turned back to them, he gave an unexpected nod of satisfaction. "He's not out of the woods yet, but I'd say the worst is over. The fever is breaking. His throat is still badly inflamed," the physician cautioned, closing his medical case, "but I see no signs of ulcers on the tonsils. And his ears are clear." Again he nodded reassuringly. "Yes, I think we can be encouraged. He's finally showing some signs of real progress."

"Oh, thanks be to God!" Nora's voice was hoarse, her entire body trembling, as she caught Evan's arm.

"N-Nora, come, sit down," Evan urged her, helping her to a chair.

As soon as he touched her, fear gripped his heart. Her dress was warm and damp with perspiration; he could feel the heat of her skin through the fabric. *"Nora?"*

She sank down onto the chair without answering.

"Nora—are you all r-right?"

She looked up at him slowly. Apprehension knotted in Evan's stomach. Her eyes were red-rimmed, her face swollen. She made a weak gesture of protest with one hand, shaking her head. "It's nothing," she said thickly. "I'm...tired is all."

Evan glanced at Dr. Grafton, who quickly came around the bed. Frowning, he stood studying Nora. "Mrs. Kavanagh?"

As if deliberately evading his gaze, Nora stared down at the floor. The doctor's frown deepened. He took her pulse, then raised her chin, forcing her to look up at him.

In that moment Evan saw for himself the flush of fever on her damp skin.

Bending over her, Dr. Grafton traced both sides of Nora's neck with his fingertips. "Sore?"

She squeezed her eyes shut, then gave a reluctant nod.

The doctor shot a significant glance at Evan. "I'm afraid Mrs. Kavanagh also has scarlet fever."

Evan shut his eyes and heaved a ragged sigh. His own throat felt swollen; his stomach lurched.

But in his case it wasn't the fever. It was fear.

᠀᠙

Ever since the message had come Christmas night that Daniel was stricken with scarlet fever, guilt had stalked Tierney like a hungry wolf.

Things had not been right between him and Daniel for weeks, not since Da's encounter with Nora and the Englishman at the Opera House. Oh, they got along well enough on the surface, all right. But his own resentment had hung between them, creating an awkwardness, a tension that had not been there before. Hunched over a kitchen chair as he pulled on his boots, Tierney brooded about his surliness and wished he could undo it.

The kitchen was dim and shadowed. Outside, heavy clouds were drawing together across the winter sky, spreading a blanket of gloom over the city that matched his mood.

He had intended to visit Daniel the day after Christmas, but what with the fierce snowstorm and working double holiday shifts at the hotel, this was the first chance he'd had. He desperately wanted to see his friend, but at the same time he dreaded their meeting. He had tried to use his Christmas gift to set things right between them, but all the while he had clung to his anger. Daniel's feelings had been hurt, and it was Tierney's fault.

But *Da's* feelings had been hurt, too. A bewildered air of rejection had hung about the man for days, making it impossible for Tierney to put out of his mind what had happened.

Yet Da's attitude had been far more charitable than his own. As Tierney might have predicted, his father had defended the Farmingtons, insisting they were good people who were only being kind to the strangers they had taken into their home. To Tierney's barbed remarks about Nora's involvement with the Englishman, his da had merely given a small shrug and a weak defense.

Wasn't it understandable, he said, that Nora and Evan Whittaker might become friends? The man seemed a decent sort, after all, and they *were* practically living under the same roof—working for the same people, taking most of their meals together, going to the same church. Why *wouldn't* they be drawn to each other?

While his father's tolerance exasperated Tierney, it shouldn't have surprised him in the least. Da held no real grudge against the British, not like most of the Irish in New York. He was always one to allow others the benefit of the doubt—even the English.

Tierney would never understand his father. He was not a man to be shamed by his Irishness or to disavow it, as did some—like Patrick Walsh.

Indeed, Da did seem thoroughly comfortable with what he was and where he came from.

But just as he was not troubled in the least by being Irish, neither did he seem to possess any real nationalistic pride or patriotic fervor for Ireland. As he explained it himself, he was both an Irishman and an American and did not know that he wished to be more one than the other.

That was the part Tierney could not accept. For himself, being an American was something that had happened to him by sheer circumstance. As long as he could remember, he had known he would one day leave America for Ireland. He might be, as his father periodically reminded him, an *Irish American*, but in his heart he was far more *Irish* than American.

Da did not understand his feelings, not at all. Nor did Daniel, although he had been born and raised in Ireland.

Reaching for his coat and cap, Tierney wished Daniel's understanding did not matter so much. He had grown used to his father's resistance; he was older and set in his ways, after all. But Daniel, more than anybody else, ought to understand.

The fact that he *didn't* brought Tierney more pain than he liked to admit, even to himself.

The steps and walk around the Farmington mansion had been cleared. There was a carriage hitched in front, and Tierney stopped for a moment to admire the small chestnut mare.

At the front door, he lifted the heavy brass knocker and rapped sharply. The stiff-necked old black man—Uriah—opened the door after a long delay. He smiled in recognition, quickly sobering when Tierney inquired about Daniel.

"Why, the young sir is still ill with the fever, I'm afraid. He's been awful sick."

Tierney shifted restlessly from one foot to the other. "D'you think I could see him? Just for a bit?"

The black man's grizzled face creased to a deep frown. "Well now, Mr. Tierney, have you had the fever yourself?"

Tierney stalled. He had *not* had the fever; that's why Da had insisted he stay away from the Farmington mansion.

His hesitation was enough to put the elderly servant on guard. His eyes narrowed as he studied Tierney. "Mr. Daniel is confined to the cottage in back. And Dr. Grafton, he said nobody could go in who hadn't had the fever."

"The cottage in back? You mean where the Englishman stays?"

Uriah nodded. "That's right. Mr. Whittaker's rooms. The doctor is there now."

Tierney considered the old man's words for only a moment before stepping away from the door. "I'll just go around back, then," he said, turning away from Uriah. "Perhaps I can at least get some news from the doctor."

Without giving the old man time to protest, Tierney tore around the side of the mansion. He slipped on a patch of ice and almost fell. Regaining his balance, he went on, slowing his pace only a little.

Sara Farmington opened the cottage door. Her eyes widened with surprise when she saw him. "Why—Tierney Burke! Whatever are you doing here? You do know that Daniel is in bed with scarlet fever?"

Impatient with the delay, Tierney gave a brusque nod. "I'd like to see him, please."

He stepped forward, trying to peer around her into the cottage. Sara Farmington moved to block him from entering. "Tierney, have you had scarlet fever?" she asked skeptically.

He shrugged. "I wouldn't remember if I had. But I'm only wanting to say hello, not to be staying."

She didn't budge. "The doctor is with Daniel just now, Tierney. I'm afraid you can't go in."

"I should be allowed to see him, I think!" Tierney snapped, irked with her unyielding composure. He did not like this woman, or anything she stood for. In his opinion, Sara Farmington represented the coddled society class of New Yorkers who could view the Irish from only one perspective: looking down their noses. She was a do-gooder old maid who compensated for her dullness by running around the city performing "good deeds." She might impress everybody else—his da included—but she did not impress *him*. Her friendliness was an act, just like everything else about her.

For a moment he considered brushing right by her. He was taller than she and a good deal wider through the shoulders. She couldn't stop him.

But this *was* her property, after all. And he didn't want her blathering to his da that he'd been rude.

Drawing a deep breath, he flashed her a smile. "Couldn't I step inside just long enough to give him a wave? So he'd know I was here to ask about him?"

Seeing her expression soften somewhat, Tierney pressed his advantage. "I won't go near him at all, I promise I won't."

After another moment, she stepped aside. "Very well," she said with a rueful smile. "But just for a moment. I'm sorry Tierney—you *do* understand?"

He nodded vaguely. Without replying, he stepped across the threshold.

He saw Nora first, perched stiffly on a straight-backed chair. He knew at once that she was ill. The doctor was standing, his arms crossed over his chest, watching her as he spoke with Evan Whittaker. The Englishman stood close to Nora, his lean bearded face drawn taut with worry.

Tierney stared at them. For a moment, he seemed to step inside his da's shoes. As he stood there watching Evan Whittaker and Nora, something deep within him wrenched and caught.

He liked Nora. Indeed, he liked her a great deal. Seeing her so, looking ill and distraught—with the Englishman standing at her side as if he had every right to be there—he felt a fierce stab of alarm for Nora, then an ever sharper plunge of outrage.

It should be *Da* with Nora now. Da should be the one looking after her and Daniel, not Evan Whittaker.

Forcing himself to look away, Tierney's gaze found Daniel. He was lying on his side in a big, comfortable-looking bed. The bed linen was tucked snugly under his chin. His eyes were shut.

He looked *dreadful*—thin, and ever so ill! His face was ablaze with the strawberry rash, and he didn't seem to be moving at all.

But as Tierney stood staring at him, Daniel's eyes fluttered open. He stared back at Tierney, his gaze slowly registering surprise. Then his mouth went slack with a weak, lopsided grin.

Relieved, Tierney grinned back and raised a hand in salute. "Well, then, and aren't you looking swell, Danny-boy? A bit like a scalded pig."

Daniel's grin tilted even more, but he said nothing.

Clearly, he was too weak even for jokes. Sara Farmington cleared her throat meaningfully, and Tierney nodded to indicate he understood. With a final wave, he turned and followed her out the door.

He started to go without saying anything more, then changed his mind. Just outside the door, he turned back.

"Nora?" he said uncertainly. "Is she—"

Sara Farmington didn't wait for him to finish. Her face reflected a weary sadness when she answered. "Yes. It's scarlet fever. The doctor just ordered her to bed a few moments before you came." She paused, glanced away, then looked back at him. "Tell your father. He'll want to know."

More troubled now than when he came, Tierney whipped around. Tugging his cap down hard on his head, he hurried down the walk without answering.

26

A Heavy Sorrow

'Tis hard to see God's lights above,
While clouds and darkness bound us;
'Tis hard to hear God's words of love
With storms like those around us.

MARY KELLY (1825–1910)

Sara Farmington sat in a dilapidated wooden rocking chair just inside the door of the hospital room. With a lump in her throat, she observed the two men in Nora's life. Whether her heart ached more for Evan Whittaker's desperate watchfulness or Michael Burke's grim mask of helplessness, she could not have said. Like two sentinels they stood, one on either side of Nora's bed, each seemingly unaware of the other's presence as they kept their silent vigil.

Perhaps the obvious anxiety of the two men only served to intensify her own fear for Nora, who had become a friend. Until taking Nora into their home, Sara had never felt the need for a woman friend. Over the years, Ginger, who had been with their household ever since Sara could remember, had become a kind of older sister and confidant. Yet, there had always been an elusive air about the West Indies housekeeper, a subtle quality of self-containment, that Sara had known, even as a child, would not be breached.

Besides, in the absence of a mother, both Sara and her brother, Gordie, had come to accept Ginger's influence in matters of discipline. Consequently, Ginger's involvement in their lives, while one of love and nurturing, was also necessarily one of authority.

In Nora Kavanagh, however, Sara had at last discovered the kind of friendship other women her age seemed to take for granted. Nora had gradually relaxed enough to laugh in Sara's presence, even to share a secret now and then. More recently, they had gone on numerous Christmas shopping expeditions together. Sara had even managed to coax her new friend into accompanying her to mission bazaars at the church and on her bi-weekly visits to Grandmother Platt—"Grandy Clare."

Grandy Clare had taken to pressing at least one gift—some small frippery or knickknack—upon the two of them at the end of each visit. Wide-eyed, Nora would balance Grandy's gift on her lap with the greatest of care all the way home as if it were a priceless, irreplaceable treasure.

Wonderfully free of pretension, Nora had an almost childlike appreciation of the smallest things that never failed to delight Sara. In spite of her widowhood and the tragedy of her life, she had somehow retained an air of girlish innocence about her that Sara suspected would never quite fade. Younger by more than seven years, Sara invariably felt herself to be the older.

Leaning wearily back in the rocker, Sara reflected on the past few days. Daniel was getting better. His skin was still blotched, and he was terribly weak from days of fever and lack of nourishment, but yesterday he'd begun to sit up for brief periods of time, had even walked around the room once or twice on wobbly legs. With the wonderful resiliency of the young, he was already taking soft food at regular intervals and showing every sign of a speedy recovery.

Sara's gaze returned to the hospital bed. She bit her lip in apprehension at the sight of Nora's small, still form, flanked by Evan and Michael Burke. For two days Nora had been like this, motionless and deathly quiet, except for an infrequent whimper or an abrupt cry of pain. While the scarlet rash that marred her pale skin was not so angry or pervasive as Daniel's had been, her fever remained dangerously high—high enough that Nicholas Grafton had warned them of the likelihood of convulsions. He made no attempt to disguise his concern about the dropsy that had set in during the afternoon, leaving Nora's face and extremities severely bloated.

After another brief examination late in the evening, he had drawn Sara to one side, warning, "She couldn't be much worse and still be alive. Her kidneys aren't functioning as they should, and it's putting enormous strain on her heart. I think we'd best hospitalize her right away."

Stunned and frightened, Sara had hurried from the cottage and gone in search of her father and Evan. Now, hours later, she sat wringing her handkerchief into a thin rope, waiting, praying for some improvement in Nora's condition. For one of the few times in her life, she felt afraid and utterly helpless.

A shadow fell across her vision, and she looked up. Michael Burke was standing in front of her. Lately, his features seemed set in a permanent frown. He had taken to passing a hand over his chest in a distracted gesture that made Sara wonder if the gunshot wound he'd received months before was still plaguing him.

"Did the doctor say how long it might be before he comes back?" he asked, putting a fist to his mouth to stifle a yawn.

Sara shook her head. "Just that he had a baby to deliver. I'm sure he'll be here as soon as he can."

He gave a vague nod, saying nothing.

The lines around his eyes had deepened with fatigue, Sara noticed, just as his normally light brogue had thickened. The poor man had neither slept nor shaved in two days; he hadn't been home since learning of Nora's illness. He looked drawn and worried and terribly sad.

He walked away, returning to his bedside vigil without another word. Watching the slump to his shoulders, Sara could not help but wonder if the ordeal of the last two days was not forcing the widowed policeman to relive the agony of his wife's death.

Eileen Burke had died of cancer years before, when Tierney was still a small boy—a prolonged, agonizing death, according to Nora. Had Michael waited beside *her* bed, as he now waited beside Nora's?

What excruciating pain it must be for such a man—a man accustomed to rescuing and taking care of others, a man who seemed to live most of his life from a position of power and authority—to simply stand by and look on as the one he loved most in the world slipped away, beyond his reach.

The likelihood that he had passed this way before, through this shadowed valley of despair, made Sara want to weep aloud for him. She ached for his pain, longed to comfort him. As she silently grieved for *Nora's* agony, so did she also grieve for Michael Burke's.

Hands clenched behind his back, Michael stood beside the hospital
bed, across from Whittaker. Other than a tacit acknowledgment of the
other's presence, neither had made any attempt to engage in conversation
since Nora's admission to the hospital. They talked with Sara Farmington
and the nurses. They spoke with the doctor. But to each other, they offered
no more than a brief nod or a shake of the head as they stood watching
Nora's agony in silence, powerless to help.

With Eileen, he had waited alone....

Tierney had been too young, too much the child, to suffer more than
brief intervals of the sickroom. Even at the end, as Eileen finally slipped
away, Michael had stood by her bed alone until it was over.

Her agony had gone on for months. Months of watching the cancer destroy her womanhood as it stripped her of her dignity, her youthful
beauty, her will to live. To Michael, it had seemed like forever.

He had done everything he knew to keep her with him, had urged her
to fight long past the time when she had the strength to fight. When she
finally gave up, he attempted to ward off the Grim Reaper for her. Eileen
had even attempted a weak joke, about what kind of foolish disease was it,
that would dare to go head-on with Michael Burke.

But she had known—they had both known—who would ultimately
win the battle. At the last, she had wanted to die, had murmured that he
should let her go, should quit fighting the inevitable and release her to
the peace of death.

He had fled the room, shutting himself inside the supply closet across
the hall, cramming a towel against his mouth to muffle the explosive cries
of his rage and anguish. When he returned to the room, Eileen scarcely
knew he was there. Minutes later, she was gone.

Never before, and never since, had Michael known such anger as he
knew during the last hours of her suffering. Anger at the demon-disease,
at the impotent doctors, at God—but mostly anger at his own unfamiliar helplessness.

Now, feeling his throat tighten with unshed tears, he drew a shaky
breath and straightened his shoulders. For an instant his gaze met and
held Evan Whittaker's. Seeing his own despair mirrored in the Englishman's eyes, Michael clenched his hands even more tightly behind his back
and looked away.

With a force of will he had mastered during the time of Eileen's illness, he put aside the image of his wife's tormented face, her pain-wracked, wasted body, the sound of her voice crying his name.

At last he turned back to Nora. Nora was still alive. As far as he could tell, she was not dying. At least she seemed no worse than she'd been when they brought her to the hospital. There was still hope for Nora.

The beginning of a prayer rose in Michael's heart, and he closed his eyes to let his spirit give it voice.

Evan supposed he shouldn't be surprised to realize that Michael Burke was praying. The man was a Christian, after all. Why *wouldn't* he pray, especially at a time such as this?

Still, it *did* surprise him, perhaps because the brawny Irish policeman always appeared to be so self-assured, so confident—as if he had any and all situations under control.

For his own part, Evan had been praying most of the evening. Indeed it seemed he had not *stopped* praying for days, what with Daniel's ordeal with this dread disease, and now Nora's.

The boy had been extremely ill—frighteningly ill. But Nora was much, much worse. Dr. Grafton's insistence that she be hospitalized at such a late hour indicated with a chilling certainty just how critical her condition must be.

For the first two hours after her admission, the private room had been alive with frowning nurses and two grim-visaged doctors, in addition to Nicholas Grafton. That Lewis Farmington had wielded his considerable influence, Evan had no doubt. An Irish immigrant on her own would not be afforded a private room, even if by some miracle there had been money to pay. But a private room *and* the finest in medical attention?

Only a Lewis Farmington could arrange *that*.

Evan could not help but wonder about the dangerously ill immigrants who had no Lewis Farmington to do battle for them. For them, there would be no hospital room, no doctor—not even a place of refuge or shelter from the cold.

Evan had seen for himself what became of the homeless, destitute immigrant who had no "people in the city"—no friends to provide haven or hope. Twice now he had visited the abysmal Five Points slum district with Pastor Dalton. He had looked into the eyes of the homeless, the ill, and the dying, and found himself devastated by the anguish and utter hopelessness that looked back at him.

He could only wonder at the courage and the vision of a man like Jess Dalton, who dared to think he could actually make a difference amid such an ocean of misery. During his last visit to Five Points, Evan had felt a stirring in his spirit that later, in the comfortable warmth of the Farmington cottage, had seemed to strengthen to a challenge. And he had known then, with no small amount of apprehension that God was confronting him, forcing him to face his feelings of horror and outrage—and asking him what *he* was willing to do to make a difference.

Until Daniel had come down with this awful illness, his intention had been to talk with Jess Dalton after Christmas about what he might do to help in the work of the Five Points mission. Now, he could not think beyond this room, this night—and Nora.

Shaky with exhaustion and at the edge of despair, Evan rubbed first one temple, then the other. He'd had one of his headaches most of the evening, vicious enough to make him sick to his stomach. No longer able to stand, he eased himself down on the chair beside the bed. Sara Farmington was seated in the only other chair in the room, a rickety wooden rocker near the door.

Michael Burke gave him a cursory look, then glanced away. Evan sighed, too weary to consider the Irish policeman's feelings about his being here. If Burke thought he'd stepped out of his place, well, then, let him. The man had no claim on Nora. At least not yet.

Unless Nora herself should tell him to leave, Evan would remain. The truth was, he was *afraid* to leave. Afraid she might simply…slip away.

He lost his breath at the thought. Squeezing his eyes shut, he swallowed hard. Did it show a lack of trust on his part, this obsessive need to stand guard over her? Was it his own fear or the Lord's urging that he continue to do battle for her in prayer?

Or…was it the fact that he loved her beyond all reason, that he could not bear the thought of being anywhere but close to her?

A breeze fanned the room when the door suddenly opened. Everyone turned to look as Pastor Dalton entered.

It seemed to Evan that whenever the tall, ruddy-faced pastor walked into a room, it somehow grew a bit brighter. It was almost as if the man wore a mantle of hope over his broad, sturdy shoulders.

No matter the circumstances, Jess Dalton had a way of bringing light to his surroundings. Even Michael Burke's bleak gaze warmed somewhat at the sight of the big pastor.

Dalton had visited both Daniel and Nora numerous times during their illness, but Evan would have not expected him to call at the hospital at so late an hour. If Lewis Farmington had sent for the pastor, perhaps Nora's condition was even worse than he feared. Evan tried to push the sickening thought out of his mind as the clergyman greeted Sara Farmington, then approached Nora's bed. "Any change?" he asked, including both Evan and Michael Burke in his nod of greeting.

The policeman shook his head. "They gave her more laudanum. She's been sleeping...a long time."

Evan stood. As always, he felt both dwarfed by Dalton's size and cheered by his presence.

The pastor's eyes went to Nora, and his soft blue gaze filled with compassion. "She has suffered a great deal—and in so many ways. My wife would say that Nora's life has been one of heavy sorrow."

As he spoke, he moved closer to the bed and clasped Nora's thin hand in his. The ghost of a sad smile went over his features as he continued to hold her hand and gaze down at her.

Finally he released her hand. Looking first at Evan, then toward the foot of the bed where Michael Burke was standing, he said, "You men look exhausted. I don't suppose I could convince either of you to get some rest?"

Burke merely shook his head.

"N-Not...yet," Evan murmured.

The pastor nodded, then gestured for Sara Farmington to join them. "Let's pray together," he said simply, motioning that they should join hands with him.

It was left for Evan to clasp the large, strong hand of Michael Burke as the four of them gathered round Nora's bed.

"Father, you know the love for Nora Kavanagh that abides in the hearts gathered here in this room," Dalton began. "Help us to remember, though, that Nora is Your child, that You love her more than we can even imagine. Lord, we pray with faith in that love, with total trust in the goodness and the wisdom of that love."

As always, the pastor's gentle voice belied his intimidating size. "We understand that it is Your right to heal or not to heal, Father. But often, when you *don't* heal, we either doubt the quality of our faith or the reality of Your mercy." Dalton paused, then went on. "Remind us of the truth, that Your sovereign will does not depend upon our faith, nor can Your mercy ever be understood by our finite minds. Our part is to trust Your mercy and acknowledge Your right to fulfill Your purposes—in Your own way, in Your own time. Surely we can do that much, Father. Surely we can trust the mercy…and the love…of a Lord who would die for us. *Surely we can trust the Lord of the Cross…*."

As Dalton prayed, the pain in Evan's heart slowly gave way to a warm, renewing peace. For the first time since the ugly disease had felled Nora, he was able to unreservedly surrender her to the Lord's mercy…to His perfect love.

For just an instant, he was even able to smile a little to himself at the irony of his hand, almost frail by comparison, clasped securely in the hard strength of Michael Burke's.

At the same time a dear, familiar hymn began to swell inside his spirit. On a long-ago golden autumn day, he had gone to South Place Chapel in London to worship. There he had heard, for the first time, a sweet and splendid hymn that had slipped into his heart and remained there ever since, like a gentle, shining gift of faith.

Never had the words sounded quite as clearly in his soul, never had they meant quite as much, as they did now.

"Nearer, my God, to Thee, Nearer to Thee, E'en though it be a cross that raiseth me…."

Until the others joined their own voices, one at a time, with his, Evan had not realized that he'd begun to sing aloud. For a moment he was embarrassed. Yet he went on, the voices around him rising and growing stronger with his.

As Jess Dalton prayed, and as the hymn rose sweetly over Nora's hospital bed, Evan did think he could sense a gathering of angels in the room and a Fatherly embrace around them all.

27

Nora's Dream

When sleep, sorrow's tomb with her flowery wand sealing,
The soft pall of silence o'er Life's battle flings,
Then glimpses of Eden in visions revealing,
O'ershadow our rest with your sheltering wings....
RICHARD D'ALTON WILLIAMS (1822–1862)

Long past midnight, Jess Dalton trudged heavily upstairs. He had his hand on the doorknob of the master bedroom before remembering that it was temporarily occupied by Arthur Jackson. Quietly he turned, then tip-toed down the hall to the guest room.

He stopped just inside the door. Kerry was curled up beneath a quilt in the enormous upholstered rocking chair by the window. She looked childlike, and troubled.

"Kerry? Whatever are you doing up so late, love?"

"Waiting for you. I couldn't sleep."

Shrugging out of his suit coat, Jess crossed the room. "And why *can't* you sleep?" Lifting her, he took her place in the rocker, then settled her snugly onto his lap.

As she often did, she replied to his question with one of her own. "How did you find the Kavanagh lad, Jess? And Nora?"

He hesitated, reluctant to distress her at such a late hour.

"Nora is worse, isn't she?" Kerry persisted.

Jess drew a deep, weary sigh, nodding. "Daniel is better. Much improved, in fact. But Nora—Nora isn't doing very well as yet."

Kerry nodded as if she'd known what he was going to say. "I had almost dozed off," she said, "but all of a sudden didn't I find myself wide awake? And with a fierce need to be praying for Nora Kavanagh."

Jess was accustomed to this sort of unpredictable behavior from his wife. Over the years, he had come to recognize her uncommon sensitivity to the urging of God's Spirit. He had learned to trust and respect what others might have deemed "coincidence."

He kissed her lightly on the cheek, gathering her more closely against him. "Nora needs all of us praying for her tonight," he said quietly. "In fact, I'm going back to the hospital. I only came home to leave a note in case you awakened, so you wouldn't worry."

Drawing back, Kerry frowned at him. "But, Jess, you've been up since dawn! Couldn't you just rest a few hours?"

"No," he said slowly, sorely tempted. "I think I'd best go back."

Her eyes went over his face with an unspoken question.

Resting his head against the padded chair, Jess met her gaze. "She's very ill, Kerry. *Very* ill."

Kerry's reply was to bury her face against his shoulder.

Neither of them spoke for the next few moments, but simply sat rocking slowly back and forth, thinking their own thoughts and taking comfort from each other. Finally, Jess stirred. Reluctantly, he set Kerry on her feet and got up. "If I sit here any longer, I'll fall asleep."

She nodded, measuring his appearance with a worried frown. "All right, then. But could we pray together before you go, Jess? I haven't finished praying for Nora this night."

In Evan Whittaker's cottage, Daniel woke with a start, sitting bolt upright in bed.

The sudden movement brought a fierce stab of pain to his head, then a wave of dizziness. Propping himself up on his elbows, he waited, listening.

For what?

His mother was in danger.

A cold touch of fear traced the back of his neck and traveled the length of his spine. He looked round the room. The candle had burned low, indeed was almost gone. In a rocking chair near the door Ginger sat, dozing. The fire barely glowed in the small fireplace across the room. Daniel felt chilled clear through.

Mother. Where was she? What had happened?

Then he remembered. They had taken her to the hospital.

A wave of dread for his mother swelled inside him. Not wanting to wake Ginger, dreading the weakness that seized him every time his feet touched the floor, Daniel quietly got to his knees in the middle of Evan's big bed. He squeezed his eyes shut and began to pray.

Nora knew this was a dream. She understood that she was more spectator than participant, more asleep than awake.

And yet she was moving. No...'twas only that the bed seemed to move. She felt bound to it, one with it. When it first tilted and began to drift, she found she could not separate herself from it. It was as if she had no power of her own, no freedom of movement.

All was darkness and shadow. And silence. Not the silence of a quiet place, but the foreboding stillness of the unknown. And she was alone. Alone as she had never been before.

At first it was terrifying. She felt herself to be entirely at the mercy of the blackness around her, yet somehow knew it held...nothing. The darkness engulfing her was damp and cold, the air itself heavy and deadly still.

After what seemed an interminable time, she gradually became aware of a faint splashing sound, like water lapping against a rocky seawall.

She must be in a cave.

The bed suddenly tilted. Terrified of falling off into the vast darkness, Nora dug the fingers of both hands into the mattress.

She felt lightheaded, then sick. Again the bed rocked, plunging her even deeper into the cave. A fierce pounding started up inside her head, a relentless volley of crashing blows, one after another. The blood in her veins pulsed with the same furious rhythm, and her heart slammed madly against her chest.

Voices...somewhere around her, there were voices. Whisperings and murmurings. Or was it only the water splashing against the cavern walls?

Suddenly, in the distance, the wall of the cave seemed to open.

Slowly, ever so slowly, a small circle of light appeared. As Nora watched, the light rose and expanded, growing larger and brighter until finally it did seem to be a spray of stars.

Wondrous sight...

She tried to sit up, but instead found herself frozen in place. Still, the light spread, filling the far wall of the cave. It began to move toward her, and as it approached it swallowed the darkness.

Again Nora strained to move, this time reaching, groping toward the light, which was coming steadily closer. It seemed to beckon, to greet her.

The murmuring around her grew louder, then ebbed and faded until it was gone. Now there came a new sound, the slow, gentle rising of soft voices singing in the distance. An entire chorus of voices, each different, yet flowing and blending as one glorious instrument. The music swelled, the rhythm thundered, a thousand voices welcoming the light with a glory that filled the cave and filled Nora's mind and her heart as if to prepare her.

Prepare her for the approaching light...

Now there was no darkness. There was only the light and its warmth and the sound of singing.

Oh, beautiful, beautiful sounds of joy!

Nora could feel the warmth, the sweet glow of the light, knew it would enfold her any moment. Anxious for its embrace, she reached out her hands, straining to welcome it—and suddenly realized it was not the light that was moving, but she herself.

At the center of the dream, she walked, then ran, toward the light. The light was everything now, it was existence itself. There was nothing behind her, nothing around her, only the light. She was inside it. She lifted her face to let it spray on her, opened her arms to let it bathe her and gather her inside its glory—

Suddenly, there was a pause in the wonder.

The sound of singing waned. The light did not recede or fade, but seemed to take a soft breath. Without actually touching her, it somehow urged her forward.

She was led through the narrowest of valleys until it widened more, still more, opening onto a brilliant, sun-washed field.

Nora stood, breathless. The field filled up her vision, indeed, seemed to fill the entire universe. There were no mountains, no rivers—there was not even a sky overhead! Only the field, mile after mile of verdant grass and boundless rows of flowers. *Eire* in all its high summer splendor had never been so lovely!

Flowers everywhere. Wild flowers of lace and delicate filigree. Exotic flowers, lush and rich blooms, heavy with fragrance. Tall garden flowers, waving, and small flowers, smiling and peeping through individual blades of grass.

And everywhere, all among the riot of colors frolicking in the field, children and grown-ups worked and played and danced among the flowers! Some were planting new seeds, others gathering bouquets. From the lips of the children spilled laughter and sparkling songs and happy sighs. Mature faces—mature, and yet fresh and young and sweetly innocent—smiled and offered a cherishing word or a touch of affection to one another as they worked and sang.

Nora was led closer, closer still. Her eyes widened with glad amazement. *Owen? Was it truly Owen, her husband?*

He stooped to gather flowers, then straightened and passed them, a blossom at a time, to a small group of laughing children.

Her children—hers and Owen's!

Nora cupped her mouth with both hands, staring at the children. Oh, wasn't it Tahg himself? Her own firstborn! But see him now, Lord—just see him now! Tall and straight and strong again—strong as he had never been in his brief, fragile lifetime! With the bloom of youth on his cheeks and a harvest of flowers in his arms, which he was scattering in the path of a small black-haired girl—

Ellie!

Ellie, her baby girl! Tears spilled from Nora's eyes as she breathed the name of her youngest child, the sound of it like a caress on her lips. Sweet Ellie, with her thick, glossy black curls, her face round and shining as she bounced and danced among the flowers strewn at her feet by her father.

Nora cried out with yearning, lunged to run to them. But the light restrained her, gently cautioned her to wait.

Wait...

And so she waited, aching and longing to join Owen and the children, yet unable to disobey the constraining touch on her arm.

Then a man appeared, a straight, tall man with clean overalls and a lustrous white beard. *Old Dan!* The grandfather, the old dear himself! He came striding across the field, strong and vigorous, healthy, as if he were in his very prime again! On one broad shoulder he carried an infant, and in the crook of his arm another babe.

The tears flowed freely as Nora cried aloud. These were her babies, then. The poor wee things who had died during their birthing. Now plump and cheerful, they cooed and sighed like new baby doves in the old man's arms.

Old Dan turned, and for a moment Nora thought he had seen her! But, no, it was as if she did not exist for any one of them; even Owen seemed oblivious to her presence.

Oh, Lord...Lord! I want them to see me! I want to go to them, to be with them.

As Nora wept, her heart straining toward her loved ones, her arms aching to hold them, others came rushing through the flowers. Leaping and laughing, they sprayed color and fragrance all about the field.

Some she did not recognize, others she did. Many she had last seen lying dead in Killala's ditches, dead of the Hunger and the fever. Now they laughed and danced in a great field of star-flowers!

Nora caught her breath at the sight of a man and a woman among the children. Thomas! Thomas and Catherine! Clad in a simple farmer's garb, Thomas's long, kind face was no longer plain and sorrowful; instead, it shone with a wondrous joy, as did Catherine's.

Thomas opened his arms and dozens of children bobbed up and down—one of them his own Katie—begging to be held. Somehow he managed to scoop them all up and give them a kiss and a hug before setting them down among the flowers.

Nora sobbed and pitched herself forward, straining, yearning to have them see her and to be a part of their joy. Yet she knew it was not to be.

Reluctantly, she held back. As she stood at the edge of the field of glory, the singing gradually swelled from clear, childlike songs to a communal anthem of praise that swept across the valley like a great and mighty wind.

Unexpectedly, Nora felt the light leave her. Cold and bereft, she shuddered, aching to follow. But there was still a caution on her to remain where she was. She could watch, but not take part.

Such a coldness, a sorrow in her soul...

The light moved across the field, illuminating the flowers and the singers in a pure, crystal glow.

Breathless, Nora blinked. When she looked again she beheld the light settling over the far end of the field—the horizon where the flowers seemed to end and yet, she knew, did not end at all.

Now every face turned to the light, and there began a veritable stampede of running feet, excited laughter, and rolling shouts of joy. Nora could see nothing but the light and the happy throngs racing toward it.

With relief, she felt the coldness in her spirit recede, sensed a suntouched smile upon her face. A gentle hand seemed to brush away her tears as her loved ones were enfolded by the golden light.

Again Nora spread her arms and reached out, tried once more to step into the field. Again she felt the kind but firm admonition to remain where she was.

For now...

Suddenly, she felt herself being turned, then led away from the glory-lighted field of flowers. She cried out, flailed her hands—and touched the hard, unyielding bed beneath her.

It was only a dream....

Only a dream...but she was afraid. Afraid of falling, falling into the darkness of the silent cave. Afraid of being alone again.

The pounding in her head returned, swelling to a deafening roar. Her heart tripped, then began to race like a fury.

The light and the flowers were fast flying away, the field growing smaller and smaller in the distance. Faster and faster she fell, spiraling, tumbling back into the unknown darkness, away from the blessed light and the happy children.

The singing stopped. The fragrance faded. The field disappeared. She was terrified. She opened her mouth to cry out, to awaken from the dream. She breathed the name of Christ and clung to its echo in her spirit.

Again came the whispering, the murmuring nearby.

The sound of singing was no more, but the words went on.

Praying...someone was praying.

Evan...

Nora felt the strength and the warmth of his love flowing over her as he prayed. *Evan...*

"*Evan!*"

28

Love Found, Love Lost

I sat with one I love last night,
She sang to me an olden strain;
In former times it woke delight,
Last night—but pain.

GEORGE DARLEY (1795–1846)

Michael felt as if someone had punched him in the stomach. His initial relief at seeing Nora return from what he'd feared to be the edge of death had been harshly replaced by an aching disappointment when she cried out for Evan Whittaker.

He had thought she was dying....

For long, agonizing moments she had seemed suspended between senselessness and a kind of terrifying nightmare world.

She had wept and cried aloud, thrashing wildly about on the bed as if caught in a trap. Groping and flailing, she would first reach out, then hug her arms to her body as if to warm herself.

Michael had truly thought she was in the final throes of the death dance as he looked on in mute helplessness. Once he had to turn away, unable to bear the all too familiar scene.

Whittaker had held her hand, his very presence soothing her at the peak of her struggle. And Whittaker's name was on her lips like a cry for help or a desperate prayer when she finally awakened.

But hadn't he known for a long time now how things were? Hadn't he at least suspected? The way her eyes softened whenever she spoke of the Englishman, the bond he had sensed when he saw them together, especially that night at the Opera House?

Because he could not bolt from the room like a thwarted schoolboy, he clenched his fists and forced a grimace of a smile. He watched the Englishman fumble to hold Nora. God forgive him, Michael even found a certain grim satisfaction in Whittaker's one-armed clumsiness!

Then an enormous tide of self-disgust rose in his throat, choking off his breath. Somehow he managed to step away from the bed and make for the door without running.

Sara Farmington had risen from her chair and stood, hands clenched in front of her, watching him.

Why must the woman always be present to witness my humiliation?

For an instant, their eyes met and held. But when Michael saw what looked for all the world like pity in her gaze, he swallowed down his pain and squared his shoulders. "The nurse said they're to be notified if there's any change," he managed to say. "I'll go."

Brushing by her, he hurried out the door before she could reply.

Sara watched his stiff-backed exit with growing dismay. When she turned back to Evan and Nora, she saw that, at least for the moment, they were unaware of anyone else in the room.

She wanted to follow Michael, but hesitated at the memory of his taut, unyielding countenance. She had no doubt that he would resent—and rebuff—any attempt on her part to ease his feelings. Yet his implacable resolve to show no emotion whatsoever grieved her more than if he had gone flying out of the room in despair.

He was a proud man, Michael Burke. Proud and unbending, despite occasional hints of an unexpected vulnerability. Perhaps the wisest thing to do would be to ignore the hurt she had seen in his eyes, the searing pain of rejection. No doubt that would be what he would want her to do.

Concern for him warred with caution; concern won, and Sara hurried from the room in pursuit.

Evan had never known the conflict of emotions that now rioted within him. Relief—blessed, heart-filling relief—crested wave after wave of other feelings, each overwhelming in its intensity. Even as he held her, felt the dampness of her temple against his cheek, his heart soared with relief and sang a song of thanksgiving.

Oh, how he did love her! And she was returned to him, returned from wherever she had gone during the awful hours of the long, agonizing night.

"Oh, Nora…I was so f-frightened! You've n-no idea how worried I've been—how worried *all* of us have b-been for you!"

"Was I really that ill, then, Evan?" Her voice was weak, her hand limp, but she was alive—alive!

He brought his face still closer to hers. "Yes, you were, and I was f-frightened half to d-death!"

Her eyes misted. "I had such a dream, Evan. Such a strange, wonderful dream."

"A dream? What sort of a d-dream?"

She turned her eyes toward the ceiling, not answering right away. When she looked at him again there was uncertainty in her eyes. "It—it may sound foolish if I tell it aloud. But to me…at the time…it seemed such a splendid thing.…"

"T-Tell me, Nora. I won't think it's f-foolish. I p-promise I won't," he said as he gently lowered her to the pillow and held her hand.

She wept as she spoke in whispers, pausing every few words to swallow painfully. The tears trailed down her cheeks as she told of seeing the family she had lost, the field of glory, the beauty and the splendor and the light.

"Oh, such a light it was!" she murmured, the wonder still in her soft voice when she had finished her telling of the dream. "Sure, and I'll never forget it! Somehow I feel it's still here, inside me." She touched her heart. "It's almost as if I'd been touched by a star."

She laid her other hand on his arm. "What do you suppose it all meant, Evan? What kind of a dream would this be?"

Evan's gaze went over her face, drinking in her wonder and making it his own. It was difficult to give voice to what he believed the dream to be. "Why…I think you m-might have had a d-dream of heaven, Nora."

She stared at him. "Truly?"

Loving the way she was clinging to his arm, Evan echoed "Truly."

After a moment, she nodded. "Evan…could it be, then, that it was a kind of gift—to dream of heaven, so?"

"A g-gift, Nora?"

"Aye," she said, again nodding as she explained. "I was allowed to see my family—all of them, even the wee babes who died in their first hours—I was allowed to see them whole and happy and rejoicing together in that beautiful, glorious place! Sure, and what else could such a dream be, if not a gift?"

Seeing the light reflected in her eyes, the smile of wonder on her lips, Evan could only murmur, "What else, indeed?"

"How could such a thing happen?" she mused softly. "How?"

Perhaps because you were so close, my love…closer than any of us knew… closer than we dared to admit….

When he made no reply, Nora seemed to assume that he, like she, had no answer. After a moment her eyes swept the room with sudden awareness. "Michael? Didn't I see Michael and Sara here, in the room?"

Evan, too, turned to look, suddenly embarrassed at the emotion he had unthinkingly displayed ever since she'd awakened. With great relief, he saw that they were alone. "They m-must have gone for the nurse," he said, turning back to her. "B-But, yes, they've b-been here all along."

Her eyes went over his face. "You were praying for me, weren't you, Evan?"

"Why, of c-course, I was praying for you, Nora. Constantly."

Nora shook her head, squeezing her eyes shut for an instant as if even so small an effort exhausted her. "No, I mean just before I awakened," she explained, opening her eyes. "You were beside me, praying."

He nodded slowly. "Why…yes. B-But not just me. We've all been praying…m-most of the night. M-Michael Burke and Miss Sara—and Pastor D-Dalton was here earlier…."

She smiled, again closing her eyes. "But it was *your* prayer I heard, Evan."

Evan's throat tightened. He had not once prayed aloud. "And you were holding my hand," she said softly, her eyes still closed.

"Yes," he murmured, "I was." Without thinking, he brought her hand to his lips and held it there. When he realized what he'd done, he was embarrassed. But Nora seemed not to mind. Her eyes were open as she lifted an unsteady hand to wipe away her tears. Then, touching her hair, she uttered a small sound of disgust. "How ugly I must look!"

Evan shook his head in protest. It didn't matter in the least that her face was puffy and peeling from the rash, that her eyes were red-rimmed and smudged with shadows of illness. She was awake, she had escaped from the clutches of the fever—indeed, from the clutches of death. She was *beautiful*!

"You wo-wouldn't know how to look ugly, Nora! D-Don't even think such a thing!"

A dubious smile touched her lips. "Ach, and would you listen to the man?"

After a moment her expression sobered. "Evan?" Her eyes searched his as if trying to read his thoughts. "Thank you."

He stared at her. "For *what*, Nora?"

She blinked, and he saw that her eyes were again glazed with tears. "For caring enough about me to pray as you did, for…holding on to me. In your heart."

"N-Nora!" he blurted out. "You are so dear to me! I could not b-bear to lose you!" Dismayed at his reckless admission, Evan quickly turned his face away.

The gentle touch of her hand on his bearded cheek took his breath away. "Why, Evan, you are dear to my heart, as well. But didn't you know?"

Evan was not at all sure he could express the words that had been in his heart for months. The hateful stammer hindered him. He felt foolish, inadequate—but desperate to finally say what was in his heart. What if he had lost her, without ever telling her what she meant to him?

"N-Nora…forgive me if you'd r-rather n-not hear me say this, b-but… oh, Nora, I d-do love you so!"

Incredibly, she smiled. She smiled directly into his eyes, a smile filled with tenderness and understanding…and something else. Something Evan had never until this moment beheld in a woman's eyes.

"And I love you, Evan, though sure, and you will think me a forward woman for saying so. In such a place as this, and looking as I do—" She gave a small, rueful shake of her head. "Aye, a forward woman, indeed."

Evan stared at her, awed by what he saw in her face, what he heard on her lips. "You…you *love* me, Nora? Truly?"

Her fingertips brushed the corner of his mouth and traced along his beard. "Aye, Evan. Truly."

Shaken, Evan buried his face in the warm dampness of her hair so she would not see him fight back the tears. "I never d-dared to hope," he choked out, "that you could *love* m-me. Never!"

"Foolish man," she murmured against his temple. "And how could I *not* love you?" Now she was holding *him*, gathering him closer, pressing her cheek to his.

Nora whispered something else, something he took to be Gaelic. Not trusting himself to look at her or to speak again, he remained still, quietly cherishing the sweet wonder of her arms around him, her face close to his. This was his deepest hope, his secret dream. A dream shared only with the Lord.

More than one miracle had happened in this room tonight; more than one infinitely precious gift had been given. He dared not speak of these wondrous things until he had offered his thanksgiving to the Giver.

When he finally lifted his head, Nora had drifted off to sleep, her lips touched with a smile.

Now Evan could weep without her knowing.

Feeling foolish and meddlesome—but determined—Sara caught up with Michael halfway down the hall.

She saw his shoulders stiffen when she called to him. He stopped, and without thinking she put a hand to his arm. His eyes went from her face to her hand. For an instant, Sara thought he might actually shake off her touch.

Instead, he merely stood, saying nothing, not quite meeting her gaze. Now that she had acted on her instincts, Sara hadn't the faintest notion what to say. Quickly, she dropped her hand away. She really didn't know this man—didn't know him at all. Whatever had made her think she could help him, could ease whatever hurt he might be feeling?

Finally he looked at her, and Sara flinched at the resentment she saw burning out from him. Wildly she searched for the right words, words that wouldn't sound as foolish as she suddenly felt.

"Michael, I..." she faltered. "I don't know what to say, exactly, but—"

"Why would you be thinking you need to say anything?" he replied quietly.

Sara was excruciatingly aware that she had overstepped the established bounds of conventional behavior, was guilty of the very thing about which her father frequently teased her: meddling in the affairs of others. Michael Burke more than likely considered her a tiresome, interfering spinster. Yet she could not bring herself to ignore his pain.

In the end, he eased the awkwardness between them. "I expect we are both feeling the same thing," he said, still not meeting her eyes. "Relief that the worst would seem to be over for Nora—and for Daniel, as well."

Sara hesitated, then nodded. "Yes. Yes, of course. But…"

She let her words drift off, unfinished, as he finally looked directly at her. His expression was not unkind, but neither was it altogether friendly. Certainly, it did not invite further interference.

"Well, Sara Farmington," he finally said, twisting his mouth in what was probably intended to be a smile, "don't you think you might as well go on and say whatever it is you're thinking? I should be used to looking the fool in front of you by now—you seem to have a way of being present on those occasions when I fall on my face."

Sara opened her mouth to protest, then stopped. *Why did I ever follow him out of the room?*

"Sure, and you're not at a loss for words?" he bit out, obviously baiting her. "That would be a strange thing entirely."

Stung by what appeared to be contempt on his part, Sara told herself not to mind, that he was only venting his anger on the most convenient target. Still, she wasn't at all certain he would not turn on her if she provoked him.

"I only wanted to say that—that I know you're disappointed…about Nora and Evan Whittaker…and I understand." She had not intended to be so blunt. But what, exactly, *had* she intended? "What I meant to say—"

He drew a deep sigh, making it clear that his patience was at the expense of great effort. "I expect what you meant to say is that I shouldn't be in the least surprised about Nora and the Englishman. And you would be entirely right. As a matter of fact, I'm not surprised at all, having seen the two of them together on past occasions—and given the fact that conditions have been made altogether ideal for a relationship to grow between them.

"However," he went on, the edge in his voice now more pronounced and the flint in his eye sharper still, "since you claim to understand how I feel, perhaps you'll allow me a bit of time to collect what's left of my pride. It will take some getting used to, I confess."

Then, giving her no chance to reply, he turned the corner of the hallway and strode resolutely toward an oncoming nurse.

Miserable, Sara stood and watched him go. Why hadn't she left him alone? It had been a mistake to confront him while the wound was still raw. She should have waited.

With a heavy heart, she started back toward Nora's room. Before tonight, she would have said that she at least had Michael's friendship. Now, because of her foolish meddling, she wondered if even *that* could be salvaged.

She had spoken the truth about understanding his disappointment—his pain. Even now, the sound of his dreams breaking, his hope shattering, seemed to echo in her own heart with a terrible finality.

29

Morgan's Promise

As a white candle
In a holy place,
So is the beauty
Of an aged face.

JOSEPH CAMPBELL (1879–1944)

Ireland
Mid-January 1848

A week after their return from Belfast, Morgan's grandfather took to his bed.

Morgan knew the man would not get up again. "Your grandfather's body has simply worn out," the physician announced. "His heart—and his lungs—can no longer bear the strain. There's really nothing to be done except to make him comfortable."

For two days now, Sir Richard had slept most of the hours away, slipping in and out of consciousness like one drifting slowly out to sea, rising and falling with the ebb of the tide.

Slumped in his wheelchair beside the bed, watching his grandfather sleep, Morgan closed his eyes, wishing he, too, could sleep away the days with the old man—or at least the nights. Determined not to become dependent on the opium, he had refused to bring even a small supply home from the hospital. He was beginning to regret the decision; last night had been yet another of many without sleep, and he knew himself to be strung with brittle wire.

Opening his eyes, he glanced down over himself with distaste. He had thinned out to a scarecrow, and felt even more useless. Until the shooting,

Morgan had not realized how much he had always taken his size and his strength for granted. He had always been a great oaf, even as a lad, but had never thought much about it one way or the other. His awareness of being excessively tall and physically powerful extended only to the practical: beds were generally too short, chairs too flimsy, and doorways too low.

Lately, however, he had come to see that indeed he had enjoyed being large, had perhaps even used it to his own advantage now and then. Now he was whip-thin, and it dismayed him to realize how weak and worthless he really was.

He hated his body, he hated his weakness; most of all, he hated this cursed wheelchair. He was insightful enough to see that all his hatred was turning inward, against himself and the things around him, because he could not direct it to the ones who had done this thing to him. Nobody was willing to talk, to point the finger. There was no reason to believe his assailants would ever be caught.

In the meantime, he did his best not to think of the future. The truth was, he could not bear to speculate on what lay ahead. As long as his grandfather was still alive, he would put on the brave face and pretend that he was doing well.

A grim smile touched his lips. What else *could* he do? His present activities were limited to wheeling in and out of rooms and hoisting a book onto his lap.

As yet he could do virtually nothing on his own. Since returning to Dublin, he'd been more or less at the mercy of a surly male attendant from the hospital. For an exorbitant sum, the man came once a day to help with Morgan's bath and "exercise."

There was no one else. Even the ancient butler had been retired. A few weeks before the Belfast trip, Parkes' poor health and crippling arthritis had forced him to take his pension and go to his sister's home in the country.

Mrs. Ryan cooked, and the day maids kept house, but certainly they were no help to *him*. Until his newly hired companion arrived, he was virtually on his own.

The thought made him scowl. Not only was he to be dependent on the wheelchair, but he would also be dependent on another man. A black servant, hired sight unseen, before they had ever left the hospital in Belfast. Joseph Mahon, the priest, had suggested the man, and in his eagerness to provide Morgan with immediate care, his grandfather had urged Joseph to make the necessary arrangements without delay.

The new companion was to have arrived before now, but with the deep snow and icy roads across the country, there was no telling when he would actually show up. *If* he showed up at all.

Sandemon, he was called. A former slave, he had been granted his freedom by the Crown while still in Barbados, and was eventually given shelter at a mission run by one of Joseph's priest-friends. When the priest left the island and returned to Castlebar, he brought the freed slave...*Sandemon*... with him.

According to Joseph, the black man was intelligent, well educated, strong, and healthy. When his grandfather inquired somewhat delicately as to whether or not the man was "civilized," Joseph had merely smiled what Morgan thought of as his "sly priest's smile" and replied, "Aye, Sandemon is quite civilized, Sir Richard. He's had the benefits of a fine education— and he's more than a little enterprising, as you'll see."

Joseph had gone on to explain that this Sandemon—a Christian man— had allegedly taken an active part in the work of the church in Castlebar. "He's as good with his hands as he is with the books—and he has a back of solid iron," Joseph assured them. "He practically built the chapel on the outskirts of Castlebar with his own two hands."

When Morgan dryly questioned aloud why the town of Castlebar would consider parting with such a wonder, Joseph had fixed a stern look on him. "Because his patron—my friend—recently died," he said. "'Tis a fate common to a great host of priests in Ireland these days," he added pointedly.

With the loss of the priest and the devastation of the town, he went on to explain, Sandemon was left without a job and without resources. He needed employment. "And he needs a home. Sure, and it would seem he might be just the man for you, Morgan. He's a great fellow—broad in the shoulder with a back of steel. And with an intellect as clever and relentless as your own."

Morgan had conceded the Great One's admirable qualities, suggesting that no doubt such a marvel as Sandemon could also cook and sew as well. "We'd best snatch him up before the Queen gets word of him."

Joseph's thin face had sobered and grown stern with rebuke. "Now, Morgan, I would say something to you: The truth is that you will be needing a strong man to help out. Sandemon will prove a good companion—you will see. You'll not find another man of his qualities so easily."

His grandfather could not wait to sign him on. The deed was as good as done that day in the hospital waiting room. Sandemon was to be "Morgan's man."

On a trial basis, of course. Strictly a trial basis.

Now, pulling himself up in the wheelchair, Morgan found himself wishing the man would hurry up and get here. Whether he turned out to be more nuisance than blessing remained to be seen. At the moment, his greatest need was for a strong back.

He glanced over at his sleeping grandfather, and regret hit him like a blow. He had known it would come to this one day soon, of course. Richard Nelson was well into his eighties and had been failing for months. Knowing it and expecting it, however, did not necessarily make it easier to face.

Leaning forward a bit in the chair, he studied the sleeping old man with a heavy heart. His deeply lined face, now gaunt and hollowed, still spoke nobility and a kind, gentle heart. The white hair had grown thinner of late, but as always traced a neat, careful curve round the high forehead and lean jaw. His frame was shrunken, his hands gnarled—but there was a dignity and an elegance about the faded Richard Nelson that even time could not altogether destroy.

So many years had been lost to them, years they might have had together, if only...

If only *what*? If only he had known sooner of his grandfather's existence? Not likely. It was only thanks to Joseph Mahon's interference—clever priest that he was—that Morgan had discovered he *had* an English grandfather. Just as it had been Joseph's doing that brought the news to Richard Nelson that his Irish grandson was about to swing. Had the old man not arranged Morgan's freedom from the gallows, forcing him to appear in Dublin as one of the conditions of the pardon, Morgan would never have consented to meet with him.

Even then, he had come grudgingly, with the intention of making the obligatory bow, only to be dismissed after the old man's curiosity was satisfied. Instead, Richard Nelson had begged him to stay.

And so he had stayed. He had stayed, and over the months had grown more than a little fond of his elderly English grandfather. Indeed, he had come to love him. He had grown close to Richard Nelson in a way he had never been close to his father.

Gently, Morgan took his grandfather's hand—a hand not unlike his own. As he studied the long, thick-knuckled fingers, a sad smile crossed his face. He was going to miss this old man, miss him a great deal.

That his grandfather would soon be gone he had no doubt. Then there would be no need to pretend, no need to play the strong man, to feign a hope he did not have for a tomorrow he could no longer bear to imagine.

He knew he should pray for his grandfather—and for himself. He had tried—many times—since the shooting. He would close his eyes and fold his hands and try to go beyond the pain, to skirt the fear, the dread of the future, the unspeakable horror of being only half a man.

He had groped like a child in the dark, wept real tears—even tried, in his heart, to kneel in faith. In blind desperation he had fallen before the throne…and found nothing there. Nothing but silence.

Joseph Mahon the priest was fond of saying that no man was alone who could hear even the faintest whisper of God.

Morgan had listened. With a spirit raw and still bleeding from its wounds, he had cried out against the pain and then waited, listening.

Joseph Mahon the priest would have said that even in the silence, God was speaking.

Hearing nothing, Morgan could only wonder with bleak despair if the wheelchair was God's final word for him.

Just outside Drogheda, Annie Delaney stopped to rest. She had thought to be in Dublin City before nightfall. She would have been, too, had she not spent such a long time marveling over the ruins at Monasterboice.

Why, she'd lost an hour or more surveying the round tower alone! Sure, and it must have loomed a hundred feet and more into the air. You could see where its cap and upper parts had been destroyed long years ago, more than likely by a lightning storm. But it was an immense wonder all the same.

These were just some of the sacred ruins across Ireland which Morgan Fitzgerald had described in this thin sketchbook published a few years past. Although Annie had practically memorized the poet's descriptions of Monasterboice and other religious ruins, she had kept the handbook carefully tucked away with her precious few other books. They were treasures, and to be cherished.

She had been on the road for twelve days now and was getting a bit impatient to reach her destination. The snow had slowed her down some. Her shoes were thin, so she had to keep stopping and rub her feet to ward off frostbite. Mostly, though, her journey had been free of obstacles. The nights had been the worst part of the trek altogether. She'd found shelter at a convent once or twice; mostly, though, she slept in barns or stables.

This evening she passed through Drogheda, which old Devil Cromwell had sacked two centuries before, butchering most of its people. Now, just outside the sad old town, she began to wish she had not lingered quite so long at Monasterboice.

Still and all, wasn't she seeing some grand sights for herself? She was gaining a much clearer understanding of Morgan Fitzgerald's love for tramping about the countryside, as had been his custom during the years before he got himself shot in Belfast.

Sobered by the memory, Annie wrapped her cloak more tightly about her throat, reminding herself of the reason for her journey. 'Twas not to be dallying over ancient ruins and crumbling relics.

She was on her way to Dublin City, she was. Fitzgerald's refusal to take her with him had been firm enough. Obviously, he'd marked her as a bit daft and not to be taken seriously. The old man had paid her even less heed.

Although disappointed, Annie supposed she understood. The old man—Sir Richard, he was called—was obviously consumed by worry for his grandson's recovery. As for Morgan Fitzgerald, more often than not he was dull with the opium or distracted with the pain.

The way Annie had it figured, by the time she arrived in Dublin City, the two of them would have had time enough to see things in a different light.

If not, well, then, she would simply find a way to get around their resistance. She would somehow have to make herself indispensable to the both of them.

She had no doubt but what she could manage. When Annie Delaney set her mind to a thing, wasn't it as good as done?

His grandfather died just before midnight. It came sooner than Morgan had expected, despite the doctor's caution earlier that evening.

Morgan was alone with him when he awakened for the last time. Dozing in the wheelchair beside the bed, Morgan jumped when the old man spoke his name.

"Aye, Grandfather," he said, taking his hand, "I am here."

Sir Richard's eyes were surprisingly clear as he turned his face toward his grandson. But his words chilled Morgan to the very center of his being. "This is the last time I will speak with you, Morgan," he said in a frail whisper.

When Morgan squeezed his hand and would have protested, the old man gave an impatient shake of his head. "I am going. And I am ready. Indeed, I am *eager* to go! Your grandmother is waiting for me, and I long to be with her...and with my Lord. But—" His voice faded, and for a moment Morgan thought he was already gone.

But with a ragged breath, the old man rallied. "My only regret is for you. I lack peace for you, Morgan—a peace I long to have before I go."

Clasping the old man's frail hand between both his own, Morgan choked on the grief welling up in his soul. "I will be all right, Grandfather," he assured him in a hoarse whisper. "I will."

Again the old man shook his head. He twisted as if to sit up, but fell back, depleted. "Listen to me, Morgan...you must promise..."

"What, Grandfather?" Morgan swallowed, his unshed tears scalding his throat.

"You must not...give up." His grandfather's gaze pleaded with Morgan, who had yet to understand what it was the old man wanted from him.

"Closer," Sir Richard whispered. "Come...closer...so you can hear."

Leaning forward as far as he could, Morgan continued to grip the old man's hand between his own. "Aye, Grandfather. I can hear you."

"Two things...you must promise me."

A fierce spasm of pain seized Morgan, rocking him with such a force he thought he would pass out. Pain in his back...pain in his heart. He could not tell which of the two would tear him apart first.

Somehow he forced the words out. "Promise you what, Grandfather?"

"Promise me—"

"Whatever you say, Grandfather—"

Morgan ground his teeth against the pain so he would not scream.

"You will build your school."

Morgan lost his breath in the furnace of pain. "My school?"

"It is a worthy dream, Morgan...young minds and young hearts...that is where the healing must begin...promise me, then, that you will build your school...."

Dazed by the pain, which was now receding, Morgan managed a nod.

"Morgan? I can't see you...do you promise..."

Morgan's face crumpled as his last thread of control broke. His tears fell over the old man's hand, and a sob tore from his throat. "Aye...I promise, Grandfather...I promise."

"One other promise, Morgan..."

"What is it, then, Grandfather?"

"Promise me...you will let nothing silence your voice—"

"I don't understand—"

"Listen...listen to me, Morgan...you are a voice for God in Ireland... you must allow nothing to silence that voice."

"Grandfather—"

"There will be no hope for our poor, lovely land...or its people...without God's voice, Morgan...do you understand?"

No...no, I don't understand, and it is beyond me to care—

"Morgan!"

"Aye, aye, Grandfather! I will try."

"You will speak for God in Ireland?"

"I will try—"

Sir Richard smiled and closed his eyes. "Yes...you...you will try. Sing for me now, Morgan...please, would you sing for me?"

God in heaven, I can't...I can't...

"Sing an Irish lullaby for your grandfather, Morgan. Sing me to sleep, son of my heart...."

Morgan Fitzgerald kissed the palm of the old man's hand, the hand of his English grandfather who had loved him so well for such a brief time. Then he dried his tears on his sleeve.

He would have time for weeping later. For now, he would sing an Irish lullaby. He would sing his grandfather to sleep.

PART THREE

SPRINGTIME ANTHEM

Rainbow Vistas

"For I know the plans I have for you," declares the LORD,
"plans to prosper you and not to harm you,
plans to give you hope and a future."

JEREMIAH 29:11

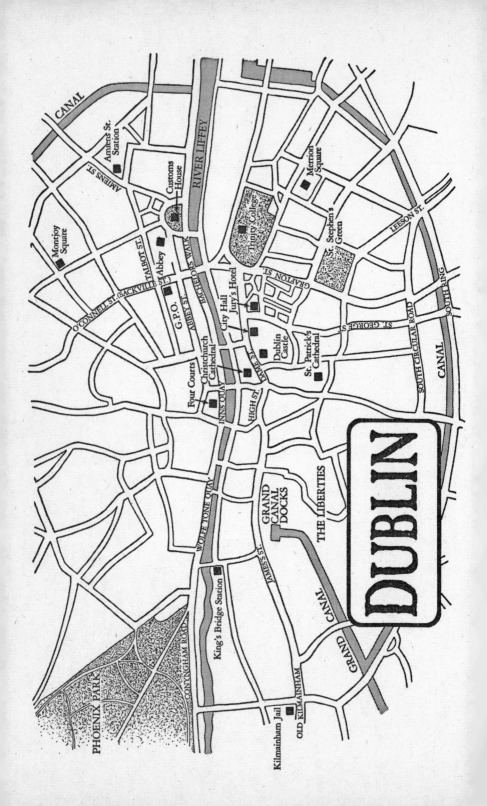

30

Dublin: Darkness and Daybreak

'Tis uselessness that slays the heart,
And loneliness the soul....
'Tis love Divine and purpose pure
That heal and make man whole...

MORGAN FITZGERALD

February 1848

It had never occurred to Annie Delaney that Dublin would have its slums.

All her life she had pictured the grand capital city as one majestic scene after another of graceful bridges, noble mansions, towering steeples, and sprawling castles—all set around the picturesque River Liffey and Dublin Bay. It may have had all these and more, but so far she had seen little that resembled the Dublin of her dreams.

She should have realized the city would host ugliness as well as beauty. But she had yet to see the beauty; instead, she had ended up in this sordid, mean district. Sure, and it must be the very dregs of Dublin City!

She had entered the city long past sunset. Much to her dismay, she had immediately gotten herself lost, stumbling into a vast maze of desolate streets lined with decaying old houses. The large, moldering structures looked as if they might have once been fine homes. Now they appeared to be crowded with derelicts who peered furtively out the broken windowpanes or shouted drunkenly from doorsteps and hallways.

Annie would have thought the slums of Belfast had steeled her for Dublin's dark side. But she was finding out that a strange city at night, wrapped in fog and unknown dangers, was a great deal more frightening than the familiar squalor of Belfast.

Her heart thudding, she appraised her surroundings. Obviously, this was a disreputable—and more than likely dangerous—area. She hadn't a thought where she was or how to find her way out.

Sure, and she would not dare to ask directions of any of the dwellers in this place! What she must be doing was to get away as swiftly as possible and find a decent neighborhood. Yet the longer she walked the wretched streets, the more she began to feel as if she were traveling in meaningless circles. It seemed as if she'd been wandering for hours, yet always she ended up back at the docks or in a tangle of dark alleys.

Cold mists draped the squalid buildings, obscuring most of their fronts and gaping doorways. In the deep, heavy fog enshrouding the streets, the gaslights were virtually worthless. Anything could be lurking nearby, entirely unnoticed.

When a voice hissed from what appeared to be an empty doorway, Annie nearly jumped out of her skin. Holding her breath, she quickened her pace.

"Hey—Lassie! We've a drop for sharing! Come in out of the cold, why don't you? Come in and warm yourself!"

The rough, sneering voice raised the hair on the back of Annie's neck. Her shoes smacked the cobbles as she took off at a full run, praying the owner of the voice was too drunk to catch her.

As she ran, she kept glancing back over her shoulder. The fog-webbed streets teemed with stalking shadows, invisible pursuers laughing at her futile attempts to escape them.

Desperately, Annie turned into an alley. Seeing nothing but blackness ahead, she slowed her pace. Was there no outlet?

She held her breath. Every building became an evil presence, every doorway concealed some terrible unknown. Watching her. Mocking her.

Annie stopped, stood still, listening. She whirled around, then turned and started running again.

Please, Lord...sir...please get me away! I seem to be in a fix here, sir! Please come and help me!

Every nightmare she had known as a child, every dark fear she had thought buried, now swept over her. Someone…*something*…would reach out any moment from one of the dark, sinister doorways to seize her and wreak terrible things upon her! She could almost feel the cold touch of evil at her back.

Running harder, she prayed incoherently. Tears stung her eyes but she blinked them back. Once she stumbled, righted herself, and lunged forward. Fear totally overcame her now, a different kind of fear than she had ever known before tonight. Not the fear tempered with anger that had given her the strength and courage to defy Tully. No, this fear was an all-consuming, shattering thing that left her breathless and weak.

Her lungs felt on fire, near to exploding, as Annie careened around the corner between two warehouses. Then she saw the faint hint of light just ahead.

Safety! Thanks be to God, she would be all right now!

Gulping for breath, Annie shot a look behind her, then quickened her run still more. She was almost at the end of the street, within full view of the gaslight, when two figures stepped out of the shadows, blocking her path.

Annie stumbled, pitching forward. Flinging her arm out, she slammed her hand against a brick wall to keep from falling. A man and a boy stood watching her, their faces leering in the glow from the streetlight.

Annie cried out, then whipped around to run back the way she'd come. She screamed at the sight of another boy, this one older, moving in on her.

Her legs shaking under her, Annie braced herself. Her mind spun, groping wildly to think of a way to escape the three. They closed ranks now, moving in on her, backing her up against the brick wall.

"Why, the lass is afraid, Con," said the man to the boy at his left. "Sure, and we've come upon her unexpected. It's only natural she might be thinking we mean to harm her."

The man smiled, and Annie's stomach pitched. Dressed in a tattered seaman's coat and cap, his leer revealed a mouth of rotting teeth. An angry gash split his face in half, running from ear to ear just above his mouth—much as the River Liffey cut Dublin City right through in the middle.

The boy called Con looked to be not much older than Annie—until she saw the wickedness in his eyes. This one would have been born old. And mean. Yet, she faced them, chin up, furious at the way her body was betraying her with its weakness and violent shaking.

"You need not be afraid of us, at all, wee lassie," the man said, his terrible smile still in place. "We've only come to see you safe home. No decent lass, as you obviously are, should be on the streets alone in the Liberties. 'Tis a wicked, dangerous place, don't you see?"

"Might be she doesn't have a home, Da," jeered Con. "Might be she's just a poor orphan girl on her keeping."

Ach, and wasn't he an ugly brute! Even the man's grizzled, divided face was a credit to this one, with his pudding gob and runny eyes. If this was a family, sure, they must have been bred in the sewers!

Annie willed her lip to stop its trembling as she faced the ruffians. The other boy, the one at the man's right, stepped up now, and for the first time Annie got a clear look at his face.

Chilled, Annie recognized the fixed, vacant stare, the foolish grin of an imbecile. This one had little mind, if any. She shuddered. Undoubtedly, he would do whatever he was told.

"Might be at that. Still, she has herself a purchase." He jabbed a finger at Annie's knapsack. "And a poke. Just be handing those over to Con, why don't you, lassie? A wee thing like yourself should not be carrying such a burden."

"Can't we just take her home with us, Da?" Con's hard eyes mocked her. "Sure, and I'd fancy a little sister."

The three laughed as if he'd made a great jest. Annie knew she had one chance, and only one. As the man reached to take her knapsack from her, she brought the stick down as hard as she could on the crook of his arm, at the same time kneeing him hard in the groin.

Caught by surprise, the man yelled and bent double, groaning with pain. Annie whipped her da's carving knife from inside her shoe.

Slicing the air with the knife, she backed off from the three in a crouch. "Leave me be, now, you scum, or I'll cut you, I swear I will! When I'm done, you'll be even uglier than you are now!"

The man was still howling with the blows she'd inflicted, but he lunged for her, and Con, eyes blazing, came at her, too. The idiot with the runny nose simply stood staring.

Brandishing the knife, Annie jabbed at the two, all the while growling at her attackers like some sort of berserk. The man fell back, but Con kept stalking, ducking, and lurching as he watched his chance to go for her.

"You're dead, you skinny little—"

He was close enough to slice. Annie slashed the knife at his ear.

He let out a shrill scream. Blood gushed, and Annie took off, sobbing as she bounded down the street. The sound of her feet slapping the cobbles echoed in and out of the abandoned buildings.

She heard shouts behind her, and cursing.

How many? All three? Or just Con with the cruel eyes?

The thundering pulse in her ears rose above the sound of running feet. Wheezing, gulping for air, Annie ignored the hot pain in her chest. Once she dared to shoot a glance over her shoulder. Only Con seemed in pursuit, but that was enough to give her an extra surge of speed. As she ran, she kept the knife at ready.

Without realizing it, at some point in the chase Annie had broken out of the mean slum streets. The residences around her were still old, but the neighborhood looked a bit more decent and cared for.

A steeple rose through the fog and Annie first thought she was seeing a vision. But when she was close enough to make out the granite spire of the tower, she prayed fervently that this was no vision but deliverance.

⁊⧪

Just after daybreak, Morgan sat at breakfast, his newspapers spread out in front of him.

He had made the mistake of picking up the London *Times* after exhausting *The Nation.* His head throbbed with growing anger. From *The Nation*, he'd learned that one Young Irelander had recently been shot, two others arrested, while raiding a food convoy on the way to a loading port. Before taking them prisoners, the troops had beaten the offenders unmercifully.

The Times, of course, reported a slightly different version of the "atrocities of the Irish outlaws." In addition, there were more of the usual remarks about the "aimlessness and laziness" of the Irish people.

With mounting rage, Morgan ignored his plate as he went on reading. Predictably, there was no mention of the fact that those same worthless Irish had been deprived of even the most basic rights of free human beings, and were now starving to death on land rightfully theirs while growing an abundance of food for England to export.

To lay a hand on these "designated" food provisions would automatically mean prison, exile, or even execution. Not long ago, two little lads were transported to Australia for a term of seven years—this for stealing a bit of corn to fill their hungry bellies.

At least *The Times* could no longer ignore Ireland's disaster altogether. With the growing international awareness that the Irish famine was reality, not rumor—and with increasing protests from both clergy and laity that England's handling of the catastrophe was nothing short of criminal— *The Times* had recently been forced to address the situation.

It was no longer enough to acknowledge the Queen's observation that there did indeed seem to be a "dearth of provisions in Ireland." The working people of England—and even a few members of the nobility—had begun to add their voices to those of other nations. The world was beginning to take note of Ireland's plight. Along with donations from a multitude of countries came demands that England institute a relief program appropriate for the Christian nation she claimed to be.

But Morgan knew with sick certainty that it would be a very long time before the worldwide aid, no matter how significant, could be channeled and dispersed to make an appreciable difference.

In the meantime, the people were still dying.

He let out a long breath of disgust, crumpled *The Times*, and tossed it to the floor. Glancing up, he saw that Artegal, the new footman, had come into the room.

Morgan sat watching the man with a mixture of mild disdain and irritation. Artegal was quietly and efficiently arranging calling cards and correspondence, presumedly separating those cards he deemed worthy of Morgan's notice from the rest.

With Smith O'Brien's help, Morgan had employed the footman a week after his grandfather's death. The man's previous service included two MPs and a lawyer. He spoke of the lawyer only when questioned, and then with thinly veiled contempt. A man of indeterminate age, Artegal claimed both English and Irish blood—admitting the Irish strain only when pressed. Apparently Smith O'Brien had thought the footman's Irish blood would give him and Morgan immediate rapport—a grave error in judgment on his part.

While willing to concede his new employee's good points—the footman was indeed efficient, quiet, and conscientious—Morgan was keenly aware of the man's less endearing qualities.

Artegal was, in Morgan's estimation, a somewhat anemic rope of a man who had never discovered that it was perfectly acceptable behavior to change the inflection of his voice now and then or even, heaven forbid, offer a civil smile.

A white specter was Artegal, with straight white hair, startling white linen, ashen skin, and pale, rather delicate hands. A ghost, though admittedly an efficient one.

The man irritated Morgan. But, then, what did *not* irritate him these days? It seemed the smallest thing could set him off. Morgan had wits enough to know his constant annoyance was merely the symptom of something else, something that burned just beneath the surface of his perilous self-control.

It was a bitter thing, admitting his own helplessness. Yet admit it he must. Even the most basic physical needs were now either difficult or impossible for him without assistance. Bathing, getting dressed, going in and out of the house—he could as yet accomplish none of these alone.

Certainly, the slender, fine-boned Artegal was no help at all in moving Morgan's bulk about. Smith O'Brien offered his services each time he called, but in spite of their friendship, Morgan could not bring himself to accept.

Fortunately, his grandfather, because of his own encroaching weakness and fear of falling, had ordered a lift installed on both stairways several weeks before his death. At least Morgan could make his way to the bedroom unassisted.

The thought of his dependency made his frown deepen. What had happened, he wondered, to the man Joseph Mahon had supposedly employed for him from Castlebar—*Sandemon*?

Just yesterday he had scrawled an impatient note to Joseph, inquiring as to this Sandemon's whereabouts. Faith, the man should have been here by now, even if he had come by way of Rome!

Artegal stole out of the dining room. Sighing, Morgan pushed away from the table and wheeled himself over to the window. In the early morning mist, the view outside was as bleak as his spirits. As far as he could see, the grounds were barren and stark, the trees stripped of all color and foliage. From this side of the house, there was nothing remotely of interest to be seen. Only winter, which showed no sign of coming to an end.

A sad smile touched his lips as he thought of the Young Irelanders recently brought down for their thievery. He missed the lads, missed the camaraderie, the laughter, the bond of purpose that joined them—and, yes, even the sense of danger and adventure.

He still had a few friends, of course. Smith O'Brien and some of the others came regularly to make sure he wasn't turning into a mad recluse. But a number of the more militant lads had disavowed him even before the shooting, put off by his increasing protests against their talk of a rebellion and his call for common sense.

He did not blame them. Perhaps the answer *was* for the people to rise— if they could muster the strength, starving as they were. Could dying in defeat be any worse than living in despair? Perhaps all that mattered was to do *something*—anything—rather than simply give up and do nothing. As he had.

Uselessness—that was the real killer of a man, Morgan thought. That and loneliness. Odd, how he had never thought of being lonely before the shooting. He had always valued his solitude, never cared much for crowds or noise, liked to go his own way as he chose. Yet now—now there were times when he felt he would surely die from the pain of his unwelcome isolation.

He sighed and stretched his arms above his head. Joseph Mahon the priest would more than likely accuse him of self-pity.

But then Joseph Mahon the priest did not have to face his future in a wheelchair.

At Artegal's discreet throat-clearing, Morgan turned. The footman stood just inside the doorway, his pallid face set in its customary unreadable mask.

"Begging your pardon, sir, but you *did* say we should be expecting a… ah…a person of *color*?" The man's thin nostrils flared slightly as if offended by an unpleasant odor.

Morgan glared at him, then gave an impatient nod, waiting.

"Yes. Well…ah…it would seem that he has arrived." Artegal made this announcement with an ominous frown—the first change of expression Morgan had detected in the man since hiring him.

"So—and about time! Well, send him in!"

The footman turned to go, but at the same time a large, dark figure stepped into view, blocking the doorway. Glancing uncertainly back at Morgan, Artegal sniffed, lifted his chin, and carefully slipped sideways past the black man.

Wheeling the chair the rest of the way around, Morgan's eyes widened at the sight in the doorway. The man was big, as Joseph had claimed—tall, with shoulders that very nearly brushed both sides of the door frame. His face, long and broad, seemed carefully molded: high cheekbones firmly sculpted, broad nose, and a generous mouth. His mustache and beard were closely trimmed and streaked with gray. Draping his shoulders was a gray frieze cape, revealing a vivid purple shirt with flowing sleeves. As he stepped the rest of the way into the room, he removed a black felt cap with a visor.

Morgan stared. It would seem that Joseph Mahon the priest had hired a tribal chieftain as his new companion!

"I am Sandemon, sir." The final syllable came dancing off his lips. "Sanda-*mohn*," he pronounced it. The black man had a big, rich voice threaded with a subtle hint of refinement—a mixture of British preciseness and West Indies lilt.

The deep brown eyes were pools of calm as they met Morgan's gaze. Then, abruptly, Sandemon smiled. A brilliant white crescent, a flash of gold, against the dark satin sheen of his skin.

"It is a pleasure to meet Ireland's greatest poet."

Morgan did not return the smile or acknowledge the compliment. "What, exactly, was your hurry getting here...*Sandemon*?" he snapped, scowling. "Or did Joseph Mahon not make you aware of the fact that you were needed right away?"

The black man's gaze remained steady as his expression sobered. "He did that, sir. But there was an unavoidable delay."

"Indeed?"

Sandemon inclined his head, holding his cap against his broad chest. "Yes, sir. Unfortunately, I was needed in Castlebar for longer than I had thought."

"Doing *what*? I've been expecting you for more than three weeks!"

The black man lifted one well-shaped brow as if to question Morgan's rudeness. "And for that I am truly sorry, sir. But I did come just as quickly as I could."

"What was so urgent that you couldn't keep your commitment to me?" Morgan pressed.

"I was needed to help tend the sick and bury the dead. Your friend, Father Joseph, said you would understand."

Morgan uttered a grunt of disgust, which Sandemon appeared to ignore. "Have Artegal show you your room and get settled in. I'll be needing you soon."

"Of course, sir. But first, I'm afraid there is a matter requiring your attention."

Morgan glared at him. "I thought Joseph explained the salary arrangements. You'll be generously paid, you needn't fret—"

"No, sir," Sandemon said, lifting a large, long-fingered hand to interrupt. "It has nothing to do with my pay."

"*What*, then?" snapped Morgan. He had been awake since long before dawn, his head pounding with a vengeance. The dread weakness was on him already, and it was not even midmorning.

"There is a...woman outside, sir," said Sandemon. "She has with her a girl-child whom the woman claims to have found near the cathedral of St. Patrick late last night." Sandemon paused. "It seems the child insists on speaking with you."

As Morgan stared, the black man added, "The child said I should tell you that Annie Delaney is here. Annie Delaney from Belfast."

31

A Demented Child in Dublin

I wish you friends whose wisdom makes them kind,
Well-leisured friends to share your evening's peace,
Friends who can season knowledge with a laugh...
Children, no matter whose, to watch for you
With flower faces at your garden gate,
And one to watch the clock with eager eyes,
Saying: "He's late—he's late."
WINIFRED M. LETTS (C. 1882)

Morgan did not wait for Annie Delaney to be ushered in. Waving off Sandemon's attempt to help, he wheeled himself out of the dining room and took off in a fury down the marble entryway.

Artegal was standing guard at the front door, open to reveal the wan, bedraggled form of Annie Delaney. The girl was filthy: muddy shoes, limp socks, grimy coat, and smudged face. Her hair, beneath the boy's cap, resembled a destroyed bird's nest.

Morgan managed to stop the chair just short of the door. When Annie Delaney saw him, her black-marble eyes brightened with a mixture of eagerness and apprehension.

Speechless, Morgan sat staring at the girl, who now lifted a begrimed hand and wiped it across her even dirtier face with a jerky motion, as if to tidy herself.

She was the picture of the scrubby orphan girl, soiled and tattered and disheveled. Yet when she lifted her chin and addressed him, an odd touch of dignity redeemed her appearance.

"Good mornin', Your Honor," she said with only the slightest hesitancy. "I'm sorry to be bursting in on you so suddenlike."

Gaping at her, Morgan was only dimly aware of Artegal's disapproving frown and Sandemon's curious smile. The disreputable child might have crawled right out of a chimney, so foul was her appearance, yet she took on the airs of a duchess!

"I hope you're feelin' some better, sir, now that you're at home," she said. Her wide-eyed, artless expression didn't fool Morgan, not for a moment. This black-eyed scamp, like most ragamuffins on their own keeping, was more than likely a consummate little chiseler.

Morgan drew in a deep breath, then leveled his most baleful glare on her. "What are you *doing* here?" Not giving her time to reply, he added, "And how, exactly, did you *get* here?"

Annie Delaney met his fierce gaze straight on, without so much as the blink of an eye. "Well, you see, sir, I thought by now you'd had the time to reconsider our discussion in Belfast, and perhaps had come to see that I can be of service to you, after all." She gulped in a hasty breath. "As to how I got here, sir—why, I walked, of course!"

Out of the corner of his eye, Morgan saw Sandemon's smile widen. At the same time, Artegal's delicate pallor turned an angry red.

"You're daft," Morgan said, not even trying to soften his tone. "You are a demented child."

"Please, sir, might I come in?"

The rascal had more nerve than wits! "No, and you may *not* come in." Morgan snapped, his hands tightening on the armrests of the wheelchair. "What you may do is to get your wily little hide back to Belfast!"

"Please, sir—" The child bit her lip, then shifted from one foot to the other.

"*No!*"

Startled, Morgan saw the black-marble eyes go moist. Oh, she was good, this one! Now they were in for a weeping spell.

Instead of tears, however, a stream of words came spilling out of the demented child's mouth like an unexpected hailstorm on a summer's day. "*Please, sir, may I come in for only a moment? I have to use the facilities, and I simply can't wait a bit longer!*"

After instructing Mrs. Ryan, the cook, to direct Annie Delaney to "the facilities," Morgan dismissed Artegal to his regular duties.

Then he turned to Sandemon. "I thought you said there was a woman with her."

The black man nodded. "There was, sir. Indeed, in the words of the child, it was this same woman who 'saved her from a terrible fate' and led her safely here, to you."

"And did the *child* happen to explain what she meant by this tale?"

Sandemon did not react in any noticeable manner to Morgan's sarcasm. Instead, the soft brown eyes held a faint smile as he replied. "Again, in the little girl's words, she was about to be abducted by 'three dastardly attackers—robbers, and perhaps worse.'"

Morgan rolled his eyes. "She *is* daft." He looked at Sandemon. "So, then—what happened to the woman?"

The black man looked toward the door. "She hurried off as soon as she deposited the girl at the door. She seemed...anxious to be gone."

"I should think so, trying to foist an orphan girl off onto a total stranger. What sort of woman did she look to be?"

Sandemon crossed his arms over his chest and lowered his head as if deep in thought. "She seemed a very young woman, sir. She had a shawl draped over her head, but I could see her hair was quite pale in color. And she was...heavily painted. Much like those referred to as 'street girls'."

"A *prostitute?*"

Sandemon nodded, frowning. "Yet she did not bear the harshness of appearance one tends to expect from that profession."

"Did she say anything to you? About the child?"

Sandemon shook his head. "Not a word. The child did all the talking."

Ignoring Morgan's muttered interruption, he went on. "The child seems to have been lost and badly frightened by some disreputable men. Apparently the young woman gave her refuge until the child's pursuers gave up the chase. She kept her there, in her flat, until dawn, then led her here." He paused. "The child insists that this woman saved her life."

"Indeed." Morgan thought for a moment. "And why, do you suppose, was this guardian angel so eager to get away?" He didn't believe the tale for a moment, but in spite of himself the scamp's ingenuity intrigued him.

Sandemon merely shrugged. "I'm afraid I couldn't say, sir."

Morgan started to make a testy reply, but wrenched in the chair when a spasm of pain seized him.

Sandemon stepped forward, but made no move to touch him. "Can I do anything, sir?"

Morgan shook his head, grimacing. "It will pass," he muttered shortly.

After a moment, the pain eased. Pulling in a deep breath, Morgan knotted his hands into fists to hide their trembling. "I don't know what to say to this demented child," he told Sandemon. "She pays no heed to reason. None at all."

The black man regarded Morgan with a considering gaze. "You have met the child before, sir?"

"Aye, in Belfast. You might say she came to visit me while I was in the hospital. She tried to convince me to bring her back to Dublin with me." Morgan smiled grimly in remembrance. "The little imp even talked to the priest, tried to convince him to intercede on her behalf."

"A clever child," Sandemon commented.

"A *devious* child," corrected Morgan.

"Do you know what the child wants from you, sir?"

Morgan looked at him. "The *child*," he said with a wicked smile, "would seem to want your job, Sandemon."

When the black man did not react—Morgan was beginning to wonder what, exactly, it would take to *make* him react—he explained Annie Delaney's insistence that she could be of "real service" to him.

"She's just peculiar enough to intrigue me," Morgan admitted. "But, of course, I cannot have her here."

"Perhaps she *would* be of some help," Sandemon offered carefully, "to you and your grandfather. If nothing else, I imagine she would provide occasional entertainment. And certainly, the child must be in sore need of a home, to make such an outrageous proposal to you."

"My grandfather is dead," Morgan said flatly, disregarding the black man's attempted expression of sympathy. "And as you can see, I cannot manage *myself*, much less take responsibility for a child—no matter how... *entertaining* she might be. Or," he added pointedly, "no matter how much she might happen to need a home."

"Of course, *Seanchai*. Still, if you are interested in showing mercy to the child, I would be glad to take responsibility for her. At least until your health has returned."

"My health will more than likely not be returning, Sandemon," Morgan grated. "And you'll be busy enough as it is without taking on a demented child." He stopped abruptly. "What did you call me?"

"Sir?"

"Just now. You called me *Seanchai.*"

"I did not mean to offend, sir. I understood it to be a term of respect, and that's how I intended it, I assure you."

Morgan waved off his apology. "You didn't *offend* me—I simply hadn't realized that your vast education included a study of the Irish language."

Sandemon smiled. "Indeed not, although I find it a most pleasing language to the ear. The word is used by many of the people in Castlebar and throughout County Mayo when they speak of you with affection. Especially it is heard on the lips of the children. Fitzgerald the Poet and the *Seanchai*—the Storyteller—they call you."

Morgan blinked in surprise. "I have written only a few stories. Most of the children's tales are simple retellings of the ancient myths."

"Ah, but they are noble, heroic stories," Sandemon pointed out. "And the people need to believe in heroes, wouldn't you say so, *Seanchai*? Especially in times like these?"

Morgan looked away, saying nothing. In truth, the black man's use of the name pleased him. Even more did it move him to hear that the children of Mayo spoke of him with affection.

"What shall I tell the child, sir?"

Morgan let out a long breath. Raising a fist to his chin, he thought for a moment. "She would be your charge altogether, your responsibility— and it would only be until we can find a proper place for her."

Sandemon inclined his head to indicate acceptance of the terms, but Morgan did not miss the slight glint in his eye. "You understand you're taking on a great burden—and more than likely a great grief. The child is demented."

Sandemon raised his head to look Morgan directly in the eye. "The child," he said softly, "is God's, *Seanchai*. That makes her our responsibility. And who can say," he added quickly before Morgan could interrupt, "but what this...demented child may not just turn out to be more gift than grief to us? Hmm?"

Staring at him, Morgan wondered if he had perhaps lamented his

loneliness a bit too soon. Might not even loneliness be preferable to the
company of a mad mystic and a demented child?

Sighing, he started to wheel himself to the library, then stopped. "The
woman," he said thoughtfully. "See that she's found."

Sandemon looked at him, then nodded. "You wish to thank her for
rescuing the child, *Seanchai*?"

"No," Morgan said with a thin smile. "I want to hear her side of the
child's story. Somehow, I think it might prove very interesting."

32

Friends and Lovers

Though you are in your shining days,
Voices among the crowd
And new friends busy with your praise,
Be not unkind or proud,
But think about old friends the most:
Time's bitter flood will rise,
Your beauty perish and be lost
For all eyes but these eyes.

W. B. YEATS (1865–1939)

New York City

As soon as they separated from the other boys after school, Tierney started in on Daniel about the wedding.

It was the same almost every afternoon. Daniel spent most of the walk home warding off questions for which he had no answers—or which he would rather not answer at all, because of Tierney's manner, which if not exactly spiteful was unpleasant all the same.

"If they're going to be living in that caretaker's cottage, I can't see how there will be room for you."

Tierney had raised this same subject before. Daniel wasn't sure what he wanted from him. He understood that more than likely he and Uncle Mike would no longer want him living with them, once his mother and Evan were wed. So why didn't Tierney just come right out and say so?

"They insist they'll make room," he answered shortly. Head down, Daniel hugged his schoolbooks to his chest and began walking a bit faster.

It was a blustery February day, as cold as it had been in December before the big snowstorm. But today there was no snow. Only gray, heavy skies that threatened more winter in one form or another.

Neither of them spoke until they reached the storefront where old John Jacob Astor had once worked as a baker's helper. Then Tierney broke the silence between them. "Is that what *you* want?" he asked abruptly.

"What *I* want?" Avoiding the other's probing gaze, Daniel kicked a rock and sent it skipping over the remains of a broken milk bottle. One of two pigs in the middle of the street gave him a blank stare, then went on with its mate to the next pile of garbage.

Tierney, too, kept his eyes straight ahead. "I mean, do you want to live there with *them*, in that cramped little cottage?"

They had reached O'Rourke's Saloon on Pearl Street. Inside, someone was banging out a raucous song on the out-of-tune piano. The boys stopped in front to listen.

Daniel groped for the right words to answer Tierney's question. The truth was, he thought it would be best if Mother and Evan could be alone for a time—without him, and without the Fitzgerald children, whom they planned to eventually make a part of their household.

Tierney said something else, which Daniel couldn't hear over the noise from the saloon. "What?"

They started walking again, slower than before. "I said, you don't *have* to, you know. You don't have to live with them. At least not yet. Da and I talked. And we'd like you to stay. If you want."

Daniel held his breath. Moistening his lips, he replied, "Are you sure, then?"

"Aye, we're sure." Suddenly Tierney stopped and turned to face him. "Look—there's something I want to say."

Daniel waited, praying this wouldn't be the start of another argument between them. They were standing in the middle of Pearl Street, amid the busy dry-goods stores and importing buildings. Businessmen and trades-people milled about, hurrying toward their shops and offices. But Daniel paid scant heed to the impatient pedestrians jostling by. He sensed that this was an important moment between him and Tierney, a moment that could mean a great deal to the both of them, depending on what was said.

"I'll not beat around the bush," said Tierney, his mouth set in a stubborn line. "All along I'd hoped that my da and your mother would marry—you already know that."

Nodding, Daniel said, "It was what I wanted, too."

"I don't like that Englishman," Tierney bit out, as if he hadn't heard Daniel. "Not a bit. And it baffles me what your mother sees in the likes of him."

When Daniel would have interrupted, Tierney simply raised his voice and pressed on. "I know you think he's a grand fellow—and it's probably best that you do. What counts is, your mother has made her choice. And the way I see it, that has nothing to do with you and me."

His expression relaxed and his tone softened somewhat as he went on. "What I guess I want to say is, I don't see why their marriage should spoil things for us. Why shouldn't you go on living with me and Da? You're my best friend, after all—and Da thinks you're swell." He paused, then shot Daniel a cocky grin. "Of course, he doesn't know you as I do."

This had to be the longest speech Tierney had ever made. Daniel was aware of how difficult it was for his friend to say such things; Tierney's blunt way of saying what he thought seldom went beyond the superficial. By expressing himself as he just had, he was allowing Daniel a rare glimpse into his true feelings. It was not to be taken lightly.

He met Tierney's gaze. "You're my best friend, too. And I'd hate it if things were any other way," he said earnestly. "I want to stay with you and Uncle Mike. But you're sure it's truly all right with him?"

"All *right* with him?" Tierney burst out. "Why, if Da had his way, he'd rope us together!" Giving Daniel's shoulder a quick jab, he added, "He has this daft notion that you're a good influence on me. As I said, he doesn't know you as I do."

In the kitchen of the Farmington mansion that same evening, Evan Whittaker and Nora Kavanagh sat holding hands and making attempts to do some sensible planning for their future.

It was a futile effort. Evan, at least, seemed to have lost the ability to concentrate on anything other than Nora's eyes and her soft, shy smile.

Just last week they had finally managed to set the date—May 15. That very night, Evan wrote an eager letter to his father, urging him to come to New York for the wedding—and to bring Aunt Winnie. He had been writing of Nora all along, of course, but making an effort not to reveal his feelings about her. It was a dizzying thing, finally being able to admit his love—and to write of their wedding!

Since then, however, little had been accomplished in the way of planning. Evan was still too caught up in the incredible realization that Nora loved him and had consented to be his wife. Nothing would have suited him better than to toss convention aside and have the wedding tomorrow. Nora was having none of that, of course, and insisted, red-faced and flustered, that he was disgracing her with his impatience.

"I d-don't agree," he told her firmly. "This is the f-first time in my entire life that I've ever b-been in love. Why wouldn't I b-be impatient to m-make you my wife? I—I am a man consumed b-by love!"

"Evan, do be serious! We have much to decide, you know." She lifted a hand to pat the neat, thick bun at the nape of her neck, threaded with a blue satin ribbon. Glancing at Evan, she broke into laughter, delighting him. He leaned closer and kissed her on the cheek.

She was lovely. There was no longer any evidence of the scarlet fever in her creamy white skin, and her dark hair held a high glossy sheen, even where streaked with gray. She was a princess in a prim white blouse, a gift to his heart, a treasure. And she was his!

But Nora was right. They *did* have much to decide, numerous questions to resolve. There was the matter of money, for example. Neither of them really had any. Evan had tucked away the small sum sent by his father in December, but the considerable savings he'd accumulated over the years of working for Roger Gilpin still sat, irretrievable, in a London bank. To attempt to withdraw it might lead his former employer directly to him—he could not risk it! He would do nothing to jeopardize what he had found with Nora.

She agreed, assuring him each time he raised the subject that they would manage nicely on their wages from the Farmingtons. Nevertheless, Evan intended to work toward the day when they could become independent of Lewis Farmington's largess.

Both Mr. Farmington and his daughter, Sara, had been good to them beyond all imagining, and Evan was deeply grateful. But he could not see himself accepting their help indefinitely.

For Nora's sake, he had acquiesced to his employer's insistence that he be allowed to "help" with the wedding—meaning, of course, that he intended to pay for the entire thing.

Because Evan wanted a proper ceremony for Nora, he had accepted what was obviously a sincere desire on the part of the Farmingtons to make them a gift of the wedding. But both he and Nora had refused the offer of a large, expensive ceremony at the Fifth Avenue church. They asked instead that Pastor Dalton officiate at a small, private wedding in the prayer chapel of the mansion.

Their suggestion seemed to please Sara Farmington to no end. The small chapel had been added to the east wing of the mansion at her mother's request, Sara told them. There could be no more perfect occasion than a wedding, she insisted, for making good use of the little chapel.

Apart from the wedding ceremony, Evan had determined to strive toward financial independence for himself and Nora. He was about to become a husband, after all—perhaps even a father, God willing. He wanted to be the head of his own family, not dependent upon another man's charity.

"Will we have ch-children, Nora?" he blurted out abruptly.

With a startled look, Nora's face flamed. Quickly Evan reached for her hand. "Oh, I'm sorry, d-dear! I k-keep doing it, d-don't I?"

"Doing what, Evan?" she choked out, still looking at him with a slightly stunned expression.

"Embarrassing you with m-my foolishness."

She smiled into his eyes, melting his heart. "Oh, Evan…I expect *I* would be the foolish one, to be embarrassed by a good man's love."

Beaming, Evan scooted his chair a bit closer to hers.

"Do you *want* children, Evan?" Nora asked softly, lowering her eyes. "What I mean is, you've already assumed responsibility for wee Tom and Johanna. And there's Daniel John to think of, too, though he will soon be a man grown."

Evan hesitated, wondering how he should answer. Nora had lost four children, after all—her oldest son and her little girl, plus the two infants who had died at birth. Perhaps she would not want to risk having another.

He waited for her to meet his eyes. When she did, he laid the palm of his hand gently against her cheek. "I w-want…whatever *you* want, Nora. That is all I will *ever* want."

Nora's gaze searched his, and at last she smiled. "Then we will be a large family, please, God," she said quietly. "For I would like to give you sons of your own, Evan Whittaker. The Lord knows this poor world needs more good men like you."

He leaned close, and—as it often happened these days—their attempts at practicality were forgotten in the sweet magic of a kiss.

Grinning broadly, Sara Farmington backed out of the kitchen before they saw her.

Her intention had been to confer with Nora about a singular problem regarding the guest list. Unwilling to intrude upon their privacy, she tiptoed down the hall in search of her father.

To her surprise, she eventually found him in the chapel. He seldom went inside the small sanctuary; it reminded him too painfully of Sara's mother. Most often, he did his praying and shared his quiet times with God in the seclusion of the library.

Tonight, however, he was sitting in the back of the chapel, his arms folded over his chest as he faced the small, plain cross that was the only adornment at the front of the room.

His face was shadowed in the dim light from two flickering candles. For a moment Sara thought her father was praying. Not wanting to intrude, she turned to go.

When he quietly spoke her name, however, she went to join him. "If you want to be alone, Father—"

"Not at all," he said, taking her hand. "I was just sitting here thinking of your mother."

Surprised, Sara examined his profile. "Are you feeling lonely tonight, Father?" she asked, concerned.

He shook his head, turning to look at her. "No, not lonely. Sometimes I just like to sit and think about Clarissa. About our special times together."

"You were very happy together, you and Mother," said Sara, squeezing his hand.

A faint smile touched his lips. "Indeed we were. Your mother was a wonderful wife—a splendid woman. Our marriage was quite the best thing that ever happened to me."

"You've missed her terribly over the years, haven't you, Father?"

He sighed. "I will always miss her, Sara. But I have memories the years can't touch."

Sara turned away, inexplicably saddened by the rapt expression on his face. Sometimes it seemed that all those around her had someone special in their life—or at least had known the unforgettable experience of loving and being loved. She rejoiced in their joy, but she could not share it. She knew God loved her, of course, and she knew that her friends cared—her father, Nora and Evan, the Daltons. But somehow, tonight, none of that seemed to matter. When she returned to her room and lay down to sleep, she would still face the unutterable isolation of her aloneness, unwarmed even by her memories.

Her father's hand tightened on hers. "Sara? Is something wrong?"

She turned to him. To her dismay, something in his gentle, fatherly expression of concern brought her feelings of loneliness rushing to the surface. She felt tears form in her eyes and blinked furiously so he wouldn't see.

"Why, Sara," her father said, cupping her chin so she could not look away, "what is it? What's made you so unhappy?"

Suddenly she felt like a little girl again. And for a moment she almost wished she *could* be. Everything was so much easier then. She had never felt alone or unwanted, hadn't worried about growing older by herself without a husband or children or the fulfillment of loving someone who loved her as well. She could simply crawl onto her father's lap, and he would rock her in his arms and make everything in her world all right again.

"Sara?" he pressed gently.

She looked at him, able to manage only the weakest of smiles.

"I'm sorry, Father. I'm not unhappy. Truly, I'm not. I think I'm just feeling very emotional because of Evan and Nora's wedding. They're so sweet together, aren't they? And for a moment it made me sad, to think of you and Mother as you must have been, the way you must have loved each other. I believe I might be feeling a bit sentimental tonight."

Her father's dark eyes, so disconcertingly knowing, went over her face. Slowly, he nodded, then pulled her head against his shoulder. "I understand, dear," he said quietly, holding her. "I understand."

Sara closed her eyes and leaned against him, summoning all her reserves to resist the temptation to let go, to let years of unshed tears fall at last. She did not—could not—tell her father how she longed to be loved, how something deep inside her cried out for her to give up being strong and capable, just for a moment. There was no one to turn to, no one to lean on, no one to whom she *belonged*.

><

Sara finally caught Nora by herself later that night in the upstairs hallway. Apparently, she had left Evan not long before, for her face was absolutely radiant.

Sara could not resist teasing. "While I know that glowing smile isn't for me, it's a delight to see you looking so happy."

Nora blushed, but continued to smile.

"Let's go to my room," suggested Sara. "I have some questions only you can answer about the guest list for the wedding."

Once they were settled on the chaise in Sara's bedroom, Sara searched the face of the bride-to-be for a moment. "You really *are* happy, aren't you, Nora?"

"Oh, of course, I am!" Nora assured her without hesitation.

But even as she spoke, something altered in her expression that made Sara frown and touch her arm. "What is it?"

Nora's answering smile was weak and self-conscious. "It's foolish entirely. I don't think I could explain." She glanced away, then turned back with a short, unconvincing laugh. "Sure, it's nothing more than Irish superstition. It's just that at times, when I'm feeling happiest, it's as if a cold, dark shadow passes over my heart. Almost as if…to warn me I mustn't be *too* happy."

Again she laughed. "As I said—'tis nothing more than superstitious nonsense. 'Too much joy makes the devil jealous,' Old Dan used to say." Her expression turned somber. "It might be I'm afraid of too much joy, Sara."

Nora sat silent for a moment, her eyes averted. Then, with obvious effort, she forced a more cheerful expression. "Now," she said, "there was something you wanted to talk about?"

Sara searched Nora's face briefly, then withdrew the guest list from her skirt pocket. "I have just a few questions. I want to be sure I don't neglect anyone you want invited to the wedding."

"Oh, Sara, you needn't do this!" Nora protested. "We really don't want anyone here but the children and you and your father—"

"Evan's father, if he comes—"

"Yes, of course. And his aunt."

"What about Michael Burke and Tierney?"

The light faded from Nora's eyes. "I—I don't know that either will come."

"Nora, have you talked with Michael? I mean, *really* talked with him, since your illness?"

Nora shook her head and looked away.

"Shouldn't you?"

When Nora looked at her, Sara hastily said, "I don't mean to interfere. But I think Michael would want to come. And I'm certain that Daniel would want him and Tierney to be there."

"I did try to talk with Michael," Nora said, "once, while I was still in the hospital, and again later. He was—he seemed in a fierce hurry to leave me. I don't think he heard anything I said. I don't think he *wanted* to."

"He was still hurting," Sara said gently. "Perhaps you could try again, now that he's had time to accept things."

Nora raised her eyes from her hands. "Do you truly think so? I'm not sure...and Tierney—"

"It may take longer for Tierney. But perhaps Michael could at least convince him to come to the wedding. I think it's important for Daniel."

Nodding slowly, Nora said, "Yes, you're right. Daniel would want him there. They're such good friends."

"So are you and Michael," Sara reminded her gently.

Nora looked at her with a thoughtful smile. "Yes. And you are a good friend, too, Sara. A very good friend, indeed." She paused. "You're right about Michael. I'll try to talk with him again soon."

"Is there anyone else at all you'd like invited, Nora? What about family or friends still in Ireland?"

The last remaining light of happiness faded from Nora's eyes as she turned her face away from Sara. "There are no family or friends left in Ireland," she said quietly. "Only one. But...he would not be wanting to come to my wedding."

33

Keen for a Fallen Friend

The valley lay smiling before me,
Where lately I left her behind,
Yet I trembled, and something hung o'er me,
That saddened the joy of my mind.

THOMAS MOORE (1779–1852)

New York City
Early March

As she dressed for her visit to Michael, Nora's hands shook so badly she could scarcely button her shirtwaist. It took her several minutes simply to get the hairpins in her hair, because she kept dropping each one she picked up.

Smoothing her collar with trembling fingers, she remained standing in front of the mirror without really seeing herself. She knew her apprehension was foolish. This was Michael, after all. He would not strike her or insult her. More than likely, she would be met by the same fixed, inscrutable expression that had greeted her two previous efforts to put things right between them.

But this time, she must find a way to break through his unyielding coldness. She *must*, for the sake of their friendship—and for the sake of Daniel John, who had finally admitted his desire to go on living with Michael and Tierney. She prayed the Lord would open Michael's heart to her this evening, that he would be receptive and at least try to understand.

Michael did not love her. Nora had known that for a long time. He cared about her, would have done anything in his power to help her—even to the extreme of marrying her. But he did not *love* her, not as a man should love a wife. Nor could her feelings for him ever be anything more than friendship.

The Lord had known. More than once, she had sensed His Spirit's restraint, the caution to make no hasty commitment to Michael.

And now she knew why. *Evan* was God's plan for her, not Michael. In her heart she saw Evan's dear, kind face that day months ago, aboard the *Green Flag*, when he had offered her his "protection" during the terrible sea voyage and for as long afterward as she might need it. He had been ill even then, ill and feverish, with the wound in his arm already going bad. Yet he had sat there, pale and miserably shy, but with an unmistakable dignity, asking her to at least consider him a friend.

She could not say, exactly, when her love for Evan had begun. It had been a subtle, gradual awakening; indeed, it almost seemed to have had no real beginning. But God had known even then that one day He would join their hearts, would allow them to share a very special love. And for that, she would be forever grateful!

Yet, just as surely as she knew she was to wed Evan, Nora believed that her friendship with Michael was not to be taken lightly, to be cast aside as if it were of no value. Michael was important to her—and important to her son. Surely a friendship such as this was a gift worth preserving. And preserve it, she would, if she could only find the way.

If her life and Michael's were to be intertwined, if they were to share her son and sustain the bond of affection that had existed since their youth, she must somehow bridge the gap that lay between them. Much depended on the outcome of this evening, and her own peace of mind was but a small part of it.

Sighing, she turned away from the mirror and started for the bedroom door. She could not delay it any longer. While she still had no idea what she was going to say to Michael, she was resolved to try, and leave the rest in God's hands.

The letter from Joseph Mahon the priest reached Michael two weeks after he had written his own letter to Morgan Fitzgerald in Dublin.

Standing in the dimness of the kitchen early that evening, Michael had to read the priest's words over twice before his mind could fully comprehend the tragedy that had befallen his boyhood friend. Even then, a part of him froze in disbelief, unwilling—unable—to take it in.

Stunned, he sat down at the table, staring at the letter that he held in front of him. He felt faint, as if all the blood in his body had drained away.

Again, his eyes went over the words. Morgan...paralyzed? Confined to a wheelchair...an invalid—for *life*?

Dear God in heaven, how could such a thing happen? And how was it to be borne by a man who had spent most of his life on his legs, roaming an entire country just for the love of it?

A painful memory flashed before Michael's mind—a younger Morgan, all long arms and legs, loping down the road with his harp slung over his shoulder and his eyes looking past the town, seeking whatever lay beyond the confines of their small village.

Another thought struck him now, and he squeezed his eyes shut and moaned aloud. The letter *he* had written, the letter to Morgan telling him about Nora and Whittaker: Would it make things more difficult still?

Inexplicably, Morgan had seemed resigned to the idea of Nora marrying his best friend—more than likely because it was a means of saving her life. But to learn that she was to wed, not Michael, but the English Whittaker—no matter how much he had liked and respected the man— what would such news do to him, coming on the heels of what he had already lost?

If only he had waited to send the letter. Yet he had believed that he should be the one to tell Morgan. He wanted him to know that he had at least fulfilled his part of his promise, that he had offered marriage to Nora, had waited months for her to decide—only to lose her to another man. There was nothing more he could have done to change things, and he wanted Morgan to hear that from *him*.

Now, the thought that his letter might only deepen his friend's anguish hit Michael like a sickening blow. He wrapped his arms around himself bracing his body against the pain knifing through him.

Oh, Morgan, you great, grand fool! Didn't I warn you that terrible, fierce island would one day destroy you? Why couldn't you have left it with the rest of us? Why couldn't you have saved yourself while trying to save everyone else?

Never before had Michael felt so far away from Ireland. Never before had he sensed so keenly the vast distance that separated him from the one man in his life he had loved as a brother.

Hugging his arms tightly to his body, he stared at the letter spread out before him. A shattering sob tore from his throat, and for the first time since the death of his wife, Michael wept.

Asking Uriah to wait with the carriage, Nora started for the front door. She stopped long enough to glance up at the window of Michael's flat on the second floor, where a faint glow could be seen behind the curtains. Drawing in a long steadying breath, she went inside.

She was uncomfortably aware that her behavior was improper—a lone woman calling on a man in his home. But she considered her friendship with Michael of more importance than convention. Indeed, she had chosen this evening deliberately, knowing both Daniel John and Tierney would be away. Tierney would be working late at the hotel, as he did every Friday night, and Daniel John had been invited to spend the evening at the Daltons, with Casey-Fitz and Arthur Jackson. Their absence would give her and Michael time alone together to talk.

Assuming, of course, that he was *willing* to talk.

She had to knock twice before he opened the door.

"Michael, I know you didn't expect me, but—"

Nora broke off, staring at him. His eyes were red and shadowed, his face haggard. He looked as if he were either ill or utterly exhausted.

He stared at her with a vacant gaze for a moment, then stepped aside so she could enter. Slowly, he closed the door, then turned to face her.

"Nora," he said dully, "Daniel John is not here."

"Yes, I know," she answered uncertainly. "I—I came to talk with you, Michael. But if this is a bad time—"

Again he stared at her. Finally, with a stiff, jerky movement, he pulled out a chair from the table and held it for her to sit down.

What looked to be a letter had been left open, and he reached now to fold it and return it to its envelope.

"Michael, I—we need desperately to talk. I know you haven't wanted to up until now, but if you would only listen to me...." Nora's words drifted off. He seemed strange, distracted; her nerve began to fail her.

As if he had not heard her at all, Michael went to stand at the window, his back to her.

Biting her lip, Nora watched him nervously for a moment, then took a deep breath. "Michael—I thought…I know you're unhappy with me, and I suppose you have a right to be. But I can't bear having this bitterness between us. I never meant to hurt you, Michael. I would *never* deliberately hurt you!"

He turned to look at her, and Nora saw with dismay that there was a great sorrow in his eyes. *Dear Lord, it is even worse than I thought!*

"Michael," she choked out. "Please…come sit down with me. Please, for the sake of our friendship—and our sons—we *must* talk to each other!"

At last he nodded and moved away from the window. "Aye," he said, absently starting for the stove, "you're right. We must talk. I'll just fix us some tea."

Perhaps he was going to be reasonable, after all. Somewhat relieved, Nora waited until he brought the teakettle and cups to the table and sat down.

She began by reminding him of how important he had always been to her, from the time they had been childhood friends growing up in the village. His silence encouraged her, and she went on, telling him sincerely how much it had meant to her, his willingness to take Daniel John into his home—and his proposal of marriage upon her arrival in America.

"But, Michael," she continued quietly, "I think I knew even then it was not to be. 'Twas not for love that you were wanting to marry me, but for the sake of our old friendship, yours and mine—and your promise to Morgan."

Puzzled, Nora saw a look of pain cross his features. But he merely nodded and went on staring at his hands, clasped in front of him on the table.

"Michael…I did not mean…to fall in love with Evan. In truth, I never thought to love any man again, after Owen. What has happened between Evan and me—I can't explain it."

For the first time since she'd begun her appeal, Michael spoke. Without raising his eyes from his hands, he said quietly, "Nora, you do not owe me an explanation. I know there is no explaining why a woman loves one man instead of another."

Nora reached for his hand, and he looked up. His eyes searched hers, but there was no anger in his gaze. Relieved, Nora squeezed his hand. "Michael, that day in the hospital, when I first came to America, and you asked me to marry you—"

Unbelievably, he smiled a little. A sad, haunted smile. "And you refused me...for the second time?"

"Oh, Michael! Do you remember the promise you asked from me that day?"

He looked at her blankly.

"You said if the time ever came when my heart sang love for a man, I mustn't let the song be silenced by uncertainty or pride. You made me promise to—to '*give love's song a voice*,' that's what you said. Even..." She faltered, then went on. "Even if the song was not for *you*...but for *another*."

His sad, sad gaze went over her face, and he nodded, smiling that same heartbreaking smile. "Aye, I did say that, didn't I? More fool, I."

"Oh, *Michael*!" Nora choked out, feeling the tears spill over from her eyes. "I'm sorry, but I do love Evan!"

He enfolded her hand between both of his. "Ah, Nora, it's all right, lass. Don't be crying, now. I've been the great fool, and that's the truth. I saw it coming, I suppose, but simply refused to face it. I was lonely, that was the thing, and I was looking to you to ease the loneliness. I thought you needed me...and I you. But it wouldn't have been right, not for you...and perhaps not for me, either. It simply wasn't meant to be, was it? I'm only sorry I hurt you as I did, with my foolish, hardheaded ways."

Such a wave of relief swept over Nora that she could no longer control the tears. She sobbed, and Michael moved to pull his chair alongside hers. Gently, he coaxed her head onto his shoulder and began to soothe her. "Ah, don't, Nora Ellen, don't be crying over it any longer. We are still the best of friends. We will forget this ever happened, and go on. You will see."

"Oh, Michael, I'm so relieved! I *hated* having you angry with me!"

"Ah, lass, there must be no more anger between us now. Not now, not ever."

Something in his voice made Nora lift her face to look at him through her tears. Amazed, she saw that his own eyes were moist. "Michael?"

He squeezed his eyes shut.

"Michael?" she said again. "What is it?"

She put a hand to his arm and felt him shudder. He opened his eyes, and they were filled with anguish.

Still clutching his arm, Nora searched his face. "Tell me."

He drew in a long, ragged breath. Then he told her the terrible thing that had been done to Morgan.

The longer Michael spoke, the louder the roar in Nora's head became. At times it almost drowned out what he was saying. But she heard the dreadful words all too clearly: *"shot...paralyzed...wheelchair..."*

"For the rest of his *life*?" she whispered, begging Michael with her eyes to tell her it wasn't so. "There is nothing that can be done?"

Michael shook his head, again closing his eyes as if to shut out the sight of her anguish.

Sick incredulity gave way to a tearing pain that ripped through her entire body. The room reeled as Nora braced both hands on the edge of the table.

"It will *kill* him!" she whispered. "He cannot bear such a thing!"

Nora scarcely heard Michael's words as he tried to comfort her. The shock had dazed her; the pain was numbing. At some point she realized her head was again pressed against Michael's shoulder, and she was keening softly as if for one dead.

She had no awareness of how long they remained that way. Michael went on holding her, the two of them at last weeping together for their old friend...for the long-legged minstrel who would no longer walk the roads of Ireland with his harp slung over his shoulder and the sun shining warm upon his face.

After hearing the Fitzgerald children's prayers, Evan worked in the library with Mr. Farmington for another hour.

Shortly before nine, he went to the kitchen to wait for Nora. When she hadn't returned by nine thirty, he began to worry. By ten, he was frantic.

Pacing the kitchen, he imagined the worst. *Burke had given her a difficult time of it. They had argued and he'd grown abusive. They hadn't argued and Nora had changed her mind, had decided to marry the policeman after all. The carriage had been waylaid by thugs and Nora was lying in one of the city streets, hurt and unnoticed.*

When he heard her at the back entrance a few minutes past ten, he flew to the door and flung it open, gathering her inside before she could even speak.

"Th-thank heaven! I was wo-worried half to death!"

Helping her with her wrap, he went on talking, rambling in his relief. "I thought you'd be b-back long before now."

Only when he had hung up her coat and turned her around to face him did he realize how utterly exhausted and wan she looked.

"Nora?"

"I'm sorry to worry you," she said, her voice low. "I didn't think to be so late."

Something in the thinness of her voice, the way she continued to avoid his gaze, sent a warning racing through Evan.

Trying to ignore his growing sense of dread, he took her hand. "You must b-be exhausted. Would you r-rather not talk tonight, dear?"

"Oh...no, I—" Finally she raised her gaze to his. The well of anguish in her magnificent gray eyes made Evan sway on his feet.

Had his worst fears been realized, after all? Had she decided for Michael Burke instead of him? Was he to lose her, even before she was really his?

"Nora, what...what is it?" His voice shook as he forced out the words, bracing himself for whatever he was about to hear.

Nora searched his face with pain-filled eyes. Unexpectedly, she collapsed against him, sobbing. "Oh, Evan!" she choked out. "'Tis the most terrible thing!"

Helpless, Evan tightened his arm around her. With growing horror, he held her as she told him of the tragedy that had befallen Morgan Fitzgerald.

Tortured by her despair and the memory of the giant, heroic Gael they had left behind in Ireland, Evan's heart bowed beneath the burden of Nora's anguish...and his own.

34

The World and Nelson Hall

I have not gathered gold;
The fame that I won perished;
In love I found but sorrow,
That withered my life.
Of wealth or of glory
I shall leave nothing behind me
(I think it, O God, enough!)
But my name in the heart of a child.

PADRAIC PEARSE (1879–1916)

Dublin

Within three weeks of Sandemon's arrival at Nelson Hall, Morgan had begun to feel as if he were living in two worlds.

Outside the estate, the world at large was convulsed with unprecedented turmoil and upheaval. A workers' revolution in France had exploded, proclaiming a republic and sending the French king scurrying into exile in England. Like a forest fire, the revolt in France sparked outbursts of revolution throughout all Europe. The flames of rebellion spread to Germany, Austria, and Italy, creating a climate of chaos and insurrection across the Continent.

The news of widespread revolution fired Irish blood with new fervor and talk of rebellion. Assuming a good harvest this year, the end to famine was in sight, excited nationalists insisted; was the time not right to plan their rising? Those who cautioned that it would take years of good harvests to inject any strength into Ireland were either wholly ignored or scorned into silence.

Factions of the Young Ireland movement heretofore split on the issue of rebellion came together, as if the revolution in France had changed everything. There was talk of shouldering pikes and guns, inflammatory literature written to fire the patriotism of young men. Even a new Irish flag was hoisted, at first with the French red, white, and blue in honor of the new French Republic. But soon there appeared the tricolored banner of orange, green, and white—to reflect the union of the parties.

In the midst of the swelling cry for insurrection, William Smith O'Brien and a few others held back, still convinced that a peasant war in the midst of the famine's devastation could wipe out the island entirely. Weeks before, however, impatient with the caution of O'Brien and others, the formidable John Mitchel had separated himself from Young Ireland. Taking his burning vision for a people's rising and his considerable talent for arousing the masses, he began a new movement—one dedicated to armed rebellion.

For his podium, he established his own newspaper, the brazen, vitriolic *United Irishman*. Soon many of the previously cautious Young Irelanders were quoting Mitchel's fiery rhetoric and calling for armed revolt.

Finally, it seemed, even Smith O'Brien surrendered to the people's mood. At a huge meeting of the Confederation, he called for an Irish army of at least 300,000 men who would "protect social order and act in defense of the country."

Reading excerpts from O'Brien's speech in *The Nation*, Morgan shook his head with dismay. *Old friend, you have destroyed yourself,* he thought. *And more than likely, the entire Young Ireland movement as well.*

The British government had already instituted prosecutions for sedition against O'Brien, Mitchel, and Meagher. The three were still out on bail, but not for long, Morgan suspected. Not for long.

Yet in the midst of the turbulence going on in the rest of the world, life had settled into an unexpectedly smooth routine at Nelson Hall. Grudgingly, Morgan had to admit the improvements could be credited only to Sandemon's influence. Unbelievably, his new companion seemed to be proving the wonder Joseph Mahon had touted him to be.

The black man had immediately set about imposing order and purpose on Morgan's days, including a new regime of daily therapy and exercise. Such a program was fundamental, he insisted, for a long-range plan of restoring Morgan to health and vigor.

The attendant from the hospital was immediately discharged. The day maids were supervised more closely; the mansion had actually taken on a neater, more cheerful appearance.

To Morgan's amazement, even the food seemed improved, not so much by variety but more by flavor and seasonings. Since he was quite certain that the dull Mrs. Ryan—queen of wilted cabbage and unsalted turnips—could not be coerced by any means, he could only wonder at what sort of ruse the devious Sandemon might have employed to inspire the cook.

The one divergence from this newly developing order was Annie Delaney. Despite Sandemon's rigid control over her, the crazed child from Belfast was a continual distraction and disruption.

Apparently, in Annie Delaney, even Sandemon the Wonder had met his match. Instructed by Morgan to keep the girl "out of trouble and out of his hair," Sandemon devised a schedule of chores for Annie. Unfortunately, she proved a monumental failure in all she attempted.

The sound of smashed crockery rose above Mrs. Ryan's fury when Annie was set to helping in the kitchen. Flowers wilted from her attention with the watering can. The fire blazed dangerously out of control when she poked the logs. The crystal vibrated in the wake of her unladylike dashes through the dining room. And Artegal, poor pale specter, froze in terror each time the girl careened into the hall after descending the steps three at a time.

The Old Ones would have said she was a faerie child. Sandemon proclaimed her as God's child. Morgan insisted she was a demented child.

No matter what Sandemon tried, the girl's appearance remained disreputable. She claimed to comb her hair each morning, yet it looked a tangled nest by the time she came down to breakfast. She swore that she bathed faithfully every other day, but the smudges on her cheeks never quite disappeared. Mrs. Ryan had accumulated some decent clothing for the girl, but on her angular frame all dresses appeared baggy, all hems hung unevenly, and half of all buttons were missing.

Yet her gap-toothed grin could somehow break through Morgan's black moods and coax a smile, no matter how firmly he resisted. At times he even caught himself listening for her approach.

He admitted it was an impractical situation altogether, having the child continually underfoot, but when he considered sending her away, he could not think where.

Perhaps it might be different if the girl were of any real help. At least that would justify her presence at Nelson Hall. But the truth was that Annie Delaney seemed to be good at nothing—nothing at all—except for making noise and breaking dishes.

When he pointed this out to Sandemon, the black man would simply nod serenely and then remind Morgan that Christian charity required no justification. Besides, he would say confidently, in time they were sure to find just the right "service" for Annie Delaney. The girl would eventually do more than try their patience, he was certain of it.

Morgan did not believe it for a moment. Sandemon pampered the girl, that was the thing. He had not missed the growing bond between the two. The child did seem to *try* to please the black man. The fact that she never succeeded did not appear to affect Sandemon in the least. He praised her for nothing, encouraged her in everything, and took an almost fatherly, forgiving view of her failures. Even when her grating Ulster accent reduced his name to "Sand-Man," he seemed inordinately pleased by the exasperating child.

Morgan knew better by now than to argue with Sandemon about Annie Delaney. For that matter, he was learning the futility of arguing with Sandemon about *anything*, anything at all.

Besides, arguing required strength, and strength was something he no longer had. In truth, he doubted that he would ever be strong again. In spite of Sandemon's rigorous exercise and therapy routine, he could not see where he had gained much, if at all. Oh, his bones had some meat on them again, and thanks to the black man's relentless nagging, his muscles were toned and gaining some use once more. But all too often he still felt as weak as a scalded cat, and the pain that wracked him daily was nearly as fierce as ever.

Indeed, he was convinced it was the pain that was keeping him so weak. Each time he thought he might be making progress, he would be seized with an agony that went on for hours and left him drained and inert for days.

'Twas the pain that had driven him back to the bottle. The bullet was still lodged in his back—and would remain so. No surgeon would touch it, they had told him in Belfast, and again in Dublin. They feared that displacing it could extend the paralysis even higher up his body—or cause his death. Morgan could not help but wonder if, like the bullet, the pain might be with him forever.

Frightened of becoming too dependent on the laudanum, he had chosen not to keep it on the premises. But one night, at the end of his wits with the white hot pain, he had decided to have some whiskey brought in.

His grandfather never touched "the creature," as the people referred to it, so there was none in the house. He could not ask Smith O'Brien, for the man was a known teetotaler and would more than likely be offended by the request. Certainly he would not ask Sandemon. No doubt the West Indies Wonder would comply, but in the process would make Morgan feel a failure and a fool.

In the end, it was Artegal to whom he turned. He knew very well his prim, pale footman took a drop every now and then—indeed, he had smelled it on his breath. When Morgan faced him with his suspicions, Artegal had at first looked offended, then anxious.

The outcome was that Morgan now had his own bottle, tucked away unnoticed in his bedroom. Each night he would pour a small tumbler full and drink it quickly, so as not to enjoy the taste. He was careful to drink only a small amount, as little as he could get by on, in order to sleep.

He was relieved at the difference it was making. A few solid hours' rest without waking in pain had to be better for him, he reasoned, than those long, wakeful nights spent in agony. If he occasionally paused before the first sip of the evening, remembering what "the creature" had done to his father, the thought did not stay his hand for long.

In truth, drink had immobilized Aidan Fitzgerald, stealing the attention and the affection that should have rightfully belonged to his sons, turning a bitter, unhappy man into a morose, defeated drunk. However, Morgan would remind himself with a grim smile, he was *already* immobilized, and he had no sons—or anyone else—requiring his attention or his affection. Besides, he had no thought of ending up like his father. He had handled the whiskey before, after all, when he was still a young rake on the road. He would handle it now. It would serve him as medicine, and nothing more, until the time came when he no longer needed it. If, indeed, that time ever came.

Sandemon had spent most of the morning on the Dublin docks and was becoming increasingly dispirited by his surroundings.

The young *Seanchai* was still curious about the woman who had allegedly rescued Annie Delaney the night she arrived in Dublin. Apparently, he had convinced himself that the child's story was too outrageous to be anything but fabricated.

For himself, Sandemon believed the child and wished only to thank the woman who had saved her. He had suggested to the dubious young master that he might do the same, if they were indeed able to locate Annie Delaney's "guardian angel."

Whether Morgan Fitzgerald realized it or not, Sandemon was convinced the stubborn giant was becoming attached to his "demented child."

It was as he had hoped: Annie Delaney, with all her curious qualities and seeming flaws, had indeed been sent by the Lord and would be used in the *Seanchai*'s healing.

If, that is, Morgan Fitzgerald did not manage to resist *her* as successfully as he had resisted all other evidences of God's grace thus far. For as was so often the case in the midst of tragedy, young Morgan seemed bent on turning away from his Lord rather than clinging to Him.

Sandemon understood. He had done the same once, a long time ago. Tormented by the fear that God had turned away from him—wasn't his personal tragedy evidence of that very fact?—he had proceeded to absent himself from God.

As for the young master—well, this one was not simply *turning* away—he was running away, at least in his spirit. And not for the first time, according to the priest, Joseph Mahon. With evident affection, the aging priest had told Sandemon something of his new employer's past, including the long years of spiritual rebellion.

Only in recent months had the prodigal returned to his heavenly Father. But the homecoming celebration was short-lived, brutally interrupted by the shooting in Belfast that had left him as he was now—a bitter man in a wheelchair, feeling abandoned and utterly useless.

There was abundant hope for the *Seanchai*, of course. He was God's child, and he had friends standing in prayer for him. Yet Sandemon could not ignore a growing fear for the anguished young poet, who was attempting to numb his pain with the lie of whiskey.

He thought he was deceiving those around him by drinking alone in his room at night. But he was deluding only himself. Most likely he was using the lingering pain of his injury to justify his dependence on the bottle.

Sandemon sensed, however, that the young master's spiritual torment far exceeded his physical pain. Such an agony would not be quenched by drinking from anything other than the Water of Life.

Sighing, Sandemon turned his thoughts from Morgan Fitzgerald to look around him. It seemed this entire country was in agony. Here, spread out on the docks beneath a dull, heavy sky, hundreds of people waited for ships to take them away from Ireland.

The depths of misery and neglect seemed no different here in the city than in the remote villages of County Mayo. Starving and ill, devastated by fever and the harsh elements, the poor souls camped on and around the docks, praying they would survive long enough to board their ship of rescue.

Sandemon wept in his spirit for the nearly naked, starving children, the bewildered, diseased elderly, the gaunt young mothers with hollow eyes. For a time he abandoned his mission of locating Annie Delaney's rescuer and joined three priests in moving through the crowds, attempting to soothe and console the suffering all around him. He prayed for the living and grieved for the dying, sorrowful but not surprised at what man's inhumanity had once more wrought in God's world.

For three days Sandemon returned to question pub owners and innkeepers along the docks, as well as numerous poor wretches throughout the disreputable area known as the Liberties. He had only the sketchiest of memories of the woman he had seen with Annie, in addition to the child's dramatic description: "Sure, and wasn't she a great, tall lady, with glorious golden hair? She had a grand cloak, remember? And she was beautiful, like a stage actress! But she didn't talk—she didn't talk at all, Sand-Man!"

On the fourth day, Sandemon felt his search might have proved fruitful. A young strumpet in the slums had reacted at once to the description the black man gave her. Suspicious and openly hostile, she proceeded to rake Sandemon from head to toe with cold eyes. "What's it to the likes of *you*? A good way to get your throat slit, in case you didn't know it, asking after a white woman in a place such as this!"

Adopting an air of exaggerated humility, Sandemon stretched the reason for his questions as far as he could without actually lying. "She did a kind thing for a child who is—important to my young master," he told the prostitute. "He is eager to find her, that he might—acknowledge her bravery."

"Bravery?" The young woman's hard eyes narrowed in speculation. "Is it a reward he's talking, then?"

Sandemon merely shrugged and gave a noncommittal smile.

She studied him for another moment. "Could be he's looking for Finola. I'm not saying it's her, mind—just that it might be."

"And could you tell me where to find this...Finola?"

The woman shrugged. "She stays at Gemma's mostly."

"Gemma's?"

She gave him an impatient look. "Gemma Malone's. She has a place with some girls upstairs at Healy's Inn. Not far from St. Paddy's—the cathedral. This time of day," she added with a sneer, "you'd find most of them at home, likely."

This one was little more than a child, Sandemon observed sadly, wondering how one so young had come to such a place. What tragedy had driven her to the streets? What lonely desperation lay behind the painted mask?

Sandemon met her gaze, and for a moment something flickered behind the hard exterior. With a courteous bow, he then raised his eyes and smiled directly into hers. "God loves you, child," he said gently.

Then he turned and walked away to continue his search.

35

Finola

Then blame not the bard, if, in pleasure's soft dream,
He should try to forget what he never can heal.

THOMAS MOORE (1779–1852)

Healy's Inn was at the fringe of the Liberties and easy to find. As the street girl had said, it wasn't far from St. Patrick's, the twelfth-century cathedral dedicated to Ireland's patron saint.

Sandemon was surprised to find the ancient cathedral located in the midst of low streets and narrow, squalid alleys. As for the inn, it was actually a run-down pub—dim interior, dilapidated stools, two or three worn-looking women drinking at a table near the bar.

Sandemon asked for the woman named Finola and was met with a hostile glare from the middle-aged man keeping bar. Thinking the fellow's unfriendliness was due to his black skin, Sandemon quickly explained that his business was on behalf of his employer. "I assure you he means only to thank the young woman," he said with a deferential smile. "Did I mention that he is the grandson of Sir Richard Nelson?"

"Aye, and the Queen is me godmother," the barman sneered.

Sandemon had not come into the Liberties entirely unprepared. He withdrew two calling cards from his shirt pocket, one with Morgan's name imprinted on it, the other bearing Sir Richard's. Extending the cards to the barman, he said quietly but emphatically, "It could be important to the young woman that she meet with my employer. He would like to thank her for a kindness."

The red-faced barman was clearly unimpressed. Picking up a used tumbler off the bar, he wiped it dry and replaced it for the next customer. "Then tell your employer," he said, turning back to Sandemon, "that *he* should come *here*."

Gathering his patience, Sandemon attempted to explain. "I fear that is not a possibility at the present time. The young master is confined to a wheelchair while he recovers from a most serious injury."

The Irishman studied Sandemon another moment. Finally, without turning, he barked an order over his shoulder. "Lucy—go fetch Finola downstairs! Tell her I said she should come."

A small, round woman with a heavily made-up face hauled herself up from her chair and started for the stairs at the side of the bar. When she returned, Sandemon recognized the tall young woman with her at once.

Today there was no shawl covering her hair, which fell in graceful, shining waves down her back, like fine spun gold. Her brightly painted face seemed a cruel mockery of her beauty and otherwise demure appearance. Clinging to the hand of the woman named Lucy, she struck Sandemon as being very shy—or very frightened.

He saw a glint of recognition in her eyes when she looked at him. Inclining his head, he straightened and repeated his explanation for coming. When he had finished, the fair-haired young woman merely stood there, holding Lucy's hand, regarding Sandemon with a clear blue gaze that reflected an unexpected innocence.

"She can't answer you!" snapped the barman.

Sandemon looked at him, and the man tapped his head with a grimy forefinger. "She's a bit slow, Finola is. She can hear you well enough, but she can't talk a bit."

Sandemon turned back to the golden young woman with the startling blue eyes. He looked at her for a moment, then said, "Please, Miss. If you will come with me, the carriage will bring you back later this afternoon. Mr. Fitzgerald is a kind man, and the little girl you helped is most eager to see you again. You will be made welcome at Nelson Hall, I promise you."

Like a child, Finola first looked at the woman, Lucy, then to Healy before turning back to Sandemon. Then, releasing Lucy's protective hand, she nodded that she would accompany Sandemon to Nelson Hall.

But the barman was having none of it. "If it's a woman your employer wants, he can have his choice upstairs! Our Finola isn't for sale!"

Drawing himself up to his full height, which was considerable,

Sandemon fixed the sputtering barman with an unwavering stare. "My employer," he said slowly and distinctly, "is not looking for an upstairs kind of woman. As I have attempted to explain, he merely wants to speak with the young woman who did a kindness for…a member of his household. Perhaps," he added patiently, "both you and Miss Finola would be more at ease if one of these…ladies…accompanied us to Nelson Hall?"

"She can't speak at all, you say?" Morgan repeated, staring at Sandemon with exasperation.

At his companion's brief shake of the head, he slammed one hand down hard against the armrest of the wheelchair. "Then why, pray, did you *bring* her here? The only reason I wished to find her was to verify the girl's story!"

Sandemon inclined his head as if to acknowledge the legitimacy of Morgan's question. "Knowing your skill at communication, sir, I thought you might find another way to converse with her. She is, as I explained, able to hear you."

Morgan shot him a dubious look. Still, there *was* the rudimentary set of hand signals he'd devised to communicate with his niece, Johanna, who could neither hear nor speak. But that had worked only because he'd spent the required time to teach her the gestures.

"Besides, *Seanchai*," Sandemon put in, "I thought the child should have the opportunity of seeing her mysterious rescuer once more. She was, as you know, quite taken with the young woman."

"Ah, yes," Morgan grated, mimicking Annie as he added, " *'Like a princess, she was. Came right out of nowhere!'*"

Sandemon merely smiled.

"Oh, bring her in, then! And fetch the girl as well!" Watching Sandemon nod, then exit with a flourish, Morgan wondered sourly if it was the purple shirt that gave the black man his air of royalty or the ever-present cap he wore as proudly as a crown.

Seated in one of the two fireside chairs, Annie watched the peculiar exchange taking place between the Fitzgerald and Finola with great delight and utter fascination.

Finola's friend, Lucy, perched on the edge of a chair near the door, observing the scene with suspicious eyes. In front of the fireplace, near Annie, stood Sandemon, hands clasped behind his back, watching with discreet interest.

Annie was pleased to see that the golden-haired Finola—who looked like a princess, and that was the truth—seemed to have gotten over her initial shyness with the Fitzgerald. And while he still appeared somewhat stunned by Finola's beauty, he was no longer gaping, but instead making the effort to communicate with her.

Indeed, the two of them seemed to have devised some odd method of talking with each other, in spite of poor Finola's inability to speak aloud. They had reached the point that, when the *Seanchai*—Annie was beginning to think of him in Sandemon's term—enacted one of those funny little hand signs of his, the lovely Finola would either smile or shake her head vigorously, then proceed to wiggle her hands and fingers much as he had.

It was a grand display to watch, and Annie was particularly satisfied to see that the *Seanchai*'s eyes held a smile when he looked at the Princess Finola.

Catching Sandemon's eyes, Annie winked and grinned. He settled a mildly reproving look on her, then winked back.

Later that night, after Finola and Lucy had been safely returned to the inn, Sandemon took a tray of correspondence upstairs to his employer, who waved it aside, saying, "I get nothing but appeals for donations. I'll look at it later. But stay—I want to talk with you."

No longer requiring Sandemon's assistance in getting dressed, he had already changed into his nightclothes. He wheeled himself over to the fire. "What they've done to that girl is a crime!" he blurted out, turning the chair around to face Sandemon.

Genuinely puzzled, Sandemon frowned. "A crime, *Seanchai*?"

"Yes, a *crime*! She's little more than a child, after all, and mute at that! This Healy—he must be as low as they come, to turn an innocent like that into a prostitute!"

Sandemon considered his outburst for a moment, then shook his head. "No," he said slowly, "I don't think that's the case, *Seanchai*."

"What do you mean, you 'don't think that's the case'?" the young master snapped, his face flushed. "The girl lives with strumpets, she's painted like a strumpet—and didn't they send her here with you, a total stranger? To the house of another stranger?"

"They sent a friend to look after her," Sandemon reminded him mildly.

"Also a strumpet!"

"I was informed that Miss Finola was...not for sale," said Sandemon. "I am convinced the young woman is no strumpet."

And so he was. There was a virtue in those clear blue eyes, a purity about the girl that clearly marked her as an innocent.

His employer fell silent for a moment. "I'll admit I find it difficult to see her in such a role. But what else could it be, then, with her living in their midst? And painted like a doxy as she was," he added, his mouth twisting with disgust.

Sandemon remained silent, for he had no explanation. "You seemed to make good progress in communicating with the young woman. Were you able to verify our Annie's account of the night in question?"

Morgan gave Sandemon a sharp look, then made a dismissing motion with his hand. "Apparently, *our* Annie told the truth," he said shortly. "No doubt that pleases you."

Sandemon could not stop a faint smile. "No doubt, young master."

"Don't *call* me that, I've told you! You're a free man, not a slave!"

"But a black man, nevertheless," Sandemon offered, still smiling.

"A fact duly noted and of no particular interest to me. Hear me, now: I want you to see what you can learn about the girl."

"Which girl is that, sir?"

"Finola, of course! I already know more than I care to know about that demented child from Belfast! I want you to find out if they're abusing her in any way—"

"By that you mean are they prostituting her?"

The young master leveled a long, scathing look on Sandemon. "I said *in any way*, didn't I? Find out what her circumstances are." He paused. "And we'll be making her a gift for rescuing that little heathen down the hall," he said dryly. "You can deliver it tomorrow."

Sandemon considered him for a moment. "Perhaps you would like to go with me? We can manage the carriage with no difficulty, I'm sure."

Suddenly gone was the note of wit, the glint of wry amusement in the eye. The reply was weary, almost sullen. "I don't feel up to leaving the house just yet."

His tone allowed for no argument. Sandemon hesitated, wanting to press the matter, yet sensing it was not yet the time. At last he inclined his head, saying, "Do you need anything else before I retire, *Seanchai*? If not, I will bid you goodnight."

Morgan dismissed him with a gesture, and Sandemon left the room. Heading toward his own bedroom, he felt vaguely disturbed at the quicksilver change in his young employer's mood. Yet he was encouraged, too, by the interest the young giant had shown in the lovely Finola.

Perhaps…just perhaps…there would be more than one young—*lass*, as the Irish would say—to aid in the sad *Seanchai*'s healing.

Morgan could not stop thinking about the unusual—and achingly lovely—young woman he had met only hours before.

Finola. Certainly she was one of the most beautiful creations he had ever laid eyes on. And that filthy barman who had told Sandemon she was slow—he was the one who was daft! It had taken the girl virtually no time at all to catch on to his abbreviated, somewhat primitive form of signing. She had all her wits and some extra, that was clear enough!

Those eyes were going to haunt him the rest of the night, he knew. The clearest blue he'd ever seen, and with a depth of innocence that could not possibly have been feigned. He sensed Sandemon was right about her not being a street girl. Yet he could not figure how she had come to her present circumstances.

About all he'd been able to learn from her was a sketchy version of Annie's story about her "robbers." Finola had heard the girl's cry when she'd stepped out onto the second-floor porch of the inn to feed the cat, had seen her running down the alley toward St. Patrick's. She had raced down the steps and tugged Annie back up to the porch, where they had waited until the girl's pursuers finally gave up and went away. Then she had led Annie to Nelson Hall.

She knew Dublin well, Finola had conveyed to Morgan. Unfortu-nately—and to her possible danger—the fair Finola seemed to have no fear of wandering about the city on her own. That bunch she lived with more than likely had no inkling of her whereabouts most of the time.

He had been unable to learn much more about her. She didn't even seem to have a last name, nor did she appear to know her own age. Yet he was convinced she was anything but slow.

The memory of the golden-haired young woman made him smile. The thought of her was a far more pleasant diversion than the ideas that usu-ally occupied his mind this time of night.

He yawned and stretched, feeling somewhat drowsy. He decided to forego the whiskey tonight. The nightly drink was quickly becoming a habit. He had been without pain most of the day; perhaps if he would read for a while, he would be able to sleep uninterrupted.

At Morgan's urging, Joseph Mahon had been sending him portions of the journal he was keeping. Morgan would read each segment, making minor editorial notes in the margins. He had not said as much to Joseph yet, but he had every intention of seeing the journal published. It was a starkly truthful, agonizing account of Ireland's misery—and it demanded to be read.

Remembering that he had left the most recent packet downstairs in the library, Morgan scowled. He hadn't the energy to go back down tonight.

Instead, he opted for a book, starting the chair toward the table by the bed. Stopping abruptly, he wheeled around to the small stand by the door and began to riffle idly through the correspondence Sandemon had left there. An envelope from the States caught his eye, and he plucked it up.

He recognized Michael's handwriting right away. Anxious for news from them all, Morgan ripped the envelope open and began to read. A faint, nagging guilt passed through his mind as he scanned the opening lines. He had not written Michael or Daniel for months. They would not know of the shooting or the fix he was in.

He pushed the thought aside. Eventually he would have to write. He could not avoid it forever. But as yet he was not ready to put his misery into words.

He skimmed rapidly down the page, smiling a bit at Michael's scrawled words about the friendship of his son and Daniel John. Moving on, his eyes locked on the first paragraph of the next page. He felt a burning in his eyes and a knife at his heart as he read the words over again. And again.

…Perhaps you have been expecting at some point to hear of an impending marriage between Nora and me. I'm sure you will be surprised—just as I was—to learn that, although Nora is indeed soon to be wed, it will be to Evan Whittaker, not to me.

Stunned, Morgan wet his lips and tried to swallow. His throat felt dry and swollen, and he could taste nothing other than bitterness as he read on.

I hope this change in what we both expected will not be a source of too much disappointment, old friend. I suppose there is no figuring why a heart feels affection for one instead of another. It was a hard thing at first for me to accept, but accept it I must, it seems. I'm afraid I haven't been too charitable about it all, for I did have my heart set on the lass, and that's the truth.

Morgan's own heart had begun to pound with wild fury. A dull ache at the back of his neck rapidly threatened to turn into a fullblown riot of a headache.

The consolation for us both would seem to be that she is happy, and that Whittaker, by your own admission, is a fine fellow—a decent man. Who would have thought she would decide for an Englishman, when she could have had the likes of us, eh?

Who, indeed? Morgan clenched his teeth against Michael's weak attempt at humor.

He read no more. Flinging the pages to the floor, he sat staring across the room into the fire.

Finally he roused. So, then, what of it? She would have married *someone* eventually. So it was not to be Michael, after all, but the Englishman. What real difference did it make in any event?

She was not his. It was not for him to question her choice. And didn't Michael himself grudgingly admit to her happiness?

Nora's happiness. That was the thing that mattered now, he told himself firmly. The *only* thing that mattered.

Spinning the chair, he circled the room once, then again. At last he wheeled himself over to the high, massive chiffonnier, where he retrieved the bottle of whiskey and a tumbler.

He poured himself a generous drink. For a moment his gaze went from the full tumbler to the scattered pages of Michael's letter on the floor across the room.

Then, lifting his glass in a bitter, silent toast, he drank to Nora's memory—and to her marriage.

His own reflection in the mirror on the opposite wall caught his eye, and he hurled his glass at the ruined man in the wheelchair. The tumbler shattered and the mirror cracked, leaving a crazed spider-web pattern across the silvered glass. Morgan watched the distorted vision of himself, caught in the web, and lifted another toast—only this time he raised the entire bottle.

36

Night Winds

Solomon! where is thy throne? It is gone in the wind.
Babylon! where is thy might? It is gone in the wind.
All that the genius of man hath achieved or designed
Waits but its hour to be dealt with as dust by the wind....
Who is the Fortunate? He who in anguish hath pined!
He shall rejoice when his relics are dust in the wind....
Happy in death are they only whose hearts have consigned
All Earth's affections and longings and cares to the wind....

JAMES CLARENCE MANGAN (1803–1849)

Hunched over the hotel desk after school, Tierney Burke was reading the *Tribune*'s account of the death of John Jacob Astor, dead at eighty-four years of age.

Astor was to be buried the next day—no doubt, thought Tierney with disgust, in a style that befitted the "richest man in America." It was said that six clergymen would participate in the funeral service, and policemen from all over the city would be in attendance to provide security. He figured his da might be one of them.

Tierney let out a muffled sound of scorn. So what good now were Astor's twenty million dollars? Everyone knew his eldest son had been a mental incompetent for years, and his second son was supposedly indifferent to his father's enormous wealth.

Da had seen the old man once or twice, when he'd pulled special duty for some big to-do. His description of Astor as an addlepated, drooling old man was enough to turn the stomach.

The entire city was in awe of Astor's wealth, his mansion at Lafayette Place, his vast holdings. Yet, apparently the old man, at least in his later years, had not been able to enjoy a bit of the money for which he'd grubbed all his life. Rumor had it that for the last few years he'd been too weak to even feed himself, yet so fat that his worn-out skin drooped like melting wax.

By his own admission, old Astor had loved money more than anything else in life. Da thought it was sad, and found the stories about the old millionaire pathetic; Tierney thought them revolting. One of the reporters at the *Herald* had said it best, calling Astor a "money-making machine," and declaring that half the millionaire's fortune rightfully belonged to the people of New York.

To Tierney's way of thinking, amassing money just to get rich was a disgustingly futile preoccupation. He'd made the mistake once of comparing Lewis Farmington with old Astor, and Da had hit the ceiling.

"There is no shame in a Christian man also being a *wealthy* man, Tierney!" he insisted, jabbing his finger in the air as was his way when exasperated. "Lewis Farmington uses his money for the good of others. Why, he and his daughter have done more for the underprivileged in New York City than we will ever be knowing, I'm sure."

It struck Tierney that the Farmingtons couldn't have done all that much, or they wouldn't be as rich as they obviously were. But he kept his feelings to himself, for Da, like Daniel, had a definite soft spot for the Farmingtons.

So far as Tierney was concerned, money was fine, and he intended to have some of it. But he would *use* his for setting things right where they had gone wrong; for bringing justice out of tyranny; for setting Ireland free.

That was one of the reasons he held Morgan Fitzgerald, Da's old friend back in Ireland, in such high esteem. Morgan and his lads had simply taken a share from those who had more than they needed and used it for those who had none—just like the Robin Hood legends. Of course, the English had been all set to hang Morgan for his shenanigans. But at least he had shown his contempt for the idle rich—and managed to accomplish a bit of good with their money before they stopped him.

The thought of Morgan Fitzgerald and what had been done to him in Belfast sparked a fresh blaze of anger in Tierney. Da was still grieving, too, from the news about his friend. And Daniel was taking it hard. He'd scarcely

talked at all for days, just sat around as if he were numb, occasionally picking at the harp, but more often staring into space. More than once, Tierney
had heard him weeping quietly in the night, when he thought everybody
else was asleep.

The high, unpleasant voice of Hubert Rossiter, the bookkeeper, jarred
Tierney rudely out of his thoughts.

He glanced up. "Mr. Walsh has some extra work he'd like you to do
tomorrow night," said the bookkeeper. "A special job."

Tierney took his time replying. "I'm on the desk tomorrow night," he
answered distractedly, glancing back down at the *Tribune*.

"Barry will cover for you. Mr. Walsh would rather you took care of the
other job."

Slowly Tierney raised his eyes from the newspaper to Rossiter. "What
sort of job might it be?"

The dome-headed bookkeeper adjusted his thick round eyeglasses, settling them more securely on his nose. "It shouldn't take long. Mr. Walsh
thought you might like to get away from the desk for a bit."

The man's habit of not looking at a person when he spoke never failed
to irritate Tierney. Deliberately, he leaned farther over the desk, bringing
his face closer to Rossiter's.

"How *far* away from the desk…sir?"

Tierney had no respect at all for the simpering bookkeeper. He knew
Rossiter for what he was—a middleman, a glorified go-between for Patrick Walsh and his varied and numerous "businesses." Nor had he missed
the fact that he made the man uncomfortable.

Rossiter glued his gaze to the open ledger in front of him. "I believe it
simply involves two or three pickups and then a delivery. Shouldn't take
more than an hour and a half or so."

"What kind of pickups?"

The bookkeeper finally lifted his pale hazel eyes to Tierney. "All you
need to do is stop at the addresses I give you on Water Street and take the…
materials…you pick up where you're told to take them."

Tierney studied the man for a moment. *Water Street.* No doubt he was
to pick up some of the take at the brothels and deliver it—where?

"I think not," he said bluntly. Ignoring the flush that spread over Rossiter's polished oval of a face, Tierney dropped back to his original slouch
and continued to read.

"You're saying you won't do it?" The bookkeeper's tone was incredulous. Tierney looked up. "Aye. That's what I'm saying."

The bookkeeper sputtered something about Tierney's not valuing his job, then disappeared into the hotel vault.

Tierney had already lost interest in the *Tribune* article. Leaning on his elbows, he pondered what his crafty employer might be up to. Walsh had plenty of delivery boys without recruiting *him*—especially when it would mean taking him away from his regular job.

Of course, these "go-between deliveries," as Tierney thought of them, most likely paid the boys a great deal more than working the hotel desk.

He was tempted. The faster he could make the money he needed, the sooner he could get out of New York. He had it in mind to leave for Ireland by the time he was sixteen—another year. Da would press him to go on with his schooling, of course, but who in Ireland would care if he wasn't a scholar?

Yet he balked at involving himself in the illegal side of Walsh's enterprises. Da was a policeman, after all—and an honest one. If he were ever to learn that his own son was working the wrong side of the law, there was no telling what he would do.

Or what it would do to him.

They were at odds most of the time, but a part of Tierney clung to a grudging respect for his straitlaced father. It was known throughout the force—to Da's disadvantage at times—that Assistant Captain Burke was not on the take and held nothing but contempt for any officer who was.

Tierney did not like the idea that the same contempt might at some point be leveled at *him.* If indeed he ever did depart from his da's unyielding code, it would not be to risk landing in trouble—or hurting his da—for a few extra bucks as a delivery boy.

Besides, he wasn't so certain but that Patrick Walsh might merely be testing him—hanging out a carrot to see if Tierney would bite at it. Walsh had a way about him that Tierney suspected bordered on game-playing: baiting a person simply as a means to test his mettle.

If that were the case, the man might just as well learn right now that Tierney Burke did not play games.

Unless, of course, he happened to be dead-sure of winning.

It was the middle of the night. Lying sleepless in his bed, Daniel stared into the darkness, thinking.

He was sure his heart had not been so heavy since the night Katie died, late last summer.

In school, at home, even on calls with Dr. Grafton, he could not seem to think of anything else but Morgan. Morgan in a wheelchair. Morgan with paralyzed legs.

He had asked Dr. Grafton endless questions, and the kindly physician did his best to answer. What he learned was anything but encouraging.

If the bullet were lodged near the spine, the doctor said, it might well be inoperable—and exceedingly painful.

If the damage to his spinal cord were permanent, then Morgan had no hopes of ever walking again. In his letter, the priest had indicated this was the case.

The image of Morgan confined to a wheelchair was almost beyond bearing. One of Daniel's clearest memories of his friend and mentor was of walking together with Morgan to the pier in the village, Morgan striding along on those great sturdy legs—like tree trunks, they were—with his harp slung over his back, as Daniel hurried along to keep up with him.

He wanted desperately to write to Morgan, but he had delayed thus far, not knowing what to say. Indeed, what *could* he say?

His thoughts went to his mother, and the ache in his heart deepened. The news about Morgan seemed to be stealing all her newfound joy with Evan. Oh, she still spoke of the wedding, and her eyes still softened when Evan was near or whenever she spoke his name. But most of the time, she seemed terribly sad, quiet and withdrawn and distant.

Daniel thought he understood what must be going through her mind. Like himself, she was no doubt wishing there were something she could do. He had even thought of going back to Ireland, simply to *be* with Morgan. He was going to need a great deal of help, and where would it come from? Shouldn't the people who cared most about him be the ones to help him?

If these were *his* feelings, could his mother's be much different, after all?

For Mother loved Morgan, too.

Daniel had known how things were between them for a long time, knew that the affection between his mother and Morgan went beyond a special childhood friendship.

Yet it would be impossible to go back. There was no money, no work to be had even if they should find a way—

He had to stop thinking about it. To return to Ireland was not even a remote possibility. Not now, at least. Perhaps not ever.

He would do what he could. He would write to Morgan, and write often, to reassure him that they still cared for him and remembered him. And he would pray for him.

He would also pray for his mother...and for Evan.

In the middle of the night, Evan came fully awake. Since the news had come about Fitzgerald, every night had been long and anxious, filled with fitful, worrisome dreams and abrupt awakenings, leaving him exhausted and on edge all the next day.

Fumbling for his dressing gown, then his eyeglasses, he got up. He lit a candle and sat down on the edge of the bed. Wearily, he raked his hand down the side of his face, thinking.

He was sick at heart about what had happened to Fitzgerald. But he was every bit as distressed about what was happening to *Nora*. Day after day he watched her grieve, helpless to ease her sadness. He prayed it was only his imagination, but he sensed that in her sorrow, she was slipping away from him, a little at a time.

He thought he would die if he lost her. Yet, he also understood her despair. She had loved Morgan Fitzgerald with a great love, he knew. He had seen for himself the bond between the two of them. An entire ocean and months of change separated them, but that bond had not been altogether broken.

He felt that Nora was torn between sorrow for the tragedy that had befallen Fitzgerald and a feeling of helplessness that she could not do something for him. Evan understood the helplessness, for he, too, wished there were something he could do for the man.

The big Irish poet would always have a special place in Evan's heart. Never had he encountered such a heroic spirit, never had he admired the courage of another human being as he had Fitzgerald's.

But his respect and admiration for the man did nothing to ease the anxiety that now plagued him relentlessly, night and day. He was terrified that Nora's memory of Fitzgerald—and her pity for him—might pull her away, might even destroy their love.

It was nothing she said, nothing she did. It was more what she did *not* say or do that struck fear in his heart. She was still sweet and gentle with him, but distracted; still thoughtful of him, but distant. She still touched his hand when she spoke his name, kissed him goodnight at day's end. But Morgan Fitzgerald had become a silent intruder in their relationship.

Evan had not even attempted to discuss the wedding since the news about Fitzgerald arrived, telling himself that Nora was too preoccupied to do much in the way of planning. The truth was, he worried that if he tried to push her, he might somehow trigger doubts, or even cause her to abandon their plans altogether.

Thus he prayed continually for the trust and the patience to give her time, the time she needed to heal and regain her affection for him.

You've already lost her....

Out of nowhere came the ugly whisper of doubt, lodging itself in his thoughts with a cold, brutal thud. Evan swallowed, bracing himself against the shudder that wracked his entire body.

Did you really think you had a chance against a man like Fitzgerald? You, with your missing arm and your weak eyes and your foolish stammer? Even with worthless legs, he's more man than you....

Evan gripped his forehead, trying to force the dread whisper from his mind. Since childhood, he had been tormented with these debilitating bouts of self-disgust and insecurity. He had believed he'd fought the final battle not long after losing his arm, going on to survive both the physical and emotional anguish that followed.

Yet here it was again, the creeping doubt, as vile and torturous as ever.

With an angry cry, he twisted off the bed and dropped to his knees. Taking off his glasses, he propped his arm on the bed to brace himself, then rested his head on his hand and sought the Quiet.

"Oh, Lord, p-please...I have been w-waiting for her all my life! P-Please, don't let me lose her...not now, Lord, p-please...not now...not ever...."

Nora doesn't love you, poor fool. She never did. She only feels sorry for you....

Evan groaned, squeezing his eyes shut until they hurt.

"Lord, I t-t-trust Your love...and I t-trust Nora's love."

Waiting, scarcely breathing, Evan felt the cold, depraved whisper reluctantly leave him. Cleansed, he murmured the Name he had clung to since childhood: "Jesus...Jesus...."

Unexpectedly, the thought of Abraham, great but imperfect saint of old, came rushing into his thoughts. Abraham who was asked to sacrifice the dearest thing in the world to him.

Be willing to give up everything... A new whisper filled Evan's spirit, penetrating the darkness.

Abraham lifted the knife in his own hand, ready to plunge it into the child he cherished.

Even those you love best...

Abraham would have delivered his own son into the sovereign arms of God.

Trust Me...and be obedient...I will not fail you.... The voice grew stronger in Evan's spirit, and he breathed a deep sigh.

Abraham's faith was proved. He was blessed; his descendants were multiplied; he became the father of all nations.

Because he trusted, and was willing to sacrifice...because he obeyed. Evan, trust Me...trust My love....

Evan laid his head upon his arm and sobbed weakly. "I *do*, Lord! I do t-trust You! Help me to t-trust You *more*. M-make me strong enough to give her up...if I m-must. Make me w-willing...and able to obey You, no m-matter what."

In the silence, still on his knees, for a fleeting moment Evan felt the soft, warm light of his Father's smile rest upon him.

37

A Conspiracy of Love

So did she your strength renew,
A dream that a lion had dreamed
Till the wilderness cried aloud,
A secret between you two,
Between the proud and the proud.

W. B. YEATS (1865–1939)

Sara had not seen Michael Burke since Nora's bout with scarlet fever—
just long enough to make her feel ill at ease when they finally met
again, the day of the Astor funeral.

Having just parted company with Kerry and Jess Dalton, she stood
outside the church, waiting for her father to finish his conversation with
Horace Greeley, publisher of the *Tribune.* Knowing Mr. Greeley's fondness for lengthy discussions, Sara sighed; she would likely still be waiting
long past the time when the other mourners had dispersed.

"Sara?"

Sara jumped, whipping around at the sound of her name just behind
her. "Sergeant Burke! I mean...*Captain*—" Flustered, Sara automatically
backed a step away.

He was studying her with a glint of amusement. "Has it been so long,
then, that you no longer remember my first name?"

"Oh...no...of course not!" As always, Sara felt clumsy and foolish in
his presence. Exasperated with herself, she forced a smile. "How are you,
Michael?"

He had grown a dark mustache, Sara noted, trying not to stare. Always handsome, he now looked even more dangerous.

"Better than when we last met," he said, smiling easily. "And yourself?"

They made pointless small talk for a few more minutes; then he inquired after Nora.

Sara frowned. "I'm not quite sure, to tell you the truth. I'm somewhat worried about her."

Immediately, his expression sobered. "She's not ill again?"

"Oh no!" Sara quickly assured him. "Nothing like that. It's just that Nora doesn't seem herself lately. For a time, she was so happy, planning for the wedding and—" She broke off, not wanting to distress him by mentioning Nora and Evan's engagement.

"And what?" he prompted her, frowning.

Sara bit her lip. "It's just that ever since the news came about your friend in Ireland, the one who was wounded in Belfast—"

He nodded. "Morgan."

"Yes. Ever since then, Nora seems so distracted. Worried. It's almost as if she were…grieving."

When he made no reply but simply nodded as if he understood, Sara went on. "Nora told me a little about your life in the village. The three of you must have been very close."

A muscle at the side of his mouth tightened, and he glanced down at the cobbled street for a moment. "Aye, we were. And it's no surprise that she would still be upset about Morgan's troubles. I've had the time dealing with it myself."

He looked up, meeting her eyes with a frank, steady gaze. "They were sweethearts for a long time. And they were friends as well. There was a bond between the two that was like nothing I have ever seen, and that's the truth. As for Morgan—" A hint of a sad smile touched his lips. "You would have to know him to understand why he is not easily forgotten. No doubt you are right; I expect Nora is grieving for the man. Knowing her as I do, I fear she may also have some wild notion of trying to help him."

"Help him?" Sara repeated. "You don't mean she'd consider going back to Ireland?"

One eye narrowed, and he nodded slowly. "It's occurred to me," he said, his expression grim.

Sara stared at him in horror. "Oh, Michael, *no*! She can't! Why, she's only recently regained her health." She paused, then added carefully, "She and Evan were so happy...until this. I *know* Nora's feelings for him are genuine!"

To her great relief, the mention of Evan didn't seem to disturb Michael. He simply nodded, saying, "Aye, that's the truth. I fear she may be thinking foolish things."

"Would it help if you talked with her?"

He shrugged. "I could try, I suppose."

"Please do! If Nora will listen to anyone, it's you."

His eyebrows lifted. "Don't be counting too much on that, Sara. Pity's a strong force in itself—one to be reckoned with. And it's not pity alone binding Nora to Morgan, that's the thing."

"But love is stronger than pity," Sara said firmly. "And Nora *loves* Evan Whittaker—I know she does."

"She also loved Morgan Fitzgerald," he said quietly.

"But that was a long time ago," Sara insisted. "And I can't believe his memory means more to her than Evan. Nora's not the sort of woman to be in love with more than one man at a time!"

His slow, wry smile brought a flush to Sara's face. "Aye, and don't I know *that* well enough?"

Sara bit her lip. "I'm sorry—"

He waved off her attempt to apologize. "No, you're right. If Morgan *is* the problem, it's more the memory of the man, I should think. Memory and pity. Morgan is not the best thing for Nora now. I doubt that he ever was. Theirs was a destructive kind of love, I always felt."

Vastly relieved, Sara pressed. "Then you *will* talk with her?" At his nod, Sara thought for a moment. "I have an idea: Why don't you come to dinner one night soon? We could make an opportunity sometime during the evening for you to speak alone with Nora—without being too obvious."

He regarded her with a curious smile. "I expect my coming to dinner might be *more* than obvious."

"What do you mean?" Sara asked, genuinely puzzled.

He tilted his head slightly, still smiling. "Do the Farmingtons make a practice of inviting Irish cops for dinner, then?"

Sara stared at him with growing irritation. "No," she countered acidly, "as a matter of fact, we don't. But we *do* make a practice of inviting our *friends* to dinner on occasion—and I *thought* that's what I was doing."

His eyebrows shot up in surprise, but he said nothing.

"If you'd be more comfortable," Sara went in a tone slightly less caustic, "bring the boys—your son and Daniel. That way no one could possibly misunderstand. It would give Daniel an opportunity to spend some time with his mother, and I'm sure we'd all like to get to know Tierney better."

"That's kind of you. But I doubt that Tierney would—"

His eyes left her as her father came walking up and touched her arm. "Sara, my dear, I'm sorry you had to wait. Captain Burke," he said jovially, extending his hand to Michael. "Good to see you again."

Growing increasingly uncomfortable as the two men exchanged pleasantries, Sara took her father by the arm. "We really should be going, Father. I have a mission committee meeting later this afternoon, and I'm afraid we're keeping Captain Burke from his duty."

Her father darted a look from one to the other.

"A moment, Miss Farmington...Sara?"

Sara shot a wary look at Michael.

"I'm afraid I didn't catch the day or time."

At Sara's blank stare, the policeman turned to her father. "Your daughter was just inviting me to dinner, sir. If you've no objection?"

Sara swallowed with great difficulty as her father responded with cheerful approval. "Excellent! Soon, I hope? What about tonight?"

"Tonight?" Sara choked out.

"Why not? Didn't you tell Mrs. Buckley this morning I wanted roast chicken this evening?"

"Yes, but—"

"Well, then?" He went on, his words, as always, spilling out like marbles from an open bag. "There'll be more than enough—and food fit for a man's appetite at that, none of that abominable stew she tries to sneak past us every now and then." He stopped. "Seven should be fine, eh, Sara?"

Sara opened her mouth on a word but swallowed it whole as her father, ignoring her, added, "And bring those boys along, why don't you, Captain? We'd love to have them!"

Michael Burke gave Sara a slow smile, his eyes glinting. "Seven will be grand, thank you, sir."

Lewis Farmington didn't know quite what to make of his daughter and Assistant Captain Burke.

The tension between the two had been unmistakable. And the attraction between them was undeniable.

As he helped Sara into the carriage, Farmington studied the broad back of the Irish policeman, who had crossed the street and was conversing with two of his men. Burke was a sturdy kind of man, one not easily swayed, he would imagine—a man who had taken his blows over the years, no doubt, but rallied nicely. Decent and sensible, he was a strong man who more than likely would prove a good husband, if somewhat immovable at times. No harm in that, though. Clarissa had often accused *him* of being somewhat obstinate, but she always seemed to like him well enough, nevertheless.

He turned back to his daughter, who sat waiting for him with a questioning smile. Straight back, firm jaw, clear eyes—wonderful girl. A bit too hardheaded for her own good, perhaps. Definitely too strong-willed to be considered a good catch by the few remaining bachelors in their own set.

Lewis had once held hopes for Judge Worthington's son, Isaac—a big, strapping blond with a good head for law and what Lewis had always thought to be a finely developed sense of morality. One night, however, in Sara's hearing, the young fool had offhandedly referred to New York's immigrant population as "filthy disease breeders." The look Sara turned on him would have withered a cactus.

But this Michael Burke now, this brawny Celt—Lewis suspected he would not be so easily dismissed. Whether or not Sara realized it, she might well have met her match in the Irish policeman. The exasperating thing about it all was that both of them seemed determined to deny their interest in each other.

Ah, well. Time and God's will had a way of taking care of human foolishness. It would be interesting to watch events unfold. Curious, how he wasn't in the least bothered that his only daughter might take a shine to a fellow like Burke—*common*, their acquaintances would call him.

Lewis supposed his own feelings about Burke had to do with what he sensed about the man. He had pretty good instincts most of the time about people—men, at least. No man with half a brain would try to figure a woman. Their mystery was part of their appeal, after all.

At any rate, he felt he could trust his instincts about the Irish policeman. And so far, his instincts seemed to be cheering the man on.

Tierney was dumbfounded by the realization that Da was actually going through with this fiasco tonight. Furious, he made no attempt to curb his temper.

They had been arguing for ten minutes or more, Tierney contending that the evening was nothing more than a tasteless joke to the Farmingtons.

"Why would you set yourself up for this? I never thought you'd actually go!"

He was standing just inside the door of his father's bedroom, watching him iron his one good white shirt. "Can't you see they're simply playing you for the fool?"

Da straightened, setting the iron down on the board with a hard thump. Shirtless, his Sunday suspenders hanging loose at his waist, he stared at Tierney with burning eyes. "That will do, Tierney!" The words exploded like pistol shots.

For an instant Tierney felt almost ashamed. With his thick dark hair uncombed and tousled, and the angry scar from his wound still blazing across his chest, Da looked at that moment more boy than man. The hurt in his eyes belied the anger in his voice, and Tierney knew he had wounded him with his words.

But it was true, all the same, and why couldn't the man see it? Inviting him to dinner at their grand mansion—as if Da were to be treated like one of their own kind! And him too gullible to see what was behind it all!

Well, *he* saw the way things were, all right! It was that ridiculous old maid, Sara Farmington! It was perfectly obvious to Tierney: She fancied Da and would amuse herself by playing the fine lady to this dumb Irisher. Even with all her money, she had obviously not been able to snare a man. So she had decided to dally with the poor, unsuspecting Irish cop.

And Da was falling for it!

"I told you," his father said with exaggerated patience, "that the three of us were all invited this evening—you, as well as Daniel and myself. The entire affair is mostly to give me an opportunity to speak with Nora. Sara is worried for her."

" 'Sara is worried for her,'" Tierney mimicked. "*Sara* has a yen for *you*, is more to the point!"

Da's mouth thinned to a slash, and his hand on the iron tightened to a white-knuckled grip. "Tierney, I'm warning you," he grated out in a deadly hard voice, "you may be my son, and you may think you're the man grown. But if you don't stop with your disgusting accusations and your spiteful tongue, I will show you what a *gorsoon* you really are!"

Tierney stood, legs apart, hands clenched, glaring at his father with a mixture of rage and frustration.

"I think," his da went on, white-faced but making an evident attempt to control his anger, "it would be best if neither of us said anything more for the time being. Perhaps you should just…leave me alone for now."

"You bet I will." Tierney shot back in a savage voice. "I wouldn't want to keep your fancy lady friend waiting." Turning, he charged out of the room.

"Are you working tonight, then?" his da called behind him.

Tierney hesitated, then said in a bitter tone, "Aye, I'm working tonight, sure enough!"

In the kitchen Daniel was bent over a chair, shining his shoes. He straightened, his face pinched in a troubled frown. "What are you so riled about anyway?"

Tierney scowled at him. "You're going, of course."

"Why shouldn't I go?"

Tierney's jaw tightened. "Aye," he grated out, "why shouldn't you, indeed?"

Crossing the room, he flung open the door so hard it slammed into the wall and bounced back. He took the steps two at a time without so much as a glance behind him.

38

The Wounds of a Friend

Thank God for one dear friend,
With face still radiant with the light of truth.

JOHN BOYLE O'REILLY (1844–1890)

When Michael and Daniel arrived, each with bouquet in hand, Sara was moved beyond all reason. That a boy of Daniel's age would bring his mother flowers—and for no special occasion—she found quite wonderful.

Michael's bouquet was for *her*, he explained, appearing stiff and uncomfortable in his starched white shirt and slightly worn suit. It was not that a man had never brought Sara flowers before tonight. She had received a few bouquets over the years.

But not recently.

Perhaps it was the sight of the two that moved her: the fresh-faced Daniel, eager to see his mother; a carefully groomed Michael, obviously ill at ease, yet just as obviously pleased with himself that he had thought of flowers. In any event, never had Sara made such a fuss over a man's thoughtfulness. And never had she been so pleased by it.

Dinner was a pleasant success, once it recovered from a somewhat strained beginning. Father, bless his heart, was at his gregarious, jovial best, regaling them with stories about his first attempts at shipbuilding—especially some of the more hilarious failures. Somehow he also managed to find just the right questions to entice Michael to talk about *his* work.

Sara noticed with relief that Evan and Michael seemed to grow increasingly comfortable with each other as the evening progressed. They even laughed together once or twice.

Nora was the quiet one at the table, Sara observed with some concern. Of course, Nora was always quiet, especially in the presence of more than one or two people. Tonight, though, her silence seemed born of bafflement rather than shyness or melancholy. She followed the banter between Sara and her father, the exchange about immigrant problems in which Evan and Michael eventually involved themselves, with watchful attention and a slightly bewildered look.

But other than an occasional soft word to her son, she merely listened from the outer fringes without participating.

When the moment presented itself to cast Nora and Michael together, Lewis Farmington did his part—as previously coached by his daughter.

"Evan, I won't keep you long, but I'm afraid I do need you for just a few moments in the library, if you don't mind," he said, getting up from the table. "Abraham Ware will be at the yards first thing in the morning, if he's true to form, and I still have to dictate the last part of our bid. Would you mind terribly?"

Even as Lewis spoke, Evan rose from his chair. The consummate assistant, he never failed to anticipate his employer's needs. "I rather expected you'd want to finish up after dinner, sir."

Both men excused themselves—Evan with a slightly uncertain glance at Nora and Michael.

"Daniel, I'm going to steal you for a moment if your mother and Michael have no objection," Sara said. "I've changed the trim on the Christmas harp you made and turned it into a decoration I can leave out all year. I want to see what you think of it."

The boy gave her a curious look, but followed willingly. On the way out the door, Sara managed to breathe a hasty prayer that the Lord would take control of the situation in the dining room.

"So, then, Nora—I expect you've been busy," Michael said as soon as they were alone. "Making your plans for the wedding and all, I warrant."

Nodding uncertainly, Nora appeared embarrassed by his forthrightness. Michael, sensing he would get nowhere by being less than direct, decided to continue in the same vein.

"I should hope so," he said, allowing himself to drink more deeply of his tea, now that the Farmingtons were out of the room. "There's not much time remaining till May."

Still Nora avoided his eyes. Staring down at her half-empty plate, she gave another small nod. "No…I suppose not."

"You didn't eat much tonight, I noticed. Wedding jitters, is it?"

Her eyes still downcast, she forced a smile. "More than likely."

"What is it, Nora Ellen?"

Finally she raised her eyes to meet his. Her expression was uncertain, guarded. "I don't know what you mean."

"You're still sorrowing over Morgan," said Michael, making it a statement, not a question.

"And you're not?" she countered sharply. "Doesn't it trouble you, knowing the state he must be in?"

Michael nodded slowly. "Aye, of course, it troubles me. Just as it troubles me to see *you* in such a state."

Fixing her eyes on the table once more, she offered no reply.

Impatient with the woman, Michael got up and went around to her. "The last time we parted," he said, sitting down beside her, "'twas as friends, isn't that so?"

She nodded, and he went on. "Then speak to me now as a friend, Nora Ellen. Tell me what's in your heart, even though I suspect I already know."

Her head snapped up, and Michael was almost pleased to see a glint of irritation in her eyes. She would likely be more candid with him if she were a bit fussed.

"And why wouldn't I be grieving about Morgan? I can't believe you're not distressed for him, as well!" she added accusingly.

Michael chose his words with care. "I am grieved for the man, sure. But I have also accepted the fact that there is nothing I can do for Morgan, other than to pray for him and perhaps write him of my concern. Do you have it in mind that I could do something more—something that has not yet occurred to me, then?"

Her shoulders slumped, and her face took on a weariness he had not seen there for a long time. "There must be something," she said dully. "Some way we could help."

Michael shook his head, holding her gaze as he took her hand. "There is not, Nora. And I think you know I am right in saying so. You are only hurting yourself by avoiding the truth."

Her eyes searched his for a moment. "We could go to him," she said quietly. "We could do that."

It was the very thing he had feared. "Of all the foolish things you have ever said, that is surely the most foolish of them all!" he bit out, his voice hard. "I can't believe you would even consider such a daft idea."

Pulling her hand away, she indicted him with a look. "Are you saying you haven't thought of it yourself? Sure, and Morgan needs his friends, at such a time as this!"

This was not going to be easy. Michael drew in a long breath, then reached once more to cover her hand with his, ignoring her attempt to pull away. Pressing his face close to hers, he said firmly, "Morgan has other friends, Nora. Friends right there in Ireland—in Dublin, if you will—who are close enough to be of help to him."

"You can't be knowing that! Besides, Morgan has never been as close to anyone else as he was to us!"

Michael sighed but did not soften. "Even if that were the truth, lass, it's over now."

The hurt in her eyes made him feel ashamed of what he was about to say. Yet it needed to be said, and there was nobody else to do the job. "What the three of us had, that's all in the past, Nora," he said quietly. "There is nothing at all we can do for Morgan now, except to support him with our thoughts and our prayers. He would not be expecting more from us, and we should not expect it from ourselves."

"How can you be so unfeeling about him?" she cried, twisting her hand free. "Sure, and the two of you were like brothers!"

His eyes went over her face—so fine, so delicate. So haunted. "And so we will ever be, in our heart of hearts. But I cannot go back to Ireland to prove it so, to Morgan, or to myself. Nor can you, lass."

"I could get the money to go, if that's what you're thinking!"

He wanted to shake her. "This has nothing to do with money. Of course, you could get it. Sara Farmington would give you whatever you asked. *She's* your friend, too, Nora, in case you haven't seen." Michael stopped, pulled in another steadying breath, then pressed on. "You cannot go back, Nora Ellen, because the man you love is *here*, in New York City. And you are promised to *him*. To *Evan Whittaker*. Or have you forgotten so soon why you turned *me* down?"

He saw tears form in her eyes and felt a pang of self-disgust that he had been so rough with her. But he would finish what he'd begun. "You refused to marry *me* because of Whittaker. Now I am reminding you that you have no call to reject *his* love for a man who never *wanted* you! You cannot do such a thing, Nora!"

Unable to bear the stricken expression in her eyes, Michael looked away.

"What did you say?" The words came as a choked whisper, and Michael despised himself even more.

But he turned back to her, forcing himself to ignore the trembling lip, the shimmering tears spilling down her lovely face.

"I said that Morgan never wanted you, Nora. And he does not want you now. Nor does he *need* you. That is the truth, and I believe that in your heart you have always known it. Morgan has ever been wed to Ireland— a fierce, jealous woman who will tolerate no other claim on a man's affections. You knew the way it was with him years ago, and you know it now. But pity has fooled you into thinking things are different. I am telling you that things are no different at all—and never will be."

Stumbling to her feet, she stood over him, eyes blazing. "You have no right to say such a thing to me!" she cried fiercely.

Tossing his napkin onto the table, Michael shot to his feet and faced her. "I have *every* right, woman! I know Morgan Fitzgerald as well as you ever did, perhaps even better. He sliced a piece from my heart now and again—not only yours! And he'd do it again, to either one of us, don't you doubt it for a minute!"

Eyes wide, Nora backed away and would have fled the room. But Michael grabbed her shoulders, forcing her to stand and listen to him.

"You'll not run from this, Nora; you will hear me! Because of what has happened to Morgan, you've somehow romanticized him in your memories until you've lost sight of the way things really were—the way things still *are*! Well, it's no different now than it ever was. Morgan being Morgan, he will somehow overcome his trouble. You wait and see if he doesn't.

But in the meantime, you must face the truth: If the man had ever wanted you in his life, he could have *had* you, long before now. The truth is that he never loved you quite enough to give up his heart's greatest passion, his *Dark Rosaleen*—his Ireland! And," Michael pressed brutally on, ignoring her sob of protest, "he *still doesn't.*

"Open your eyes, woman! You have the love of a good man now, a man who would give up his very life for you! Don't be so foolish as to cast that love away. Leave Morgan to Ireland and the Lord, and get on with the new life God has granted you."

Spent, he dropped his hands from her shoulders and stood watching her. Nora hugged her arms to her body as if to keep herself from shattering, but she did not weep. Instead, she stood, trembling, staring at him as though he had struck her.

Michael knew he had done all he could. Perhaps he had thrown away their friendship forever for the sake of the truth. He could no longer bear the raw look of betrayal in her eyes. "Make our excuses to the Farmingtons, if you will," he said shortly. "Tell Daniel I will wait for him outside. We must be leaving."

Turning, Michael left the dining room without looking back. But the memory of Nora's stricken face was engraved upon his heart.

⁂

Tierney Burke found Rossiter soon after he arrived at the hotel. The bookkeeper sat hunched over his ledgers in the back office, leafing through the pages as carefully as if the answers to life's greatest mysteries were at his very fingertips.

Rossiter looked up with annoyance when Tierney entered. "You're late. There's been nobody at the desk for more than ten minutes."

"And there is no one in the lobby to need a clerk at the desk," Tierney countered.

"Mr. Walsh expects his employees to be prompt."

"I'll work late. I wanted to ask if you still need a boy for those deliveries tonight."

Rossiter frowned. "Deliveries?"

"The pickups on Water Street you asked me to do," Tierney reminded him impatiently.

The bookkeeper looked him over. "As it happens, we do. But why would you care?"

Tierney shrugged. "I can do the job, after all," he said casually. "If you want."

Rossiter's eyes narrowed. "Why the change of heart?"

Tierney leveled a cold stare on the man. "Why not?"

Michael retreated to the quiet of his bedroom as soon as he and Daniel returned home. Weary and drained from his row with Tierney and the confrontation with Nora, he sank down into the rocking chair and closed his eyes.

Still troubled by Nora's resistance to his words, he was more troubled yet by Tierney. He could only pray that the boy's bitterness and streak of rebellion would not be his undoing.

Tierney had accused him more than once of not understanding him. Tonight, for the first time, Michael admitted to himself that the lad was probably right.

There was an anger, a deep-seated resentment in the boy that both baffled and frightened him for his son. Try as he would, he could not understand Tierney's volatile temper, his unreasonable bitterness. Nor could he fathom his undisguised hatred of people like the Farmingtons.

It was not merely the fact of their wealth, Michael sensed, although that was a part of it. More to the point, he believed it was what the Farmingtons represented. To Tierney's way of thinking, Lewis Farmington—and even Sara—had somehow attained their success, their status in society, at the expense of the less privileged.

The boy had created a simplistic formula—and a dangerously faulty one, Michael believed—equating wealth with the evil oppressor, and poverty with the innocent victim. Michael had been a policeman long enough to know that Tierney's view was extremely naive. Evil abounded on both sides of the dollar, and he for one would not want to try to figure where it thrived best.

Rocking slowly back and forth, he sighed. He did not know what to make of Tierney. The boy had more than his share of good points. Hadn't the teachers at school often commented on the lad's sharp wits, his natural leadership ability, his protective instincts for the younger, less confident boys?

But he had his faults, too, and some were more prominent than others. His unpredictable fits of temper, a strain of spitefulness—even a trace of bigotry, Michael thought with despair.

In addition, Tierney's opinions were often unfair and shortsighted—like his contempt for the Farmingtons. Yet Lewis Farmington's works of Christian charity were widely known, even in the recesses of the Five Points slums. And as for Sara—she was a woman deserving of respect.

For the first time since their meeting, Michael allowed himself to think freely and honestly about Sara Farmington. For months, he had been committed to marrying Nora, to giving her a home and his name, just as he'd promised Morgan he would. But by Nora's choice, he was now free of that commitment.

Thinking about it, he had to admit that Sara Farmington had intrigued him from their very first meeting. In the grime and dust of a tenement hallway, he had watched her stoop down to offer kindness to a filthy, neglected child. The months of getting to know her better had only increased his admiration for her.

There was a strength about Sara, coupled with an unexpected gentleness, that appealed to him. In addition, he knew her to possess a seemingly unshakable faith—and an indomitable will. Yet she was never less than delightfully feminine. Her grace of figure was not one bit marred by her slight limp, any more than her allure was weakened by her wit. She was womanly, bright, interesting—and more than a little attractive.

Suddenly, Michael found himself thinking about Tierney's accusation—that Sara had a…a *yen* for him. As infuriating as he found the boy's insinuations, he could not deny half wishing his son were right.

Getting up from his rocking chair, he stretched and gave a small, self-mocking laugh at his foolishness. Lewis Farmington would more than likely have a stroke at the thought of an Irish cop taking a fancy to his only daughter. Still, the man was never anything but cordial when they met, and he had been downright friendly throughout dinner tonight. In truth, Michael liked the millionaire shipbuilder a great deal—and he sensed he had Farmington's respect as well.

That doesn't mean he'd take kindly to your courting his only daughter....

Michael twisted his mouth at the thought. Sure, and what did it matter what Farmington might think? To court a millionaire's daughter was a luxury hardly covered by the wages of an immigrant policeman. Besides, what gave him the cheek to think Sara herself would welcome his attentions? She was an heiress, after all, living on a level of society an Irish cop could never aspire to.

Besides, didn't the woman freeze in her shoes every time he came near? It seemed he had only to call her name and she lost her powers of speech. Still, there had been a time or two when she'd colored so prettily in his presence, he'd half thought—

He was being a great fool, and that was the truth. Disgusted with himself, Michael jerked down his bed linens with a fury. Straightening, he shook his head at the reflection in the mirror.

꿈

Later that night, after Michael and Daniel had gone and Nora had made her weak excuses to the Farmingtons, she lay in a crumpled heap atop her bed.

She could not rid her mind of Michael's words. They had pierced to her heart, where they continued to stab at her with what he had called the *truth.*

Evan had come to the door at least twice, knocking and calling out to her, but had finally gone away when she begged him to leave her alone. Later, she had sensed Sara's presence outside the room, but finally her footsteps, too, moved on down the hall.

Nora lay there for what seemed an interminable time. As she heard Michael's words sound over and over again in her mind, her anger and shock began to fade. In their place came a gradual, painful awareness of the validity of what he had said. It was a truth she had long known, had even faced, years ago. But as Michael had said, Morgan's tragedy had somehow distorted reality for her. She had idealized and romanticized their old friendship and the love they had once shared into something it never was, and could never be.

And by doing so, she had risked the gift of Evan's love.

Slowly Nora sat up, rubbed her face between her hands, then reached for a handkerchief to wipe away the tears that remained. Suddenly she realized what a hard thing Michael had done for her this night—a thing only a true friend could bring himself to do.

He had freed her, Michael had. Brave enough to make her face a painful truth she had almost forgotten, he had risked losing their friendship in an attempt to free her from a deadly trap of her own making.

And, she thought ruefully, it wasn't the first time, now, was it?

How often, when they were growing up together in the village, had Michael rescued her from some danger of her own doing, then shaken her by the shoulders and rebuked her for her foolishness?

Even then, young as they were, Nora had sensed that Michael's fierce reprimands were born of his concern, his affection, for her. And so it was now. No one but Michael could speak to her so, could pass beyond her wounded anger to reach her heart.

Michael, her friend and her brother. Her protector. Michael, who at times had served as her conscience.

Getting to her feet, Nora touched the bun at the nape of her neck, wondering if she dared go to Evan so late.

Of course she could. He would be waiting, more than likely. Waiting and wondering. And worrying.

Suddenly, she was desperate to have him hold her, to press his cheek gently against hers and whisper his shy endearments against her hair.

Hurrying from the room, Nora raced down the stairs, grabbing her wrap from the coat tree in the hall. Once outside, she ran the entire distance between the big house and Evan's cottage.

When he opened the door, his anxious frown gave way to astonishment as Nora flew into his embrace.

39

Wishes of the Heart

The harp that once through Tara's halls
The soul of music shed,
Now hangs as mute on Tara's walls
As if that soul were fled.
So sleeps the pride of former days,
So glory's thrill is o'er,
And hearts that once beat high for praise,
Now feel that pulse no more!
THOMAS MOORE (1779–1852)

Dublin
Early April

From his bedroom window, Morgan watched the scene outside with a glint of amusement.

True to his word, Sandemon had at last found a "service" for their demented child from Belfast. It was an extra grace that this service happened to be safely outside Nelson Hall.

Annie Delaney had been appointed official groom to Morgan's horse, Pilgrim. This morning, she stood with Sandemon near the stream that flowed along the west side of the grounds. The great red stallion nuzzled the girl's hand as she stroked his immense head, her expression rapt.

That the cantankerous Pilgrim had taken a liking to the girl was a wonder indeed. Yet, watching them, Morgan could see for himself Sandemon's claim that the lass could do most anything she liked with the horse.

It could only be, Morgan thought wryly, a friendship made in heaven.

The feisty stallion was not one to tolerate authority; besides Morgan and one or two of the lads in Mayo, Pilgrim had suffered few hands at his bridle, even fewer bodies on his back. But for his own mysterious reasons, he seemed to adore Annie Delaney. Sandemon claimed the big brute practically purred like a contented cat at the girl's slightest touch.

The child suddenly screwed her face into a fierce glare as she peered up at Sandemon. Morgan smiled and shook his head. More than likely, she had been given an instruction not to her liking. As always, the tall black man remained intractable in the face of the girl's mulishness. He stood as if waiting, one hand extended, until Annie finally relinquished Pilgrim's reins.

They moved away from the stream, Sandemon leading the stallion in the direction of the stables. Annie ran along behind, scooping up papers and other debris blown onto the grounds during last night's wind.

Morgan craned his neck to watch until they were out of sight, then leaned back in the wheelchair and closed his eyes. What he would give to feel the power of old Pilgrim beneath him again! How he missed the freedom, the exhilaration of riding the great brute across the mountains of Mayo. Only now, with the experience forbidden to him, did he admit to himself that sitting on that stallion's broad back had been, in some primitive, inexplicable way, a kind of rite of his manhood. Never did he feel quite so free, so completely and wonderfully a man grown, as when he and Pilgrim went thundering across the countryside, the wind in his face, the sun clinging to his back, and the high hope of living in his spirit. Knowing he would never savor such a feeling again made the memory all the more poignant. And painful.

Opening his eyes, Morgan wiped the back of his hand over his perspiring forehead. The hot pain in his back was on him already, and it was only midmorning. Though it attacked less frequently these days, its force had weakened not at all.

He needed a drink. But it was early yet, too early. If he started in now, he would be useless the rest of the day.

A dry, bitter laugh escaped him. As if he could be any more useless than he already was!

What was there to do, in any event? For the most part, he'd lost interest in reading. Aside from Joseph Mahon's journal, much of what was brought to his attention was the same raving political rhetoric. By now he could recite most of it from memory: *The rebellion will come. The people will rise. Young Ireland will lead. Ireland will be free.*

He had been a part of all that once. No longer. Smith O'Brien and one or two others among the lads continued to hound him to take up his pen again. He still had a voice, they insisted.

A voice, but no words. They did not understand that he no longer had anything to write. He had nothing to protest, nothing to defend, nothing to say. His journals lay empty, blank pages on a tidy desk. His harp lay silent—a dead, voiceless thing propped up in the corner of the room to accuse him.

The days passed in a meaningless succession of routine. He ate his meals, read his mail, endured the exercises Sandemon forced on him. He sat in the infernal wheelchair, his torso and arms growing stronger and more powerful through Sandemon's therapy, his legs hanging heavy and useless, his mind as dull as stale soda bread.

If he cared to, he worked a bit on Joseph's journal or told the girl a story in the library after dinner. She begged for the stories, did Annie. The ancient legends and tales. The adventures of Cuchulain and Finn mac Coul, the heroic exploits of the Fenians, the tragic love story of Deirdre and Naisi. It mattered not how many times she had already heard them told. The child was a sponge, soaking up whatever he was willing to offer.

Which was little enough, Morgan admitted to himself guiltily. Hadn't he seen her hunger, her yearning for the books, her thirst to learn? That she was clever and quick-witted enough, he had no doubt. But Annie needed more—wanted more, he sensed. The lass hungered for acceptance, for companionship—for *involvement.* She required more of him than he was able to give, more energy, both physical and emotional, than he could muster. It simply was not within his power to be all the girl needed him to be.

At night he drank. The whiskey helped some; it eased the pain, allowed him to sleep, to forget—for a few hours, at least.

Occasionally, he still tried to pray. But his prayers were lifeless things, like his legs. He sent them up from a leaden heart, felt them bounce back from an empty vault.

More than once he had asked for a sign of God's presence, a reminder that He had not abandoned Morgan Fitzgerald altogether. At times he thought if he could gain even the faintest glimpse of divine control in the chaos of his life, an assurance of peace beyond the pain—perhaps he could somehow summon the strength to endure without going mad.

But the echo of silence was his only reply, deepening his despair, his feelings of utter helplessness and hopelessness.

Less and less frequently now did he make the attempt to approach the throne. He was quite certain God did not notice. Or if He noticed, He did not care.

⚜

Annie Delaney and Sandemon worked in the stable until late morning. As always, Sandemon supervised Pilgrim's grooming. At the moment, he had left Annie to her work and gone to the other side of the stable, where he stood talking with Colm O'Grady, the full-time groom.

Annie carefully combed Pilgrim's mane, relishing the silken weight of it. She loved every part of her duties as groom: the pungent smell of hay and warm animals in the stable, the way the horses had come to recognize her and welcome her—and especially the opportunity to become friends with the Fitzgerald's grand and noble stallion.

She was careful and conscientious in her new capacity. The great red stallion was the first animal for which she had ever taken responsibility, and she was resolved that in this area—unlike the other projects at which she'd failed so miserably—there would be no room at all for finding fault.

So far, Sandemon seemed satisfied with her efforts, which pleased Annie. They had become great friends, she and the black man. He kept a firm hand with her, sure, and gave little quarter where mischief was concerned. But he was kind, too; kind and helpful and genuinely interested in her as an *individual*—Sandemon's word. Annie could talk to him about most anything she chose, and he would have a comment, an observation, or at least a question.

She hadn't decided which of the two was the most clever or the wisest—Sandemon or the *Seanchai*. She supposed the *Seanchai* had the most classical education. Certainly he was more the scholar when it came to history and culture.

She suspected, however, that Sandemon had great wisdom, the kind of wisdom that had little to do with book knowledge, although he was obviously an educated man. Sandemon knew about nature and time and God. He understood tides and seasons and animals and trees.

And he understood *her*. As for the *Seanchai*, while he was kind enough in his own gruff way, he seemed to find her little more than an amusement in his life—and at times an annoying one, at that. Obviously, he had no real interest in getting to know her as a person. He would listen to her chatter, cast a wry face at her shenanigans, and at times would even tell her stories, making the giant warriors and the faerie people of the ancient legends come alive.

But in spite of his tolerance, he did not care to know the *real* Annie Delaney, and his indifference grieved her. The *Seanchai* was a true hero, a great man, and she was devoted and indebted to him. In the beginning, she had hoped he would come to depend on *her* and even want her as his friend. As time went on, however, she had come to see such a possibility as more and more unlikely.

Perhaps it might have been different had it not been for his terrible tragedy. Sandemon said that tragedy worked in different ways upon different people. With some, he said, it acted as a separator—dividing them from their family, their friends, and even from God. With others, it seemed to draw them closer to their Creator and those who loved them.

It had been his experience, said Sandemon, that often the physically strong, the self-reliant, tended to draw away during their troubles. Perhaps because they had so cherished their own strength, their personal power, they found it difficult, if not impossible, to rely on others.

That being the case, it made perfect sense that the *Seanchai* would have the hard time of it. Annie sorrowed for what he had lost, longed to comfort him. But how could she comfort him when he refused to take her seriously?

Still, she had no room to complain, for hadn't the man taken her in, given her shelter and work to do? The both of them, the *Seanchai* and Sandemon, were kind to her. Indeed, through their kindness Annie was beginning to find her own healing—from her mum's hard heart and from Tully's brutality.

For the first time in a very long time, Annie lived without fear. She was finally learning to trust again.

"You will comb that poor horse bald if you do not give him a rest," Sandemon observed mildly, coming to stand and watch.

Annie looked at him blankly for a moment, then at Pilgrim's mane, which indeed she had been combing steadily for a long time. Grinning, she rubbed the great stallion's nose, then put away the comb.

"What's on with Old Scratch?" she asked, motioning to the black thoroughbred on the opposite side of the stable. Annie didn't like the horse, which, according to Colm O'Grady, was stabled there as a favor to one of Sir Roger Nelson's influential friends. The high-strung, nervous animal seemed to live in constant protest of his confinement. Annie had told him off once or twice, but he ignored her entirely.

Sandemon's gaze traveled to the horse, then back to Annie. "Bad blood in that one," he said soberly. "You keep your distance, hear?"

"I expect I will," said Annie. "He doesn't like me a bit more than I like him."

Sandemon nodded. "We should go in now. The *Seanchai* may need me."

"Aye. But one last lump of sugar for Pilgrim before we go," Annie said, digging down in her pocket.

"You spoil that stallion shamefully," observed Sandemon as they left the stable and started walking toward the house.

"I'm thinking he might be lonely," said Annie. "He must miss the *Seanchai* in the worst way."

Sandemon regarded her with a thoughtful expression. "Yes," he said gently, "I imagine he does."

After another moment, his face creased with an inscrutable smile. "I might know a secret," he said.

Annie's ears vibrated, and she stared up at him. "What *sort* of a secret?"

The black man shrugged. "I might know a special date."

"A special date, is it? What kind of a special date? Tell me, Sand-Man!"

"What if I knew the *Seanchai*'s birth date? Hmm?"

Annie stopped walking and yanked at his sleeve to halt him.

"How would you know such a thing?" she asked eagerly.

"His friend the priest provided me with certain pertinent information when he employed me."

"*Per-tin-ent?*" echoed Annie. "Isn't that what the *Seanchai* says I am sometimes?"

"No, child, that's *impertinent*," Sandemon replied, still smiling. "There's a great difference."

"So, then, when is it? The *Seanchai*'s birthday?"

"Soon. Next month, in fact. We should be planning a gift for the occasion, don't you agree?"

"Aye, and a very special one, Sand-Man! Something very special indeed!"

Already Annie's mind was working, trying to think of something that would make the *Seanchai* happy.

"I might have an idea," said Sandemon. "But it would require a great deal of work—and we have little time. Still, if you would help, we could probably have it done by then."

Shifting eagerly from one foot to the other, Annie beamed up at the black man. "Sure, and wouldn't I be *wanting* to help, though? What sort of idea is it, Sand-Man? Tell me!"

He put a finger to his lips. "Quiet, now, child, else the *Seanchai* will know we are conspiring. This will be our secret, yours and mine. Not even Artegal is to know."

"Especially Artegal." Annie wrinkled her nose. "He'd spoil it all on purpose if he got wind of it. Just because it's our idea. He doesn't like either of us, you know." She paused. "For that matter, he doesn't even like the *Seanchai*."

Sandemon looked at her. "I fear you're right. He seems an unhappy man."

Again Annie scowled. "He is a hateful man. A cold man altogether." Tugging on his sleeve, she started up with her nagging again. "Now tell me your idea for the *Seanchai*'s gift, Sand-Man!"

"You agree to help as much as is needed?"

"My hand to you, I'll not rest until the gift is done!" Annie pledged solemnly.

Sandemon smiled at her. "Very good, child. Here's what I think we might do."

❧

After dinner that evening, Sandemon accompanied Annie to the library in search of a book.

Other than a warning to the child that she take care, the *Seanchai* had given them both free access to the shelves, which held thousands of books of all description.

As she almost always did, the child selected a book of Irish folklore for her own reading. At Sandemon's invitation, she began reading one of the tales aloud to him while he browsed the poetry shelves.

She was reading to him a tale about the exploits of one named *Oisin* in the Land of the Ever Young when the *Seanchai* wheeled into the room and sat, just inside the door, listening.

The child stopped and looked up, but the *Seanchai* gestured that she should go on. "Finish the tale," he said quietly, smiling.

The child's face lit up like morning sun as she read on. She read the story fluidly, easily, almost as if from memory. When she had finished, the *Seanchai* motioned for Annie to bring him the book.

He glanced down at it, then looked up at the child. "As I thought," he said. "These stories are in the Irish."

Annie nodded. "Aye, sir, but Sand-Man does not know the Irish."

Still regarding her with a curious look, he said, "And so you translate into English as you read." Sandemon heard the note of surprise in the other's voice. "You know the Irish well, lass. Who taught you?"

"Me da," replied the child with obvious pride. "Mostly from *your* poems and other writings, sir."

The young master stared at her. "From *my* writings?" Sandemon could have sung for joy at the warmth reflected in those eyes, eyes so often clouded with pain or hardened with bitterness.

The two men exchanged a look over Annie's head. "This is a clever child," said the *Seanchai* dryly. "She reads the Irish and translates it like a scholar. Not a common thing these days in Ireland."

Sandemon slanted a glance at the child, gratified by the beaming smile on her face. "I have wondered why such a thing should be, sir—why more of the children aren't fluent in their ancestral language?"

The *Seanchai* let out a sharp sound of disgust. "Perhaps because the British set out to systematically destroy it! For generations it was either illegal or impossible to teach the language. If you weren't arrested for trying, you were caned and ridiculed. These days there are few scholars remaining who would be competent to teach it."

Sandemon considered his words. "To abolish a people's national language—would that not serve to shatter their unity, to fragment their culture?"

"Ah...you see behind the veil," answered the *Seanchai* cynically. "No language, no nation."

Sandemon leveled a steady gaze on his employer. "Then," he said carefully, "it would seem to behoove those few scholars who *are* adequate to teach—to do so." He paused. "Wouldn't you agree, *Seanchai*?"

The man in the wheelchair fixed a withering look on Sandemon but said nothing.

Sandemon remembered something the priest in Mayo had confided to him. "It would seem to me," he said casually, "that a fine school under the supervision of learned men could accomplish much in the way of preserving Ireland's culture for future generations."

The *Seanchai* surveyed Sandemon with narrowed eyes. "Perhaps," he bit out. "But I, for one, would not have the energy to administer such a school." A shadow flitted across the face of the young master, a fleeting, haunted look, as if he'd felt the chill of a ghostly presence.

Sandemon was not yet ready to drop the subject. "Perhaps when you are stronger again you will want to give it further thought. We must work doubly hard at your therapy in the meantime."

He half expected his employer to wheel himself out of the room in a temper. By now he recognized the first signs of agitation and restlessness that seemed to come upon his young master each evening. He knew the signs for what they were, and it concerned him greatly. The man reminded him for all the world of Old Scratch, the hot-blooded thoroughbred who constantly threatened to break down the confining walls of his stable. But in the young master's case, even if he were to break free, he had no place to run to, and no legs to run with. He was most certainly trapped, and the futility of it plagued the man's great soul like a curse. Unable to run, he took his flight by other means.

But this time the *Seanchai* did not flee the room. Instead, he turned to regard the girl with a measuring look.

"Perhaps," he said distractedly. "For the time being, however, I'm considering the instruction of only one student. It would have to be a clever child, don't you see—one eager to learn. And," he added, still watching Annie, "one willing to live within the confines of Nelson Hall, since my travel is somewhat restricted." He paused, letting his words hang suspended like a challenge.

Surprised and profoundly pleased, Sandemon shot a look at the child. She was gaping with utter astonishment at the man in the wheelchair.

"*Faith*, sir! You wouldn't be thinking—it's not *me* you're meaning—"

With his large hands on the armrests, the *Seanchai* leaned forward slightly in the wheelchair. After a moment, he said something in the tongue of the Irish. The child, wide-eyed and flushed with excitement, wiped her hands on her skirt and then answered. In the Irish.

Slowly, the *Seanchai* nodded, then turned to Sandemon. "This child," he said, "insists she would like to be my student. What do you think? Can she manage the necessary time from her everyday duties?"

Sandemon inclined his head. "Certainly, sir," he said, restraining his desire to shout. "We will work out a schedule right away."

Much later that night, after reading from the Scriptures to the child and talking with her about the Savior's love, Sandemon sat at the small desk in his room, his Bible open in front of him.

His legs were too long for the low desk, and when he moved he invariably bumped his knees. But the room was quiet, the fire was warm, and the Spirit was especially close to him tonight. He felt the peace of the Lord and was content.

His thoughts went to his young master just across the hall. The *Seanchai*, he was in much, much need of prayer—one of the reasons the Lord had sent Sandemon to Nelson Hall, he knew. Praying for this stricken giant, this tortured, heroic soul, was an adventure in faith and a challenge. He could scarcely wait to see what God had in store for his wounded warrior.

Then his mind went to the child. Remembering the look of pure joy and amazement that had crossed her elfin face earlier in the library, he smiled. Perhaps the first step had been taken toward what he hoped would eventually be a very special relationship.

His smile broke even wider at the thought of the birthday gift he would make—he and the child—for the unsuspecting *Seanchai*. Unable to control his joy any longer, he got to his feet. He stretched his arms and his spirit up, up, until he stood poised on the balls of his feet, reaching and laughing aloud in pure delight, rejoicing in the presence of his Lord.

After a moment, however, his exultation ebbed, and he clasped his hands tightly together. With his head bowed low, he stood in front of the fire and took up his praying again.

He prayed for the lonely, frightened man across the hall who thought he had nobody to share his life with, to warm his world. Who thought nobody needed him, when all the time there was a young, tender soul in desperate need of his attention, and so near at hand at that.

Sandemon knew Annie's story, and it grieved his heart. She had confided in him her mother's blaming rejection, the drunken stepfather's abuse. She told her tale awkwardly, with obvious embarrassment—but without any real anger or bitterness.

Sandemon had considered sharing what he knew of Annie's background with the *Seanchai*, yet held back in the hopes the two would eventually grow close enough that the child herself would tell him.

In the meantime, he was doing what he could to lead the girl closer to Jesus. She was a believer, with a true reverence for God and a respect for holy things. But as yet she possessed no real insight into the loving heart of the Lord. It was pure pleasure and delight for Sandemon to guide one so young, so in need of acceptance and affection, to the open arms of the Savior.

As he did every night, he now stormed heaven's gates for his disconsolate young master, the fallen patriot who believed himself abandoned by his Creator. He interceded for the sad, angry poet who thought his words would sing no more.

He was careful to remind the Lord about the whiskey that was becoming, he feared, a nightly ritual. Sandemon suspected the drink was more than a painkiller by now; more than likely it had become a substitute for facing reality. There needed to be something soon to take its place, to free the *Seanchai* from its grasp, or he might go the way of the poor, sad man who had been his father—the man described with such compassion by the priest in Mayo, the man who had failed both his sons in such a sorry way.

Once more Sandemon prayed for the salvation of the dark-eyed, brave little girl whom Jesus had charged to his responsibility. The child who just might be—*please, Lord*—a part of the young master's healing.

Suddenly, Sandemon was struck by the image of another young girl. Caught off guard, he remained quiet, waiting. The memory of long golden hair and a clear, innocent gaze passed before his mind.

The silent Finola. A princess with no voice.

What, Lord? Sandemon questioned. *What of the lovely Finola?*

As he waited, listening, expecting, Sandemon felt a gentle warmth and light settle over him, draping his spirit with insight and assurance. At that instant he lifted the mute young woman with the golden hair before the throne, convinced beyond all doubt that in a way as yet unseen she, like Annie Delaney, would be an instrument of healing in the life of Morgan Fitzgerald.

40

No Hope Apart from God

His songs were a little phrase
Of eternal song,
Drowned in the harping of lays
More loud and long.
His deed was a single word,
Called out alone
In a night when no echo stirred
To laughter or moan.

THOMAS MACDONAGH (1878–1916)

The next few days were happy days for Annie Delaney. She spent her mornings in the stables, tending to Pilgrim or helping Sandemon with the wondrous birthday gift for the *Seanchai*. She labored hard alongside the black man, for now that she had caught his vision of the gift, she could not wait to see it done and presented.

Afternoons were spent at inside chores, which, to Annie's relief, were few—both because of her clumsiness and because she was busy elsewhere, usually at her lessons with the *Seanchai*.

In the evening, she was mostly on her own, unless there were stories to be told in the library.

Sure, and if she could have ordered up the routine of her days, she would not have asked for more. Best of all, even more than the time spent with Pilgrim, she loved her studies. Having the full attention of the *Seanchai* as he instructed her, receiving a rare word of praise from him when she excelled, had quickly come to be the brightest part of her day. A word of encouragement from the *Seanchai* or a smile that clearly said he was pleased with her progress would send Annie flying to her room afterward, where she would immediately set to poring over her lessons with more fervor than ever.

Sandemon teased her, saying that she would turn into a bookworm and get lost wiggling through a hole in the stable. But Annie could tell he was pleased with things as they were. In fact, he seemed as happy with all the attention the *Seanchai* paid her as he was with the reports of what a good scholar she was becoming.

Annie would not have thought she could bear more joy. But this morning Sandemon had made a suggestion that had her jumping out of her skin with delight.

"A *birthday party*! Truly, Sand-Man? A real *party*?"

He lifted a hand to caution her. "A very *small* party. The *Seanchai*, as you well know, has little patience with crowds or clamor. We will prepare a simple event for the three of us—a special time to acknowledge his birth date and to give him his gift."

"But you're supposed to invite guests to a party, aren't you? Even a small one?"

He shook his head. "Not this time, child. We must respect the *Seanchai*'s feelings. Unless Mr. Smith O'Brien should happen to return from Paris before then, it will be only the three of us."

Annie pursed her lips, thinking. "I know someone else we could invite. Someone I expect the *Seanchai* would like to have at his party."

Sandemon frowned, but before he could protest Annie went on. "Sure, and Finola would come, were we to ask! And don't you think the *Seanchai* would want to see her again? He seemed to like her fine, as I recollect."

Sandemon was quiet for a moment. Despite her excitement, Annie forced herself to hold her tongue. She was learning not to press when the black man was thinking.

Crossing his arms over his chest, he seemed to consider her suggestion. Finally, he offered a faint smile. "Could be you're right, child," he said slowly. After another moment, he gave a small nod. "Yes, perhaps your idea is good. Here's what we will do, then. This afternoon, while you and the *Seanchai* are busy with your studies, I will go into the city and pay a call on Miss Finola."

Annie scowled at him fiercely. "I'd thought to go with you."

"You have your studies," he said firmly. "Besides, it wouldn't do for both of us to leave the *Seanchai* alone for too long a time. What if he needed help and neither of us were here? And," he added, cutting short Annie's objection, "the area in which Miss Finola lives is not a proper place for a child."

"I'm not a child!" Annie retorted. But she knew from the raised eyebrows and the slight tightening around his mouth that further argument would be a total waste of time.

The more Sandemon thought about Annie's suggestion to invite Finola back to Nelson Hall, the more the idea took on merit. On the way into Dublin, he considered the consequences, and could think of only one unpleasant possibility: What if the *Seanchai* felt they were interfering in his life and grew angry?

Sandemon was used to the young giant's temper, and routinely ignored it. But nothing must be allowed to halt the growing relationship between the *Seanchai* and the child. There was no telling who would ultimately benefit most from it, but that both would be greatly blessed, he had no doubt.

Somehow, though, Sandemon did not think the *Seanchai* would mind their inviting Miss Finola. In fact, recalling the uncommon warmth that had filled the young master's eyes during that first encounter with the mysterious young woman—and remembering his own recent inclination to pray for her—Sandemon began to wonder if the child's idea might not be truly inspired.

Annie had hoped the *Seanchai* would be in the mood for storytelling after dinner. Ever since Sandemon returned with the news that Finola had accepted their invitation to the party, she'd been far too restless and excited to think of much else. Perhaps one of the *Seanchai*'s stories might help to take her mind off the party—and the wondrous gift she and Sandemon were making.

Her hopes were dashed, however, not long into the meal. In fact, she didn't even suggest a story, seeing the way things were with the *Seanchai*.

He was irritable and short all through dinner, scarcely finishing his tea before muttering an excuse and wheeling himself out of the room.

Sandemon helped him onto the lift, then took Annie to one side in the library. "He has asked to be left alone," he told her. "I'll check on him once more, and if he still doesn't want me the rest of the evening, I'm going to go out to the stable and work on the gift."

"I'll go with you, then."

He shook his head. "No, child," he said. "He might become suspicious if he should discover both of us gone this time of night. I won't work long—perhaps another hour or two. I want you in the house so you could fetch me if he should call. Stay in your room where you can hear him."

At Annie's nod of assent, Sandemon followed her from the library. "Stay upstairs now, mind," he cautioned her again before starting toward the back of the house.

In his bedroom, Morgan wheeled himself toward the desk where Joseph Mahon's journal lay open, its pages in disarray, accusing him.

He had neglected his usual reading for some nights now, unable—or unwilling—to steep himself any further with Mayo's misery. Tonight, however, he knew himself to be too restless for sleep. A storm was brewing; in the distance he could hear the approaching thunder. His skin seemed to crawl with an energy for which there was no outlet. Every nerve in his body screamed for release. If he went to bed, he would do nothing but thrash about, so he might just as well return to the priest's dolorous writings.

He had the monster of all needs for the whiskey tonight. Before he started in on the journal, he set out his flask and tumbler at the ready. He would wait another half hour or so, he told himself. He would read for at least that long without the drink.

It had occurred to him only a few nights past that he was starting his drinking earlier each night, consuming more and more all the time. Last night he had promised himself with fierce resolve to cut back.

He was growing dependent on the stuff, just like his father.

The ugly truth was that he was gradually becoming a drunk—a secret drunk, but a drunk all the same.

It was no secret from Sandemon, of course; the black man knew, had to know from the smell on him every morning. But he said nothing, gave no indication that he noticed. Morgan could not help but wonder why.

Before he began to read, Morgan braced his hands on the armrests of the wheelchair, half-rising to stretch the muscles of his body. Too soon, his legs collapsed, sending a wave of familiar frustration crashing over him.

His back was aching tonight—not bad, but enough to justify taking a drop right away.

No. He would wait.

His eyes slid to the flask near the journal. At the same time, he noted with distaste the trembling of his hands on the pages. How many times had he seen his father's hands tremble in just the same way?

His mouth was dry, his throat hot, but he forced himself to ignore the flask.

He could easily envision Joseph Mahon the priest, his silver head bent over the pages, the pen propped in his frail, unsteady hand, writing laboriously, painstakingly, late at night.

When else would the man find time? He spent his days and most of his nights with "his people," the villagers of Killala.

The priest continued to pour out his life for them, as if he hoped by killing himself he might make a difference.

Yet Morgan knew in his heart that indeed Joseph *had* made a difference—in some instances, the difference of life or death. In truth, if ever a body of men had showed themselves heroes, sure, and countless priests and Protestant clergy throughout Ireland had done so. Many had given up their own lives in the act of caring for the sick, feeding the hungry, and ministering to the dying. Morgan had heard of case after case where the priest or pastor was all that stood between the people and the graveyard.

In his own experience, he had never known such an utterly selfless human being as Joseph Mahon, whose words as he read them played sorrowfully upon his heart:

> In spite of their unmitigated suffering, I have yet to hear a resentful or bitter word raised against the Lord. These poor ones understand that it was not their Lord who brought this pestilence upon them, but unprincipled men, even evil men. They know with certain assurance that it is not Providence that has ruined our country, but the greed and apathy of man. And their quiet acceptance does defy all human understanding....

Nor do they seek for supernatural signs of God's remembrance or miraculous wonders that prove His power. Unlike Jacob of the Bible, they do not attempt to take hold of God's favor, to wrestle Him into a blessing or gain a sign of His protection in their agony. Even those who stand to lose most, who at one time were the most vigorous and self-reliant, refuse to surrender to hopelessness or despair. Indeed, out of their very weakness, their abject humiliation, has come the greatest triumph of faith I have ever witnessed....

Morgan's heart swelled, then began to hammer wildly as he brought the pages even closer to his eyes. The words seemed to darken and intensify in front of him as he read on:

It is a wondrous thing they do, these abased and despised. The comfortless reach out to comfort...the suffering reach out to console...the dying reach out to the living with triumphant words of conviction and the assurance of God's love!

Perhaps it is because in their agony they have finally glimpsed the truth, that only those without God are truly helpless, and only those separated from His love are truly hopeless.

The level of dependency on the Lord, the unshakable faith in Him which I have encountered as a priest this past year has convinced me that there is no strength apart from the Lord's presence, no hope apart from His promises, and no peace apart from His love.

There is a triumph in these lives that cannot be explained in mortal terms. It does seem to me, simple priest that I am, that in the very act of reaching out with mercy to others, they attain a kind of merciful healing for themselves.

If Joseph himself had stepped off the pages of his journal and hurled the words in Morgan's face, they could not have resounded louder in his mind, would not have pierced his heart with such a force.

His eyes locked on the words before him, and he read them over and over again. With each reading, they echoed more loudly, more clearly, in his soul.

A wave of shame washed over Morgan. All his life he had used the power of his presence and the power of his pen to help others—to try to change the fate of his dying Ireland. Yet suddenly, with the loss of his legs, he had simply turned inward, wallowing in misery and self-pity like a pig in the mire. He had let go of the Cause and embraced the bottle, wanting nothing but to forget. Sure, and Morgan Fitzgerald had given up to die, hadn't he, now?

And all the time, right here in his own house, a little piece of his beloved Ireland was waiting, looking to him for help and love and protection. There *was* something he could do, something he should be doing, after all! He had made a promise to his grandfather—a promise he'd done his best to ignore. But now here it was again, facing him down in the wee demented lass from Belfast, challenging him to fulfill what he had promised—to Grandfather, to himself, to his land, to his God.

Morgan began to weep—not for the loss of his legs, but for the loss of compassion.

Through his tears, he stared at the flask of whiskey and the glass in front of him. With an almost brutal force and a wail of despair, he flung out his arm and sent the flask and tumbler crashing to the floor.

A violent urge to go to his knees seized him. Half-blind from scalding tears and burning remorse, he clung to the desk, twisting his body free of the chair. He tried to kneel, but slipped and lost his balance altogether. He managed to crawl to the foot of the bed, where he stopped. Doubled over, he curled himself against the bed like a sorrowing child.

There he prayed, a prayer unlike any other he had ever voiced. Allowing himself to be wrapped in the love of his Savior, he acknowledged that he was indeed helpless—but not without hope. He asked the One who had lamed the demanding Jacob as a constant reminder of his weakness and need for God, to use these lifeless legs of his as a constant reminder that he, too, was utterly dependent on the same God.

"Let me never forget that, like the afflicted people of Joseph Mahon's journal, I have no strength apart from your presence...no hope apart from your promises...and no peace apart from your love...."

The obscure uneasiness he'd been feeling earlier continued to nag at Sandemon as he worked in the stables. With the approaching storm, a vague heaviness had settled at the very center of his being, intruding on his peace, pressing him to do—what?

He had worked much longer than he'd anticipated. Glancing at the inexpensive pocket watch the priests in Barbados had given him years before, he saw that he had been gone from the house for well over two hours.

Too long. An urgency now overtook him, a need to return to the house. No doubt the *Seanchai* was still cloistered in his room—drinking the entire time, Sandemon feared.

He straightened and tossed a piece of leather onto the floor. He must leave the stables—now. He wiped his hands on his trousers, then picked up the lantern to leave.

The exasperating thoroughbred—"Old Scratch," the child called him— picked that moment to raise trouble. Squealing and snorting like a crazed demon, he began to bump at the door of the stall, his hoofs pounding the floor in a frenzy.

Sandemon gave an impatient sound of disgust, then started toward the front of the stable.

"You are a devil, I think," he muttered, approaching the horse, who tossed its mane and snorted excitedly.

"You'll get no sympathy from me this night, Old Scratch," he said, near-ing the front of the stall. "I do not coddle horses, especially bad-tempered ones like you."

The words he spoke were anything but kind, but Sandemon uttered them in gentle tones, hoping to soothe the beast. Instead, his presence seemed to agitate the animal that much more.

Suddenly, the horse snorted and reared up. Sandemon caught a flash of red, bright and wet, on the thoroughbred's left front hoof. Hanging the lantern on the wall of the stable, he continued to reassure the horse in soft words, watching him closely as he drew near.

Again the thoroughbred reared, and this time Sandemon clearly recog-nized blood on his hoof—enough blood to indicate a serious cut or injury.

No wonder the poor beast had turned more temperamental than ever! His foul disposition only masked a frightened animal in pain.

Immediately sympathetic to the thoroughbred, Sandemon eased the rest of the way up to the stall.

"Poor boy...poor boy," he murmured, carefully releasing the board that secured the door of the stall. "Sandemon will help you. Hush now...."

Unexpectedly, the horse quieted, all the while watching Sandemon through wild eyes. Even when the black man opened the stall door and put one foot inside, the thoroughbred followed his movements in total silence.

Sandemon never once stopped his murmurings as his gaze traveled down, from the horse's head to the hoof that needed tending.

Slowly, cautiously, he extended his hand to gentle the horse.

And he knew in an instant he had made a foolish mistake. The thoroughbred reared at his touch, shrieking like a creature out of hell.

On instinct, Sandemon threw up his arms to protect his head, whipping his body hard to the side of the stall. He crashed into the wood, then bounced off. Again he lunged to the side of the stall, trying to hurl himself out of the way of the horse's flying hoofs.

Instead, he stumbled, lurching directly into the thoroughbred's path. An incredible blow knocked the breath out of his body, sending him spinning out the open door of the stall.

Sprawled on his back, he stared up. The last thing he saw was the belly of the devil horse as he reared up, screaming, over Sandemon's head.

41

Secrets of the Lonely Heart

Lone and forgotten
Through a long sleeping,
In the heart of age
A child woke weeping....
The darkness thickened
Upon him creeping,
In the heart of age
A child lay weeping.

GEORGE WILLIAM RUSSELL (A.E.) (1867–1935)

Annie sat up, vaguely aware of the noise that awakened her. A peculiar noise, something not quite...right.

When Sandemon hadn't returned after more than an hour, she had fallen asleep, a book still in her hand. Now, glancing around the dimly lit bedroom, she pushed the book aside, waiting for her eyes to focus.

The candles had burned low. Outside she heard the rumbling of distant thunder, the soft patter of rain.

Was that what she'd heard, then? Only an approaching storm?

Still drowsy, she lay unmoving, listening. She thought there had been a crash—had it been thunder?—just before she'd awakened.

Perhaps she had a dream. Rolling over, she lay listening to the rain. She had always found it a mournful sound, the falling rain, and yet it lulled her, like a sad song that would not be ignored.

There came a muffled cry, like someone weeping. Annie sat up. Then she heard a thud. Inside the house, or out? She could not tell.

Now a banging—louder this time. Outside, she thought.

Leaping from the bed, she ran to the window, pushed the draperies roughly aside. The window was swollen, and she had to force it open.

On the rain-heavy wind came a loud neighing and the scream of a terrified horse. Something was wrong in the stables! *Sandemon! Sandemon and Pilgrim!*

Leaving the window open, Annie ran from the room. In the hall, she stopped, frowning. Strange sounds were coming from the Fitzgerald's bedroom. Muffled noises, like someone talking to himself. Then a loud thump, and still another.

Annie's eyes darted from hallway to the stairs, then back to the *Seanchai*'s room. She had promised Sandemon to stay near, in case the *Seanchai* needed help. She must see to him first!

Sprinting down the hall, she charged into the *Seanchai*'s bedroom. With her hand still gripping the doorknob, she stopped, her eyes widening in horror.

The room reeked of whiskey. The *Seanchai* was on the floor, crouched and trying to pull himself up into the wheelchair. A pool of whiskey and broken glass spread across the carpet in front of the desk.

With both hands braced on the seat of the wheelchair, the *Seanchai* stared at her from the floor. His eyes were red, his copper hair wild, his clothes disheveled.

"Annie!" He gave a short laugh of surprise. "Thanks be! Help me, lass! Hold the chair so I can get into it!"

He was drunk!

Annie's legs seemed sunk in lead. She could not move, could only gape at the man on the floor in growing terror. He was sprawled between bed and chair like a common drunk!

Like Tully!

"Annie? It's all right, lass; just hold the chair. I didn't fall, I was just—"

Drunk...drunk, like Tully...his clothes in disarray. She couldn't go near him...he was drunk...he would hurt her.... Repulsed by the sight of him clawing at the wheelchair, sickened by the familiar sweet and smoky smell of the whiskey, Annie fled from the room, screaming.

The *Seanchai*'s cries for help echoed behind her as she went flying down the stairs and out of the house.

"Annie! Come back! Come back, Annie!"

She ran as hard as she could to the stables, screaming all the way across the grounds. A cold rain pelted against her face, and a bolt of lightning lit up the sky with an eerie blue light.

"Sand-Man!" She must find Sandemon! He would help her! He would keep the drunken *Seanchai* away from her!

Tearing into the stable, she saw Pilgrim first. The big red stallion was carrying on something fierce, screaming and pounding the floor of his stall in a fury.

She shushed him, but didn't tarry. Her eyes went to the empty stall where Old Scratch was supposed to be.

He was gone! Heading toward the stall, Annie stopped, frozen by the sight of Sandemon lying on the floor of the stable.

Annie screamed his name and pitched toward him. Dropping down on her knees, she began to shake him. The black man's eyes were closed. A trickle of blood wound its way down the side of his face.

Sobbing, Annie continued to shake him, calling his name. *"Sand-Man! Wake up! Wake up, Sand-Man! I need you!"*

Somebody was shaking him, screaming his name. Groaning, Sandemon opened his eyes. The world was spinning crazily. He put out a hand to stop the spinning. *"Sand-Man!"*

The child was screeching at him, crying and tugging at his arm. "Oh, Sand-Man! You're not dead! Thanks be to God…you're not dead at all!"

He moaned, squeezed his eyes shut against the noise of frightened horses and the child's shrill cries.

"Hush, child! Of course, I'm not dead! Hush, now, or I will die from all the racket!" He caught her hand. "And stop shaking me, foolish child!"

Sandemon's eyes began to focus. The spinning slowed. His ribs hurt with each breath, and his head felt as if it might explode. He tried to push himself up, but the stable tilted in front of him.

Staring at the girl, he put a hand to his head. "What is *wrong* with you, child? Stop that screeching! I'm all right, didn't I tell you? At least I will be, once my head clears."

She was sobbing uncontrollably, gripping his arm. "What happened to you, Sand-Man? I thought you were dead! Old Scratch is gone, and Pilgrim was in a panic! And the *Seanchai* is drunk, and—"

Sandemon caught her by the forearm. "What about the *Seanchai*? What are you saying, child? Is he all right?"

She stared at him, then wailed, "He's *drunk*! On the floor! He tried to make me help him, but I couldn't—"

Sandemon stared at the child with rising dread. "On the *floor*—" Rolling to his side, he grasped her arm. "Help me up!" Clambering to his feet, he swayed, ducked his head down until he was steady.

"We must get to the house at once! Come, child! Hurry!"

⁂

In his room, Morgan had finally managed to get himself into the wheelchair. Avoiding the broken glass and the pool of whiskey, he was wheeling toward the door when it crashed open.

Sandemon stood framed in the dim light of the hallway. But a different Sandemon, this. His face streaked with dirt and sweat, a cut over one eye, his purple shirt smudged with dust.

"Are you all right, *Seanchai*?" The black man's gaze jerked from Morgan to the breakage on the floor. "What happened?"

"Bit of an accident, is all!" Morgan snapped. "What's wrong with you? What's all the commotion?" He stopped, seeing Annie lurking behind him. She was staring at Morgan, her eyes filled with fear and disgust.

"Annie?" Morgan reached out a hand to her. "Come here, lass. What's gotten into you?"

The child hung back, dark eyes flashing.

"You're not hurt, *Seanchai*?" asked Sandemon.

Morgan looked at him, "Hurt? No, I'm not hurt, why—" Morgan's gaze went back to the child, and understanding began to dawn. "I was trying to get back into the chair when she found me. It must have frightened her, seeing me so..." He let his words drift off, unfinished in his humiliation.

Sandemon scrutinized him for a moment. "You're not drunk," he murmured, then blinked, his eyes taking on a hooded expression as if he knew he had spoken out of turn.

"No, I am not *drunk!*" Morgan shot back. "I haven't even had a drink!"

He followed the black man's gaze as it traveled to the broken glass and the whiskey on the floor.

"I threw it!" Morgan snarled.

"You *threw* it?" Sandemon repeated skeptically.

"Aye, I threw it," Morgan repeated, softening his tone. Sagging in the chair, he added, "I'll not have it in the house any longer."

Looking up, he saw something glint in the black man's eyes.

The two men exchanged a long look. Then Sandemon gave a nod and turned to the girl for a moment. "Go back to your room, child," he said softly. "I will come to you as soon as I have cleaned up in here."

Annie didn't move. Her dark eyes went from Sandemon to Morgan, then back to the black man.

"Go with her," Morgan said quickly. "You can clean this up later."

"Seanchai—"

Morgan shook his head, made a dismissing motion with his hand. "It's all right. Take care of the child."

Sandemon gave a nod, then put an arm around Annie's shoulder. "Come, child," he said gently. "Everything will be all right now. Come with Sandemon. You must rest."

After bandaging the cut over his eye, Sandemon returned. He started right in cleaning up the whiskey and broken glass.

"Is she all right?" Morgan asked tightly, staring out the window into the rain-veiled night.

"She will be. She was almost asleep when I left her." Sandemon's voice was muffled by a drumroll of thunder.

Lightning streaked over the stables and bounced toward the stream. Morgan wheeled the chair around from the window and sat watching Sandemon.

"What happened—why did she tear out of here as she did? She seemed frightened out of her wits!"

Sandemon, poised on one knee with rag in hand, looked up. Finally, he gave a weary sigh and got to his feet. "This will wait, I suppose. First I will tell you about Annie. I should have told you sooner." He paused, giving Morgan a hard look. "Perhaps then you will tell me why you threw the whiskey across the room instead of drinking it, hmm?"

They talked for a long time. After Morgan had heard the story about Annie's drunken stepfather and uncaring mother, he held his head between his hands, grieved beyond words.

"No wonder she ran…no wonder." He looked up at the black man, who now sat at the desk across from him. "I have been the great fool, Sandemon. And not for the first time in my life."

Sandemon stood and walked to the window. With his back to Morgan, he stared out on the night. Outside, the storm had subsided, but a steady rain continued to fall. "All men are fools at times, *Seanchai*," he said quietly. "There is no escaping that part of our nature, I think."

Morgan looked at the broad back, the regal head. "I can't imagine you ever playing the fool, my friend."

The black man turned, regarding Morgan with a look of great sadness. "I was the greatest fool of all, *Seanchai*. I confess to you that no greater fool ever walked."

Morgan regarded him with curiosity. "What is your story, Sandemon?" he asked softly. "You involve yourself in the lives of others—and I mean that kindly—you live out your days *doing* for others, taking care of them. But you speak not at all of yourself. Why is that?"

"Perhaps my past is a hurtful thing, *Seanchai*. More to the point, it would serve no purpose to share it."

Unwilling to infringe upon the solitary man's privacy, Morgan remained silent. But he wondered. He knew he would always wonder.

"I want to see the child," he said. "Will you go with me?"

"She may be sleeping," Sandemon cautioned.

Morgan gave a nod. "It doesn't matter. I need to be with her. But I don't want to frighten her again. You'd best go with me."

"It was only a momentary thing, *Seanchai*," Sandemon offered. "It will be forgotten by the morning sun."

"Not by me," Morgan said, his voice low. "I will not forget this night, I promise you."

When they entered the bedroom, they found the child sleeping.

Wheeling up beside her, the *Seanchai* sat staring at the thin, elfin face, the thatch of dark, tousled hair, the long eyelashes brushing her cheeks as she slept.

For an instant, the man in the wheelchair met Sandemon's eyes across the bed. Carefully, then, he took the child's hand, enfolded it in his own much larger one, and brought it to his lips.

"I will make it up to you, Annie," he murmured. "If you will but forgive me for my foolishness, I promise I will make it up to you. The pain of your past...my neglect...everything. You will never have to be afraid—not of this great fool, not of anything. You have my word, child."

The girl sighed in her sleep, and the *Seanchai* leaned over to brush an unruly strand of dark hair away from her forehead.

Still holding her hand, he leaned back in the wheelchair and looked at Sandemon. "I am going to need your help," he said wearily. "Giving up the drink—and becoming a father for the first time: a formidable task for any man."

Sandemon gave a wry smile. "I will count it all joy, *Seanchai*."

He left the two of them alone then. Closing the door quietly behind him, he paused in the hallway. After a moment the *Seanchai*'s soft voice could be heard, singing gently in the language of the Irish.

Sandemon smiled and went on. He did not have to speak the tongue to recognize a lullaby when he heard it.

Wedding Gifts

Had I the heavens' embroidered cloths,
Enwrought with golden and silver light,
The blue and the dim and the dark cloths
Of night and light and the half-light,
I would spread the cloths under your feet:
But I, being poor, have only my dreams;
I have spread my dreams under your feet.

W. B. YEATS (1865–1939)

New York City
May

Evan's father and aunt did not arrive in New York until the day before the wedding.

Waiting on the dock with Evan and Lewis Farmington, Nora could not say what rattled her more—the thought that today she would meet Evan's family or the fact that tomorrow she would be his wife.

Added to the turbulence of her emotions were the memories called up by New York Harbor. It was largely as she remembered it from her own arrival—teeming with immigrants, clamoring with the press of bodies. A veritable riot of alien languages, a profusion of color, the flags of nations. Ships disembarking or setting sail. Crying children, frightened mothers, the bewildered elderly. Laughter and wailing, terror and confusion.

It had been almost a year since she had first stepped off the *Green Flag* to be met by Sara Farmington, then a stranger to them all. The thought of everything that had happened since then set Nora's mind to spinning.

Illness and death. Tragedy and happiness. New friends. Love. And soon—a marriage!

Many a change had awaited them in this new land, yet today Nora could say in all truth, *"Thanks be to God, for He is good."* In the midst of it all, He had been there, loving them through the worst and the best of it.

Now she stood bracing herself for yet another new experience—meeting Evan's family. She prayed they would not despise her entirely. What must they think, after all, of his marrying an Irish widow he'd met aboard ship?

Even with her future husband on one side of her and Mr. Farmington on the other, Nora felt fearfully exposed, vulnerable. Nervously she smoothed her hair, then fidgeted with the bow at her throat.

"Nora? Why, you're t-trembling!"

She looked at Evan to find him watching her with a concerned frown.

"You mustn't be f-frightened, dear! I've t-told you, my father is a kind, quiet m-man. And you'll love Aunt Winnie—everyone d-does."

Nora managed a weak smile. How many times during the past week had poor Evan attempted to soothe her nerves? "I'm sorry," she said, her voice low. "I simply can't help it, Evan! I want them to like me!"

"Of c-course, they'll *like* you, N-Nora! They will *love* you—how can they h-help themselves? Now then," he said firmly, "I insist you stop f-fretting. You'll m-make yourself ill."

"He's quite right, you know, Nora," Lewis Farmington put in from her other side. "You'll charm them at once! Just see if you don't."

"Here they are now!" Evan cried, urging Nora forward, through the teeming crowds on the dock. *"F-Father! Aunt Winnie! Over here!"*

Swallowing down her apprehension, Nora allowed Evan and Mr. Farmington to draw her through the crush of people milling about the dock, near the gangplank. At the sound of Evan's voice, an elderly silver-haired man lifted a hand, while the extraordinarily attractive woman at his side broke into a near run, tugging the man along with one hand while she waved broadly with the other.

Evan gave a strangled cry. Nora stopped, tears burning her eyes, as she watched him close the distance between him and his family. His aunt, a diminutive flurry of pink and white, came flying, flinging her arms around Evan, sobbing and laughing all at the same time. Then Evan turned to his father, and Nora lost her breath at the look that passed between them.

Evan's father, a slight, slender man much like Evan, looked a good deal older than his sixty-nine years. As he stood staring at his son with tear-glazed eyes, a tide of emotion seemed to flood his thin, deeply lined features. His gaze rested only briefly on Evan's empty sleeve before he opened his arms to his son with a choked cry.

Lewis Farmington took Nora's arm, and they stood watching the two men embrace. Again, Nora whispered, *"Thanks be to God."*

Beside her, her employer added a quiet, *"Amen."*

By now Evan's aunt was fairly dancing about the two men as they continued to cling fiercely to each other. After a moment, Evan turned, his eyes searching for Nora. By the time she and Mr. Farmington joined the others, there was scarcely a dry eye among them.

Except for Lewis Farmington's gaze, which, Nora noted, seemed fixed in place on the petite and vivacious Aunt Winifred.

That evening, Lewis Farmington hosted a lavish dinner for the wedding party at the mansion. Sara observed with interest that, while she was at one side of her father, Winifred Whittaker Coates had been conveniently seated at the other. With even greater interest, she observed the almost instant rapport between her father and Evan's aunt.

Considering the attractive widow more closely, Sara was impressed. Evan had indicated that his aunt was in her late fifties, but she could have easily passed for a much younger woman, with her dancing blue eyes, blonde coiffure gently threaded with silver, and an almost maidenly figure. At the moment, she and Sara's father were debating the comforts and discomforts of shipboard travel. Father's intent expression, Sara thought with amusement, seemed to indicate he found the widow's every word a veritable treasure.

At Sara's left sat Michael Burke, a surprise guest. Invited only the day before by her father—at both Nora and Evan's request—he seemed tense and jumpy, although disconcertingly attentive throughout the meal.

Sara was glad she had worn her blue satin, for Michael had complimented her at least three times throughout the evening. Still, she could not ignore the fact that he seemed far more intent on watching her father than in talking with *her.*

In the library, Lewis Farmington felt as if he were holding court. Not that he minded, of course. The fact was, he was enjoying himself immensely!

First he met with Nora and Evan—a brief meeting, but one that gave him enormous pleasure. "A wedding gift," he said, handing Evan an envelope. "From Sara and me."

When the two lovebirds tried to express their thanks, he waved them off. Clearing his throat loudly, he said, "The two of you—and the children, of course—have become very special to us. Naturally, we wanted to make you a gift of some sort."

He gestured toward the envelope in Evan's hand. "You can open it later, when you're alone. But it takes a bit of explaining, and that's why I wanted to see you for a moment. You'll find a deed in there," he said, again pointing to the envelope. "A deed to a house I used to own in Brooklyn. It's not a large place, but it's had good maintenance and it's in a respectable neighborhood. It's yours. I want you to have it."

Good heavens, Nora looked about to faint! And Evan looked little better.

"Now don't take on! I understand that you're not quite ready to assume the financial burden of a home and the support of the children just yet. You're welcome to use the cottage just as long as you like, and we want to continue helping with the children, if you'll allow it. The deed is simply your assurance that, when the time comes, and you're ready for a place of your own, there will be one waiting for you. There's a nice quiet fellow who works at the yards living in it just now; he'll take good care of it until you move in."

He stopped for a breath, and both Nora and Evan began protesting in unison. He ignored them. "Now see here," he said firmly, "if you're serious about providing a home for Little Tom and Johanna, you'll need a bit more room than what you have in the cottage. This is our wedding gift to you—Sara's and mine—and you'll insult us greatly if you refuse it. It's no mansion, after all—just a nice clean little house, where you'll have a bit of room and some privacy. It's for the children, too, you understand."

He stopped, and to his dismay felt tears rising to his eyes. *Good heavens, he was taking on like a father!*

Clearing his throat again, Lewis squared his shoulders. "I want you to know…that I wish you both the very best, and that Sara and I will be always here for you if there's ever anything you need. Anything. We'd be proud if you'd consider us your family, here in America."

Bless them both, he had to get them out of the room before he started weeping in earnest!

Next to enter the library was Michael Burke. Lewis hadn't been the least surprised when Burke caught him alone after dinner and requested a private audience. He'd been expecting it. The last two times he had seen Sara and the Irish policeman together, the sparks flying between the two would have set an iceberg ablaze!

Ushering Burke into the library, he motioned him to take a seat. When the younger man declined, Lewis chose to remain standing also. Backing up to the cold fireplace, he gave Burke an encouraging smile. "Well, then, Captain—tomorrow is the big day! I trust you and your son will be here."

Burke stood near the desk, back straight, hands clasped behind him. "I'll be here, of course. As for Tierney—I don't believe he can make it."

"Too bad. Daniel will miss him, I'm sure." Noting the other's strained expression, Lewis moved to change the subject. "I believe you mentioned wanting to speak with me about a matter of some importance, Michael— you don't mind if I call you *Michael*?"

For an instant Burke's eyes lit up with what almost appeared to be gratitude. Immediately, however, his expression sobered. "I'd be pleased if you would, sir."

Waiting, Lewis sensed the enormous stress the policeman seemed to be under. "Well, then—what can I do for you…Michael?"

Burke's prominent Adam's apple worked up and down with difficulty as he cleared his throat. "When you hear what I am about to ask, no doubt you will think I have colossal gall, sir."

Lewis Farmington lifted his eyebrows. "Indeed? And here I thought I had the corner on gall—or so my business acquaintances tell me."

The policeman forced a smile. "Still—what I wanted to say—to ask about, that is, concerns your daughter."

Lewis fought to keep his expression noncommittal.

"I…ah—" Again the policeman cleared his throat. "I should explain, sir, that I know it's a bold thing I'm asking. In truth, I'm in no position at all to be making such a request."

Poor fellow. Obviously, he was on unfamiliar ground altogether. Lewis doubted that this strapping Irishman was much accustomed to humbling himself. He sighed. It seemed there was nothing like a woman to bring a strong man to his knees.

"You see, Mr. Farmington, sir, I'm fully aware you may find my request insulting—because of my being, ah—"

"Irish?" Lewis finished helpfully.

Burke's eyes widened. "Sir?"

With another sort of man, Lewis might have done nothing to ease the policeman's struggle—indeed, he might even have prolonged the agony a bit, to test his mettle. But the truth was he found it almost distasteful that a man of Burke's obvious caliber would need question his acceptability as a suitor.

Therefore, he decided the captain's misery had gone on quite long enough. "You're wondering how I would feel about an Irish policeman courting my daughter. Isn't that it, son?"

Burke went white, but to his credit, he never so much as flinched. "Aye, sir, that's it, right enough. And I'd understand if you think I'm half-cracked in asking."

Lewis studied the straight-backed Irishman with interest—and no small degree of admiration. "Perhaps you'd best tell me the nature of your intentions."

The Adam's apple worked again. "The honest truth, sir?"

"Exactly that, son. Give it to me straight."

"I'm looking for a wife, sir. Any woman I end up courting, 'twould be with an eye toward marriage."

"I see." Lewis measured the strong jaw, the dark eyes, the firm chin. "You're some older than Sara, I believe?"

"Yes, sir, I expect by a number of years. I'm well past thirty-six, you see."

Lewis nodded. "That's almost ten years' difference. A significant gap."

The policeman's mouth drew down slightly.

"But not necessarily a problem," Lewis added. "There were eight years between Sara's mother and me and we had a wonderful marriage. The Daltons come to mind as well—she must have been little more than a girl when he married her, and there's certainly no denying their happiness. Still, you've been married before and have a son who's almost grown."

"Aye," said Michael Burke, his mouth thinning. "And I'll not mislead you, Mr. Farmington. Tierney's a bit of a problem these days."

An honest man. Straight and direct. "Well, show me a boy his age who isn't a bit of a problem these days. Still, it wouldn't do to count on a wife being of much help with the boy. He's almost a man."

Burke inclined his head, his expression somewhat grim. "Aye, I'm well aware of that, sir." He paused. "Begging your pardon, Mr. Farmington, but Tierney has nothing to do with my reasons for wanting to court your daughter. I'm taken with Sara, and that's the truth."

"You've made your peace about Nora, then?"

The policeman nodded and managed a smile. "I'm happy for her and Whittaker. I can see that it's best."

Lewis regarded him with a thoughtful gaze. "I don't suppose you'd happen to know if Sara is *interested* in your courting her?"

The other hesitated. "I'd like to think so, sir. But I can't say for certain, no."

"Hmm." Lewis laced his fingers over his middle. "Well, I suppose there's only one way to find out, now, isn't there?"

The dark eyes glinted. "Sir?"

Lewis fingered his watch fob, then locked eyes with Burke.

"Let me just say this, Michael: Sara is my only daughter, and I'm understandably protective of her. I'd have no qualms about dealing harshly with any man who even thought of taking advantage."

At Burke's red-faced attempt to protest, Lewis waved him off. "I'm not worried about the likelihood in your case. I'm simply telling you I won't be underestimated when it comes to my daughter. As for finding out if Sara would welcome your attentions, I suppose you'll just have to give it a go, now, won't you?"

The years seemed to fall away from Michael Burke. "With your blessing, sir?"

Lewis grinned at him. "Godspeed, my boy. Godspeed."

The truth was, Lewis was itching to get this discussion over with so he could get back to Winifred Whittaker Coates.

Later that night, after his father and Aunt Winifred had retired to their rooms in the mansion, Evan asked Nora and the children to join him in the cottage.

Although Nora was far from easy in her mind—tomorrow was her wedding day, after all—at least her fear about Evan's family had been vanquished. His father had been sweet, almost shy in his kindness to her. And his Aunt Winnie—well, it was just as Evan said: Nora adored her!

Wondering what Evan was thinking on this, their last night to live apart, Nora searched his eyes as he took her hand in front of Daniel John and the children. He smiled at her, his gaze going over her face with tender affection.

"There is something I wo-would say to you," he began quietly, turning toward Johanna and speaking slowly, that she might better understand his words. "Just b-before we left Ireland, I p-promised Morgan Fitzgerald, who is very d-dear to us all, that I would t-take care of you—every one of you—as if you were m-my own."

He paused, giving Nora's hand a gentle squeeze. "Now that Nora and I…are to be m-married, I feel that, in a very special way, you *are* m-my own. You have become m-my family…and I love you all. I know I can n-never take the place of your father, Daniel—or yours, Tom and Johanna. But I hope you will at least allow m-me to be your friend."

Nora's heart swelled with pride and thankfulness as Evan went on. "Tomorrow, Nora and I will vow b-before God to love and care for each other for the rest of our lives. But t-tonight, in your hearing, and b-before God, I want to renew the promise I m-made in your behalf many m-months ago. I vow to you all that I will love you and care for you as if you are m-my own. For indeed you are m-my own…and for that, I am grateful beyond all words."

That night, alone in his room—the *last* night he would be alone in his room, Evan reminded himself thankfully—he read the letter that Daniel John had handed him just before leaving the cottage with Nora and the children.

"It is from Morgan," the boy had said, handing Evan the envelope. "He sent a gift as well, but asked that I keep back the gift until the wedding day."

Now, seated at the table in his room, Evan opened the letter somewhat hesitantly, uncertain as to what he might expect from the great Gael who had held such a deep love for Nora.

He need not have feared. The first few lines left little doubt as to Fitzgerald's intent.

> And so, Evan Whittaker, you are an Englishman who keeps his word, after all. For didn't you pledge to look after my loved ones as if they were your own? And it would seem that indeed you are about to make them your own!

The letter was brief, but reassuringly warm, filled with the big Irishman's wishes for their marriage and their future.

As Evan reached Fitzgerald's final words, he could only smile. Indeed, he could almost imagine the glint that might have danced in those piercing green eyes when the man penned his closing thrust:

> That you are a noble man, I have no doubt, Whittaker. I believed that when I entrusted you with my family, back in Ireland, and I believe it now. I know, too, that you will cherish Nora and be the devoted husband to her she deserves. Mind that you do, my English friend, for there is no ocean wide enough to keep you safe from me should you ever do less.
>
> With that in mind, I embrace you both and pray the Lord's blessing upon your love and your wedding day.

Evan laid the letter in front of him, on the table. His eyes misted as he sat staring at it. "God keep him," he finally whispered, touching the letter with gentle fingers. "God keep us all."

The Wedding Day

Hold the gift with reverent hands,
For it is holy....
MORGAN FITZGERALD (1848)

The wedding day dawned with a warm and honeyed May sunrise.
In the Farmington mansion there was much excitement. Daniel John, who had spent the night there, did all he could to keep Little Tom in tow, but the tyke was spinning like a top by midday. Even Sara Farmington was a flurry of nervous excitement, hurrying from one room to the next, helping Nora dress, seeing to the flowers, nagging her father, and listening to Evan's Aunt Winifred regale the maid with backdoor tales of wayward British nobility.

By early afternoon, Sara was quite wild, and had decided that if and when she ever married, she just might brave the scandal of elopement.

Nora's fingers were numb, her knees jelly. Only Sara's timely appearance in the doorway saved her from utter hysteria. Between the two of them, they finally managed to secure the countless pearl buttons of her wedding dress, with time to spare for the veil.

"I should not have agreed to a veil," Nora worried. "I am no young virgin bride, after all."

"You are still quite young," Sara said firmly, inspecting the veil and Nora's hair. "And you are Evan's bride. It's entirely proper that you wear a veil."

"Such an expense," Nora fretted.

"A worthwhile extravagance, surely."

"I am going to be ill," Nora warned.

"Nonsense! You are going to be married."

"Aren't you listening to me at all, Sara? I am terrified, and that's the truth!"

A pearl-studded pin in her mouth, Sara stepped back for a better look at her handiwork, then moved to tuck the pin in one last place. "More to the point, you are absolutely lovely."

Brushing a stubborn wisp of hair away from Nora's temple, Sara met her eyes. "You'll not faint, surely?"

"I might. I'm mortal ill."

Sara shook her head. "It won't do. If your groom is even half as anxious as rumor has it downstairs, you will be needed to prop him up. Now, then, take some good, deep breaths and let's go."

"Go?" Nora stared at her.

Sara patted her arm. "Yes, dear. Downstairs. To the chapel. It's time."

Nora attempted a deep breath, as Sara suggested. A sharp pain sliced the breath into ragged gasps. "It's as I said." She put a hand to her heart. "I am mortal ill."

Sara laughed at her. "You're impossible!" she scolded, tucking Nora's arm securely inside her own. "Now come along. We can't very well have a wedding without a bride, can we?"

In the wing off the chapel, Lewis Farmington peered closely at Evan's silk tie. "We haven't quite got it yet, I'm afraid," he said, frowning. "Let's have one more go at it."

Quaking, Evan lifted his chin and suffered his employer's thick-knuckled ministration.

"It's quite all right to breathe, Evan," his employer remarked, standing back to inspect his work. "Ah! Perfect!"

"I am qu-quite ill."

"Nonsense! You can't be ill! This is your wedding day!"

A thought suddenly struck Evan. "Father—and Aunt Winifred?"

"They're already seated. Your father is feeling better. Winifred says he's fine now. Just exhaustion from the voyage, I'm sure."

"The ring?"

"Daniel has it, safe in hand. Really, Evan, you must relax. You should enjoy your own wedding, son! Besides, if Nora sees you in such a state, it might make her think you have doubts."

Evan tightened his jaw. "Yes…y-you're right, of c-course. I mustn't let her kn-know how anxious I am. She m-might misunderstand."

"Quite right!"

Evan moistened his lips. "D-Daniel?"

"On his way. With the ring. Deep breaths, now, Evan. I'll see you smiling and relaxed before we go in."

"Go in?"

"To the chapel, Evan—into the chapel! You're about to be married, remember?"

Lewis Farmington patted Evan on the back. Evan's knees threatened to buckle, but his employer caught him just in time and prodded him forward to the door.

ॐ

At the front of the chapel, Jess Dalton was taking great pleasure in anticipating the ceremony. Every wedding at which he officiated was special to him, of course, for he was a dedicated believer in the blessings of matrimony. But this particular ceremony was going to be a pure delight to his heart. Evan Whittaker was a fine, godly man who loved Nora Kavanagh to desperation. And Nora—a gift of a woman, no less. The two of them had gone through much suffering together, which would only serve to make their joy even sweeter.

He beamed out upon the cozy chapel with its small scattering of invited guests. On the third row back sat his own wife, the remarkable Kerry, beside a wide-eyed but smiling Arthur Jackson. The boy appeared a bit dazed by all the finery around him, yet he seemed to be enjoying what he called the "goings-on."

Jess slanted a look at the ashen-faced groom to make certain he was still on his feet. With both Lewis Farmington and Daniel Kavanagh flanking him, he appeared reasonably secure. At least for the time being.

The processional music swelled from the organ, and the guests drew a collective breath of excitement.

Jess turned his gaze to the back of the chapel, where the beginning of the procession was now in view. Sara Farmington, elegant and quite lovely in the softest of blues, approached, her slight limp somehow giving her all the more charm.

Behind her came a smiling Johanna Fitzgerald, sweetly young and pretty in cream and blue lace, her dark red hair falling in soft curls around her shoulders. Wee Tom, as they called him, bounced cheerfully along behind his sister, quite the little man in suit coat and breeches—Sara Farmington's doing, no doubt.

Another swell and salute of the organ, a rustling of the guests, and the bride herself at last appeared. Nora Kavanagh was a vision in ice-blue silk and pearls, the veil scarcely concealing her enormous, anxious eyes.

Escorting her was the brawny, strong-featured Michael Burke. Straight and proud in a dark suit and starched linen, the policeman beamed a thoroughly Irish smile as he delivered the bride safely to her white-faced groom.

Nora managed surprisingly well throughout most of the ceremony, hardly stumbling over her vows at all.

She did not even weep until toward the end, when Daniel John stepped out from Evan's side and retrieved the Kavanagh harp from a small alcove near the front. Touching her arm, then Evan's, the boy murmured, "This is Morgan's gift, sent with his love. I will present it to you as he requested."

Nora's eyes filled even as her son shouldered the harp and began to strum it softly. Evan's hand gripped hers as Daniel John first read Morgan's words in the Irish, then began to sing them in English:

> *For love and love alone will ever be the vow that joins you....*
> *Hold the gift with reverent hands, for it is holy.... Be so much one*
> *you taste the tears and breathe the fragrant joy of living from a single*
> *cup, a golden chalice overflowing...*

At last Michael handed her over into Evan's keeping. For an instant, his strong hand lingered on her arm, and their eyes met. In that moment the miracle of friendship spanned an ocean as three hearts touched, joined by memory and an enduring legacy of love.

Outside the mansion, the sun was a golden lamp. The warm spring afternoon was quiet and sweetly scented. Sara Farmington stood at the shoulder of Michael Burke, waiting for the first appearance of the new Mr. and Mrs. Whittaker.

As the doors to the chapel were flung open, Nora and Evan came forth for all eyes to behold, resplendent in their happiness. They stepped onto the brick walkway just outside the chapel. Then, bathed in the golden warmth of the sun and their newly found joy, they stood, smiling shyly at their well-wishers.

Suddenly, from a gentle rise on the east grounds, a low hum sounded. The hum deepened to a drone, rising up, spreading and flowering into a joyous Celtic wail. Everyone, including the newlyweds, turned to look.

Across the green lawn of the Farmington estate came a fully kilted piper, strutting, head high and proud. He stopped a short distance from the mansion, piping an ancient tribute to the new bride and groom.

Sara's gaze traveled from the piper to Nora, whose face was a shining wonder, stunned and tearful, as she clung to the arm of her smiling groom.

Overwhelmed with the glory of the moment, Sara watched as Nora turned her shining but questioning eyes on Michael Burke. He met her look with a slow, pleased grin and a jaunty wink.

As the wail of the pipes died away into the hush of the gentle spring afternoon, Sara felt Michael's eyes on her and turned to meet his gaze.

"However did you manage—" She stopped. "Of course! He's a policeman, isn't he? The piper?"

"Aye, just another Irish cop," admitted Michael, studying her with a most peculiar smile.

"That was really quite wonderful," Sara stammered awkwardly.

Michael Burke turned the full power of his Celtic smile on her—a dangerous smile, beneath that dark, rich mustache. "Sara, lass," he said softly, "there is little an Irishman cannot manage, once he sets his mind to it." He paused, studying her for another moment. "You'd do well to remember that in the days ahead."

Taking her arm, he tucked it firmly inside his own. Then, together, they went to congratulate the bride and groom.

By choice, Evan and Nora spent their wedding night in the cottage. Perhaps one day they would accept Lewis Farmington's offer of a wedding trip. But for now they felt they should stay close to the children, to reassure them that they were family and would not be separated.

They approached the cottage still enfolded in the excited happiness of the day. Someone had been there before them, had made of the small rooms a warm and inviting hideaway for love. Candles glowed beside the bed, which had been turned down to reveal soft quilts and plump pillows. Through an open window, the mellow spring night bathed the room with gentle fragrance.

Standing at the threshold in the open doorway, Evan stared inside, then at Nora, hoping she could not sense his growing anxiety. "I...I'm sorry, I c-can't carry you across the threshold, Mrs. Whittaker," he said, searching her face.

Nora smiled into his eyes, then took his arm. "Sure, and you're not superstitious, are you, Evan? And yourself not even Irish!"

Inside the room, Evan took her veil and placed it carefully on the coat tree. When he turned back to her, Nora had gone to stand at the open window. The curtains billowed about her with the breeze, casting shadows in the path of the flickering candlelight.

"'Tis a beautiful night," Nora said softly.

"A beautiful day," Evan put in inanely. He was suddenly gripped with terror, seized with fear that he would prove a disappointment to her.

What if she could not bear the sight of him? The missing arm, the angry scar—what if he *repulsed* her?

As if she had heard the panic in his voice, Nora turned about to face him. Avoiding her eyes, Evan went to the desk and removed a small package.

When he straightened, she had come to stand beside him.

"Evan?" Her voice was soft, questioning.

Still avoiding her gaze, Evan pressed the package into her hand. "I... this is for yo-you...a wedding gift," he stammered.

Nora looked from him to the package in her hand. "What is it, then, Evan?"

"Open it," he said, motioning to the package. "Please."

Keeping her eyes on his face another moment, Nora slid the paper away to reveal a small jewelry box. Staring down at it, she lifted its lid with a soft cry. Ever so carefully, she removed the delicate pearl brooch. "Oh, Evan, isn't it lovely!"

"It was...my m-mother's," Evan explained. "Father brought it with him. For you."

"Help me," she said, placing the brooch at the throat of her wedding gown. With fumbling fingers, Evan held the material in place with his one hand while Nora pinned the brooch.

"I feel so grand," she said, again smiling into his eyes.

"You're...ex-exquisite, Nora," Evan choked out, unable to take his eyes from her. He wanted desperately to touch her, yet he was afraid to move.

She came to him and caressed his soft bearded cheek with her hand, leaning against him.

"Nora—"

Nora lifted her face to his, and his world spun. Lost in her eyes, he pulled her closer. "Nora...d-dearest..."

Nora searched his gaze, all the while tracing the line of his lips with her fingertips. Evan thought his heart would explode from the nearness of her, the fragrance of her hair, the warm sweetness of her breath on his cheek. "Oh, Nora...I th-think I shall d-die for the love of you!"

She lifted her face and met his lips. His mind exploded, and he went on kissing her until he lost his breath.

"I love you, Evan," she whispered at last. "I will always love you." With one hand on his forearm, she eased out of his embrace. "I will draw the curtains," she said quietly.

Evan moved to snuff out one of the candles on the bedside table, then went around to extinguish the other one.

"No, Evan," Nora said softly, turning from the window to face him.

He stared at her. "I thought...I thought you wo-wouldn't want the light...that you'd rather not see..."

Miserable, he let his words die away as he stood with downcast eyes.

"Oh, Evan...Evan, you foolish man." Nora came to him, again melting into his embrace, clinging to his shoulders. "Did you think your arm would make a difference, and me loving you as I do?"

He lifted his gaze, captured by the warm tenderness in her magnificent eyes. "I was afraid you'd simply n-not tell me. I can keep it covered, Nora...I understand—"

She placed one hand over his mouth. "Hush, now, my dear, foolish husband! Hush..." Her lips replaced her hand, and they kissed again.

"Leave the candle burning," she whispered against his cheek. After a moment, she gently freed herself from his embrace and helped him slip out of his suit coat, then his shirt.

When she pressed her lips with infinite gentleness to the dread scar, Evan squeezed his eyes shut to absorb the healing warmth of her love.

As his wife removed the brooch and began to undo the myriad tiny pearl buttons at the front of her wedding dress, Evan reached for her. Lifting her hand to his lips, he brushed a gentle kiss over her fingertips.

"I'm not...entirely helpless," he said softly, unfastening first one button, then another with a surprisingly steady, if somewhat clumsy, hand. Nora smiled, and he could see his love and desire reflected in her eyes.

For the first time since the surgery that had claimed his injured arm— perhaps for the first time in his life—Evan Whittaker knew himself to be a whole man.

Ride with the Wind

To him who is able to keep you from falling
And to present you before his glorious presence
Without fault and with great joy—
To the only God our Savior
Be glory, majesty, power and authority,
Through Jesus Christ our Lord,
Before all ages, now and forevermore!
Amen.

JUDE 24-25

Dublin

Morgan hurried through the rest of the papers, signing his name with a flourish—using the new pen Smith O'Brien had presented him for his birthday.

Gathering up the sheaf of papers in front of him, he stacked them, glancing over the two at the top of the heap. Authorization for Cusack, a Dublin barrister, to pursue legal steps for Annie's adoption. The final bid from O'Toole Bros, to start the necessary renovation on the east wing next month—for the school.

At the moment, he would complete only those matters requiring immediate attention. At Sandemon's and Annie's insistence, he would be at leisure for the rest of the day; apparently the two had planned some sort of a surprise for his birthday.

Hearing a door slam somewhere in the house, then the sound of running footsteps, he replaced his pen on its brass stand, waiting. As he had anticipated, Annie came crashing into the room, out of breath and somewhat wild-eyed.

"It's time, *Seanchai*! Can you come now?"

"Is this a safe venture?" Morgan queried, smiling at the excited child.

"Oh, it's grand!" she exclaimed, still winded from whatever exertion she'd been up to. Running around behind him, she grabbed hold of the wheelchair. "We can go faster if I push you!"

Morgan knew better than to protest. Gritting his teeth, he held on and suffered a frenzied exit from the library, shaking his head as they streaked down the hall to the dining room.

They screeched to a halt just inside the door. Sandemon stood smiling near the food-laden table. At his side stood the lovely young woman named Finola. Although he had not seen her for nearly two months, Morgan had not forgotten the golden-haired beauty. He found himself inordinately pleased that she would be present for his birthday.

Amid Annie's ravings, Sandemon's laughter, and Finola's shy smile, Morgan leaned back and prepared to enjoy the fact that he was growing older.

Much later, feeling, in his own words, "fattened for the kill," Morgan was taken for another ride by the highly excited Annie Delaney. By God's grace, Sandemon saw fit to take control of the chair before the child had a chance to hurl him down the ramp off the back stoop.

Annie ran on ahead, quickly disappearing. Part of the surprise apparently included a visit to Pilgrim, for they were headed in the direction of the stables. Pleased, Morgan sat up a bit straighter in the chair, watching for Annie to lead the stallion out to meet them, as she usually did.

He stole a glance at Finola, walking alongside him. *What is her story?* he wondered. *What lies behind that unfathomable blue gaze? What took her voice, yet left her with a smile that could charm the bees or melt a man's heart?*

As if sensing his eyes on her, she looked back at Morgan with a questioning expression. Caught gawking at her, he would have looked away. But Finola smiled, catching him up in the warmth and quiet glow that seemed to radiate from her.

Inside the stable, Morgan turned toward the stallion's stall, only to find it empty. "Where is he?" he asked Sandemon. "Where's Pilgrim?"

"Waiting for you, *Seanchai*."

Sandemon stopped the chair. "A moment, *Seanchai*, if you please," he said, disappearing around the center row of stalls.

"What are they up to, do you know?" Morgan asked Finola.

She shrugged, turned both hands palm up, and smiled.

She knew, all right. Morgan was sure of it.

"Can you wheel yourself over here, *Seanchai*?" Sandemon called.

"Of course I can wheel myself over there!" Morgan snapped. "I only require help when a devious companion or a demented child intends to have some mischief at my expense."

Followed by Finola, Morgan stopped the chair as soon as he turned the corner. In front of him, in an empty space where there was no stall, stood Sandemon, looking mightily pleased with himself. Above him, bolted onto the rafter, was a block and tackle, threaded with heavy rope. The entire apparatus included two pulley wheels and a wide leather seat attached to two ends of rope—something that looked like a child's tree swing, only sturdier.

Only now did Morgan see Annie. Wearing a face-splitting grin, she was standing off to the side, holding Pilgrim's reins. Catching sight of Morgan, the big stallion tossed his head and gave a welcoming snort.

Morgan sat staring at the lot of them—the horse, the child, and Sandemon. "You are having great sport, I can see. Am I to simply sit here, then, like a great lump, or will you be telling me what you are about?"

Bouncing from one foot to the other, Annie giggled. Sandemon and Finola smiled broadly.

Feeling greatly disadvantaged, Morgan cast a withering glare on them all.

"This is our gift to you, *Seanchai*," Sandemon finally said, gesturing to the contraption.

Did they think he knew what it was, then? Not wanting to hurt their feelings, Morgan managed a smile. "It seems a fine gift," he said uncertainly. "You made it, did you?"

"Sand-Man and I!" Annie cried out. "We've been working on it for weeks!"

Morgan gave a wise nod. "I've no doubt. Well, I am—impressed. And grateful, of course."

Annie giggled again, louder this time. "He doesn't know what it is, Sand-Man," she said. Sandemon nodded, smiling.

Morgan shot a wary look from one to the other. "Now that's the truth," he admitted. "I don't know what it is."

Nobody offered to enlighten him. At last Sandemon stepped up, bending forward from the waist and looking directly into Morgan's eyes. "What it is, *Seanchai*," he said softly, "is a means of putting legs beneath you again."

Morgan narrowed his eyes and lifted his chin. "Legs?" he repeated skeptically.

"Four of them," Sandemon said, straightening. With no further explanation, he wheeled Morgan up to the seat of the swing. Then, stooping, he slid a rock under one wheel of the chair to brace it.

Now he turned and held out his arms to Morgan. "If you trust me, *Seanchai*, you can ride your fine stallion again," he said quietly.

Astounded, Morgan stared at the black man's arms extended toward him, then transferred his gaze to Sandemon's face. The dark eyes regarded him with a watchful expression.

"If I trust you?" Morgan repeated softly.

Sandemon nodded, waiting.

Morgan moistened his lips, then held out his hands to Sandemon, like a child.

A slow smile broke across Sandemon's face. With strong arms, he lifted Morgan up, out of the wheelchair, into the leather seat of the swinglike contraption. "Hold the ropes tightly, *Seanchai*. We are going to lift you up, just high enough so that Annie can lead Pilgrim underneath you. Then I will lower you into the saddle. See, he is ready and waiting for his master."

His throat swollen, Morgan looked at the wide-eyed Annie, then Pilgrim, then back to Sandemon. "Aye," he said, gripping the ropes. "This might work."

The sleeves of Sandemon's purple shirt billowed out, as slowly, carefully, he pulled at the rope, hand over hand. Morgan felt himself rising, looked nervously down at his limp legs swinging uselessly over the stable floor. At the same time, Annie began to move, her eyes on Morgan, suspended above the ground.

Looking down, Morgan swallowed hard. "Sure, and there are those who have always said I would swing one day," he cracked weakly.

Sandemon now secured the rope around a pole and held it, waiting until Annie brought the stallion to a halt, directly beneath Morgan.

Once the horse was in place, Sandemon slowly, ever so slowly, lowered Morgan down into the saddle.

Morgan's arms trembled as he touched the leather saddle, felt the strong, hard-muscled back beneath him. Pilgrim gave a small puff of pleasure, as if to welcome him.

It had been so long....

Feeling the familiar power of the big red stallion under him, Morgan was overcome. Rather than disgrace himself with tears in front of Finola, who was watching him with shining eyes, he cracked a smile.

Sandemon came alongside and put a hand to Pilgrim's neck. "You know you cannot ride alone," he murmured.

Morgan nodded reluctantly.

The dark eyes probed his. "Will you ride with a black man then, *Seanchai*?"

Morgan met his gaze. "I would ride with Black Cromwell himself," he said in a soft voice, "to fly free of that chair for a day!"

Sandemon threw back his head and gave a deep-chested laugh. "Child!" he shouted. "Bring the mare!"

Leaping up behind Morgan, the black man wrapped his arms securely around his middle. "Today we will fly, *Seanchai*! You and I together, we will fly!"

They sat waiting for Annie and Finola to mount a soft-eyed chestnut mare, then walked the horses out of the stable.

Side by side, the horses took the pathway leading away from the stable at a slow walk. Annie looked over at Morgan, her face about to crack for pure joy. "Have we made you happy, *Seanchai*?" she asked, beaming.

Morgan looked at her, then at Finola, seated demurely behind her on the mare. "You have made me happy, child," he choked out.

His muscled arms around Morgan, Sandemon dug his heels into Pilgrim's flanks, and they broke into a trot, then a canter. Green-leafed trees and budding flowers swept by them. Morgan smiled at the chatter of birds, gulped in the sweetness of May.

Laughing, he shouted, "I would ride harder, Sandemon!"

"Then, ride, *Seanchai*!" Sandemon cried, urging the stallion into full gallop. "Ride as hard as you want! Ride with the wind! I will not let you fall."

With a Dublin springtime sun falling warm on his shoulders and a gentle wind at his back, Morgan rode away from Nelson Hall, out into the countryside. Sandemon's strong arms held him safely in the saddle as they went flying over the green fields Morgan loved.

As they rode, a soft voice came singing to Morgan's heart. Like an echo from the upper air, it whispered: *Ride, Morgan! Ride with the wind! I will not let you fall....*

Discussion Questions
for *Heart of the Lonely Exile*,
Book Two of The Emerald Ballad Series

1. Evan Whittaker tells Daniel John that to guard against despair and disillusionment Daniel must "hold the hope of heaven in his heart." What did he mean by this? Did Evan's explanation help you understand what is meant by a "pilgrim soul"?

2. Pastor Jess Dalton's sermon on unconditional love convicts Sara Farmington of a sin she suddenly realizes she's harbored for years. What is that sin?

3. In a bitter tirade, Michael Burke questions Pastor Dalton about God's church.

    "I would ask you this, Pastor: Where *is* the Lord's church? Where was it—other than for a brave few, of course—when the Irish were dropping by the thousands along the road, dying of starvation and the fever...Where is the church when the black slave is torn away from his wife and his babies and put in chains, or when he's beaten to a bloody pulp for accidentally looking into a white man's face...Where has it been? Where, exactly, is it now? Right now?"

    The pastor's blunt, incisive answer catches Michael up short and stirs an unfamiliar fire in his spirit.

    Do you recall at least a part of the pastor's answer to Michael? Did it speak in any way to your own confusion or questions about God's church?

4. In the scene between Evan Whittaker and Lewis Farmington in which Farmington gives Evan advice about "courting" Nora, he asks Evan a pointed, significant question.

    "How, exactly do you see yourself?...as a *man* who has only one arm? Or as *only* a one-armed man? It will make all the difference, you know."

What's your explanation for Mr. Farmington's meaning?

5. What traits does Daniel John see in Dr. Nicholas Grafton that create in him a desire to be the same kind of physician as his mentor?

6. The child Annie Delaney from Belfast learned to read from the pages of Morgan Fitzgerald's poetry. Through the years he's become a folk hero in her mind. What "outrageous" idea does she come up with after Morgan is wounded? And how does her proposal turn out?

7. Two people invade Morgan Fitzgerald's life, and he's never quite the same after their arrival. The child Annie Delaney and the enigmatic Sandemon each bring what at times seem to be opposite qualities into Morgan's world. How do you view the differences they make in his life?

8. "Finola" may be an example of how God can bring beauty out of ugliness and light out of darkness. How so?

9. The words of Morgan's friend Joseph Mahon pierce his heart and help him finally to accept the reality of his descent into alcoholism:

> "The level of dependency on the Lord, the unshakable faith in Him, which I have encountered as a priest this past year, has convinced me that there is no strength apart from the Lord's presence, no hope apart from His promises, and no peace apart from His love."

How does he react to these words and to Annie Delaney's fearful rejection of him—and what is the decision he makes and shares with Sandemon?

10. What is Lewis Farmington's wedding gift to Nora and Evan? Why would a gift of this nature be particularly poignant and meaningful to these two immigrants?

A Note from the Author

When I first began to research the idea for the first book in this series, *Song of the Silent Harp,* I discovered a strong religious thread throughout the history of Ireland. I hope I have communicated to my readers a clearer understanding of how Christianity influenced the lives of some of America's Irish ancestors.

During those years of study and writing, I became aware that it is virtually impossible to separate the past from the present. The struggles and successes, the trials and triumphs of our forebears, make up not only a rich heritage but also contribute in immeasurable ways to what we—and our world—are today. Like young Daniel Kavanagh, I believe that, from God's perspective, yesterday, today, and tomorrow are one vast *panorama,* a continuing epic that our Creator views in its entirety, from the dawn of time through the present to eternity.

Further, history *does,* indeed, repeat itself. Most experiences of the past continue to happen. The horrors of famine and hopelessness that surround many characters in An Emerald Ballad still exist. Month after month, year after year, the innocent victims of war, disaster, political indifference, and oppression go on suffering and dying, just as they did in Ireland during the Great Famine.

Government programs and private charities cannot begin to meet the escalating demand for worldwide assistance. I believe the Christian church should be at the very front of international rescue operations, for it is the *church* that bears the responsibility—and the privilege—of giving love to a world that needs it.

I invite you to join me in finding practical ways to help through your church of favorite charity. There are many organizations that provide an opportunity to put faith and love into action. One person *does* make a difference.

BJ Hoff

OTHER FINE BJ HOFF BOOKS PUBLISHED BY HARVEST HOUSE PUBLISHERS

RACHEL'S SECRET

Bestselling author BJ Hoff delights with her compelling series *The Riverhaven Years*. With the first book, *Rachel's Secret*, you'll discover a community of unforgettable characters, a tender love story, the faith journeys of people you'll grow to know and love, and enough suspense to keep the pages turning quickly.

When wounded Irish American riverboat captain Jeremiah Gant bursts into the rural Amish setting of Riverhaven, he brings chaos and conflict to the community—especially for young widow Rachel Brenneman. The unwelcome "outsider" needs a safe place to recuperate before continuing his secret role as an Underground Railroad conductor. Neither he nor Rachel is prepared for the forbidden love that threatens to endanger a man's mission, a woman's heart, and a way of life for an entire people.

WHERE GRACE ABIDES

In this compelling second book in the The Riverhaven Years series, you'll get an even closer look at the Amish community of Riverhaven and the people who live and love and work there. Secrets, treachery, and persecution are a few of the challenges that test Rachel's faith and her love for the forbidden "outsider," while Gant's own hopes and dreams are dealt a life–changing blow, rendering the vow he made to Rachel seemingly impossible to honor.

The Amish community finds their gentle, unassuming lives of faith jeopardized by a malicious outside influence. At the same time, those striving to help runaway slaves escape to freedom through the Underground Railroad face deception and the danger of discovery.

SONG OF ERIN

The mysteries of the past confront the secrets of the present in bestselling author BJ Hoff's magnificent Song of Erin saga.

You'll be intrigued by this panoramic story that crosses the ocean from Ireland to America. In this tale of struggle and love and uncompromising faith, Jack Kane, the always charming but sometimes ruthless titan of New York's most powerful publishing empire, is torn between the conflict of his own heart and the grace and light of Samantha Harte, the woman he loves, whose troubled past continues to haunt her.

AMERICAN ANTHEM

At the entrance to the city, an Irish governess climbs into a carriage and sets out to confront the man who destroyed her sister's life—a blind musician who hears music no one else can hear…

On a congested city street, a lonely Scot physician with a devastating secret meets a woman doctor with the capacity to heal not only the sick…but also his heart…

In a tumbledown shack among hundreds of others like it, an immigrant family struggles to survive, and a ragged street singer old beyond her years appoints herself an unlikely guardian . . .

So begins *American Anthem,* a story set in 1870s New York that lets you step into another time to share the hopes and dreams and triumphant faith of a people you'll grow to love.

> "An eloquently told story that weaves
> history, music, faith, and intrigue…
> an absolute pleasure."
>
> *Christian Retailing*

> "The story gently unfolds with intriguing characters, and the sound of music,
> which Hoff manages to make fly off the pages with her
> glorious and passionate descriptions."
>
> *Christian Library Journal*

Great reviews for BJ Hoff's MOUNTAIN SONG LEGACY trilogy...

BOOK ONE...*A DISTANT MUSIC*

"BJ Hoff always delights readers with her warm stories and characters who become part of your 'circle of special friends.'"

JANETTE OKE, BESTSELLING AUTHOR OF *LOVE COMES SOFTLY*

"For this Kentucky woman, reading *A Distant Music* was like driving through the eastern hills and hollers on a perfect autumn day, with the scent of wood smoke in the air and the trees ablaze with color. BJ Hoff's lyrical prose brings to life this gentle, moving story of a beloved teacher and his students, who learn far more than the three Rs. I brushed away tears at several tender points in the story and held my breath when it seemed all might be lost. Yet, even in the darkest moments, hope shines on every page. A lovely novel by one of historical fiction's finest wordsmiths."

LIZ CURTIS HIGGS, BESTSELLING AUTHOR OF *THORN IN MY HEART*

"As always when I open BJ's books I'm drawn into a place that is both distant and at home...as I tell my husband, I wish I could create the kinds of characters B.J. does because I fall in love with them and want them always as my friends."

JANE KIRKPATRICK, AUTHOR OF *LOOK FOR A CLEARING IN THE WILD*

"In some ways, *A Distant Music* is reminiscent of the Little House series. Each chapter recalls the details of an event or some characters dilemma. Eventually, though, Hoff connects all the threads into a solid story whose ending will deeply touch readers. *A Distant Music* should find an eager audience."

ASPIRING RETAIL MAGAZINE

BOOK TWO... *THE WIND HARP*

BJ always does a great job of drawing her readers into the lives of her characters. I'm sure that there will be many who will be eagerly pleading to know 'what happens next.' I will be among them."

JANETTE OKE, *LOVE COMES SOFTLY*

"BJ Hoff continues the story of Maggie and Jonathan, who must endure their share of trials before reaping their reward. Though this novel is historical, BJ Hoff deals with issues that are completely contemporary...Kudos to the author for charming us again!"

ANGELA HUNT, BESTSELLING AUTHOR OF *THE NOVELIST*

BOOK THREE... *THE SONG WEAVER*

"Like a warm visit with a good friend over a hot cup of tea, *The Song Weaver* offers comfort and satisfaction...and you don't want the visit to come to an end."

CINDY SWANSON

"BJ Hoff is a master at characterization, and her stories are rich with insight. I love the historical setting and learned something new about the role of women in that society."

JILL E. SMITH

"*The Song Weaver* is the last book in the Mountain Song Legacy Story, and I hate to see it end. I'll miss Maggie and Jonathan and all the others...A very satisfying end to a special series. She never disappoints."

—BARBARA WARREN

To learn more about books by BJ Hoff
or to read sample chapters, log on to our website:

www.harvesthousepublishers.com

HARVEST HOUSE PUBLISHERS
EUGENE, OREGON